Volume 29

Secrets

Satisfy your desire for more.

Sweet-Talking the Opposition by Saskia Walker

Journalist Eliza Jameson is on assignment on a luxurious Rhine river cruiser when she finds the perfect distraction on board — old flame, Marcus Weston. To play him at his own game, she decides to call the shots, but Marcus has his own agenda. In the ensuing battle, who will end up on top?

Chimera by Nathalie Gray

From the overcrowded slums of a future Earth, he rose as the perfect tool of lethal justice and deception. Cold and stoical by choice, alone by circumstances, he will neutralize any and all threat to his client then move on. But when his next assignment involves a popular politician who's as smart as she's attractive, the greatest betrayal would be to deny his heart.

Edge by Dominique Sinclair

Catlina Demarco, the first woman trained by the Department of International Intelligence, has left the agency. Agent Noah Tyler, her former partner and lover, is the last man she expects to show up with handcuffs and intent to bring her back. Forced into the jungle by three armed banderos, Cat finds her and Noah once again working as partners, their thoughts as one, their bodies craving, their goals conflicting.

Beast in a Kilt by Nicole North

Scottish Lady Catriona MacCain has loved Torr Blackburn, a fierce Highland warrior, since she was a young lass. When Catriona's family promises her in marriage to a detestable chieftain, she needs Torr to save her. But he's been cursed by a witch and doesn't believe himself worthy of the virginal Catriona. However, she's determined to seduce Torr and claim him.

Saskia Walker
Nathalie Gray
Dominique Sinclair
Nicole North

Volume 29

Secrets

Satisfy your desire for more.

Red Sage Publishing, Inc.
P.O. Box 4844
Seminole, FL 33775
727-391-3847
www.redsagepub.com

SECRETS Volume 29
A Red Sage Publishing book
All Rights Reserved/July 2010
Copyright © 2010 by Red Sage Publishing, Inc.

ISBN: 1-60310-009-1 / ISBN 13: 978-1-60310-009-0

Published by arrangement with the authors and copyright holders of the individual
works as follows:

SWEET-TALKING THE OPPOSITION
Copyright © 2010 by Saskia Walker

CHIMERA
Copyright © 2010 by Nathalie Gray

EDGE
Copyright © 2010 by Dominique Sinclair

BEAST IN A KILT
Copyright © 2010 by Nicole North

Photographs:
Cover © 2010 by Tara Kearney Adkins; www.tarakearney.com
Cover Models: Krystle Hoshowski and Nimai Manrique
Setback cover © 2000 by Greg P. Willis; GgnYbr@aol.com

Printed in the U.S.A.

Book typesetting by:
Quill & Mouse Studios, Inc.
www.quillandmouse.com

Contents

Sweet-Talking the Opposition

by Saskia Walker

To My Reader:

Dear Reader, when these two characters decided to take up residence in my imagination I thought they were perfect for each other, but they had other ideas. They just wanted a quick fling, but I wasn't going to let them get away with it. I decided to trap them together on a boat, for a week, to see what happened. I had such a lot of fun watching as Marcus and Eliza's story unfolded, and I hope you do too!

I'm indebted to Andrea Mason at Page and Moy River Cruises for her help with information for this novella.

Chapter 1

Eliza Jameson stared at the River Queen in dismay. There, amidst the crowd of passengers, photographers, and members of the press milling on the dockside, was Marcus Weston, the serial seducer she'd rather stupidly had a fling with two years before. Surely he wasn't going to be on board as well? Marcus was the most talked-about travel journalist in London, and the chances were he was writing up this inaugural voyage, just as she was. She noticed he had a backpack slung over his shoulder, and she gave a deep internal groan.

"Great, that's all I need," she muttered under her breath, hoping he hadn't seen her and she could sneak on behind him without being spotted.

Too late. He lifted a hand in greeting, and then smiled over at her and stood by as if waiting for her to join him at the end of the gangplank. Heat rushed to her face, and she had the urge to take flight. Behind her, the taxi that had brought her to the Amsterdam dockside from Schiphol airport revved up and sped away. So much for that.

Marcus was waiting for her to respond. She forced herself to nod politely, telling herself to get a grip. How awkward could it be? Plenty awkward. He would tease her about her new job, she had no doubt about that, but she also knew she was woman enough to face up to him. She simply had to pull herself together, and fast. Snatching at the handle on her suitcase, she ignored his insinuating stare. She was here to work. Her job was to record the features of the cruiser for a travel guide, and a beautiful cruiser it was too.

She focused on the gangplank as she approached, evading his stare. Festooned with flowers, a banner on the near side was emblazoned with the words *Maiden Voyage*. The launch gleamed white, pristine amongst the other multi-colored boats on the busy Amsterdam waterways. Being aboard the River Queen would be a treat. She would just have to ignore Marcus' presence. This was her first assignment for a new job. She couldn't afford to mess up.

As she approached him, she lifted her chin to mask her emotions and tried to look as nonchalant as possible. "Marcus Weston, fancy meeting you here."

"Fancy." He gave her a mock bow, making no effort to hide the fact he was giving her a thorough once-over, appraising her from top to toe. It was a possessive look, too, obviously so.

He had a damned cheek. It was as if he assumed he could have her easily, because he'd had her before. He was the sort of man who thought he could charm the clouds out of the sky if he wanted to. It made her blood boil. Even so, memories of a crazy weekend at a newswriter's conference in Zurich edged into her mind. She'd had too much champagne, and when he approached, curiosity got the better of her. They spent a large part of that weekend in and out of her bed—and in the ladies cloakroom at the conference facilities. They even had a quick tryst while waiting for their flights back to England. The whole experience had been powerfully sexy and hauntingly memorable. He'd made it clear it was a fling, though, and she'd thought about him too much afterwards. That part wasn't so good.

She needed to warn him off straight away. She let go her case and put her hands on her hips with a wry smile. "If I'd known you were going to be on board, I would have chosen a different departure date. You're too much of a distraction."

He chuckled. "And there was me thinking I'd have been much more agreeable about coming on the damn trip, if I'd known you were going to be on board. You're just the sort of distraction I enjoy." He lifted his eyebrows and glanced at his watch, clearly amused by her attitude. "Now, tell me, why are you holding up the departure, hmm, Ms. Jameson, gossip columnist extraordinaire?"

He was trying to flatter her, but she was no longer a gossip columnist. He was right, though. The last of the passengers had boarded. The thrum of the engines was growing, and a nearby officer in a white uniform looked over at them with a frown. She shot Marcus an annoyed glance. "Something, or someone, made me hesitate. I was hoping this would be a nice, relaxing cruise."

His eyebrows lifted, the corners of his mouth curling into a wickedly sexy smile. "If that's meant to be a challenge, I can think of numerous ways to help you relax."

"You would take it that way." She shook her head. She'd meant to emphasize the fact she wanted to be alone.

It was what had drawn them together the last time—a tedious conference, a mutual taste for adventure. Looking into his eyes, she could tell he remembered. Damn him. He was so self-assured—not to mention devilishly attractive, with his thick dark hair, challenging eyes, and a broad, suggestive smile designed to make women melt.

Before she had the chance to say anything else, he dropped the backpack slung over his shoulder and ducked down. Her legs went from under her when he lifted her into his arms. He looked directly into her eyes, his face close to hers. "I can't have you hanging about here, complaining about my presence on board. That wouldn't be good for my reputation."

"Reputation?" She laughed dismissively, annoyed that he'd already got his hands on her. She couldn't afford to be toyed with by this man, not again. It was far too risky. "Put me down," she demanded. "There's no need for this."

He ignored her request.

"Can we get some help with the bags," he called out to the officer who was standing by. The man nodded and gestured up the gangplank to another uniformed staff member, who darted out from the cruiser and picked up their luggage.

Marcus carried her up the gangplank. He'd barely changed. A little more weather-beaten, perhaps. His strong, chiseled features were so familiar, and his handsome mouth was giving her such a knowing smile that she narrowed her eyes at him disapprovingly. "You're treating me as if I'm a helpless woman, I'm not."

"Oh, you're not helpless, I'm well aware of that. But you were exhibiting some unusually indecisive behavior, and we can't have that."

She pursed her lips, glaring at him. His dark hair looked as if he'd just ruffled it with his fingers, and she remembered how it felt. His smile grew wider, and she realized she had instinctively looped one hand around his neck, while the other rested against the wall of his chest. She glanced away.

"Ah, honeymooners," the purser said with a grin when they reached the plush interior reception area.

Marcus stiffened in response, stopping dead in his tracks. He looked amazed, almost betrayed, by the other man's comment. Wasn't that just typical. Eliza laughed wryly. He was a dedicated bachelor and a notorious womanizer. He would hate that assumption.

"Nope," she replied to the purser, putting Marcus out of his misery. "Not honeymooners. Mr. Weston was merely assisting me."

Marcus quickly took her cue and set her down.

"It would have been fun to hear you squirming out of that one, Marcus, just for the entertainment value." She tapped him on the chest. "I should have let you deal with it."

The bemused look on his face was too funny. No, she definitely wasn't going to let him get the better of her, not this time. She handed the purser her ticket.

Marcus nodded knowingly, his equilibrium quickly restored. "That's what I remember about you, Eliza. You're so full of surprises." He put his hand on her arm, stopping her when she went to move away. "But you aren't getting away that easily. I have a duty to ensure you get that relaxing cruise you were after. My masculine pride insists upon it."

The purser handed her back her ticket together with a key and a welcome pack. He gave her directions along the corridor to the main deck, where her cabin was located, before taking the ticket Marcus held out to him.

Marcus hadn't asked if she was here on a commission. He'd make fun of her novice state as soon as it occurred to him, and she wasn't going to give him a chance to do that. She bent to pick up her suitcase.

Marcus drew it away from her. "Allow me."

She reached out to snatch it back, but he moved it further away. She stared at the humor sparkling in his eyes—the challenge, the promise. He was so damn sure of himself. It roused the militant feminist in her, and yet, at the same time something in her core responded to his sheer, relentless masculinity, evoking a dangerous cocktail of sensations.

The level of noise and movement around them had increased. She noticed that the other passengers were mostly couples, honeymooners and retirees, which was to be expected. The purser was indicating the gangplank be removed and glanced back at them with a frown, clearly wondering what the problem was. What could she do? If she let Marcus escort her, he'd know where her cabin was located—but he was the sort of man who could find that information if he wanted it, anyway. Rather than make a scene over the case, she gave him a nod and let him follow her with it.

Walking with as much poise and nonchalance as she could muster, she followed the purser's directions across the reception area and along the elegant, carpeted corridor. Numbered cabin doors lined the space to left and right. Her mind ticked over fast as she counted the numbers down. Meeting him, here and now, was the last thing she'd expected. She'd often wished she'd never met him at all, because he made all other men she met pale into insignificance. Didn't he just know it, though? Despite her annoyance, the memories swamped her—torrid and arousing memories. Marcus was still the only man who'd given her a multiple orgasm, and the only one who'd suggested sex outside of the bedroom. That had thrilled her deeply. As much as she hated to admit it, she hadn't met anyone since Marcus who'd obscured his memory enough for her to consider dating. Two years on. That was pretty bloody annoying.

They'd bumped into each other a couple of times in London since then. Once at the theatre, another time at a party. Both times he'd been accompanied by stunning women. It was hard not to be bothered. This time he seemed to be alone, but she'd vowed never to get involved with a man like him again. He was a serial seducer. She was just one of many women he'd unleashed his charms on. But he was close behind her—a handsome, red-blooded man—and right now his attention appeared to be all hers.

Could she really resist?

Did she really want to?

She stopped outside her designated cabin. "Thank you," she said, and turned her back against the door, her mind racing while she looked at him standing there and eyeing her up. Away from the hubbub of the reception area, the tension between them escalated, his masculinity omnipresent. Her senses were filled with it, her womanly center keenly attuned to the presence of so much testosterone. "I'll take it from here."

His eyes twinkled. "I was so pleased when I saw you climbing out of your taxi."

He'd been watching her? That surprised her.

"And you're traveling alone," he added, in an insinuating tone. "It'll be good to catch up with each other."

Don't let him get to you, she told herself. Easier said than done.

He dropped his bag to the floor, put one hand against the door by her head, and leaned closer. She noticed he hadn't put her case down, but held it as if it were a bargaining tool while his large, muscular body engulfed her much smaller form. The scent of his cologne washed over her, the gap between them minimal. He breathed against her hair, inhaling deeply. "My cabin is three doors back, but I'd love to see how big your bed is."

So much for keeping her head. It was spinning. She gave as dismissive a laugh as she could muster and flashed her eyes at him. "You think I'm just going to fall on my back for you?"

"You did last time."

He had the nerve of the devil himself. She wasn't able to deny the remark, though. "Don't take anything for granted, Marcus."

"Come on, Eliza, you're woman enough for another round, surely?" He gave her a knowing smile and then ran one finger over her tightly pursed lips. Then, lowering his head, he kissed her neck—just barely, and it was so tantalizing.

When he breathed subtle kisses over her skin, her eyelids dropped with pleasure. Her blood was racing, her core melting, and her back shifting against the cabin door. Resist him, she urged herself, but did she really want to? Mercifully, voices at the end of the corridor filtered into her consciousness. Other passengers approached. She broke free, grappled her key into the lock. Moving quickly, she opened the door. "Thank you for bringing my case. Now just put it down, Marcus, please."

He had other ideas. He was looking past her, at the bed. "These cabins are surprisingly big." He gave a husky laugh, his glance surveying the entire cabin, with its en-suite bathroom and floor-to-ceiling sealed window overlooking the water and the passing scenery. He walked past the end of the nearest of the twin beds and put her case on the luggage rack. "More like a five star hotel room than a ship's quarters."

The stretch of his body when he moved fascinated her. His tall frame was nimble, panther-like. On the surface he was sophistication personified, and yet a raw energy shimmered beneath what was visible. She took a deep breath, inwardly refusing to enter the cabin until he'd left it.

"I'd like to give your bed a try." He looked at her when he spoke, not the bed.

She laughed softly, shaking her head. It was what he'd done in Zurich, insisting on her bedroom, not his. Was he guarding his own territory? Why? It had to be strategy. Yes, and if he never let the female enter his space, then he could love and leave her, come and go as he wished in her space. How about turning the tables on him, play him at his own game? She looked at him, brooding handsomely while he undressed her with his eyes. She should be able to do it. She should be able to match him—have him and walk away. Yes, why not? She'd have to keep her head, not let him get under her skin, but the cruise would be even more fun if she had Marcus Weston to toy with in her spare time. She just needed to formulate a strategy of her own.

The boat had started to move, and she held onto the doorframe while she got used to the odd sensation. The hum of the engine made itself felt within her body, purring internally. She pointed at the floor outside her cabin, where he had left his bag. "Out, Marcus."

He hesitated, one eyebrow lifted, his expression part surprised, part admonishment. Then he walked out, pausing alongside her, his eyes narrowed. "We'll discuss it over dinner then, shall we?"

He wasn't so sure, now. She liked that.

"You're so demanding." She met his stare and anticipation ran in her veins. "You want to watch that habit." Smiling, she stepped past him and into her cabin, closing the door behind her as she did so.

Strategy. She was perfectly capable of inventing her own.

That evening, Marcus glanced around the swish restaurant while making a quick checklist in his head. Pleasant ambience. Smart staff, expensive décor, extensive menu, an up-market city restaurant atmosphere. Unbelievable. It wasn't his sort of thing at all. This time last week he'd been paragliding in Queenstown, research for a feature on New Zealand adventure sports for the leading men's UK health magazine. A sedate river cruise was the last thing he aspired to cover. He could have been in India, right now, on a train through Rajasthan. That was his next big write-up for the Sunday press, something he could really sink his teeth into.

He could have drafted a feature on this dainty affair after a quick dockside reconnaissance mission and a glance through the stats, but the cruise company had insisted he partake of a complimentary week-long cruise on the Rhine and Moselle rivers to get the full impact of the luxury cruise. Bungee jumping and rock climbing were more his sort of thing, but he'd had to stand in for a fellow travel journalist. Not a lot he could do about it. Frank was having a hernia operation. If this was his usual lifestyle, Marcus couldn't help wondering how he'd got the hernia in the first place. This was pure, unadulterated luxury, a chance to sit back and be pampered. A week of such behavior was a truly alien experience for Marcus.

"Good evening, Sir." The headwaiter arrived by his side and ushered him into the restaurant. "Will Madame be joining you later?"

Madame? Marcus stared at the waiter for several second, uncomprehending, before he realized the waiter was indeed talking to him. The man had made an assumption. Hazard of the environment, Marcus suspected. Couples seemed to be the norm. He glanced at the man's name badge.

"Hans, there is no Madame. I'm traveling alone, although that may change." He smiled. He'd spied Eliza seated at a table.

The headwaiter blushed, adjusting his bow tie to cover his awkwardness. "Please forgive my error, sir, I—"

Marcus shook his head, putting up one hand.

"No worries. I can see your usual clientele will be couples." It paid to be on friendly terms with the staff. He'd be able to quiz the guy for any information he might need later on.

"Would you prefer a river view?" Hans gestured to a couple of free tables next to the windows.

Marcus was, however, looking beyond him at Eliza. He knew a potential playmate when he saw one. Her independent comebacks hadn't fooled him for a minute—she was as interested and curious as he was. Right now she was chatting to a couple at the next table to hers, as well as to the wine waiter, animatedly, while discussing the wine list. The couple and the waiter were lapping up her attention, and Marcus wasn't surprised. She looked hot.

He nodded in her direction. "I see a friend," he said, winking at the headwaiter.

He savored the anticipation as he made his approach. When he'd seen her on the dock, her blonde hair, longer than he remembered it, was wisping around her shoulders. She had it pinned up now to expose her rather beautiful neck. Everything else was just the same as he recalled, and stunning, too. The combination of bright green eyes and a vivacious smile was forever eye-catching. The independent, mischievous sparkle she radiated was suggestive of an attitude she lived up to on intimate acquaintance.

Her slip of red dress looked about to drop off, which appealed to Marcus immensely. It dipped between her breasts, swaying when she moved. He wanted to feel her supple, feminine body in his arms again. He was pretty sure she was thinking the same thing. The chemistry had been electric the first time they met, and it had hummed back and forth between them outside her cabin, like live wires crackling across the ether. Even now, with her bright, self-assured poise as she watched him making his approach, there was something palpable humming in the atmosphere between them. Reciprocated desire. He was sure of it.

Marcus smiled. *I'll have her on her back before midnight.*

"Care to share your holiday time with a work colleague?" he said when he reached the table.

She looked him up and down with a smile and mock suspicion. "Are you working right now?"

He glanced down and noticed her dress finished high on the thigh. Nice. "Let's just say I'm working on an attractive side project."

He grinned at her, and sat down at the seat opposite.

"I should turn you down for being so arrogant and making assumptions." She was smiling as she picked up her wine glass.

"But you're not going to."

"If I do decide to spend time with you during this trip, we do it on my terms." She sipped her wine before continuing. "If you agree, you're welcome to join me."

That was quite an air of authority she had going on there. He nodded, impressed. A waiter delivered a smoked salmon starter to Eliza. With a dramatic flourish, he also presented Marcus with the menu.

"I'll have whatever the lady has ordered. She has good taste." He smiled for her and her alone. A lingering memory of her lying on a bed, panting, after their first sexual encounter in Zurich played in his mind as it had done many times since. In the image her arms were out, hands still clutching at the sheets even though he'd pulled out. He'd looked down at her, admiring the view. Her pert breasts looked fabulous in the aftermath of hot sex, the nipples dark and jutting. Her green eyes were wild with pleasure, and her cheeks flushed. The way she looked at him in those moments after sex had brought him back to being hard faster than he ever had before. That kind of thing stayed with a man.

Now here they were again, thrown together, and she was looking like the most sophisticated date a man could possibly wish for. She looked dressed to kill, literally, as if she'd just stepped out of a film noir. Her hair was pinned up somehow and there was a slim choker around her neck that constantly drew his eye. The dress she wore was sheer class, simple but elegant, with a low scooped neckline. She had a mischievous twinkle in her eyes, as if she had a secret. It seemed to tap into his libido, because the fact that she was slightly removed made him want to possess her all the more.

He settled into his seat. "Are you enjoying your cabin?"

She nodded, her expression somehow knowing.

Looking into her eyes, he had the feeling she knew what he intended to say next, but he said it anyway. He was a straight-to-the-point type of a bloke. "You'll have to give me the guided tour, later."

"Pushy sort, aren't you?" Humor filled her expression.

His starter arrived and he waited until the waiter had gone before continuing. "You're an attractive woman. I want you. If I'm not wrong, you're also attracted to the prospect of some bedroom action. What's to apologize about?"

She gave a breathy laugh, and he noticed a slight flush on her cheeks. "Bedroom action," she repeated. "There you go, racing ahead and making assumptions. On my terms, remember?" She gestured at his plate. "Now, eat."

He wanted to eat, but preferably her, and she was sparring with him. That had the effect of making him even keener to get her on her back. He wolfed down his salmon rather indelicately, watching as she continued an earlier conversation with the couple at the next table. Her sultry, knowing attitude toward him made his blood pump hard, while the reference to her terms set his mind racing. What did she have in mind?

She'd ordered lobster for the second course. He approved. The wine was good, too, and, with Eliza on board, maybe this wasn't going to be such a tedious commission after all.

"Mmm, this is so good." She gestured at the plate with her fork, her face filled with something akin to orgasmic pleasure.

He hardened immediately. Putting his fork down, he pushed his plate away. He never could eat when he wanted sex. Besides, she was far more interesting than mere food, and so sexy. Her hair looked as if one pin stopped it from falling over her shoulders. How was a man supposed to think about food with a vision like that in front of him?

"What do you think of it all?" She gestured around the restaurant.

He took another mouthful of wine and glanced at the various couples surrounding them while he let the flavor resonate. "The last restaurant like this I set foot in was in North London, and it was my parent's fortieth wedding anniversary."

She looked surprised. "Your parents have been married forty years?"

"Yes."

"I'm surprised."

"Why?"

"Oh, I don't know. Not what I expected to hear. You've bucked the family trend, is that it?" She laughed softly. The idea obviously tickled her.

"You could say that. They've done the job of being married really well." He shrugged. " Just seems like it's hard to get it that right, you know."

Curiosity filled her eyes, and he cleared his throat, wondering what the hell he was on about it. It was something he rarely ever thought or talked about. It didn't usually crop up, but he had inadvertently led the conversation to it. Now he had to lead it away. "What about you? What's your background?"

She paused before responding, and for a moment he thought she was going to push him about his previous remark, but she obviously decided against it. "I have two brothers, and our mother brought us up on her own. She's pretty grounded. She taught us how to be independent."

"That figures. I've seen that independent streak in your articles."

"What do you mean?"

"You don't write like other gossip columnists. Your opinion is more obvious. And sometimes you like to push it a bit, don't you?"

"I guess. I'm surprised you read my columns. I didn't think you'd be into that sort of thing."

"No, I'm not into the celeb stuff. I only read it because I know you."

She looked amused, and that secret thing was back in her eyes. "Know me?" she quizzed mockingly. "Marcus, I assure you, you don't know me as well as you think you do."

"That sounds like a challenge."

"It might be, or it might be a promise." Her eyes flashed.

She was reeling him in, but he liked it. "Tell me more, then. How did a single mother go about making her daughter so strong-minded and independent?"

"Oh, practical things, I suppose. My mother is a staunch believer in arming us with survival skills. My brothers learned to cook alongside me. She made sure they could take care of themselves. I got to join them on a car maintenance course, just stuff like that."

"You mean you can change my spark plugs as well as turn me on? What a woman."

The insinuating and amused expression in her eyes made him realize how well they understood each other. She responded to his flattery with knowing looks, and then teased him for being so blatant. He liked the fact she wasn't a simpering sort, and he liked her sense of humor. The attraction was strong, and they had a lot in common. Attitude, in particular. But they really didn't know these things about each other. They hadn't had this kind of time alone, before. At the conference in

Zurich mealtimes had been busy social occasions. In the bedroom it was all about fire and sass.

He spoke about his siblings, and then listened when she talked about her teenage years growing up on the Welsh border country, dreaming of going to college to study journalism. What she said about her upbringing really did fit. She came across as independent. Confident in herself, without being pushy. She hadn't called him after the conference. Suddenly, he wondered why she hadn't.

Other women tried it, thinking he'd slide into another night when it was offered on a plate. Doubt edged into his consciousness. Was she just playing with him here? He felt sure she wanted him, but she was being guarded. He wanted to know.

"Thank you," she said when he topped up her wine.

"I want to keep you satisfied in every way."

"Oh, you are, and I'm sure you will tonight, too."

Result! He relaxed back in his seat.

Her lips glistened when she smiled his way. So sexy. He wanted to feel her soft, feminine body wrapped around his, and soon. He wanted to clear the table off with one swoop of his arm and have her right there and then, with that little dress of hers pushed right over her hips. A picture of her bent over the table with him thrusting into her from behind popped into his head.

She stared at him searchingly.

Their eyes locked, and her lips parted invitingly. Did she even know how hot she looked? He shook his head at her, shifting in his chair, and she nodded. She'd felt it too.

She pushed her plate aside. "I've had enough food. I want you now."

He folded his napkin. "That's music to my ears."

When he set the napkin down, she put her hand on top of his, making him pause. Then she leaned closer, her eyes flashing and cleavage tantalizing. "On my terms, remember? Do you think you're man enough to stick to my rules?"

He didn't have a clue what her rules were, but the challenge in her voice acted like pure adrenalin to his already fired-up libido. "Let's go somewhere more private, and I'll be sure to stick to you and your rules"

Chapter 2

Something electric had shot between them back there in the restaurant, and he'd hardly got her out of the place before he pushed her up against a service door in the corridor and kissed her. Eliza moaned and pulled away from his forceful kiss. She put her hands against his chest, and her legs almost slid from under her. His hands cupped and kneaded her bottom under her skirt.

He squeezed her buttocks firmly, opening her up with probing fingers. Her breath caught. "Do you think we can make it to the cabins?"

A devilish grin arrested her attention. "I want to have you right here and now."

He shoved one knee between her legs so they moved apart, making her gasp aloud. She had to clutch at his shoulders to maintain her balance. Intense heat had been building between her thighs over the duration of the meal, and his knee wedged in there was far too suggestive. Her sex contracted with need. She fought the urge to grind against him. Clearly, that was what he was inviting her to do.

He jerked his head back toward the restaurant. "I wanted you in there, over the table. I have never forgotten how good your derrière looked when I fucked you from behind."

Biting her lip to stop herself groaning aloud, she shut her eyes for a moment. It was so damn hard to stay cool while he was so bloody full on. She'd barely held it together during the meal, but she needed to be levelheaded if this was going to work out the way she wanted it to. Luckily, someone tried to push open the service door they were leaning against, and she rocked forward into his arms. Marcus grinned.

"Come on," she said, laughter escaping her. She pulled his hand, moving faster than he. That was brief. Soon, a possessive hand around her hip urged her to match his long strides. She counted the cabin doors and took a deep breath. This was the crucial part. When they got near his cabin, she stopped and turned toward him, grabbing him and kissing him full on the mouth, forcing him to a halt. He was taken by surprise, and this time she was the one who backed him up against the wall. "Hey, you haven't heard the rules yet, you might not want to—"

"Tell me," he demanded, huskily, "and hurry, before I strip that dress off of you right here in the corridor."

She put one hand over his cock, massaging it through his trousers. "First, we use your cabin. Second, I get to call the shots on what happens once we get in there."

He had his hands locked around her hips again, and he pulled her in, holding her hand tight against his impressive erection. A frown quickly formed on his forehead, though. "My cabin?"

She forced herself out of his grip, stepping back and tugging on his tie suggestively. "Come on. Your cabin is nearer, and I want you right now!" She set off. "You're not going to let a needy girl down," she added over her shoulder, "are you? That would be terrible for your reputation."

He paused for a split second and then caught up to her when she closed on his cabin door. She was gratified to see he was groping in his pocket for his key.

Inside, the cabin was lit by the occasional lights on the shore. They created slow-moving patterns of light through the space. He reached for the light switch.

"No, leave the light off. I like it this way. It's sexy." She walked into his cabin and dropped her evening bag on the chair. "There are two rules you have to agree to follow."

She delivered the line and then strolled into the center of the space, willing herself to see it through. If he played along, she could do it. If he laughed at her, or didn't want her enough, she would fail. She didn't want to fail. She wanted to know what it would be like to conquer a dominant man like Marcus. Pivoting on one tall heel, she turned to look at him.

"Two rules for my fantasy to be realized." She folded her arms and eyed him up and down.

"Rules?" he repeated, stripping off his tie and throwing it on the floor.

He was so aroused he wasn't thinking fast. She nodded. Dark slivers of anticipation raced through her veins. The constant, low hum of the engines through the cruiser only seemed to make her more sensually aware. She took a deep breath. "Do you agree to follow the rules?"

It was the only way she could deal with it, but she wasn't going to say that. She wanted him to think she was sure of herself, that she had the upper hand and knew what to do with it.

Marcus gave a quick shrug. "I'm game if it means I get to be inside you."

He'd much rather be in control. She knew that. But he clearly wasn't going to let it worry him, not when he was all fuelled up. He wanted her—that gave her strength, and it gave her power.

"First, you must do everything I ask. Follow my every instruction."

"Ah, I see. In that case, I am your servant." He licked his lips, his hungry gaze covering her body.

She turned away, and gestured to the back of her dress. "Unzip me, please."

He moved behind her and lowered the zipper to the small of her back. She could feel the weight of his hand unmoving there at the base of her spine, and his breath hot against her shoulders. He rested a kiss on her neck, a fleeting touch that sent skitters of sensation under her skin. Her backbone seemed to melt. She swayed, her eyes closing.

"That's enough." She turned away, holding the dress loosely in place with her hand. "The second rule...you are not allowed to touch me, or touch yourself, unless I say so."

A flash of confusion crossed his face, but he quickly masked it. His body emanated tension. There was a more serious look in his eyes now, and his voice when he replied was husky. "It'll be hard to keep my hands off you."

"Do you agree?"

The tension escalated.

"I agree."

Lowering the dress from her shoulders, she let it drop to the floor and stepped out of it. He stared at her, transfixed, slowly taking in the whole ensemble, from the polished elegance of her shoes, up the length of her legs and all the way up to the neat line of her choker, devouring everything in between—from stockings to lace G-string to lace balconette bra, just as she had intended.

His hands clenched at his sides. "Making me promise not to touch seems like a pretty mean thing to do, Eliza."

"Maybe." She bit her lip to stop from smiling, then threw her dress over the back of a chair, being sure to show him her derriere, as he called it, as she did so. She'd been unsure whether she could pull this off, but the way he was looking at her was making her even hotter, while keeping him at bay made her feel emotionally guarded and safe, too. When he was in charge he overwhelmed her and left her vulnerable. Not that she didn't like that. She liked it a lot. Too much, in fact. Right now, though, she wanted to try this tactic. It had a built-in reward all its own. Besides, it was a secret fantasy, and it was making her incredibly horny. "Do you still agree to follow the rules?"

His eyebrows flickered, his eyes dark with lust. He was taut as a bow. "I agree."

Power throbbed in her veins, her body hot and clutching inside, hungry for him. He was so male, so strong, and he was agreeing to do her bidding. She wanted him ever more with each passing second.

"You understand you are here for my pleasure." Her voice was barely above a whisper when she delivered her planned lines. "You may experience pleasure along the way, if I happen to toy with you…." She paused. It was her intention to drive him to the brink of distraction. "But please try to remember to exercise your self-restraint. My pleasure must come first."

He stared at her for the longest moment before he replied, "I'll try to please."

She leaned forward to kiss him briefly, her mouth opening, her tongue teasing against his. Oh yes, she could tell just how hard he had to fight the urge to take charge.

She forced herself to step away, pivoting on one heel. "If you do well, your efforts will be rewarded." She eyed him up and down. "Take off your jacket and shirt. I want to look at your body."

"I feel like a gigolo," he said with a slightly nervous laugh.

"Now you've got the idea." She flickered her eyebrows.

Unbuttoning his shirt, his smile tight, he pulled the white cotton free of his belt. His pecs flexed as he moved. The muscles in his belly rippled when he stripped, his body hard and powerful beneath the sophisticated suit and tie. Lust grew inside her. Her body yearned to be against his, her nerve endings running riot beneath the surface of her skin. He was so intently focused on her while he stripped that she had to force herself to take regular breaths.

She gestured at his belt. "Drop the pants."

Before he did so, he pulled a couple of condoms from his trouser pocket and threw them on the bed.

"Came prepared, huh?"

"Why not? I was hoping to get another taste of you. You're one gorgeous, sexy lady, and I want you." His hands were on his belt, his eyes on her as he hauled it off, flipped open the button on his fly, and lowered his zipper.

His remark let loose a sense of pride in her chest, and increased the damp heat between her thighs. When the trousers had been kicked off, she gestured at his shorts, where his erection strained. "And the rest."

He removed his tight black jockeys and when his long, thick cock bounced free, she inhaled deeply. She didn't let go that breath until his socks were also gone and he was completely naked. She gave a deep sigh of pleasure and circled him, admiring his body. "Looking good, Marcus, as ever."

"Why, thank you. I like to please."

Her fingers itched. She paused and reached out, touching him. His breath hissed out when her fingertips met his warm skin. She traced the muscles of his arms, following the lines down and laying her fingers over his. He flexed his fingers ever so slightly, lifting hers with his own. She met his gaze, and the question was there on his face. Accusing, inviting.

"Be careful, you almost broke a rule."

"It was involuntary. Honest." There was a note of humor in his response, and his body leaned her way.

She laughed softly and trailed her hands over the bone of his hip, where the smooth plane of his abdomen was broken by the sweep that curved slightly into his flank. His cock was so erect, so ready. She moved close against him and her hand rested in the dip of muscle on his buttock, her fingers caressing the lean, tight shape of his bottom. His cock twitched against her belly. She paused, her body against his, tempting him to break the rules and touch her. He looked down into her eyes. She could see the tension in his smile and the unmistakable glint of sheer lust in his eyes.

"You're being very well behaved," she whispered. "Chances are, you will be rewarded."

He swallowed but didn't reply. Restraint emanated from his every pore.

She stepped behind him and ran her hands down from his firm buttocks along the back of his taut thighs, bending to embrace the calf of his legs with her palms. Then she moved up again and her hands curved into the insides of his buttocks and up to the base of his spine, circling in the dips on the small of his back. His body vibrated under her touch. She stroked her hands over his back, slowing when the flesh rippled at her touch. Admiring the perfect symmetry of his shoulder blades, she turned him to face her again.

"Do you want me?" she asked.

He arched his eyebrow at her when she moved her hand over his cock, stroking it. His mouth twitched on one side. He nodded.

"Where do you want me?" She hated the fact she could hear the tremor in her own voice, praying he didn't notice. "Show me where."

His eyes narrowed and he nodded down at his groin, to where his jutting cock pointed into her hand. She repeated her request. He closed one hand around the stem of his erection, over hers.

"Right here." His voice was quiet, and his hand moved up and down. In the dim light, his eyes looked black with lust. His hand slid hers expertly in a light grip on his long, thick cock, in slow, even strokes.

She felt it inside. She glanced up.

His mouth opened and his neck arched back. He fixed her eye with his, staring blatantly at her. Oh, he knew she wanted it, and he thought he was gaining on her.

"I want you right here," his hand closed tight around hers, squeezing his shaft, and held still. "I have to have your sweet, warm body wrapped around me, and soon."

Breathless with need, she forced a response out. "I think you're making too many demands."

He groaned.

"On the bed," she instructed, pushing him against it with her hand against his chest. He stepped back until the edge of the bed hit against the back of his legs. She pushed. "Lie down."

He did so with a low curse, his hands splayed on either side of him as if to resist grabbing her. He stared at her, eyes wild—all man, all ready—his cock rigid and jerking against his belly. Her sex clenched at the sight, a nagging ache pounding out an erratic beat deep inside. She paused long enough to kick off her shoes and peel off her damp G-string and bra.

"You have great breasts," he whispered, staring at her.

Focus, she told herself. She had a plan to execute. Stockings next. Lifting one foot onto the edge of the bed, she rolled her stockings down, first one, then the other, making sure he was watching. Then she climbed over him, stockings still bunched in one hand. The head of his cock shone with a drop of his dew. She bent down and kissed its swollen tip, tasting his essence with her tongue, sweeping over the firm surface in circular movements. She reached for his balls and savored the movement of them in her hand, while she sucked gently at the end of his shaft. He moaned. Taking him deep into her mouth, she gloried in his hardness.

"I'll come if you keep doing that. Please. Stop." Each word was torn from him. Poor baby, he was so close. "Your pleasure first, remember," he added, his chest heaving, his eyes narrowed.

"How astute you are," she murmured, amused at his craftiness. She climbed over him and separated the stockings she had bunched in her hand to tether him to the polished chrome frame that bolted the bed to the cabin wall. He muttered something incoherent, watching her movements with a dark glint in his eye. He strained up against her. The rush she felt was unreal. All that male strength and power, tethered, was outrageously sexy. She felt light-headed, as if it was only the heavy throbbing inside that anchored her. She grabbed for a condom and quickly rolled it onto his cock. Breath hissed out when she stroked it in to place. Then she straddled him, her fingers slipping inside her hot, wet sex, and up to where her clit was ticking like a bomb, longing for contact.

He watched her touching herself, his cock hard against the back of her hand. "Let me in, Eliza, please." His voice was gruff.

She lifted the crown of the cock into position, gasping when its broad head pressed against her opening, and then sank down onto it, slowly, savoring every ounce of sensation when it filled and stretched her. Her head fell forward and she stared down at him. This gorgeous sexy beast was—for the moment—in her charge. Her sex clenched and her entire body suffused with heat, her hips already rolling to increase the pressure of contact.

"Eliza," he breathed, eyes rolling, hands tightly fisted against the chrome bar. "Oh, Eliza."

She gripped the chrome bar as well, and rode him up and down. She moved slowly at first, then built speed until it was fast and frantic, her body reaching for its climax.

"Oh yes." He groaned, eyes closing. "This is crazy, but you're so hot, and—fuck it—it's damn good."

"Isn't it just," she gasped, stripped bare of her armor in the act. Her thighs trembled. "You fill me so well," she added in a low whisper. A hot, heavy weight built inside her, its release growing imminent. Her sex tightened, released, and clutched around the bulk of his cock as she ground down onto him, her movements becoming purely instinctual.

"Christ, Eliza." His eyes were bright. The muscle in his tethered arms ridged, his body arching up from the bed. "What are you doing to me?"

His cock was like hot steel inside her, then it began to reach and lurch.

Her climax rolled up, swamping her senses, her entire body trembling. Her hands around his head, she arrested him with a hot, wet, breathless, possessive kiss. Confused emotions welled inside her, and she clutched at him. She forced the feelings back. Pull away. But he returned her kiss fiercely, and when she drew back to look down at him, stroking his hair, he shook his head as if unable to speak. His eyes were filled with pleasure, but also with admiration and passion, explosive passion. And, boy, it was going to be hard to leave—but she had to, because all she wanted to do was stay.

What the hell? Marcus felt as if he'd been hit by a truck. That had been intense, one of the most full-on orgasms he'd ever had. He looked up at her admiringly when she untied his wrists, and the first freed hand moved straight to her bottom. She glanced down at him, but didn't say anything as she untied the other stocking.

He was just about to grab her and roll her into his arms when she got off the bed. Marcus watched, perplexed, when she began putting on her clothes. "What are you doing?"

"I'm going to bed in my own cabin. I want an early start for my sightseeing tomorrow." She answered without looking at him.

Rising up onto his elbows, he regretfully savored the sight of her as she pulled on the skimpy red dress.

"Why don't you stay? I'll be ready for another round soon." He tried to make it sound as suggestive as possible, but she seemed intent on her plan to leave. Something didn't quite fit. He was sure she'd enjoyed that just as much as he had.

She flashed him a smile. "Maybe I'll hold you to that offer tomorrow evening."

"Why not sooner, like now?"

"I need sleep. I want to up bright and early to see Cologne in the morning."

"Cologne?"

"Our first port of call. We're docking there tomorrow." She glanced in the mirror, shaking out her hair and straightening her dress. "Why don't you join me? We could mooch around the sites together, get some lunch, try out the local beverages."

He gave a soft laugh. "Tourist stuff? No way. I have a good book with me, and I intend to sit on the sun deck and read it."

"You don't feel the need to check the place out for your article?" Mischief shone in her expression, but she was avoiding eye contact.

"I don't have to check it out. I've toured this region. Cycling holiday with my father, years ago. I had enough of rustic towns and castles to last me a lifetime, believe me."

She slipped her feet into her high heels, which made her skirt swish fetchingly around her sleek thighs. "Ah," she said. "For a moment there I thought you were resting on your laurels."

Marcus shifted uncomfortably, sitting up properly and leaning forward on the bed. Was he too complacent? Before he had a chance to reply or quiz her, she waved at him, using just her fingertips.

"Sleep well, and get your stamina levels up for tomorrow." She winked and blew him a kiss before heading out the door.

He stared at the closed door for several long moments before he dropped back down on the bed. Maybe she was right. He was treating this commission like a walk in the park, something he swore he'd never do when he started out in this trade. But he had a good reason. He knew this area. He'd been here before.

He shoved her comment out of mind, rearranged the pillow into a bunch under his neck, and breathed in deeply. The lingering aroma of her perfume—and the delicious smell of aroused woman and spent sex—filled his senses. He groaned. He'd be waking up with a storming erection in a couple of hours, and the illusion of Eliza being there and ready for him. But his bed would be empty. After tonight's unexpected, revelatory sex session with her—and with it being so fresh in his memory—it was a lethal combination of elements sure to drive him crazy.

Reaching for the lights, he flicked them off. Images of Eliza riding him, writhing in pleasure, filled his mind. He started to get hard again. A session like that deserved a second round. Why the hell had she left right then? It unsettled him, just as her remark about him resting on his laurels had. This whole week seemed designed to frustrate him. He was covering the most sedate commission he'd ever been sent on, and now the woman he wanted had "terms" and an agenda of her own. She'd better be ready for a come back round the next day. Turning over on his side, he thumped the pillow, forcing it right where he wanted it to be, and squeezed his eyes tight shut, willing himself to sleep.

When he breathed in, he could smell her.

His cock twitched.

This wasn't going to be easy.

Eliza's legs were weak and she struggled unsteadily with the key to her cabin. Resting back on the door when it shut behind her, she laughed softly and congratulated herself. She'd done it, by god, she really had managed to pull it off.

It had been worth every moment. The look on his face...and the way he was when he came. She gave a triumphant smile, feeling as if she were a huntress who'd felled the fastest panther on the face of the earth. She had wanted him, and it was good. But she'd protected herself, too. He was too damn attractive, and he magnetized her in dangerous ways. It had been hard to walk away, very hard. The last thing she wanted was to be left vulnerable, though, or to find herself caring, but she'd proved to herself she could protect her emotions this time. She'd started out on the right foot.

Not only that, but it didn't seem to have occurred to him that she was working. That suited her fine. Undressing, she hummed, her body warm in its sensual afterglow, her sense of pride at top notch. After visiting the bathroom, she sauntered back to her bed. When she slipped between the rather cool sheets, she tried to ignore the fact they would look and feel a whole lot better with Marcus in them.

Chapter 3

Marcus awoke when the cruiser's engines lulled. Rolling onto his side, he glanced at the bright sunlight flooding into his cabin. *Eliza.* He turned back, but the space on the bed where he'd hoped to see her was empty. With a wry smile he got out of bed, wrapped a sheet around his waist, and looked out at the town from his massive cabin window. It was day two, had to be Cologne. Yes, he'd been there, and remembered it vaguely. His cabin was too far away from the spot where the gangplank would be to see the passengers alighting. He'd been hoping to catch sight of Eliza before she headed off. Stroking his chest idly he remembered her fingernails raking over him as she came. His cock hardened, making him sigh.

He'd just have to wait. She seemed keen to have another session later. Maybe it would work out well. It was the sort of attitude he'd admire in a guy. *Yep, I can make it work.* It was a perfect arrangement.

Either that or it would drive him insane.

He stuck his head out the door and sought out the steward, Ivan. Ivan was removing a tray from outside a cabin further down the corridor. Marcus waved and asked him to bring coffee. The steward smiled and nodded. After Ivan disappeared from view, Marcus watched the other passengers dressed for a day exploring ashore. His gaze darted toward Eliza's cabin to his right. She could have called, awoken him with sexy looks and promises for later, before she'd gone. He shelved his disappointment and headed for the shower.

The coffee had arrived by the time he emerged. He dressed and tried to set up his laptop on the narrow dresser in his cabin. He wasn't comfortable there so he took it to the bed, smiling wryly at the pillows and thinking again of the night before. What a woman. What a surprise. They'd had good sex when they'd been involved before, but the fantasy she'd pulled on him last night had been red hot. It demanded a response from him, as if she had laid down the gauntlet. He picked up the pillow and breathed in, unable to resist. Her scent was still lingering faintly, and it made him want her. He shook his head and stuffed the pillow behind him. It would have been so much less distracting had they gone to her bed.

Picking up his cup, he took in the aroma of the coffee. He rolled a slow, deep draft around his mouth and cradled his cup awhile before putting it aside and beginning to write. Thoughts about the cruiser came easily, but when he read his notes, he found he'd described the setup in much more decadent and suggestive tones than he would normally use. It suited the luxurious vessel, but it also suited his current wish to have a certain vibrant, sexy woman with him.

After he'd drafted the outline and noted some key catchphrases, he used his mobile phone to touch base with a couple of colleagues in his office in London. He almost mentioned he'd bumped into Eliza but decided discretion was the way to go. Women appreciated that. He could tell the guys later.

When he turned off his phone he noticed the engines were silent now, the corridor hushed. Most of the passengers had gone ashore. It occurred to him she was playing hard to get to screw with his mind. Didn't seem like her style, though. He almost wished he'd gone with her or found a clever way to keep her by his side. Maybe he should take action on that point. If he found ways to make her chill out and relax, she'd spend a little more time with him. He headed off to the on-board Jacuzzi to see what he could do about getting some private time for them later that afternoon.

After a light lunch accompanied by a crisp Belgian beer, he took his Tom Clancy novel out onto the sundeck, where a conservatory-like affair sheltered passengers from any autumnal breezes. He turned a chair so he could see the gangplank, and settled down, occasionally glancing up to watch who came and went.

When he glanced at the Cologne skyline, he found himself wondering what Eliza was up to. The museums, perhaps, or the the city cathedral. He'd visited it with his father. So, if this was Cologne, tomorrow was...where? He had to get a grip on the itinerary. She was right. He thought about the Rhine route, fixing it in his mind. Bonn, tomorrow would be Bonn. He remembered his father taking him to see the birthplace of Beethoven there while lecturing him on making something of his life and pursuing an academic career. The memory stirred a wry smile. His big thing had always been sports, but he did have a knack with English language, and his father had wanted him to work on it, maybe go into linguistics. That was never going to happen, and it became a major bone of contention between them. He'd been a rebel. Maybe still was.

Hourly cruisers passed by, filled with tourists. These were day-trippers, and many of them stared at the River Queen with interest as they passed. Marcus scowled. He was a traveler, not a tourist. He lifted his book in front of his face, occasionally glancing past it. He wasn't sure what time they were due to depart, but the increased numbers of passengers returning to the vessel around four o'clock suggested it might be imminent.

Sure enough, he caught sight of Eliza on the shore, several fancy shopping bags in tow. God, she looked good, all energetic and alive, her hair loose and brushing over her shoulders as she chatted with other passengers. He stood up and waved, closing his novel. She caught his wave and returned it.

"At last." He sauntered down to meet her.

"To what do I owe the pleasure of this welcome?" She met up with him in the reception area, handing him her shopping bags and taking off her sunglasses.

"I have plans for you to welcome you back on board."

"Ah, you missed me. How sweet." Her expressing was mischievous.

He ignored it. "I've booked us some private time in the Jacuzzi, which I'll follow up by a massage from yours truly followed by a long, slow appreciation of your body before dinner."

"I do like a packed schedule."

The invitation in her eyes made him grin. "I'll give it to you, lady. But we'll have to head down soon. We'll start at the Jacuzzi. And we'll finish in your cabin."

Her eyebrows lifted, and she smiled a secretive smile. "Lead on. I'm fascinated."

Five minutes later they were strolling from the cabin area toward the on-board Jacuzzi room on the lower deck. Eliza was wearing a fluffy white robe which only seemed to emphasize her petite form.

She glanced at the towel he had tied around his waist with a dubious expression. "You've got no shame, parading along the corridors in a towel."

He shrugged. "I didn't bring a robe. Usually I don't have a need for them on the sort of commissions I undertake."

"I can see that. I do hope you've got shorts on under it."

"I'd rather not have, but we'll be subject to closed-circuit television, so I had to do the decent thing." He winked, put his arm around her waist and led her toward the staircase.

The room housing the Jacuzzi was tiled with marble on the floor and walls. Large enough for six people, the Jacuzzi itself was sunk into the floor of the room and bubbled invitingly. Eliza dropped her robe, revealing a silvery-white bikini that made him to do a double take. With her pale blonde hair and green eyes, she looked lithe and somehow delicate. He reached for her but she moved too fast and had climbed into the Jacuzzi before he could get hold of her. The look of her body moving through the water to the opposite side was so hot, he was surprised the water didn't steam. Dropping his towel, he glanced at the security camera regretfully.

He took a seat facing her, content for the moment to look at her. She rested her arms along the sides of the Jacuzzi, her wet hair clinging to her throat. She stretched her neck, purring as the water frothed up around her breasts. A siren, that's what she looked like.

She smiled across the Jacuzzi at him, and he felt the touch of her foot against his knee. "This is a real treat. Thank you."

"After your performance last night, I had to make a good comeback."

"Oh, I see. You thought that was a challenge?"

Reaching through the water, he grasped her ankle before she could pull her foot away. He drew her across the small pool toward him, reeling her in by the leg. He liked the way he could grasp her body easily when she moved across the Jacuzzi, mobile and sylph-like in the warm, bubbling water. She didn't put up a fight, so he settled her on his lap. "Yes. I'd pay highly to get you alone."

"And there was me thinking an orgy in the Jacuzzi would be more your sort of thing."

Slightly perturbed by her remark, he quickly corrected her. "No way. I'm a one-on-one lover, especially when that one is you."

She laughed and touched the end of his nose affectionately. "The big bad wolf has another side to him. You're just a soft pooch underneath it all, aren't you, Marcus Weston? I bet you secretly dream of smoking a pipe and having your slippers beside the fire."

He laughed it off, but he wasn't sure which of those remarks unsettled him more—the reference to the orgy in the Jacuzzi, or the image of slippers by the fire. He kissed her quickly, to stop himself saying anything else. She was a crazy, curious sort of a woman. Fascinating, though. What was it about her? There seemed to be no escape from the knowing look he saw in her eyes.

"You know as well as I do, I'm not the settling down type. However, when I'm with a woman, I want to give her my full attention."

"Loyal to the current owner, huh?"

"You've got a mischievous side to you I didn't know about."

"You're catching on." She turned to face him, latching her hands on his shoulders, deftly slotting one leg on the other side of him so she faced him with her feet on either side of his hips on the spa seat. She swayed on him, moving her hips back and forth.

The ability to think straight melted away when he felt the weight of her body, and the heat and pressure of her pussy through the thin barrier of her swimsuit, right up against his shorts. He was hard as rock, and it was only a sense of decorum that prevented him from getting his cock out there and then, and sliding it home.

He ran one knuckle down the front of her bikini bottoms, enjoying the whimper she gave when he rolled it over her clit. Stretching back, she pivoted her body against his hand, her hands locked on his shoulders.

"You have great breasts."

She gave a dismissive laugh and then moved as if to float away from him. "You're full of it."

That wasn't good. He pulled her back into his lap. "I mean it."

"Men prefer big boobs with cute nipples. I don't even have cleavage."

"Don't tell me what I prefer. Besides, you do have cleavage. I spent half of the meal last night hauling my eyes out of it, trying to avoid a slap."

She glanced back at him. "My breasts are tiny, and I'm too skinny. You saw a shadow, that was all."

"You're not skinny, and your breasts have attitude, just like you. I love them."

He leaned down and sucked the nub of one nipple through the fabric of her bikini top. He felt her tense and then relax in response, and her hands moved over his back restlessly. Through the fabric, he could see and feel her response, her nipple peaking and jutting through the thin material.

"Marcus, the camera." Her voice betrayed her anxiety.

"It's behind you." He pointed it out and then turned his attention to the other breast, gratified to feel her hands clasping his shoulders ever tighter. The scrape of her nails ensured his erection wasn't going to simmer down anytime soon.

A moment later, when he looked back at her face, he noticed a new sense of vulnerability there. She was aroused, her pupils dilated and her lips softly parted. But there was something else there. Eliza didn't look so self-confident now, and there was also a sense of wonder in her expression. He liked that he'd affected her that way, and he moved his hand under the water to cup her pussy through its Lycra covering.

The bump of her pubes felt firm and yet malleable. He squeezed, reaching under her and pressing the fabric into the dip where her body opened, the palm of his hand pressed hard against her clit.

She rocked, her eyelids lowering, a blush rising into her cheeks. "Marcus, I'm really aroused. You're going to have to stop."

He didn't want to stop. The need to give her a length—and soon—was far too pressing. "I want to be inside you. I loved the sound you made when you put my cock inside you last night. I want to hear it again while I let you have every inch of this hard-on you've caused."

A low moan escaped her, and she bit her lip. Her hips writhed and her eyes darkened. This wasn't going to work. She was ready now. And so was he.

"I've made a big mistake," he muttered, low. "We should have shagged first, before the Jacuzzi."

Breathless, delighted laughter escaped her mouth. She shifted and grasped him in a hug, kissing him, her wet hair clinging to his face as well as her own. He eased her back into the water and returned her kiss as he rose to his feet with her captured in his arms.

"Come on, back to the cabin now."

She nodded, and the look on her face showed him she wanted it is much as he did. He watched while she stepped out of the water. Her body seemed to shimmer, the silver bikini iridescent in the artificial light.

Following her, he snatched for his towel, tying it securely around his waist. "You look like Ursula Andress walking out of the sea."

Eliza put her hands on her hips shook her wet hair back. "Why thank you. You're doing a fair impression of Sean Connery yourself. Is this some adolescent fantasy of yours, me Ursula, you 007?"

"Maybe," he replied, laughing. "We can recreate the scene when we get to your cabin."

"Your cabin." She gave him a winning smile as he started to object. "I don't have any condoms in my cabin," she added, "and I bet you do."

The mention of condoms was far too enticing to his cock. "Too right I do."

He took her hand. They darted to the door and up the stairs to the main deck. There seemed to be people milling about everywhere, and the engines had started up. The boat was on the move.

"We're going to get a few stares." She glanced down where the towel was tied around his hips, and her slim eyebrows lifted. "Better hope your towel stays on."

He grabbed her in his arms, lifting and carrying her as he walked down the corridors toward the cabins.

"I can walk," she exclaimed. "In fact I can run."

"I am well aware of that, but I'm hoping they'll be so busy looking at you, they won't look at me."

"Ah, I see. Your, er, problem hasn't gone away, and I'm some sort of decoy."

He flashed her a warning glance. "It's going to be an even bigger problem as soon as I get you alone."

People watched them pass with surprise. Some laughed.

"So much for relaxing in a private Jacuzzi." With her arms locked tight around his neck, Eliza chuckled softly against his chest where she had hidden her face. The sound was infectious and even as he shook his head at her remark, he couldn't get the grin off his face.

"Honeymooners, got to be," a loud voice declared behind them. Marcus rolled his eyes and Eliza looked up at him, her expression filled with humor.

"What the hell is wrong with these people?" The door of his cabin was just ahead. This time he didn't care that it was his space rather than hers. It was nearest, and there were condoms. Plenty of them.

"What do you expect them to think when they see you slinging me around like some possessive caveman?"

"Caveman?"

"I'm teasing—hey, slow down. We're at your cabin."

He stopped. "Grab the door handle. It's not locked."

"You can put me down now. No one will see your problem."

As soon as he set her down, she opened the door and darted across the room, giggling, throwing off her robe as she went. The door slammed shut behind them, and he dropped his towel, running after her. She was busy clambering onto the bed on her hands and knees. He got there in time to grab the bottom of her bikini and haul her back to the edge of the bed with the scrap of material captured in his hand, revealing her gorgeous bottom while he pulled at the fabric. Collapsing in fits of laughter, she struggled against his grip, trying to scurry up the bed.

"No way," he told her, "you don't get away that easy, not after teasing me about my so-called problem." He held onto her hips, stripping the bikini bottom down her thighs as he hauled her back. "You're going to have to help me with my problem first."

Swaying, she flashed a killer look over her shoulder at him, hair hanging over her face.

He trailed his fingers along her nether lips. "Slippery."

"Your fault," she declared in mock chastisement, and then caught her breath when his finger met her swollen clit. He stoked it back and forth, back and forth, until she was shaking visibly.

"Please, Marcus, inside."

Moving one finger into her opening, he took a moment to admire the view. God she was beautiful. "Here?"

"Yes!"

Then she wriggled her sexy bottom and he couldn't wait any longer. He dropped his shorts. "Condom. Don't you dare move, I want you right there." Stumbling over to the bedside cabinet, he hauled the drawer open. It came right out in his hand and spilled its contents on the floor. "For crying out loud, how hard does this have to be?"

"It already looks hard enough to me, big boy."

Oh god, the way she was looking at him, those mischievous eyes focused on his erection. He snatched up a condom and scooted back into position. Taking a deep breath, he rolled it on, and then rubbed the head of his cock up and down her slit. She was slippery, an invitation he wanted to savor, when everything about her made him rush.

"Oh," she moaned. Her head swayed from side to side and she moaned again when he pressed at her opening, slowly easing inside. That first tight grip of her body on his trapped his breath in his lungs. Holding her tight, he eased in. Just an inch, then another, savoring each hot embrace.

"God, Marcus, that is too good."

"Can you take more of me?"

A breathless laugh escaped her. "I don't know, really don't know. But I want it. Feels so good."

With one sure thrust, he was buried to the hilt. His eyes flickered shut. She was hot and tight, clutching him invitingly. Staying deep, he moved in short strokes, each contact forcing his orgasm closer, ticking on as sure as a detonation timer. She writhed and moaned, her delicious body eating up everything he had to give and making him want to roar. He cursed. The rhythmic clutch of her body was going to make him come, and fast.

Soon the base of his spine was throbbing, his entire body taut with the build up. And then Eliza was there and crying out, tight and hot as she came—release, clutch, release. The dam inside him gave way, a ferocious orgasm breaking free. White light blazed through his mind. In those moments, he was only aware of extreme pleasure, and her voice crying out his name.

Chapter 4

Two days later, Eliza awoke with a languorous stretch and glanced around her cabin with a smile. She'd pulled it off yet again. The condom excuse had turned out to be a good one, but then yesterday he started carrying them everywhere. She'd had to pretend she'd left something in his cabin the night before. Once in there, she'd distracted him, and he soon forgot where they were. It was always hard to leave him afterward, though. It was a fine line she was walking.

Buzzing with energy, she got up and prepared for the day ahead. Soon she was wandering the pretty streets of Bonn. Being on board the River Queen was no problem whatsoever. In fact, it was fun having Marcus around and "ever ready." Because of her hyper streak, she didn't need much sleep, which was just as well because she was making notes for her report on the cruiser before dinner in the evening, or early in the morning, before they docked at their next destination. The three aspects to her day—work, sightseeing, and playing with Marcus—were a great combo. And, even though the fondness she already felt for him was growing, she was pretty sure she had a handle on it. Her time with Marcus was a treasure. Live for the moment, she reminded herself from time to time, even though she was constantly looking forward to seeing him after her time away from the river cruiser.

Bonn was an attractive city, and she found a great lingerie shop on her travels. There, she treated herself to some goodies, and found a bra that gave her a respectable cleavage. She'd almost believed what Marcus had said about her boobs, the day before. Charm personified, that's what he was. Still, in the moment, it made a girl feel good, and as long as she didn't take him too seriously, she'd be okay.

Oddly enough, Marcus was on shore when she returned, lurking at the end of the gangplank as he watched the approaching passengers, his hands in his pockets. He smiled when she approached, seemingly anxious to see again. Not exactly what she expected from the man who roved off so willingly from his conquests. Perhaps he was the one growing bored on the cruiser. He'd seen the stop-off towns before and seemed pretty reluctant about doing so again, but here he was on dry land. When she approached him a moment later he slipped a somewhat possessive arm around her waist.

"This is lovely," she murmured after she returned his kiss. The feeling of his hand gripping her possessively was divine. "Like being greeted on the doorstep after a long hard day at the office."

The remark had slipped out of its own accord. She hadn't even thought it through. His eyebrows lifted and he stared at her, but he didn't respond. As they walked toward the cabins she was fatally aware of his hard, eager body against her side and of how much she wanted him.

"Got anything interesting in those shopping bags to show me?" His voice was husky and low.

Watching the cabin numbers as they passed, she reached into one of the bags and pulled out a skimpy little black lace item. "What, like this?"

His eyes lit. "Very nice. I can't wait to see it on."

"I had a hunch you'd say that."

She stopped outside his cabin, drawing free of his hand, and fluttered the lace teddy at him. It had an open crotch. He glanced past her toward her cabin, the muscles in his cheek working.

He'd planned to push her on, she realized. Still trying to stick to his old habits. Naughty, naughty. Breathless with anticipation as to whether she could pull it off again, she waved the teddy at him, gesturing at the open crotch, then nudged him with her hip and did something vaguely suggestive with her mouth.

He grappled for his key.

Success.

❦

What was it with Eliza? By the fourth day, Marcus was still trying to figure her out. She couldn't sit still for a minute. He'd heard that about her from their mutual colleagues after the first time in Zurich. He hadn't spent enough time with her to know if it was her personality, though. He liked the active approach to life, of course he did, but he knew how to relax in between. Or, he use to, but not on this trip when she wasn't around, apparently. She'd infected him with her energy or something. Freakin' annoying. But being around her was good. She was like a fine wine—no, champagne. Then there was the fact she seemed to make friends with just about everyone in the cruiser. It perplexed him, although he figured it had to be some sort of inherent part of being a gossip columnist.

This just wasn't his idea of a perfect trip, but if she wanted to go hiking off around the sites all the time, that was up to her. He would have preferred a bit more of her company on board. Actually, a lot more. Even his Jacuzzi idea had failed to be the relaxing sojourn he'd planned. Not that he was complaining about how it had gone. He just thought it would have unfolded more at a more leisurely pace.

Before he knew it, he found himself on shore the next day, edging into the pretty town of Rudesheim. Tall, regular houses painted white and dotted with tiny windows characterized the romanticism and history of this region. He remembered badgering his father to visit the medieval torture museum here. That hadn't gone down well. His father had, however, introduced him to the excellent Riesling and Pinot Noir wines of the area, which he supposed was the gift of a more lifelong pleasure. Maybe if he bumped into Eliza they could do some tasting together. He scanned the groups of visitors milling about the place, searching for her.

They only had the morning in Rudesheim, but it was smaller than the other port towns so Eliza had time to gain the flavor of the place. When she started to make her way back to the River Queen, she bumped into Marcus rambling around a street market adjacent to the docking area. She waved, and he stopped browsing, or whatever it was he was doing. His gaze fixed on her as she approached. Her steps hastened.

Bob and Janine, the couple from the next table, overtook her and called out in greeting. Janine waved her shopping bags at Eliza, and Eliza reciprocated, lifting a gift bag. Janine cheered. It had become a bit of a routine between the two of them, much to Bob's amusement. As Eliza walked over to Marcus she noticed he looked fascinated by her exchange with Janine. He hadn't taken any notice before.

"Are you okay? I mean, you're on dry land."

He shot her a wryly amused look. "I thought we could do some wine tasting."

"What a lovely idea, but there isn't time. The cruiser leaves soon."

He shrugged it off, but she sensed he was disappointed. Interesting.

"So, you get to relax this afternoon," he asked, "after all your hard work sightseeing and shopping?"

That tickled her. "We're not done yet."

His face dropped.

"It's the Rhine gorge next. We'll be passing along it this afternoon after lunch. That's why we only have a half-day here. We could see it together from the deck."

He considered for a moment, nodded, and then relieved her of her shopping bags and carried them on board for her. Eliza felt as if she had made some sort of breakthrough, even though she had no clue why, or what it was she was breaking through.

Two hours later, they were on deck with the other passengers gazing at the majesty of the Rhine gorge—the most outstanding stretch of scenery on the trip—and they were doing it together.

Eliza clung to the railing on the deck, fascinated by the view as they passed through the gorge. The steep inclines on either side of the river were cleverly covered in terraced vineyards, and periodically were overlooked by historic castles. Some of those castles were in ruins, but most were just as they would have been in medieval times. Small, pretty villages appeared along the river's edge, giving the gorge a storybook appearance. Eliza felt as if she had been transported back in time.

At first Marcus stood next to her and when the crowd grew, he moved behind her to allow others to take his place, one hand resting on her shoulder.

"It's beautiful," she commented looking over her shoulder at him. "Have you seen this part of the river before?"

"No, last time I was in this region it was a cycling trip. We did this part of it by train and missed out on this. It is beautiful, yes."

He had relaxed, she noticed, and he was almost as entranced by it all as she was.

She watched him observe the scenery and it struck her how well he suited the backdrop. That was what he looked like, a lord or a king from one of the medieval castles on the hillsides. All rugged power. That was why he was so alluring, all the old world charm behind his contemporary attitude. The combination was downright irresistible. No wonder he could have any woman he wanted.

He caught her looking. "What?"

"I was just thinking how much this setting suits you."

"Maybe up there." He nodded to a rocky outcrop. "With my climbing gear."

"I meant more like you being the king of the castle," she teased.

"Oh, I don't mind the idea, what with all those pretty village maidens to pursue."

They were just messing around, joking. So why did his throwaway comment hurt?

"Look ahead." He gestured past her, distracting her. Two castles faced each other across the river, like two lovers separated but gazing at one another. The crowd around them chatted and gushed, their cameras clicking away, video cameras raised over the crowd to capture the view.

"This must be the cat and mouse," Marcus said.

"Cat and mouse?" When she looked back at him she saw a flicker of amusement in his eyes.

"Yes, I believe the castles are called the Burg Katz and the Burg

Maus."

"And there was me thinking they looked like lovers looking longingly at one another. But I suppose some lovers do act like cat and mouse with each other."

"They certainly do." He brushed her hair back from her face where the breeze had blown it.

Touched by the gesture, she looked up at him. Their eyes locked, and his expression grew serious. It caused a fluttering emotion inside her, and a wistful sense of yearning passed over her.

"You're missing the pretty scenery." He gestured in the direction of the riverside. He moved to stand behind her again, his hands on her hips drawing her in against him.

His body was hard and warm behind her, and when his arms gently enclosed her, it made her snuggle closer. Not thinking, she kissed his forearm where it crossed over her chest. It felt so good, and for a moment Eliza shut her eyes to the scenery, savoring the feeling of being in his arms. He seemed to be all around her, and how good that felt.

When she opened her eyes and rested her head back against his chest, he pressed a kiss to her forehead, and then another one against the side of her cheek. Emotion welled inside her. It was too perfect. It was also a transitory moment, never to be repeated, and she had to face up to it. Staring out at the rich green outcrops of forest surrounding the castle on their side, she realized what was happening. Somewhere along the way she must have let down her guard, because she liked him way too much. Stupid, stupid woman. Even though she knew it was true and she should take action to protect herself, she couldn't even bring herself to pull free of his embrace.

Mercifully, a wine waiter passed amongst the passengers shortly afterwards, and they separated to lift a glass. "You got your wine tasting after all."

"Yes, indeed." He chinked glasses with her and stared at her, eyes narrowing. "Are you alright?" He reached out his thumb and gently wiped the corner of her eye.

"Just moved." She gestured at the riverbank. "By all of this."

He nodded slowly, thoughtfully, and then he bent down to kiss her mouth. He did it so softly, so gently. Her lips parted under his, and when he cupped the back of her head, drinking her in more urgently, she all but melted. The blissful rising sensation in her chest was mirrored by a sinking feeling that was much more realistic. She needed to back off.

When Marcus drew back he looked at her strangely. "Do you want to catch some time alone before dinner?"

He gave her a warm, suggestive smile. He was thinking about sex, and deep down she was, too. She wanted him, but she forced herself to take a deep breath and pretended to misunderstand him. "Time alone?

Yes. I'll catch forty winks and see you at dinner, okay?"

Before he had a chance to talk her around, she handed him her glass and squeezed her way through the crowd. It was the only sensible thing to do.

❧❀(ᴗ)❀☙

"Work. I'm here to work," Eliza told herself in her cabin an hour later.

She'd been staring out the window out for ages, barely seeing the cabin-level view. What had happened between them? Where had she gone wrong? She'd let her guard down somewhere along the way. Spent too much time with him, most likely. She'd tried to maintain a balance, but when they were together it was so good. She had to distract herself, and the best way to do that was to put a bit of distance between them.

She set up her laptop and began typing up some of the notes she'd made. Making good progress, she began to feel a bit more together, and then there was a knock on the door.

She figured it was the steward, but when she opened the door, she was surprised to see Marcus standing there. He was dressed for dinner and looking gorgeous, his hair still wet from the shower, a purple shirt over black trousers giving him a deliciously dark look.

"Is it time for dinner already?"

"Not yet, but I thought I'd help you get ready." He winked.

She glanced over her shoulder. The laptop was open on the dresser. "I wasn't expecting you."

"Not harboring another lover in here on the side, are you?" He grabbed her playfully and kissed her on the tip of her nose. "I came down to tell you I decided to go on the excursion with you tomorrow, if you'll have me along."

"I'd love that," she blurted, surprised but pleased. So much for her new resolution to spend less time with him.

He glanced around the cabin and closed the door. "Hey, what are you working on?"

"Just a few notes."

Marcus was already over there, still happily smiling while he was scanning the information on the screen. What would he say when he found out she was documenting the trip? He'd be surprised. It probably hadn't even occurred to him that she was working, not just having fun. She'd have to come clean about her new job, and she really hoped he didn't tease her too much about it. She'd lose her nerve with the report if he did.

His expression slowly altered and he stood up straight, turning to look back at her. "You're not on holiday at all. You're covering the maiden voyage, just as I am."

"Well, not exactly, but kind of."

"Eliza, you led me to believe you were a tourist."

"No, you assumed that."

He shook his head at her, his expression darkening by the moment. "So this is why you didn't want me in your cabin, in case I found out what you were really doing here."

"Actually, no, that wasn't why I kept you out of my cabin." It was a very different reason indeed.

He didn't even seem to hear her response. "I have no idea how you celebrity journalists do things, but if there are other travel journalists covering the same subject, it's a territorial thing." He frowned at her, annoyance festering in his eyes. "I'm not comfortable consorting with the opposition."

"Marcus! I'm not the opposition." His remark really stung, but if he didn't take time to get to know a woman properly, he was bound to get himself into situations like this. Perhaps he had done so before, and that was why he kept his relationships brief. She folded her arms, looking at him with a sense of pity.

He shook his head. "But you are opposition. That's how it works in this field. You should have announced yourself. It was unfair of you not to do so."

She could have interrupted him, pointed out she wasn't a competitor and it was a different kind of reporting that she was here to do. But she didn't because she knew she should be backing off anyway. Instead, she forced her emotional armor into place and let him roll with his assumptions, just as he had at the dockside in Amsterdam.

He held up his hands and looked her up and down with regret. "I'm sorry, Eliza. This arrangement isn't going to work any more."

Arrangement? That's all it was to him. Of course it was. She pursed her lips, using her annoyance to quickly shield the wobbly emotions she felt. "It wasn't going to work anyway," she responded coolly. "This is probably for the best."

He stared at her, as if shocked she hadn't put up a fight, and then gave a curt nod, and left.

Eliza stared at the door as it shut behind him, and then threw up her hands. "Men!"

Chapter 5

Marcus picked up his coffee cup and took a quick swig before tucking into a large omelet and a stack of toast. He'd skipped dinner the night before, slept badly, and now he was starving. He surveyed the nearby couples taking breakfast together, frowning while he did so. There were dozens of them, happily flirting over the food as if they'd been at it like rabbits all night. Why had he failed to notice all these couples flirting with each other the day before?

Because you were too busy doing it, as well, and you were happy then. That didn't help his grumpy mood. Even though he hated to admit it, he sorely missed his time with Eliza. Why hadn't she told him? And why was she even doing a travel feature? He kind of wished he'd hung on long enough to find out, but he'd been so taken aback, his instinct was to draw a line in the sand.

There was no sign of her. He'd been up since dawn, pacing the deck with one eye on the restaurant. Maybe she'd skipped breakfast to avoid him, which was probably just as well, seeing as some perverse urge had led him eventually to sit at the table they usually shared. Maybe she planned to pick up something at their stop, wherever the hell it was. He peered out at the pretty town where they had docked a half hour earlier. Cochem, he recalled.

He fidgeted and took another mouthful of his coffee, inwardly groaning when he saw Hans making his way across the restaurant toward him. No doubt the man was about to inquire if Madame would be joining him soon.

One of the other passengers reached out to distract him when he walked by.

"Hans, can you tell me what time the excursion to the castle kicks off?" The passenger spoke in enthusiastic American-accented tones. It was the woman at the next table, the one who Eliza had been speaking to. Janine, or Jane, was it?

Marcus glanced out of the window while he listened to Hans give his reply. Eliza had wanted to see Cochem castle. Was she out there now, just the way she had been the previous few days? Had she been able to push this thing between them to one side, all cool and efficient? The idea of her being so level-headed annoyed him, because he was feeling less so than he ever had. If it had been a male colleague, he'd have known how to handle it. Territories would have been guarded, a contest unleashed. The fact it was a woman—and it was Eliza, whom he'd been enjoying—rattled him. But she hadn't been rattled. He remembered the steady, knowing look in her eyes when he'd caught her out, as though she wasn't surprised by his reaction.

Some little devil urged him to follow her around Cochem. Why? He didn't need to see the place for himself. Or did he? Doubt niggled at him. Who the hell was she working for, anyway, a direct competitor? Curiosity about her new job mingled with the basic to desire to see her.

The couple at the next table hurriedly rose to their feet, the woman wrapping her half eaten breakfast croissant in a serviette as they left. Hans was directing them toward the exit to shore. Apparently the excursion was beginning imminently.

Eliza would be on the excursion as well. He wanted to see her, and he probably shouldn't let her out of his sights. He swallowed down the rest of his coffee.

"Marcus Weston, I didn't know you were on this jaunt."

Just as he stood up to leave the table, a familiar face confronted him, a slim bespectacled man with a keen expression. It was Jonty Sullivan, a travel journalist who worked for a group of Northern and Scottish newspapers. "Jonty, what a surprise. I had no idea you were on board."

Jonty gave a sheepish grin. "I've been using a lot of the time to clear my backlog of paperwork. Between ourselves, the number of couples aboard was doing my head in. I've been taking most of the meals in my cabin." Jonty glanced down at the unused setting at the table opposite Marcus. "You know what it's like."

Marcus hadn't known what it was like, not until this morning. He gave a tight smile. "Covering the trip?"

"Of course, why else." Jonty considered him for a moment. "Look, I know it's not de rigueur but seeing as we're both onboard, why don't we get together this evening for a few drinks or dinner?"

The irony hit Marcus hard, and he just about managed to shrug and nod. Beyond Jonty, he noticed the couple from the next table had already disappeared out of the doorway. He had to make a move. "Sure, sounds like a great idea. I've got to head out now, but I'll catch up with you this evening."

Jonty nodded and waved a newspaper as Marcus headed off, apparently overjoyed at the idea of a potential traveling companion.

The irony made Marcus shake his head. He hadn't known how lucky he was, hooking up with Eliza. Working his way quickly through the reception, he strode down the gangplank, barely noticing the friendly greeting of the uniformed officer who stood dockside. The man gave him a well-rehearsed announcement as he passed. Marcus forced a smile, dodging the guy's speech to look past him. There were several other launches docked alongside theirs, and gaggles of tourists moved toward the town area, where two small hopper buses awaited them.

He glanced back at the officer. "I haven't booked, but I'd like to join the excursion. Which one is our designated tour bus?"

Tour bus. The idea of it seemed ludicrous to him, the furthest thing from what he normally did. He wanted to catch up with Eliza, though, and she was bound to be on it.

The officer's expression changed and he looked quickly at his watch before gesturing at the bus parked at the corner of the nearest street. Its door was just swishing shut. "The tour is due to leave just about now."

Marcus' mouth twitched. "Where's it heading?"

The officer nodded up the hillside. "To the castle." As the bus started to move off, he looked apologetic. "The town itself is popular with passengers, too."

"The castle will do just fine. I'll make my own way there. Thank you." Marcus strode after the coach as it trundled around a corner into the town.

"Who needs a coach, anyway?" He glanced up at the castle. It was perched on the hillside, practically on top of the village. He broke into a jog. The route was steep, but that was much more his cup of tea. This was something he could get his teeth into.

Weaving his way through the narrow town streets, he followed the street signs to the Burg castle. The town was already busy and he had to dodge groups of tourists. As he jogged up the winding road that led to the castle he remembered being there before. He and his father had left their bikes in the town and walked this same path. On the one hand it seemed so long ago. On the other it felt as if nothing had really changed.

Before long his muscles were warm and limber, his body enjoying the workout. His temperature was rising and he was only just beginning the climb. Checking the distance, he slowed his pace, measuring himself. He didn't want to arrive at the castle a panting wreck.

By the time he reached the portcullis at the summit, he saw that the bus had unloaded and a tour guide was in the throes of welcoming the passengers. He pushed his hands through his hair and slowed down to a saunter, taking long, deep breath to steady his heart rate. Several of the alighting passengers were already taking photos of the medieval portcullis complete with its crumbling tower while listening to the guide's introduction.

Marcus hung back until he had cooled down and then approached the group cautiously, casually putting his hands into the pockets of his jeans and milling among the vaguely familiar faces from the River Queen. The exercise had given him a bit of an adrenalin rush, and he had the urge to hunt Eliza down and carry her off.

The couple who had asked Hans about the tour at breakfast glanced over at him. The man frowned, but his wife nodded and smiled. The guy must have remembered he'd been at breakfast. Marcus nodded back. He couldn't help being amused by the guy's curiosity. He was no doubt wondering how Marcus had got up here so quickly. Not on some damn tour bus. No way.

Eliza was on their other side, surveying the castle as she smiled at the guide's humorous commentary. She looked perfectly at ease, although it was difficult to tell behind those sunglasses. She was beautiful. Not in the glossy, in-your-face kind of way that he usually went for. He liked glamorous women, at least he'd thought he did, but Eliza's quality was somehow subtler. She wore a simple dress with thin shoulder straps and no make up. Her hair was blowing in the gentle breeze afforded by the hilltop position, and she looked as if she could be advertising the benefits of good, clean, fresh air. When she turned her attention back to the guide, she glanced over and noticed him. Her smile faded, but when the group moved on, Eliza did not.

She was waiting for him. Marcus approached her, pleased that he'd had those few moments to catch his breath after the jog up the hill.

"Eliza, hi." He faltered, suddenly bereft of words. *Goon, if Jonty Sullivan can make exceptions, surely I can?*

Taking off her sunglasses, she revealed a wary expression. "Marcus, you came after all. I'm glad. Did you want to brush up on the castle?"

"No. You—I came up here because of you." He blurted the words.

"Me?" Her expression was so gently surprised and open, that triggered something in him—the urge to show her how much he meant it. He stepped closer and placed his hands on her shoulders. "Yes, you. You crazy seductress, you."

She laughed softly. "Seductress. Who, me? I thought I was the opposition." Her eyes twinkled in the sunshine and she felt so soft under his hands, he wanted to wrap himself in her.

"I overreacted. I'm sorry."

"Marcus, maybe things are different in your neck of the woods. With celebrity news it's a free-for-all." She grew serious again. "I should have told you, but I didn't because I'm nervous about what I'm doing here. It's new for me, and I thought you'd tease me. I don't want to mess up."

He drew her against him, feeling awkward and humble at the same time. "I'm so sorry. I've been an idiot. Look, maybe I can help you."

She looked up at him. "Thanks, I really appreciate that offer, but it shouldn't be necessary. I'm not even doing what you're doing, I'm detailing for a travel guide."

He groaned. "How the hell am I going to make this up to you?" He could hear the trip in his own voice even as bent to kiss her. Her lips parted in surprise under his, and he felt her resistance mount and then slacken. That shift made his need to possess her rise.

Behind them, someone cleared their throat. They pulled apart. The tour guide had returned and the rest of the group were gathered some forty feet away, watching them, amused.

The guide grinned, all shiny white teeth and sun flashing off her designer shades. "Honeymooners, yes?"

"Not again," he muttered.

Eliza smiled over at the guide. "Sorry! We'll catch up right away." Then under her breath, clearly amused, she whispered, "it's a natural assumption, given the circumstances."

She hadn't corrected the guide. What was the point, though? Everyone just seemed to assume that if you were touching a woman you had to be on your honeymoon. Looking into Eliza's eyes, he found himself wondering if they really did look like honeymooners. She did look like a happy bride. Before he had time to ponder that thought any more, she touched his arm and winked.

"If you want to make it up to me, come on the tour." Off she went.

Eliza strolled in the wake of the group, glancing back over her shoulder and winking at him, full of suggestion. It just made him wish they hadn't been interrupted. If the guide hadn't noticed they'd been left behind, he could've had Eliza halfway back to the town by now, back on the boat and under him, where—quite frankly—he wanted her more every minute. He felt a complete goon about yesterday and wanted to make up for lost time. She was playing with him, but hell, he was past caring. He just wanted to be around her.

Eliza had caught up with the guide and was chatting with her. Fighting the urge to rebel, Marcus stared at the two women as they disappeared into the castle. He wanted to walk in the opposite direction. Either that or throw her over his shoulder and leave. Instead, he trailed after the group, staying at a bit of a distance but keeping Eliza in his sights.

She smiled over at him when she saw he'd followed. He sighed. What the hell was this woman doing to him? He was tagging along on a tour group. The idea of it was absurd.

Numerous tour groups servicing a range of different languages milled about, passing from one viewing point to another. As their group trundled under the Lion's Gate—an ornate archway featuring heraldic lions—Marcus realized that the castle interior was smaller than he remembered. Although it was practically a small village in itself with

numerous separate buildings, life had made a difference to his percep-
tion of it. When he'd been here as a teenager, he'd never dreamt he'd
be chasing up here after some woman. Life played some odd tricks on
a man.

The group moved quickly once inside the main building, and he
guessed that each party had been allotted a certain amount of time. He
might not have to wait too long to whisk Eliza away. The group paused
inside a large room and the guide reeled off another stack of facts. Eliza
glanced over her shoulder with a flirtatious look in her eyes, capturing
his attention inside a heartbeat. The bare skin of her shoulders looked
so inviting, he ached to touch and hold her against him as he had done
the afternoon before when they passed through the Rhine Gorge. It had
felt somehow right to have her there against him. The mere swing of her
hips made him desire that connection in a more carnal way. His libido
had never been so hard to control.

"I want you," he mouthed.

She eyed him up and down and then, separating from the group,
sauntered over to a window overlooking battlements and a patch of
grass. She glanced his way again. Was she inviting him to follow? He
did, and she headed off in the opposite direction from the party. Where
was she was headed? He strode faster to catch up. The noise of the tourists faded into the distance. When Eliza stepped into the corridor, she
broke into a run. He could hear her laughing as her footsteps retreated.

"This has certainly livened up the guided tour." He broke into a jog.
She was fast. By the time he got to the stone staircase, she'd turned the
landing below and was disappearing from view.

"You can have me if you can catch me," she called up to him.

"Oh, I'll catch you all right," he shouted, snatching at the metal
banister when he rounded the next landing, taking the stairs two and
three at a time.

༚ࢶ(༖༙)ࢶ༚

Eliza darted out of the building and down the worn stone steps into
The Falconry, a grassy patch of land adjacent to the main keep. Her
breath rasped in her lungs, her blood rushing. So much for cooling
things off. She couldn't help herself. Marcus had been so adorable, and
he looked so wired, his eyes flashing at her every time she'd looked
round at him. She couldn't resist hunting a place for them to be alone.
She'd spied The Falconry from the window above. Now that she was
down here she saw that a great big wrought iron aviary ran along the
length of one wall, in front of which was well-tended grass, and, beyond that, a low chain fence. Wilder greenery lay beyond it, outside the
castle grounds.

She thrilled at his approach, his posture bold and self-assured. He was so darkly handsome, his body clearly defined by black jeans and khaki t-shirt. Just seeing him close the gap between them tugged at something in the pit of her belly. Pursuing her. He was truly pursuing her. Her body burned up with pleasure. She stepped over the small fence. The wilder grass was on a steep slope, but there were trees and shrubs beyond and the grass was long enough for cover. She struggled through the grass hoping there weren't any nettles.

"Gotcha," he shouted.

She cried out with pleasure when he grabbed her around the waist. Glancing back, she saw they were just out of the view of anyone who might visit The Falconry. She dropped her shoulder bag and threw herself down on the wild grass.

Marcus followed, growling while he playfully bit against the soft skin on her collarbone. "There's never a dull minute with you, Eliza Jameson."

He stared down at her, his expression almost brooding.

The way he looked, all deep and thoughtful, took her breath away. She was weak. She simply couldn't resist him. Plus, he brought out her naughty side so it was impossible to do anything but enjoy. She sighed.

He looked concerned. "You okay?"

"Yes, this is just so good, so much fun." She stroked his face, savoring the moment.

"It certainly is." He moved his fingers down the soft skin of her neck and cupped her breasts through the fabric of her dress. He fondled her through the skimpy material. "What, no bra?"

"That's the good part about having small boobs. Don't have to wear one all the time."

"They're not small. They're pert, deliciously pert." He growled low in his throat.

He really meant it. He did like them. Eliza felt wildly naughty, and moved his hands, pulling down the fabric to bare her right breast.

He grinned and ran his thumb over her nipple. "You're so bad."

"Maybe you bring it out in me." Her nipple tingled deliciously, heat firing from the contact of his thumb on her sensitive skin. "Maybe that's why I didn't wear a bra."

Narrowing his eyes, he looked at her with mock suspicion. "That seems to suggest you knew I'd come after you."

"I didn't know you would, but in my fantasy you did."

"I want to make all your fantasies come true." His tone had changed again. "I missed our time together last night."

"Me, too," she whispered, unable to maintain her guard.

He eased the spaghetti straps off her shoulders. "Oh, yes, I love the way this dress works." He pulled the soft, stretchy fabric down to her waist, watching as her other breast was also freed from constraint.

The air tickled over her naked flesh. "Are you sure no one can see," she murmured, glancing around, concerned. The tall trees between them and the town below masked them from view. But what if someone else ventured out here from the castle? She knew she had to risk it, just to be with him again, but the thought made her even more urgent.

He scanned the area, and then he flickered his eyebrows. "I suppose we might be seen."

Her heart beat faster still, the possibility of being caught making her hornier than ever. She pulled at him with needy hands, and he ducked his head and teased each nipple with his tongue, moving from one to the other. His face pressed into the soft skin of her cleavage, breathing in and moaning against her. His attention was too delicious. Her nipples had peaked and her breasts ached in his hands, sending rivers of heat through her body.

Vaguely, she heard the breeze stir the grass, the far distant sound of voices, and then his hands were on the hem of her dress and everything else faded away. The swish and sway of the fabric over her legs electrified her skin, and then his strong hands firm against her naked thigh sent her to fever pitch. He eased her panties down the length of her legs and then ran one finger over her pubic bone, and down, in between her nether lips.

"You're so beautiful," he whispered, kneeling up and staring at her for several long moments before ducking down to place a kiss on her clit. When she felt his mouth touching her there, she clutched at handfuls of grass. She caught her lower lip between her teeth. His breath was warm on the tender, anxious skin between her thighs, his lips and tongue deliciously moist.

He kissed and sucked her clit, gently at first, then more firmly, his tongue roving back and forth as his hands stroked her thighs. When she gasped and murmured involuntarily, his tongue retraced those most sensitive places, pushing her to climax. Eliza heard her own urgent cry of release being carried away on the breeze. Her thighs shuddered, and she bit her lip, drawing blood.

Her eyes stayed closed until he cast her in shadow. He'd knelt up to roll on a condom, and he looked every bit the king of the castle. The weight of his body between her trembling thighs and the hard nudge of his cock made her moan with pleasure.

"Yes, now," she whispered.

"I'm here," he paused, kissing her, "right here." He sighed deeply when he filled her.

She locked her legs around him and pushed his jeans lower on his hips with her heels, feverish with need. "Hurry, Marcus, hurry."

He reached for her breasts, sliding his hands over their hot, damp surface. His eyes were locked with hers, urging them both on. They thrust together as one. His cock was rigid, pounding inside her. The climax was coming fast. His fingers snaked into her hair where it fanned out against the grass, meshing with her in every way. The sounds in his throat were raw, both pleasured and pained.

She felt her sex begin to contract and spasm, and her hands moved over his shoulders, clasping at him. He tensed and came, his fingers flexing and pulling in her hair. Sensation shot through her in a series of hot waves assaulting her entire groin. He laid close over her as if he wanted to draw out the moment of powerful unity. He had one hand in her hair and he rubbed his stubbled cheek against hers, whispering her name.

In that moment, she felt so richly pleasured, yet so emotionally naked.

Chapter 6

"I could stay here all day." Marcus admired the camber of Eliza's breastbone yet again. She'd retrieved her underwear and pulled her dress back into place, apparently worried about being caught half-naked, but one strap still hung down over her shoulder, making her dress slip to one side.

"I think we've almost done that already," she responded.

"True." They'd basked in the sunshine for quite some time, teasing and touching one another.

She looked wonderfully languid, a rarity for her, and she yawned in the cutest way, her lips going into a small "o" before opening out. She shielded her eyes with one hand and looked at the sky. Tensing, she glanced at his wrist, then sat bolt upright and grabbed the bag she'd thrown aside earlier.

"What's up?"

"I'm looking for the time, and neither of us seem to have a watch on."

"I left the cruiser in a bit of a rush," he explained. "Chasing after you."

"That's right, blame me." She pulled a phone out of her bag and then her face fell as she stared at the screen. "Oh, my god! We're due back at the River Queen. Like, now."

"We can make it. Come on." He took her free hand as she gathered her bag up and straightened her dress.

They hastened through the grass and climbed over the low fence.

A cluster of people had gathered in front of the aviary for a demonstration. A man dressed in a green uniform had a falcon perched on his outstretched arm. He frowned over at the pair of them climbing the fence. The assembled group followed his stare in surprise.

Eliza giggled as they darted past them and ran up the steps.

"I bet I look a real state," she said as they darted through the building into the central courtyards.

Marcus looked her over as they hurried along. "Like a woman who's been well sated. I approve."

"Stop it," she retorted, chuckling. "You're making me lose focus and we've got a cruiser to catch."

They egged each other on until they rounded a corner, meters from the spot where the buses dropped off. That's when they almost ran into the tour guide who'd been leading their party earlier. When she saw them, her eyebrows went up.

Eliza stumbled to a halt and stared at the guide as if she were the prophet of doom. "Oh, no. It's gone, hasn't it?"

The guide nodded.

Marcus looked from one woman to the other. "What do you mean, it's gone? The cruiser can't leave without all the passengers, surely."

Eliza gave him a slow a nod. "They can. If you're not back, they still have to leave on time. They tell each and every passenger what time we need to return. It's our responsibility to get back to the cruiser on time."

Marcus was about to object when he remembered the officer at the end of the gangplank. There had been an announcement when he'd ventured on shore. "I had no idea it was another half-day trip."

"The cruiser heads north again today, back up the Moselle and onto the Rhine."

That should have been music to his ears, but unfortunately they weren't actually on the damn boat. If this got out, his reputation would be in ruins.

The guide was stifling a smile, watching to see how they coped with their situation. Charming. He had the feeling they weren't the first passengers to get themselves into this situation.

"Where does the cruiser stop next?" Even as he said it he knew he sounded like an idiot who had no clue what the bloody time was or where the hell he was. An award-winning travel writer who hadn't a clue what the itinerary of his trip was? Great, just great. His father was right. He was a loser.

"Dusseldorf." Eliza looked more woebegone by the second.

He wanted to kick himself. Yes, he should have known where the next port of call was. He was cruising here, but not in the way he was meant to be. *Get a grip.* He'd once taken charge and led a party out of a botched jungle trek. In comparison, this was a walk in the park.

He directed his attention to the tour guide, who adopted a schoolmarmy expression when confronted directly by him. She obviously blamed him, the one who'd been hanging back from the pack. "We can get a train to Dusseldorf and pick up the cruiser there, right?"

Even while he asked, he hated himself for not having remembered the basic rules of good travel practice, nor the time spent in this area with his father.

"Of course," the guide said, efficiently, flicking open her phone. "I'll arrange for a taxi to take you to the station."

"Good, thank you." He checked his back pocket for his wallet and then wrapped his arm around Eliza's shoulder, drawing her in against him. She looked like little-girl-lost, despite being Ms. Independent. "Don't worry, sweetheart, we'll cope. Besides, I've always preferred a customized holiday to a package deal." He winked down at her. "It'll be fun."

She stared up at him for the longest moment, green eyes glistening, then broke into the most beautiful smile and snuggled in against his shoulder. For some reason, that made him feel a whole lot better.

The train was smart and fast, but they had to stand in the corridor until a large school party disembarked at Koblenz. Marcus enjoyed the motion of the train and watched Eliza stare out the window, her eyes gleaming like emeralds in the afternoon light. Her hair was held back from her face by her sunglasses, which she'd pushed into her hair when they boarded the train. Admiring her profile, the soft line of her neck, and the fall of her hair against it, Marcus felt somehow intoxicated by her.

It wasn't how he expected to feel. She'd stood up to him, told it like it was. That was difficult to take sometimes. But she was forthright and he respected that. It was more than that, though. What was she thinking? She was so far away, staring out the window as she was. She looked as if she wanted to jump out and run away from him. It made him uncomfortable. She lowered her eyelids and glanced his way as if she'd become aware of his scrutiny. When she met his gaze, there was an aura of acceptance about her.

"What?" She touched her hair self-consciously.

Caught staring, he didn't know quite what to say. He didn't want to tell her what he was really thinking, so he gestured at the sunglasses resting in her hair. "Just wondering why you do that."

Her hand rose to her hair. "Oh. I forgot they were there." She shrugged and folded them into her hand, dropping them into her shoulder bag. "Just seemed like the instinctive thing to do with them at the time, I guess. When I'm not thinking straight…."

When she looked at him again there was both wariness and longing in her expression. He couldn't tell why, but she looked vulnerable. Not weak, but somehow tender. It stirred something inside him, and he moved without thought to close the gap between them.

He stroked her upper arms gently. "Look, I'm really sorry I overreacted yesterday. I should have known you were working. It's no big deal, really."

"It isn't," she agreed. "I'm not even writing a travel article. I'm doing the stats for a travel guide. If I manage this, I get to do more research for guide books. It's a new job for me."

"Ah, shit. I feel even worse about it the more I hear. I'm sorry. I should've known you weren't competing."

"Even if we were covering the same thing, it would come out differently, don't you think? Your articles are all about capturing the flavor, the energy, the rush."

He should thank her for restoring some foundation for his ego, but since she'd been the one to knock him into touch, he hung back. He had been resting on his laurels. She was right about that. Just because he was at the top of his game, it didn't mean he could relax. He had to stay sharp and be fresh.

He stared at her for several fascinated moments. What was it about her? Her independence was at the forefront and, only in rare moments —like when they found they'd missed the cruiser—had he sensed any vulnerability in her at all. She was different in other ways, too. Women usually massaged his ego, but for some reason Eliza constantly teased him and made him rethink things he was sure about, or thought he was sure about.

He was the first to admit he enjoyed a challenge, and she was persistently challenging him. Not in an outright way, like a colleague or another bloke would. It was an odd sort of thing, but it was getting under his skin. She fascinated him, and yet he had the feeling she could just walk away from him at any moment. She'd told him how her mother had made them all independent, and she made him feel it every day when she got off the boat left him. Most women fitted around what he wanted to do. Not this one.

She was following her own thoughts, and then laughed softly and nodded at the window in the door. "I just caught sight of the river. It's funny, us missing the boat."

"Yes." He glanced out and saw flashes of water through the trees growing between the rail track and the riverbank on this part of the track. "We'll just have to say we wanted to rewrite the trip for ourselves."

"I guess we will."

"Being with you has been the best thing about this trip," he added.

She looked at him and her lips softly parted. He couldn't resist ducking down to kiss her and touch her face with his hands. His cheek brushed against hers when he moved away.

She sighed. "This is all my fault. I should be on the boat detailing right now, not out seeing the sights. I don't need to do that for my job." She shrugged. "I just can't sit still for long. Being on the boat would have driven me mad if you hadn't been there."

"Me, too. You made it a helluva lot better. God knows, I like to be doing stuff, too." He shook his head. "I wasn't even meant to be doing this job. I'm covering for someone else."

"Ah, that explains it. I thought it was a bit tame for you, yes?"

"Not tame, not with you on board."

"That's nice to hear." The warmth in her expression made him feel better.

He shook his head. "The irony is, I wanted to get off the boat as well, but I had a rather tense time with my father around these parts when I was turning sixteen."

"The cycling trip?"

She'd remembered. He nodded. "He was using it as an excuse to talk to me about German culture and linguistics. He wanted me to apply myself to my studies. I was into the cycling. He wanted me to go into academic work, like him, but it just wasn't me."

"That would have been difficult."

"It never really got any easier. He scorns journalism." He paused. That part was hard, and he didn't even know how he'd got into telling her this. "I stopped trying to please him years ago."

He almost said more, how he lived his life differently in every way from his father, but he felt as if he might look rather juvenile with this rebellious chip on his shoulder after so many years, and he didn't want Eliza to see that. It had become important, what she thought of him.

Eliza was watching with a steady, understanding expression. It was as if she knew him already, understood him in mysterious ways. That was both comforting and disconcerting at the same time, and he wondered if that was why she was different from other women he'd known. Whatever. It wasn't altogether unsettling, which it should have been, given that he'd exposed so much about himself.

"What about you? Why did you change track? You're a great celebrity writer. You always made me chuckle."

"Thank you, Marcus. That means a lot." She stroked his arm. "I didn't want to get stale, I guess. This job was a chance to prove I was good at getting solid facts instead of running around chasing gossip. It's a big change in one sense, although it's not really that different."

"I'm sure you'll be great at it. You're a talented lady. You proved that during our first night on board."

"I'm glad you approved." Her expression didn't look as teasing as she sounded. She had a wistful look about her.

Marcus took a deep breath. He'd be all over her as soon as he got her alone. He wanted to make this up to her, badly. "We'll be in Dusseldorf soon. The cruiser won't arrive until morning. Let's get a meal and book into a hotel for the night, somewhere with a big bed where we can put yesterday's disagreement and today's faux pas behind us in style."

A shadow passed over her eyes. She masked it quickly and nodded, but drew back from him slightly. He didn't miss that. What was wrong here? His gut tightened. Didn't she want him any more? Had he blown it with her? More to the point, why did that matter so much?

"Are you okay with that?" He asked the question tentatively.

She was silent a moment, then nodded. "Yes, let's do Dusseldorf in style."

Marcus felt something hankering inside him, a need, and a deep sense of yearning. He wanted to keep her safe in his arms. He buried his face into her fingers and kissed them.

Marcus opened the bedroom door and glanced inside. "Excellent. Very comfortable."

He held the door open for her, ushering her inside. He'd been so charming. Every moment had made her feel special. The room was luxury personified, all rich colors and decadent fabrics. She dropped her bag on a chair when she sauntered in. She heard him lock the door, and then he closed on her. Arresting her from behind, he ran his hands over her hipbones, his mouth descending to kiss her neck.

Melting, she closed her eyes. It felt so good. He wanted sex to ease his ego, she knew, and she needed to pull back. But she wanted a last taste of him. That was what it was going to be. She'd vowed that much back on the train. Her plan to stay immune had failed hugely. She couldn't help it. She liked the man a lot. Every touch made her crave more of him and his crazy macho ways, but all he wanted from this or any conquest was the moment. He was the sort of man who made her match up to him, someone she could thrive off. In return, she'd confused him, and that had been good for him. But it still came back to what he needed for security. Sex. It wasn't as if she didn't want that, too, because she did, and badly. However, it wasn't medicine to her. It was a drug. It would only make her crave more.

He squeezed her against him. "The bed looks inviting."

It did. It was at least six feet wide and covered in a deep burgundy quilt and white, lace-edged pillows. An image of Marcus sprawled on the bed came into her mind, a dark panther barely sated from their lovemaking. She wanted to make that image real more than anything. Wanted to take a mental snapshot of it, one that would last forever.

"You're so adorable." He captured her ear lobe between his teeth and tugged gently.

She shivered at the touch of his teeth on her flesh. He walked her toward the bed and eased her down onto it. His hands delivered an alluring caress to her body as she lay back on the covers. Concentrating on his touch roving over her hipbones through her dress, she absorbed the heady sense of being physically adored. She was going to absorb every precious moment. Then the shutters would go up and the self-protecting armor would snap firmly in place. Meanwhile, this was one for the memory chest.

He pulled his t-shirt over his head and cast it aside. "I should have ordered champagne for the room."

Eyeing his bare chest, she reached out for him. "I just want you."

He touched her hair with his free hand, running his fingers down its length. The simple gesture felt somehow incredibly intimate. "I want that, too. I missed you so much last night."

Bending over her, he lifted her chin and looked deep into her eyes. For a moment she almost let herself believe the raw emotion he expressed.

Reaching into the pocket of his jeans before he cast them aside, he dropped a half-dozen condoms on the bedside table.

"Planning a long night?"

"As long as I can make it." He returned her smile and then undressed her, peeling off each item slowly, as if he wanted to watch her body revealed.

When he took off his jeans and his glorious cock bounced free, she sighed deeply. "Marcus, please, you're torturing me."

"Oh no, that's not what I intended. Looks as if I got something wrong here."

His tone was teasing, but once again she felt the subtle irony. Did he even know what he was saying? It made her want to grab him, hold him, have him fast and hard, and then walk away. Being with the man was like running on hot sand, exquisitely painful and shifty as hell.

Before she had time to bristle, he kissed her breastbone, moving side-to-side, caressing each curve and indentation. Her sudden resistance melted away just as fast. Her hipbone was kissed and licked until she whimpered. The arch of her foot got a special rub, and each little toe had its own moment of adoration. She writhed on the bed, and when his hand finally closed over the soft down covering her sex she trembled with anticipation.

Quicksand. I'm sinking.

She didn't care any more. Marcus, the sex god, was in full flow, and she was a mere mortal, powerless to resist and lost to sensation.

"Feeling less tortured?"

She nodded, her hair a mess, spilling half across her face, but before she could speak he began to kiss her across her belly. He buried his face deeply in her pussy. She clutched at the bedcovers when his tongue circled her clit, and then roved up and down her sex folds before pressing inside her intimate places.

"You taste as sweet as nectar, Eliza."

When he darted his tongue inside her again, she groaned and latched her hands over his back, her nails drawing across his skin. She caressed his neck and then slid one hand down to feel the hard, defined muscles on his chest. His name echoed silently around her head, and her heart brimmed with longing. She tilted her head back. Her fingers entwined in his hair.

He lifted his head, his lips shining with her juices. "You're all woman, and I want to be inside you."

"I want you, Marcus, and I…." Her voice faltered. "I don't want to waste a moment."

"Neither do I." His voice was hoarse as he rose up over her.

She reached her hand down to feel the size and power of his erection.

He groaned. His hands clasped at her waist before running tantalizingly over the surface of her breasts. Eyes wild, he grabbed for a condom and then climbed between her open thighs again, his cock seeking her center. Rising up on his arms, his body looming over her again, he paused briefly to look at her. His eyes were bright and focused, intense.

"Marcus," she moaned with a plea in her voice. She clutched at him when his hardness nudged into her. With one strong thrust, his cock was buried to the hilt inside her, and her body closed around him.

"You're so beautiful, so hot," he whispered between slow, deep thrusts, his hands lifting her bottom to gain better access.

"You make me hot."

He thrust deep against her, reaching for her over and over. Her heels on his buttocks pushed him harder. A pant escaped her throat each time their hips met.

She clutched his body molded inside hers. Each stroke reverberated through her most tender, sensitive places. She looked up into his eyes. Recognition and shared pleasure shot between them. Their strides grew fevered and he ground his hips into her. She tried to resist, tried to make the moment spin out, but the tight feeling of imminent climax built. Her reactions became mindless, a blur of sensations assaulting her.

"Now, Marcus." The hot tide of pleasure that rose over them was so large, she all but drowned in it.

He responded visibly, locked into the experience every bit as much as she was, his climax surging up to meet hers. His upper body lifted, his arms gleaming in the bedside light, the muscles in his neck corded. She ran eager hands over his back and hips and around his hard, tight buttocks, pulling against his body. She cried out, clutching onto him.

Pleasure spiraled through her and she was lost to the power of the moment. Small, involuntary sounds of relinquishment emerged from her open lips. She turned her face away into the pillow, closing her eyes, because even as she came a second time she knew without any shadow of a doubt that she was hopelessly in love with him.

Chapter 7

Eliza watched as the River Queen docked at Dusseldorf. The sleek white liner was like an old friend now, and the sight of it made her smile fondly.

Marcus put his arm around her shoulder and drew her in against him. He nodded at the boat. "I never thought I'd be so glad to see the bloody thing."

"Yes, it's a relief, although I expect we're in for some ribbing from the other passengers."

"True, but I'm sure we can handle the infamy." He glanced down at her, and he looked happy.

All she could feel was a growing sense of pain taking root inside her. It was the knowledge that this would soon be over. She'd stupidly thought she could handle it. She couldn't. Now, her goal was to pull together her every scrap of independence and guard her heart.

He kissed her forehead. "Once we get back on board, we'll grab a long hot shower and then snuggle in bed."

Snuggle. That sounded so good. No wonder his career as a serial seducer was so successful. The man was charm personified. She flashed him a knowing look, but she couldn't face flirting with him so much any more. Okay, what she most wanted was to bury her face against his collarbone where she could breathe him in and savor the feeling of being in his arms. Instead she polished up her emotional armor and looked away, toward the deck. Some of the passengers were gathering there, eagerly surveying the scenery of the new port of call.

"I bet Bob and Janine noticed we weren't there last night," she commented.

"Bob and Janine?"

"The couple who sit at the next table. The American couple."

"Ah, yes." A frown gathered on his forehead. "Oh, lordy, that's reminded me of something I was supposed to do last night."

"What?"

"Jonty Sullivan is on board. He's a travel writer."

"I've heard of him."

"We often compete for the same commissions. Turns out he was given a complimentary place on the trip as well. I bumped into him yesterday."

"And?"

A sheepish look had taken up residence on his face. "I said I'd meet with him last night."

The irony of it really tickled her. "He'll think you stood him up. Serves him right for thinking he could collude with the opposition."

He grinned. "You know, if you were competition, I'd have to watch my back. You're far too knowing."

She shrugged.

"Although in some departments, your devious behavior is much appreciated." His dark eyes were filled with suggestion, his mouth lifted at one corner as he considered her.

Narrowing her eyes, she looked at him accusingly. "Now why is it I believe you're thinking dirty thoughts?"

"Come back to my cabin and you'll find out."

Eliza quickly stifled the urge to agree. She couldn't trust herself any more. Lifting her hand, she shielded her eyes from the sun, and from him. "Hey, a woman needs to get a bit of sleep occasionally, especially when she's been kept up all night."

She watched as the gangplank was put into position.

"Okay," he responded, reluctantly, "but keep in mind I do intend to keep you up all night, all over again."

Mustering up a smile, she inwardly wished she didn't want that so much.

⁂

Marcus found himself singing, both in the shower, and afterward while he was getting dressed. He was hurrying, too. The sound of passengers returning to the cruiser after the Dusseldorf stop had awoken him. Refreshed from the sleep, he wanted to get back to Eliza. He felt mellow and yet high at the same time, much like he did after undertaking extreme sports. That same incredible sense of well-being and achievement suffused him, like a physical rush and a feeling of being sure in yourself. It was because of Eliza.

"Better than bungee jumping," he murmured to himself with a chuckle.

Checking his appearance in the mirror, he adjusted the collar of his shirt and ran his fingers through his hair, noticing how relaxed he looked. This had been fun. Yes, even when he was running up that bloody hill in Cochem it had been fun. He'd never wanted to run up a hill to get to a woman before. It felt good. She felt good.

He wondered if she'd continue seeing him when they got back to London. They hadn't last time. He wasn't sure why, but he really hoped they would this time around. It wasn't just that she was hot. She surprised him by being independent and yet playful. The need he'd felt to be inside her the night before was intense. Something unique, he couldn't deny that. Hell, he didn't want to.

As he walked toward her cabin, he was whistling to himself. He knocked and then called her name through the door to let her know who it was. There was no answer. He knocked again.

Maybe she'd popped out to get a coffee or something. He shoved his hands in his pockets and looked down the corridor, expectantly.

A couple of minutes later he was pacing up and down in front of her cabin when Ivan, the steward, emerged from the service room at the far end of the corridor. Marcus jogged toward him. "Hey, Ivan, have you seen Eliza Jameson? She doesn't seem to be in her cabin."

Ivan stared at him silently for a moment. He looked as if he didn't know quite what to say. "Ms. Jameson has gone, sir."

Gone? There had to be some mistake. "Ah, no, we weren't on board last night, but we rejoined the cruise today." He shrugged, pretty sure everybody on the cruiser must have heard the story about them missing the boat by now.

Ivan shook his head. "I'm sorry, Sir, but she left about fifteen minutes ago. I believe she's traveling back to England by rail."

"She can't have gone, we were supposed to…." Incomprehension swamped him. It was fast followed by blind panic. It couldn't be so. They were having so much fun. He glanced back down the corridor. "Show me her cabin. There has to be some mistake."

Down the corridor, Ivan opened the door to Eliza's cabin and stepped back to let Marcus pass. Marcus stared at the empty space, trying to grasp what was happening. It was true. Her stuff was gone. The bed was still neatly made from the day before. She'd never gone for a nap at all.

Ivan left, closing the door as if he sensed Marcus wanted to be left alone. He did. The only person he wanted to be with was Eliza, but for some obscure reason she'd gone. Emotion churned inside him, a sense of loss tinged with anger and confusion. Why had she left?

It was then he remembered how she'd been that morning. She'd been slightly withdrawn over breakfast. Her normal joie de vivre was masked by something thoughtful, like a sense of misgiving. He'd assumed she was tired, but he understood now. She'd known then she was leaving. She'd planned it. There was a weirdly tight feeling in his chest.

That was when he saw a piece of paper on the dresser, where her laptop had been two days before. His name was written on it. Walking over, he stared down at it for some time before he picked it up and opened it.

Marcus, if you find this note you will know I've gone home early. I think it's for the best. Thank you for a fabulous time. You made the trip outstanding in every way, and I'll always remember it.

Take care of yourself.

Eliza.

For the best? He wanted to know why. Why, when things were going so well between them, had she gone? He wanted her back.

How hard could it be to catch up with her? She had a maximum twenty-minute head start for the station. He darted to the door, but just as he reached for the handle, the engines churned and that familiar vibration rose through his feet and legs. It was too late. The cruiser was leaving Dusseldorf, and he was stuck on it. If she was trying to avoid him, she'd planned this perfectly.

"Great. Just great." He glared at the moving scenery outside while he worked through the situation. Okay, so she had a head start. He'd get off at the next stop—wherever the hell that was—and catch up with her. Even if he had to damn well swim the channel, he would find her. He wasn't just going to let her walk off on this thing between them. No way. It was too good, so why ruin it? He wanted her, and he was pretty sure from her reactions she'd been enjoying him, too. Whatever had made her leave, he wanted to resolve it. He was one hundred percent hooked on Eliza Jameson, and he didn't intend to let her get away that easy.

Chapter 8

"Eliza, just pick up the damn phone and talk to me."

Eliza glared at the phone. How the hell had he found out her number, anyway? from a mutual colleague? Wherever he'd obtained it, he'd been tenacious in using it, filling her answer machine to overflowing with demands she speak to him.

She paced the length of her apartment, trying to ignore the way his voice affected her. Both tension and desire gripped her. Her hands ached to lift the phone and talk to him.

"You have to speak to me. I need to know why you took off on me. What the hell is going on here?"

That triggered something. Annoyed at his demands, when he'd done exactly the same to her the time before, she snatched up the phone. "Marcus, there's nothing 'going on here.'"

"Eliza, thank you for answering." Relieved, he was deeply relieved, that was obvious. "Why did you leave?"

"I left as a measure of self-protection." She pursed her lips and mentally kicked herself. She'd had no intention of even answering the phone, let alone explaining herself, but the man was so damned compelling.

"Self-protection?" He sounded bewildered. "You need protection from me?"

She'd dropped herself right in it now. "No," she said, her voice low, a lump in her throat, "against my feelings for you."

"You have feelings for me?" He was smiling, she could hear it in his voice. "In that case, just let me see you and we'll discuss this."

"Oh, no," she responded, shaking her head, "I know you, Marcus. You think you can pour some sugar on me and make me sweet. It was fun while it lasted, but the longer it goes on, the worse I'm going to feel."

"Why?"

"Because you'll just walk away when you've had enough, and I'll get hurt."

"And it was okay for you to do exactly that to me on the cruiser?" He sounded annoyed now.

That was low. "It's what you did last time, had me and then waved goodbye." Exasperated, she left out a huge sigh. The tension had been building ever since he started calling her, or maybe even before.

"No," he responded, "this was—"

"I need to pull my life back into order," she interrupted. "Let's just drop it. Goodbye, Marcus."

She put the phone down, keeping her hand firmly on it as her heart thudded in her chest. She thought he'd just let it go like the last time. Apparently he had to be the one to end it, but she couldn't let herself be at his mercy like that.

When the phone started ringing again, seconds later, she pulled the plug out of the wall. All the emotional armor in the world wasn't going to protect her if he kept this up, but she had to try. Every moment they spent together had deepened her heartache. Falling for a serial seducer was bad news. Real bad news.

She flicked on the radio. The sound of London traffic reports barely touched her consciousness as she stared out of the window and paced her apartment. Being back in London was supposed to make all of this go away, but it wasn't helping.

She'd got home near dawn that morning and put the finishing touches to her report before sleeping restlessly for a couple of hours. In two days she was due back in her new office. With that to ground her, everything would be fine. She opened the window to breathe some fresh air.

An hour later she was staring with unseeing eyes at the flickering TV images of the weepy romance movie about to begin. She flicked through the channels, looking for something emotionally sturdier. She needed comedy. The nearest she could find was the latest cook-yourself-thin program. She sat up with a sigh. She grappled for the chocolate box she was working her way through and started on the second layer. Why, oh, why had she trusted her herself to get involved with him again?

Halfway through the cook-yourself-thin show—and another few choccies down—there was a rap at the door. Her breath caught in her throat as she stared across the room at the door. Unfolding her legs, she reached for the remote and muted the sound, glancing back at the door as she did so. It could be Marcus. The temptation to creep over and take a peek out of the peephole was massive. *Don't do it. It'll only make you feel even worse, if it is him.* But what if it wasn't him? Anyone else would have phoned first, but her phones were all switched off. None of her friends would be able to check on her. Maybe one of them was worried. Could be. It was the end of the workday. She hesitated, and then the knock came again, more tentatively. Marcus would knock with determination.

Standing, she crept closer to the door, trying to sense who it was out there. When she got near, she heard a rustle. It made her pause. Was the visitor going away? Curiosity had her in its grip, and she darted over and leveled up to the peephole.

Flowers filled her view, a profusion of colored blooms wrapped in smart delivery cellophane. She sighed, bit her lip. He hadn't been able to talk to her, so he'd sent her flowers. Maybe it was an apology that would give them both closure. God knew she could do with that.

"Yes," she called out, still unsure, "Who is it?"

"Flower delivery for Eliza Jameson," a gruff voice announced.

She unlocked the door and took the bouquet.

"Thank you." She breathed in the sweet scent of the bouquet. At the same time, a foot was wedged into the door. A ghastly understanding hit her. She'd seen that shoe before on the River Queen.

Acting on instinct, she tried to ram the door shut, crushing the flowers against the doorframe as she did so. A man's hand appeared around the edge and the door moved in her direction with a startling amount of force. How dare he? She stomped on that familiar foot, and there was a strangled cry from beyond. Both the hand and the foot disappeared. Throwing herself against the door, she locked it, triumphantly.

"Eliza!"

"That was a dirty trick!" she shouted, taking another quick look through the peephole.

"The flowers weren't to your liking?" He actually sniggered, even though he was massaging one foot. This was all a big joke to him.

A tight fist of emotion lodged in her chest, something closed in on itself for protection. She couldn't let it break free. That would be too painful and humiliating. She turned away from the peephole and leveled her breathing. "You know what I mean. Go away, Marcus."

"You're a stubborn woman, Eliza Jameson."

"I'm glad you noticed. Now get used to the idea."

Silence.

She could feel the tension building through the door. She closed her eyes. Knowing he was back in London and right there outside her door had hit her oddly. She wanted nothing more than to open the door, run into his arms, and hug him and kiss him. However, she'd made her vow, and it was the sensible thing to do.

Marcus glared at the door. "This is war, Eliza!"

He stomped off down the corridor, wondering if he could bribe the caretaker of the building to give him the master key. Probably not.

Her floor was too high up for him to scale the building. A couple of floors lower, maybe. He had another idea though, and he grinned as he reached the lift and pressed the call button. This was just the sort of challenge he enjoyed.

He'd gone. It was just what she wanted, but Eliza was left feeling wretched. She headed to the shower for a first-class pampering session. An hour later she returned to her sitting room in her pajamas and noticed the abandoned bouquet lying on the floor. She walked over and picked it up, forlornly plucking out the broken stems.

A cold draft hit her and she looked over at the open window. Summer had truly gone now and there was a nip in the air. She put the beleaguered flowers down on a nearby chair. As she headed over to the window, she heard noise outside. Curious, she glanced out. A crowd had gathered in the street below and several of them were pointing up in her direction.

Odd. She stepped back and away from their gaze. Then her eyes widened as Marcus descended into view outside her eleventh floor window.

What the…?

He wore a helmet and was winching himself down a rope in some sort of body holster. Drawing to a stop outside her window, he rested his feet on the frame and then signaled to someone above. Eliza stared at him, aghast, as he opened the window wider and filled the space, sitting on the window ledge and dangling his legs inside.

"Eliza, sometimes a man has to play dirty to get his point across. I promise I won't step inside. All I'm asking is that you hear me out."

He grinned, and she became aware he was looking her up and down, taking in the full spectacle of her dressed in cutesy white pajamas covered in big red lipstick kisses.

She glared at him. The pajamas were her special treat. They made her feel loved. No doubt he thought it was a hoot. "You've got a damned cheek barging in here."

"What's a man supposed to do when you won't answer the phone or the door?"

"And you think being aggressive and forcing your way in my window is going to help?"

"Eliza, I don't abseil down a building for just any woman. Now hear me out!"

She folded her arms across her chest. "Okay, two minutes. What is it that you want to say so desperately?"

Resting his hands on the window frame, he stared at her intently. "I wanted to tell you I figured out why they kept calling us honeymooners." He paused, watching her, pacing his words. "It was because we were so happy. We looked happy, and we were happy."

She knew that already. That wasn't the issue. "And?"

"I don't want it to end, and I don't believe you wanted it to end either. I don't understand why you left."

She shrugged, unable to deny what he said.

"If you didn't want to see me, you could have just said so." He looked annoyed. "Leaving the cruiser was a bit over the top, don't you think?"

"I had to get away."

"Why? Why did you leave without saying goodbye, damn it—without saying anything." He looked really angry, which surprised her.

"I didn't think you'd care. You didn't the last time around, when the boot was on the other foot and you walked away from me in Zurich."

"Was that what it was about, revenge?"

"No, but—hell, Marcus, you just waved as we parted at the airport. We were both going to London, but you didn't want to know."

"But this was different. We got to know each other this time. We were different." His eyes looked darker than ever, almost black, and the way he was looking at her made her feel exposed.

"It wasn't different." Her voice faltered.

"It was different. Look, I know I'm an idiot, and I know I've never had a serious relationship in my life, but I did want to see you after the first time." He took a deep breath. "This isn't meant to be an excuse, and I know this is going to sound really bad, but usually women get in touch with me."

She rolled her eyes. "Ooh, Mr. Luvaluva." She couldn't resist, the barbed remark was out. "Am I supposed to be impressed? Maybe fight for you?"

"No. I told you, it's no excuse. I'm just trying to explain that I thought you weren't interested. When I saw you on the dock in Amsterdam I wanted you so much, I gave it another shot."

Could it be true? He really thought she wasn't interested because of her brave face when he hadn't asked for a follow-up.

"Look, I'm admitting I'm in the wrong, but I'm not entirely to blame here. Your so-called independence is a front for your stubborn streak. If I can give a serious relationship a try, you can stop being so bloody independent and give me a break here."

Eliza swallowed. He was serious. He really was. All the tension in her body stepped in the elevator and took a ride to her feet, leaving her weak and shaky.

"Eliza, do see what I'm trying to say here?"

She just about managed to nod. Her sense of misgiving, and the need for security and her independence was still there, but her desire for him pushed its way to the forefront. It wouldn't allow her to deny this chance, not now, not after what he'd said. *Say something, before he walks away.* She opened her mouth, but when she tried to speak her voice sounded small. "So, where do we go from here?"

Gazing at her earnestly, he unclipped his helmet and dropped it onto the floor inside her space. The action was somehow significant. She stared at the thing when it rolled toward her, but didn't say anything. His expression relaxed, and he gave a slow, seductive smile. Shouting up to his accomplice, he unhooked his harness. A moment later the rope and harness was winched away, and Marcus dropped down into her apartment.

Dressed in climbing boots and khaki combat trousers with his shirt-sleeves rolled up, he looked downright gorgeous. The last thing she was prepared for was Marcus Weston standing here in her space looking so good and smiling that smile at her. She felt unarmed and vulnerable, and it was the last thing she wanted to be when he approached her. The tightness in her chest grew, and she fought the urge to run and lock herself in her bedroom. But before she knew it, he had his hands on her and he was holding her around her upper arms. He clasped her gently at first, then more securely, forcing her to look at him.

"Eliza, I understand this situation more than you give me credit for. Much more. I know I haven't been model boyfriend material, but I was gutted when you left. I wanted to see more of you, not have you walk out on me."

She'd never seen him look the way he did right then.

"Hell, I want to take you back on that boat."

Giving him a small, hopeful smile, she mustered a response. "The boat you hated being stuck on?"

"That one, yes."

Oh, but she was stripped raw. They both were. It was about saving dignity now and handling this with care. "But, everybody thought that we were honeymooners," she sparred gently.

"I was getting used to it." He kissed her softly, his mouth brushing over hers. "I want to do it all over again, be called honeymooners, be together, really together."

He looked at her so seriously she knew he meant it. Was she willing to explore that?

"So," he said, "how do I prove this to you? Tell me, Eliza, I want to know what to do. Help me."

She considered his exquisite, demanding question. "We could go on a date." The fist in her chest slowly unfurled, sensitive, vulnerable, yet somehow calm.

His eyes lit. "Yes, let's do that."

He stepped away and took a seat.

He meant now.

He sat back and flickered his fingers at her. "Better change before we hit the town, even though the jammies are adorable."

Resting his arms along the back of the sofa, he smiled and glanced around her apartment. When she didn't move, he glanced at his watch. "You're going to have be quick, I have plans for the night." He flickered his eyebrows. "The whole night."

"Marcus!"

"Oh, and I have a rule of my own."

"What?" She was strangely eager to hear his proviso.

He stood up, snatching her back against him, his hands around her shoulders, his expression determined. "This has to be the first of many dates. You understand me?"

Eliza nodded. The thing that had been lodged in her chest opened and began to radiate heat and pleasure, and when he kissed her and held her in his arms, her fate was sealed. He stroked her hair, her face, her throat, showing her with tender care how much he wanted her. She was powerless to do anything except enjoy and accept, and when she left him to get ready for their first date, it was with shaking hands, with tremulous but unguarded emotions growing inside her—hope, desire, and love.

This time she let those emotions grow, pushing back her fear and her need for independence, because she knew the man of her dreams was out there on her sofa.

And he was waiting just for her.

About the Author:

Saskia is a British author who lives with her Real Life Hero, and their big black cat, on the edge of the Yorkshire moors. Because of her parent's nomadic tendencies, Saskia grew up travelling the globe—an only child with a serious book habit. She dreamed of being a writer when she first read romance at the age of 12, and finally began writing seriously in the late 1990s. Since then she's had numerous stories published on both sides of the pond.

Chimera

by Nathalie Gray

To My Reader:

Chimera is about the forbidden fruit, that minute of intimacy carved from danger, that stolen glance and stubborn hope it's going to be all right as the enemy reloads its guns. All of which are bigger than yours. *Chimera* is love in the face of bullets. But primarily, it's the story of a woman who shares her sanctuary while the man she loves shares his wounded soul.

Chapter 1

He was blind. Eyes wide open yet he couldn't see a thing. Voices, smells of camphor and ammonia, but no image. Where was he?

Burning pain shot up his nape. As a needle would. A click from inside his skull made him blink and work his jaw against the strange pressure accumulating in his ears and behind his eyes. How could something click inside his head? Nausea rose in his throat. The last thing he remembered was sitting inside the shuttle on his way from New Heraklion for some planet-side vacation. Then this.

"Is he linked yet?" a man asked. Thirties, educated, careful. Familiar. Was the man talking about him? Linked to what?

"No," replied a woman. Gravelly voice. Older. A smoker. "You'll know when he is."

"Download complete," chimed a computer-generated, genderless voice.

He tried to sit but couldn't even move his hands. Panic bubbled closer to the surface. He pushed it down. No time for that. Later. Always had to be calm, focused and alert so he could do his job. People depended on him, dammit.

Maybe he wasn't blind. Maybe they'd just put something over his eyes. Had he been kidnapped by some renegade force, maybe a terrorist group or rogue political party? Well, he wasn't going to make it easy for the fuckers. They'd better have strapped him tight if they meant for him to stay.

Grunting, he curled his torso up by a few inches so he could rub his face against his shoulder, and then wished he hadn't. His world vacillated. He squeezed his eyes shut against the nausea.

Just breathe.

Panic made a grand comeback, and this time, this time he couldn't push it down, just like when he'd been a scared little boy who'd had to stuff teddies and pillows in all the menacing recesses of a too-large bed. Only way to stop the monsters. And even then, sometimes that hadn't stopped them. They'd wait for him to fall asleep so they could crawl out from underneath the bed and claw into his skull, plaguing him with nightmares.

Terror seized him by the throat. His breathing accelerated. A moan escaped him.

He could talk!

"What's going on with him?" the man asked. "He's not awake, is he?"

"Of course he is," the older woman snapped.

"My god. Will he remember this? Won't he fight it when it's time?" Fear rendered the man's voice high-pitched and made him instantly contemptible.

"Do you think they would believe him? After he's been triggered, he'll have six hours before the implant self-destructs and leaves nothing behind. As for fighting it, no one has ever been able to. Pain is a great motivator."

His heart beat so fast that it hurt. "Where am I?" he managed to croak. His throat burned.

"Your code name will be *Chimera*." The woman smelled of ashtray and old-woman perfume, a mix of roses and some unknown chemical.

Code name? What the hell for? Chimera. How suited to the monsters plaguing him.

Another intracranial click came a split second before the word *Chimera* blazed like white-hot steel behind his eyelids. Then pain hit. Hard. In his brain, over his face, every limb. He heard a man screaming, and realized with shock it was him.

He was suffocating!

Between desperate gulps for air, he felt something that had been lowered against his face, some kind of lid or cover. It didn't quite touch his nose. He started panting. His breath hit him in the face, smelled of medication and sour beer. But he never, ever drank alcohol, because of his profession and certainly because he'd been raised in a household of drunks.

A moment later, something whistled near his forehead, sending a tiny ribbon of air down on his face. A sweet smell filled the container around his head. Pod, stasis chamber… or coffin. He felt sleepy. Stopped screaming.

Inside, the computer voice accompanied him into oblivion.

"Launch sequence activated."

15 June 2377, 0600 hours GMT
New Heraklion Station, Mars orbit
12.6 light-minutes from Earth
"How long to the spaceports?" she asked, smoothing a crease in the

collar of her suit. She'd better look sharp. The media would be waiting for her to slip up.

Her assistant checked his watch. Expensive, like everything else the handsome blond owned. "Twenty minutes. I can't wait to get there."

"Not me. This will be the last twenty minutes of peace for a long, long time. Let's enjoy it." She closed her eyes briefly and stifled a yawn.

Months of campaigning, of sleepless nights preparing for the Planetary Commonwealth summit, had led to this. In thirty hours she would address the gathered prime ministers, chancellors, presidents and emperors. In thirty hours she would stand at the lectern, New Heraklion station's Lady Mayor Selene Delian, in the unsympathetic glare of Earth media, and either make history or make a fool of herself. Either way, it would end tomorrow at high noon. As in the old days.

"I wish we'd gone over the Asian campaign summaries one last time." Raphael's strained voice forced her out of her pleasant reverie.

She had so little time left for just sitting in a shuttle and closing her eyes. Even for ten seconds. Neither of them could afford that luxury. Red rimmed Raphael's blue eyes as it did hers. He pinched the bridge of his nose and made the synthetic leather squeak when he shifted in his seat.

She knew he didn't drink but tapped the console by her elbow. "Want something to wake you up?"

"No, thanks. I didn't have breakfast. Just forgot, can you believe that?"

"Yes, I can." She hadn't forgotten breakfast. It would take more than the fate of three million lives, not counting pets, to make her forget to eat. Ha. But she'd chewed her thumbnail down to the quick.

"We've been over these reports enough times," she assured him. "We wouldn't learn anything new. Plus, it's not as if they're supporting us out of the goodness of their hearts. They want our osmium."

Commerce. The number one reason for Earth's opposition to New Heraklion's bid for independence. Harder than diamonds and used in a panoply of alloys, osmium was the station's main export.

"Are today's news clips in yet?" she asked to keep him occupied. Should he become restless, he'd make *her* tense, and then their merry-go-round would mutate into an argument about some column of numbers or other. Raphael was dogged if nothing else. The one trait they shared.

He flicked on his portable scriptex. His was the best and newest model, of course. Hers was old but reliable. She wondered what that said about her.

He thumbed the screen and rolled his eyes. "Asses."

"What? Worse than usual? Wait, am I a loose cannon, a maverick or a glorified activist today?"

He turned the playing-card sized item so it faced her. On the full-color screen a headline read, "Selene Delian: Heroine or Gorgon?"

"Gorgon, huh? Much better than Dragon Lady."

"They take shots at you because you don't have rich sponsors." Raphael scanned the rest of the news, snapped his scriptex closed against his thigh, and sighed. "Gorgon," he mumbled, shaking his head.

Because of her non-affiliation with either of the two main political parties back on Earth, she represented a threat to both. Hence the hostile media. She knew the game. She'd been raised in it. Independence had been her parents' cause, and now it was hers.

Selene couldn't help but laugh. "At least it's imaginative."

They shared a quiet smile. After turning thirty-five the year before, she'd made a pact with herself to not let the damn tabloids get to her. She'd succeeded. Mostly.

Outside her tinted window, she spotted one of the giant hoverboards splashing the summit in vibrant colored light. Her hair looked red enough to set fire to something. A Russian doll in a suit. "Is Hector waiting at the dock?"

Lips pinched, Raphael nodded. No love lost between her assistant and the chief of security.

Her thoughts uncontrollably turned to Hector's second-in-command. Now *there* was a mystery. Hired from a security consultant corporation, the best in the business according to Hector, Agent Corinth remained an enigma even after almost a year with her team. She didn't know his real name, only his designation, because the Aegis Corporation wouldn't divulge anything about their agents. She'd never even seen his face, always hidden by the ID-suppressant helmet and the antireflective face shield. Although she understood the logic behind the safety protocols, she'd still love to see if his face matched his fit and firm physique. A shiver tightened her nape.

"We're there," Raphael said, scooting forward in the seat so he could open the shuttle door.

She wanted to tell him it was no use. Agent Corinth would get it, as he always did. She hadn't opened her own doors since his arrival.

Selene craned her neck to see their platform. To see *him*. Many people were gathered there, dock workers, the press, and some of her staff. There! She spotted a familiar black silhouette standing near the edge, his face shield angled up toward the shuttle. A tingle of excitement and affection rippled through her.

The sight of Agent Corinth, her silent anchor in the raging sea, warmed her heart. If chaos, assassinations and upheavals filled her life, he represented stability and a quiet strength on which she could count.

One night, after a particularly tough teledebate with Earth's most vocal detractor of the station's independence, she'd spent so long in the ladies' room that Agent Corinth had knocked on the door before poking his head inside. She'd been fighting the tears. Losing. Quietly joining her by the vanity, he'd put a gloved hand on hers and stood there squeezing, which had given her not only strength but solace. She could be someone else than New Heraklion's feared Lady Mayor. She could just be Selene. And every chance she had, she sought the quiet man's presence. A small nod from him, a look her way. Within a couple of months, she'd caught herself yearning for more than a stolen glance here or there. A low, simmering fire burned beneath the surface. Had their situation not been the way it was, she would have pursued the matter. But she could only watch. And so she did.

As her chauffeur maneuvered the shuttle closer to the docking station, Agent Corinth backed away from the steel handrail, his face turning this way and that. Scanning. She wondered if the man ever let his guard down, even for one second. Probably not. A shiver of longing prickled down her back, like a caterpillar on stilettos.

They were leveling off with their assigned launch tube, the concrete platform a mere ten feet away, when a violent jolt shook the shuttle and with a curse threw Raphael back into his seat.

"What the hell?" Selene propped one hand against the window for support.

The shuttle pitched forward, leveled, and scraped the platform. Yells could be heard outside. People ran from the platform. Another jolt rocked them and this time, gunshots drowned Raphael's voice. "Julie!"

The shuttle careened in a lazy rotation. Selene stood unsteadily. On the other side of the thin window dividing the passenger portion of the shuttle, their chauffeur was collapsed against the controls. The young woman's nape had been reduced to a mass of dark red pulp. Through two holes shaped like spider webs in the windshield, air whistled angrily.

"Julie!" Selene clawed over the seats to reach the chauffeur section.

After a second or two of frantic tugging, she managed to pull down the clear plastic partition and squeeze inside, avoiding as much as she could the blood splattered in a long line across both empty seats.

"Selene!" Raphael yelled. "What are you *doing*?"

Without their chauffeur's handling, the shuttle's rotation accelerated and tightened into a spin. Three hundred feet below them loomed the station floor, twelve feet of armored concrete braced with three-inch steel rods. She should know, she'd signed off on the spaceports renovation project. She was flooded by the urge to squeeze her eyes and wait for the messy end, but she fought it. With all she had. And her with a fear of heights!

Reaching over Julie's slumped form, Selene grabbed the bloodied altitude lever and yanked up. Too hard. The shuttle nose-climbed. She heard tumbling behind her, and then Raphael's voice rising in pain. The sound of things breaking rattled in the back. Suddenly, sparks flew off the consoles, which went dark for an agonizing split second before flashing back to life, but with all systems reset. Oh, no.

"Raphael! Help me!"

"Level off!" he yelled. "Level *off*!"

"I can't!" With the short-circuit, everything would be on manual. She'd never flown manually before.

Snarling, she reached over Julie's inert form—poor kid hadn't even reached twenty-five—and was shoving a foot between the chauffeur's legs when a muffled *thump* above her head momentarily distracted her. What now?

"Hold on!" she yelled to no one in particular. If she could just stabilize the shuttle, maybe they wouldn't—

A pair of black boots landed right on the hull closest to the windshield, six inches from her face. She let out a yelp of fright and threw herself back against the seat. Blood slicked her hands. Before she could do anything else, gunshots disintegrated the windshield in a rain of plastic diamonds that littered the seats and all three foot-wells. Moving as a cat would, a man dressed all in black slipped into the cockpit. She cocked her foot back, ready to kick the intruder as hard as she could. If they'd come to finish the job, she'd make them earn it! But he was no assassin come finish her.

"Agent Corinth!"

He'd *jumped* from the platform?

"The system's down! It shorted!" she added, happier to see him than she'd ever been before. And there'd been times when she was in fact so glad to see him she had to actively fight the urge to wrap her arms around him and lean her head on his chest. As she would an old friend. Or a man for whom she'd developed feelings stronger than friendship.

So that Agent Corinth would have room to sit at the controls, she braced her foot against the useless console to drag Julie's body with her, and lost her shoe in the process.

While she pushed and squeezed her chauffeur out of the way, Agent Corinth grabbed the altitude lever and smoothly brought the shuttle's nose up level, then slid into the empty, bloodied seat.

More gunshots. The window by her head exploded in rough little bits that got into her hair and clothes. With one arm shielding her head, she fiddled with the door in the hope of unlocking it before they hit the ground, where she doubted they'd be in any shape to do much more than crawl out. If they were lucky.

"What the hell's going on!" she shouted.

Beyond the passenger window, concrete pillars holding the space-ports loomed close. Too close. Damn. With the tip of its stunted wing, the shuttle scraped a pillar with a geyser of sparks and a long wail like a dying beast. The smell of fuel tickled her nose. "The wing! Fuel is leaking out!"

Agent Corinth nodded. They swerved back to avoid coming in contact with more pillars on their way down to ground level. Manually.

She'd never seen anyone pull that off. Hydraulics without sensors would be of no use. No one could fly without sensors and guidance systems. In this part of the station, they could hit anything from the osmium preprocessing factory to a scrap yard. It would be a messy landing.

And who the hell fired at them?

A black dot at the edge of her peripheral vision made her turn just in time to spot two small shuttles zooming out from the shadows between two pillars. Irregular flashes brightened the open cargo doors and illuminated people standing there, firing weapons at unseen targets. No. At *them*.

"Hang on!" Agent Corinth growled.

Even after a year, she wasn't accustomed to the helmet's computerized voice, another safety measure to protect Aegis agents' identity. She'd often wondered what his real voice would sound like. Was it soft or rough, deep or high?

Below the shuttle's nose, the ground spiraled up at them with frightening speed. Two hundred feet. One hundred. Fifty, twenty. To the onlookers, they must have resembled an out-of-control, silver spinning top. Alarms wailed and chimed from the consoles, adding to the impotent roar of the shuttle's engines. Their stabilizers and attitude jets must have been fried during the short-circuit. Agent Corinth pressed the pedal to the metal, but had no steering.

The ground filled the windshield. Oil-stained concrete. Machine parts. God, they wouldn't land, they'd *crash*. The press would capture every crunchy second from the platform above.

At the last possible second, Agent Corinth yanked on the altitude lever while simultaneously kicking at the pedals. Against the odds, their shuttle decelerated and caused her insides to squish down and her legs to feel like lead. The craft's nose came up, up, its angle allowing the skids to touch down first. Which they did. Hard.

The interior rattled. Polymer moldings and trims broke off the frame. After the initial hit, one of the skids must have collapsed, for the shuttle tipped hard toward the passenger side and almost spilled her out the broken window. She barely hung on to the frame and the loose seatbelt.

Not a second later, a series of small eruptions pitted the shuttle's nose in a line coming straight at the cabin. The attackers in the two shuttles she'd spotted earlier were firing at them again. They had their fingers to the trigger and weren't letting go.

Agent Corinth leaned forward with his gun pointing out of the broken windshield. "Stay down!"

She crouched down into the foot-well. In the back, Raphael yelled a warning a split second before another string of eruptions thudded against their hull. She spotted the two shuttles circling. Buzzards. She cringed when a few bullets hit the roof. The smell of fuel made her gag. The tanks!

"We have to get out," Agent Corinth said above the wail of police sirens growing in the distance. "*Now.*"

She'd long learned to trust his judgment. Selene pulled on the handle and kicked the door wide, half sliding and half rolling out of the tilted shuttle onto the concrete. Dust and debris ground into her palms and knees. Behind her, she heard the familiar whir of her bodyguard's breathing through the helmet. He didn't even sound winded.

"Stay close."

"Raphael," she said under her breath, pointing at the back door below the wing just as it opened. Out stumbled her assistant, his usually perfect hair mussed and his face pale and tight. He crawled to her on all fours along the shuttle's warm hull. All three of them hid behind the hull with the thick, short wing as cover.

"What the fuck is going on?" Raphael snarled, the smooth voice hoarse and tight. "Who's firing at me?"

She wanted to remind him *he* wasn't the target, but just shrugged as she hunkered down by Agent Corinth's side and waited. The faint smell she'd come to associate with him floated to her through the fuel and dust. Peppermint and aftershave. A clean, honest smell.

"Stay under the wing," he said. "They're waiting."

Selene looked around, hearing the attackers' shuttles but unable to spot them. Maybe they thought no one had survived. But thanks to Agent Corinth's fine handling, they had. The police sirens grew louder.

"Where are they?" Raphael demanded, craning his neck to see beyond the wing. "We can't stay here. The shuttle could blow up."

Agent Corinth shifted legs. "We stay. It's safer here than out there."

Selene nodded. She was staying right here under the relative shelter of the shuttle's wing. And Agent Corinth's protection.

From what she could see, they'd crash-landed in a scrap yard, with bits and pieces of shuttles, machinery and other vehicles in various states of deconstruction piled and strewn in no obvious order. Finally she spotted the two enemy shuttles and pointed with a bloodied finger.

"There," she whispered although she knew, intellectually, the attackers couldn't hear her.

About a hundred feet above, their pursuers converged and flew in circles. One shuttle veered off and disappeared between support pillars, its white-hot thrusters blazing long after the sound had receded to a faint drone. Its companion kept circling, probably looking for a better angle. Then it, too, vanished underneath the spaceports. She'd never realized how dangerous the station—or The Hive, called that because of its shape—and its spaceports' underbelly could be. Any sort of craft could hide undetected in there. She'd ask station security to review the schematics for ways to do something about this. Another bullet on her to-do list.

"They're gone." Raphael poked his head above the shuttle wing, an easy reach with his height. Selene, on the other hand, could practically walk under it while carrying a raised umbrella.

The shuttles' departure didn't convince her. Call her cynical. "They're waiting to finish the job. Trying to lure us out."

Her bodyguard nodded.

Raphael wiped his mouth with the back of his hand. "We should try to make a run for it."

The sirens intensified. The police were close now.

"No." Agent Corinth's robotic voice left no room for debate. To her incredulity and annoyance, Raphael threw the man a dirty look.

"Waiting will only—"

"Quiet," Agent Corinth replied. "I'm trying to listen."

Raphael crouched. "We can't just *sit* here!"

Just as Selene hushed him, the sound of thrusters roared right above their heads. The sudden heat from the engines buffeted them despite the relative cover of the downed shuttle's wing. The roar was deafening. She yelped in spite of herself, squeezed her palms to her ears. Dust and debris whipped at her.

A pair of men stood in the gaping cargo door, one holding some type of long-range gun and another with his arm cocked back, ready to lob something.

"Watch out!" she yelled.

The one with the gun took aim. Selene cried out as a small blast of concrete erupted right by her knee and sent fragments onto her black suit. In a strange moment of stupefaction, she thought she'd been sprinkled with brown sugar. Raphael scooted away from her as the next bullet hit, even closer this time despite her efforts to make herself as small and tight as possible. Cornered. She gritted her teeth. The next bullets would hit their mark.

Faster than she thought anyone could move, Agent Corinth jumped in front of her. In a fluid motion he leveled his gun, all eleven inches of a

matte black affair, and fired one economical shot. Only one. The target-
ed man had been about to throw something at them, but he shuddered
and fell backward, releasing the object behind him into his shuttle. A
thunderous roar and a ball of fire stabbed out through the windshield
and cargo door.

Heat engulfed Selene, similar to opening an oven's door but a hundred times worse. The attackers' burning shuttle pitched forward, its
thrusters like infernal mouths, and spiraled a few times before crashing
between piles of other carcasses deeper in the scrap yard. Smoke rose
in thick roiling fists. The stench of electrical fire stung her nose. She
coughed and rubbed her eyes.

Still standing protectively in front of her, Agent Corinth backed up
a few steps without turning his attention from the spot where the other
shuttle had disappeared. He patted the air with his gloved hand, indicating she should stay down. She wasn't going anywhere. Had no such
intention. Not without him.

Never without him.

Chapter 2

Sirens wailed as police shuttles came swerving in through the smoke, landed, and disgorged uniformed men and women who rushed in every direction, their guns ready and faces hard.

Nerves finally hit Selene. She started shaking and could barely stand when Agent Corinth offered his hand to her, which she took, squeezing it tight for a few precious seconds. He could do this for her, probably without even knowing it. He could shut out the world and create an instant and quiet bubble around her that was as much solace as it was liberation. She focused on his hand and let the stillness suffuse her. For a moment only. A treasure.

Then too early, she had to let go and dust herself off before someone could snap footage of her crouched by the shuttle and sell the crunchy video to the media, who'd love nothing better than to show the Dragon Lady in a less-than-flattering position. Only last month, she'd had to stop Agent Corinth from demolishing a reporter who'd taken a few compromising shots of her coming out of the gym, red-faced and wearing baggy sweatpants. She'd never seen a bodyguard react so violently. He hadn't stopped punching until she'd pulled him by the sleeve. And even afterward, his face shield had been on the reporter all the while he was walking away. She'd gone to bed that night filled with relief, yes, but also with quite a bit of gratification. It felt good to be protected, sheltered, once in a while. The media must have learned a hard lesson, because not one of them had physically approached her since.

She stood, trying not to step on broken glass from the shuttle window. Something was pressed into her hand. She looked down, noticed her lost shoe there. Agent Corinth shielded her while she used the shuttle as support and slipped her black pump on.

"Thanks," she said, straightening.

He nodded, his back to her, the ever-watchful guardian.

"Not just for the shoe," she added with a tap to his forearm.

He turned his face slightly, covered her hand with his own. The glove creaked when he squeezed. The tiny sound sent a jolt of awareness through her. Even as she stood on the site of a crash landing—her own—and people milled about the place, she felt so cocooned by this man's presence that a small sound like a glove creaking triggered an emotional flare. She yearned to stay this way, but couldn't, of course.

Within seconds the press shuttles began to land. Reporters quickly spotted her and would have converged on her had Agent Corinth not ushered her past a police cordon and into one of their shuttles. The tinted windows prevented anyone from snapping pictures. She let Raphael handle the press outside. His hair was close to immaculate once more. How did he do that?

"Are you all right?" Agent Corinth asked. The robotic voice coming out of his helmet sounded strained. He sat on the seat closest to the shuttle door. Near the front, the comms unit crackled with police jargon.

Selene nodded. She realized her hands were shaking and forced them flat on her lap. "What about you? Are you hurt?"

A small shake of his head.

"But then again," she went on lightly, "you're dressed for success."

Dressed for success. Ha. Body armor, the old debate. For years, Hector had tried to convince her that she should wear bulletproof armor. Because walking around with ceramic mesh plates hidden under her suit was a good idea? Not quite. Plus, if she showed fear, if she let the public know how much of a target she was for her opponents back on Earth, her people wouldn't feel safe. The last thing New Heraklion needed was for its citizens to start smuggling guns from Earth to the station.

She tried to smile, but her chin quivered and she ended up coughing to hide the strain. There'd been foiled attempts before, some vandalism, threatening letters, but never any physical action taken against her. Someone had shot at her, for god's sake! Her shuttle had crashed. They could've died. Agent Corinth could've died.

Julie did die, and only because she'd been between a bullet and Selene's head. Such a waste.

From her hands, the shakes began to spread through her body. As much as she hated herself for her emotional reaction—albeit normal and expected—she couldn't stop the downward spiral into after-shock trauma.

Breathe.

It didn't work. Heat wafted from beneath her shirt collar, spread up her neck, warmed her cheeks and tightened her forehead. On its heels, waves of frissons. She no longer shook, she literally *quivered*. Faced with her frailty, her mortality, she tried to fall back on the anger fueling her campaign. It could keep her going now even though all she wanted was to lie down somewhere nice and warm, somewhere secluded most of all, and read a good book. She couldn't remember the last time she'd read *words*, not rows of numbers and statistical data crunched by her team and re-crunched by Raphael in his zeal to impress her. She wanted peace, for god's sake! Was it too much to ask?

Across from her, face hidden behind the antireflective face shield, Agent Corinth sat silently watching her, which she knew by the set of his shoulders and the angle of his chin. His gloved hands were balled into fists. Mr. Steady Hands. She shouldn't study him so intently, shouldn't admire the way his black uniform clung and tugged over his body, or the way the ribbed armor on every joint, from wrists to knees, accentuated the man's compact musculature. She shouldn't try to guess his age or the color of his hair and eyes, or wonder if dimples graced his smile when something pleased him. She shouldn't. But she'd been doing it. For months.

Julie. Gone. Just like that.

Tears stung her eyes. Selene averted her face so he wouldn't see, even if she knew he still could.

Through the window, she spotted Raphael drawing near and extending a hand toward the shuttle door, members of the press dogging him and snapping pictures or video footage. With the angle, they'd see her cry. Not acceptable.

"Damn," she muttered, wiping the moisture from her eyes. But before her assistant could reach the handle, Agent Corinth deftly thumbed the control and locked the door.

The handle rattled with impotent *thunks* as Raphael tried to open it.

Agent Corinth didn't seem to hear. Or to care.

She took a deep breath and whispered a tight, "Thank you. Again."

There was so much more she wanted to say. Had been meaning to say for some time now. This man, this ever-attentive, silent man stirred something in her, illuminated parts of her she didn't know existed. Even though she'd never even seen his face. She felt more a woman around him than she had with anyone else. To Raphael, she was his boss, to Hector, a daughter figure, and to her lovers, a means up the social ladder. To the rest, she was the stubborn, steadfast Lady Mayor who'd run a campaign on a tenth of her opposition's funds, had been elected and would now bring the distinction of nation-state to New Heraklion.

But to Agent Corinth, she represented something that had to be protected. While she realized it was his job and nothing personal, she sometimes enjoyed deluding herself that he fostered private reasons for protecting her. That he felt *something* for her. Just as, deep down in a place she kept secret and hidden, she did for him.

Without the usual internal battle she waged whenever she thought of him, she reached out and patted his knee. "What would I do without you, Agent Corinth?"

Silence answered her.

She brushed the last of the moisture from her face, took a long breath. Their moment was over.

"You'd go on," the metallic voice murmured after awhile. "A lot of people depend on you. And need you. You're their light."

"Their light?"

He nodded. "Like a beacon. People need that."

Heat like a fever engulfed her. "Do *you*?"

"Yes."

The sibilant hissed because of the helmet, but it was still the most important and rewarding word she'd heard in a long time. Ignoring the implication of this short little word proved impossible.

Could it be?

"I'll send Aegis a message," he went on. "They'll hunt down those who did this."

Back to business.

She felt as if she were sliding back into a hole from which she'd climbed with great difficulty. Oh, well, she'd climb it again. And again. She was mature enough and self-aware enough to realize the sort of yearning she felt for Agent Corinth couldn't be harnessed or stifled, ignored or denied. It was part of her. She had to accept it and not fall into the easy trap of fatalism. Not her style.

"You're not the only one who needs a beacon," she murmured.

Her heart skipped a beat when he leaned over, his face shield closer to her face than it had ever been before. She could smell him, peppermint and aftershave. Liquid drumbeats swooshed in her ears. Anticipation and hope fought against reason, senses against the intellect.

After a few seconds, he seemed to deflate from the inside and sat back in his seat, a fist around the handle. She heard it creak in protest.

"The show has to go on," she said, forcing a smile when it was clear he would say nothing more. She pressed the heel of her hand to her forehead to squeeze back the headache. "After the summit is over, I'm taking a vacation."

A series of tiny jolts lifted Agent Corinth's shoulders, and she realized he was laughing.

"Do you like the beach, Agent Corinth?"

The silent laughter stopped. Was it her imagination, or had his shoulders drooped a little?

Without looking at him, she removed her bloodied jacket and used it to wipe the blood off her hands—as much as she could, anyway—and then rolled up the bloodstained cuffs of her shirt. She smoothed her hair back. With her jacket in a tight roll under her arm, she scooted forward in the seat. Back to normal.

A vision flashed in her mind's eye. The back of Julie's head reduced to red pulp. A shiver shook her. No, not back to normal. God, what a waste. And so young. When she returned to the station, she'd have to pay her condolences to Julie's father, an ex-police officer. She hated her job right now.

"Did I miss anything?" she said to Agent Corinth.

After a small shake of his head, he unlocked the door to Raphael's and a dozen other voices.

The noise swarmed her. She stood, knowing she looked dignified and nonplussed despite the assassination attempt, and answered questions posed to her. "No, this latest incident would not stop her from representing New Heraklion at the summit," and "Yes, she was still boarding her cruiser and leaving for Earth as scheduled."

A continual buzz of chaos around her swirled and twirled, colors and sounds. But at the center of it all stood a lone figure, an anchor, solid and strong, a constant amidst the permutable rest. A faceless friend.

The clump of journalists shuffled backward as she made her way to another armored shuttle. She answered a few more questions to give Agent Corinth time to properly inspect it, then at his subtle nod, bid the press good day and boarded the craft.

New Heraklion, in all its industrial harshness, spread below her window as they rose in a steady climb to their assigned launch tube. While Selene waited for the telltale puff of the skids touching down, she cut a quick glance at her bodyguard. The face shield was turned toward her. Out the corner of her eye, she spotted Raphael staring hard at Agent Corinth, and to her shock, she couldn't explain the malaise that gripped her.

When the door opened, in barged Hector with his usual grimace and a string of curses peppering each step. She'd had to apologize to many a foreign diplomat for Hector's behavior. Secretly, she enjoyed his frankness despite his lack of a basic sense of timing. She'd never hire anyone like him, but she wouldn't fire a dear friend either, and not only out of respect for her parents' memory. Plus, he was due for retirement in exactly fifty-four days, according to the countdown calendar he kept pinned to his office door. Subtle, as usual.

"I can't turn my back for a goddamn minute without some cretin getting it into his head to take a shot at the only cursed politician in human history who actually does what she says she'll do?" He shook his balding head and snaked an index finger into his shirt collar to loosen it. "Where's the goddamn rack when you goddamn need it? I heard about Julie. Everybody else all right?"

"Dodging bullets, crashing shuttles. Couldn't be better," Raphael muttered. "Can't wait to sleep my way to Earth. Bye, Selene."

She had the distinct impression he purposely avoided coming near Agent Corinth when the pair reached the hatch at the same time. Her bodyguard took a step back and let Raphael go first, waiting with his head tilted to look outside. After the familiar nod from Agent Corinth, she followed.

She let Hector vent some more as she dodged members of her staff on her way to board their private cruiser—an ugly thing that resembled a giant silver larva—and then navigated the narrow passageways to her cabin. Behind her, only Hector followed close enough for conversation.

"I'm not going to take the stasis aids," she said without turning around. Journey to and from Earth meant at least thirty-six hours of tedious space travel, and it had become common procedure to lie in stasis pods and enter a deep, chemical sleep. The sleep also allowed passengers to escape the temporary but disconcerting zero-g as ships switched to dormant mode to save on electricity and fuel. She didn't mind weightlessness and could work strapped at her desk without difficulty.

"Got some things to work out?"

"Yes. And I need to write a letter to Julie's dad." She had a lot of bullets to tick off her list, and even more to process mentally and emotionally. Someone had tried to *kill* her. Not just threaten her. "But you guys go to sleep. Get some rest while you can. It'll be a zoo when we land."

"You should have the medics check you out."

"I'll be fine, thanks. Just need a hot shower."

"He won't like that."

"I know."

In front of her cabin, she put her hand—which shook still—on the access panel, but waited outside when the door slid into the bulkhead. The cruiser's previous owner had decided on a nineteenth-century art nouveau look, and as much as the black, white, and gold color scheme appalled her, she was too frugal to change it. A black silhouette at the edge of her peripheral vision stopped as well.

"I want some time alone," she said loudly enough to be heard by both men. Julie's death and the attempt on her own life had truly rattled her. She doubted she'd be able to sleep, stasis aids or not. Her stomach knotted, and her nape ached from tension. She could've died. *He* could've died. Raphael as well.

Poor Julie.

"You know," Hector said, rubbing his chin until skin wrinkled under his fingers like old, pink leather, "maybe I ought to rethink my retirement. Wait a few months."

"You're already at the top, pension-wise—"

"I meant for you. I'd stay for *you*, to make sure my replacement—" Hector stopped abruptly when she smiled. "Teasing an old man isn't funny. Especially not today after…. Shit."

"You're not old, just well matured. Like wine."

He shook his head. "Oh, Mia got to you too, did she? I have to tell The Wife to stop washing our dirty laundry in public."

Selene patted his shoulder. "I'll tell Mrs. Teos you called her 'the wife.'"

"You don't think she knows?"

"Look, I'll be fine in my cabin. I won't come out and I'll block the signal to my access panel. Okay?"

Hector cleared his throat. "Yes, ma'am. You're the boss, ma'am."

That made her grin. It took a moment for Agent Corinth to follow Hector away. As she was entering her cabin, she cast one last glance down the passageway and caught him looking back at her.

Someone breathed against his nape. He shivered. He knew who—*what*—stood close enough for him to feel and smell it. They'd found him. Even here in space, they'd found him. They. The monsters.

He stood in a cabin not his own, looking down at *her* as she slept in her stasis pod, her red hair in a frizzy cloud around her round face. A porcelain doll. One he had to break.

The word *Chimera* blazed like his own personal sun behind his eyelids. It stabbed into his brain, chased shadows into the furthest recesses of his psyche to illuminate with pitiless clarity every sordid thought he'd ever had. Every fear as well.

"Kill her," the voices murmured behind him. If he turned around, would he see them? He'd never been able to. They always knew when he was about to look back and slunk out of the way.

The whisper grew in intensity. "Chimera. Chimera. *Chimera.*"

His brain felt too big for his skull. Pressure intensified behind his eyeballs and in his ears. Something popped in his sinuses. Tears welled in his eyes and it wasn't all because of the sinus ache, either.

He didn't *want* to kill her. He couldn't. It wasn't right. They'd been together for a while, and if people didn't entirely trust him or even like him, he doubted anyone suspected he would kill her.

Behind him, the breathing intensified, whistled and wheezed before turning to chuckles.

"You're weak," they whispered. "You always were."

15 June 2377, 0800 hours GMT
Athenian, Cruiser-class, leaving Mars orbit
12.6 light-minutes from Earth

Within the hour, Selene stepped out of a tepid and weak shower that had nonetheless invigorated her body. All the blood had washed away, except in her memory where it still glistened bright red.

Dressed in her worn robe, she poked her head outside, looking down both sides of the deserted passageway before placing her palm on the access panel. A quiet moment alone, finally, even if she doubted it would be peaceful. Just as she was about to deactivate the panel, a dark spot darted at the edge of her vision. Damn, was someone still up?

Cursing, she retreated into her cabin, donned her "sexy" gray tracksuit and old flip flops—the attire that had so excited that reporter—and stepped into the passageway, mumbling under her breath as she reached the first perpendicular corridor. Closed doors all around. Deep rumbles from the cruiser's engines rose from the soles of her feet up her calves. Somewhere below deck, a metallic *clunk* made her start.

She fought the urge to say hello because it was just too lame. No one else but her staff was here. It was *her* cruiser, for god's sake!

Still, a tingle at the base of her nape forced her to quicken her pace. Gray polymer bulkheads, an art nouveau lounge with acid-green plastic couches, and finally the industrial-looking galley revealed no one.

As it did about fifty times a day, her stomach grumbled.

"I'm up, might as well eat." She had plenty of time before the ship powered down and disabled gravity.

She was coming back with a pair of sandwiches on a plastic plate, an apple—synthetically grown but it would have to do—and a bottle of water when she caught the first sign. A presence, stirring like tendrils, spider-webbed through the air. It reminded her of when she'd fluff her blankets and let them float down onto onto the bed, the subtle rustle and movement of air.

She swallowed, heard the saliva gurgle down her tight throat. Sweat tingled along her spine and seeped into the waistband of her pants, creating a frisson that forced her to clench her jaw. Damn. She licked her suddenly dry lips, checked behind her. *For god's sake, get a grip.*

Fear turned into trepidation when a smell drifted to her. Peppermint and aftershave, but mixed with fresh soap.

"Agent Corinth?" she called.

Around the corner near her door, her bodyguard stepped into the passageway and shook his head. "Your panel was unlocked."

Despite the technology deforming his voice, she heard the gentle chiding in his tone.

"You want to give me a heart attack?" she blurted before chuckling. "*Man*, whew!"

She joined him by her door. His nearness sensualized her. The sight of him, that compact, muscular body, his pleasant smell, so familiar, comforting, arousing….

She forced her mind away from the tempting vision it had conjured for her. "Didn't Hector tell you it was all right to get some rest? You're up before I am and go down only after I do. If I'm tired, you must be dead on your feet."

"He told me to use my judgment. I did."

Agent Corinth leaned forward for a quick peek at her cabin. On his epaulet gleamed the black-on-black Aegis logo of a sword piercing a globe. He nodded the all-clear.

"What about you?" she asked, looking into the antireflective face shield. She'd become used to addressing it directly and no longer felt as though she were talking to herself.

"I'll stand at the door." His voice was so low she could barely hear it.

"And while gravity's down?"

"I'll float by the door."

She grinned. "Ah, come on. You don't have to. At least come in for some water."

"It's better if I stay outside." He retreated by a step, reached for the access panel.

"Come on, just a few minutes. No one is trying to kill me on this ship, right? You personally checked every rivet. Don't deny it. I know you did."

The set of his shoulders relaxed. Was he smiling? "Hector won't like it."

"He told you to use your judgment. And you are."

After a quick check on both sides, Agent Corinth followed her into her cabin. Despite not saying a word and standing pole-straight just inside the doorway, his presence filled her cabin as it did her senses, charging them to the point of nervousness. She felt comfortable around him, but so aware. Hypersensitive.

"Do you trust me, Agent Corinth?" she asked as she put her meal on the coffee table in front of the couch. An ugly, olive green polymer *thing*.

"Yes."

So un-politically brief and to the point. Refreshing. But then again, she hadn't expected anything else from him.

Her hands shook. By the angle of his face, she knew he'd noticed it. "Would you trust me with your name?"

While he stood immobile, barely inside the cabin, she busied herself with setting up the coffee table. She retrieved a set of plastic utensils from the service panel, poured water into two acrylic tumblers made to resemble glass, cut the apple in halves, which she set on napkins, and then put a sandwich beside each. A table set for two.

His hand twitched by his side. "Why are you doing this?"

"I'm hungry. I know that's nothing new, but I figured you would be, too—oh, damn." She slapped her hand to her mouth. "The helmet. Sorry."

"You can't see my face." Agent Corinth took a step forward. The shoulders, much wider than his hips, gave his silhouette a tempting V-shape. "It's against regulations."

"I know. I forgot. Sorry." She crossed her arms, feeling not a little foolish. "Here. Have a seat."

With the mix of quiet strength and grace she'd admired for a year, he sat on the very edge of the couch with his back straight and his gloved hands on his lap. Those deft, steady hands. Muscled thighs pulled at the uniform above the knee guards. That damn helmet.

"This is just too silly." Before she could change her mind or berate herself for taking a chance at souring what they had—*if* they had anything—she marched to the access panel, locked the door and killed the lights.

Darkness descended abruptly on her cabin, as if a blanket had been thrown over her head. "There. Now eat up before we start floating around chasing our food."

"You're bending the rules, Miss Delian." In the darkness, his robotic voice sounded amused.

"No." She felt her way back to the other side of the couch. "I'm using my judgment."

A faint rustle and a click indicated the man was doing *something*. She hoped it was his helmet she heard on the floor.

After a bit of patting around the table, she located one of the glasses and took it. "Cheers."

"Cheers."

She'd often tried to imagine how he sounded when he didn't wear his helmet, but she hadn't been prepared for the soft, smooth voice that rose in the darkness and caressed her entire being. Verbal velvet. The guy would make a great singer. Such a melodious voice.

Heat spread through her limbs. After she heard the sound of swallowing, she could hardly focus on her own glass, let alone anything else. Liquid heat gathered between her thighs. A small sip was all she could manage.

"Perseus Samaras," he murmured gently.

His name. God, he'd shared his name with her. The value, the sheer emotional significance of such simple act as revealing a name convinced her that if nothing else, at least he trusted her. With his real name, with a precious sliver of himself he wasn't allowed to give. She'd treasure it always, even if nothing ever came of their—whatever they had.

"Perseus," she repeated, smiling. "What a great name."

"Try growing up with it."

They shared a quiet laugh.

"Why did you choose Corinth?"

"I didn't. Aegis assigns us designations, usually ancient city names so they can't be traced to anything recent that might give the agent away."

"I've always liked that. Corinth. It has a nice ring to it."

After a short silence, she heard crunching. Perseus had started on the apple. Heat spread from her thighs to her belly. God, she was so turned on it hurt.

"How long have you worked for Aegis?" she asked between nibbles of her apple half. She was hungry, but no longer for food. Needs knifed her. Ones she couldn't satiate.

"Right out of high school," Perseus replied. "They offered scholarships and a quick way out."

"Out of what?"

Movement heralded a wave of heat by her arm a second before a hand touched her on the wrist. She shivered.

"Sorry." He snatched his hand away. "I was looking for the napkin."

"Here, take mine."

"Thanks."

She proffered it in his general direction with her arm in full extension, and then sighed when he touched her shoulder. His warm fingers tentatively grazed down to her wrist, over her knuckles, before slipping the napkin from her hand. By that time, she was trembling head to toe. Pushed to their limits, her senses fired frantic messages to her brain, which could no longer process anything beyond the basest urges.

God, she wanted this man. The very one she wasn't allowed to have. The forbidden fruit.

Perseus swore he was having a heart attack. It was all he could do to keep his breathing from betraying him. He'd spent months working for her, and only gradually got to know Selene Delian, the plain-spoken, defiant, stubborn, honest, compassionate, smart Lady Mayor who would take New Heraklion to status of nation-state. If he cared little for the fate of the station—a black hole could swallow it whole and he wouldn't miss it—he cared a helluva lot more about its leader. Plus, Selene Delian always said what was on her mind. He respected that.

He admired no one as much as he did her. No one else he knew threw themselves into their duties the way she did. With passion, with determination. And physically, she filled to the last comma his ideal woman. She reminded him of a classical beauty, back in a time and place where women were celebrated for their curves and ampleness, their strength tempered with femininity. Simply touching her hand brought him in reality ten times the pleasure he'd often fantasized about. And a thousand times the guilt.

He dabbed his mouth with her napkin, put it on the table. Economical movements. Keeping things controlled. Worse than defusing a bomb. He mustn't lose his focus for even one second.

What they did was dangerous. On many levels. First and foremost, if anyone learned Perseus had removed his helmet in a client's presence—even in the dark—and revealed his name, Aegis could fire him. He doubted they would, but a severe reprimand wasn't out of the question. And second, he preferred to hide his face so she wouldn't *know*. Wouldn't see the effect she had on him. He could hide his attraction if she couldn't see his eyes, but without the helmet, she would know right away.

He wouldn't risk that. More than mere lust—even if her short and curvy physique called to him in a siren's song—his attraction for her transcended carnal needs. He had a major crush on his boss. How lame.

Perseus Samaras, Aegis Corporation's top-rated close protection agent, had let his guard down one single time in almost twenty years. He'd lost perspective back in the passageway when she'd called his name. How had she known it was him? One last check on her had revealed a door unlocked and an empty cabin. What if whoever had attacked her earlier had placed operatives inside the ship as well? Just thinking about it made him sweat. So her empty cabin had pretty much caused him to panic like a greenhorn. Goddammit. If they'd been anywhere else than on her cruiser, he would have pulled his gun and started running. For a minute, he'd feared the worst, just as he'd done when her shuttle started to dip below the docking station. Hell, he'd jumped without even thinking. She could have *died*. He wouldn't even consider that thought for a second. She couldn't die. She was the light. He hadn't lied to her. His beacon of light.

But here he was, sharing a meal in Selene Delian's darkened cabin.

"You're very quiet," she whispered.

Even though he couldn't see her, he knew she was smiling. "Not that you're usually loud, mind you."

"I was thinking about who paid those throwaway mercs to shoot at you. They had to have access to the spaceports, and connections to smuggle guns on-station. That takes money. And power. It had to be the Planetary Commonwealth."

She sighed.

He hated himself for reminding her of the day's events. Someone had taken shots at the station's Lady Mayor, for fuck's sake! Who would do that? And she'd taken it with exemplary calm and bravery, as he'd known she would. Hell, she seemed to have taken it better than he did.

Those mercs had almost succeeded. Rage boiled his blood. He wanted to kill them with his bare hands, make them last long and hard. He took a deep, calming breath.

"Are you all right, Perseus?"

His name in her mouth sounded so good to him. "Yes. I'm sorry for bringing it up."

"It's part of your job to worry about these things. And it's part of mine to pretend it doesn't affect me." Her chuckle sounded strained.

A true lady and all woman.

But lately, the stress was starting to become more of an issue for her. Shadows underlined her usually clear eyes. The last couple of weeks had been the worse, with Earth media going for the age-old sensational headlines. The personal ones. So what if she carried more weight than the acceptable norm for public figures, these anorexic dolls with fake breasts and faker teeth. Pale imitations of real women, if anyone asked him. She wasn't eighteen! She had curves. The devil knew she had them. Plenty of luscious curves. Her voice rising brought him back to the here and now.

"An elected government wouldn't gamble its party's standing just to get rid of me. PC doesn't think I'm that important."

"You *are*."

"Bah."

He knew she must have just done that thing with her hand, the gesture she used to indicate she wouldn't touch that argument. A sort of "get out" flip of her hand that highlighted the incredibly smooth-looking skin of her wrist. He loved her wrists. So graceful. Such a tapered and inviting end to her lovely arms.

He shifted on the couch. Getting hard wasn't in his plans for the day, thank you very much. Neither had getting invited into her cabin been on the agenda, either. What the hell was he doing here?

Playing with matches.

"You *are* important," he repeated, hoping she wouldn't hear the fire in his voice, or would attribute it to something other than his own very personal views of her. She couldn't know. "To a lot of people. You're a symbol."

She chuckled. "A symbol of what? That big girls aren't always funny?"

She'd taken self-deprecation to an art form. She'd often awed him with her quick wit and charm when dealing with delegates or political allies and opponents, her speech peppered with the occasional cynical darts. That might be part of the problem, in fact. She spoke her mind, wasn't part of any political party back on Earth, and was beloved by the people. No wonder someone was after her.

"You're a symbol of how the good guy can win," he said. "That not every race is rigged. People love you here, even if Earth media don't."

"They don't love me," she replied, her voice nearer. "They know I can bring them something they want. It's all about needs."

The urge to argue that point of view made him sit forward on the couch. His knee brushed her leg. He felt her shivering.

Oh, hell.

As much as he hated himself for it, his instinctive reaction was gratification. It satisfied his male ego like nothing else that he could make her shiver this way and that her body would respond to such simple contact. His mind didn't agree, though.

"You *are* important enough, believe me. PC isn't above political assassination."

"I'd rather not talk about that right now, okay? There will be only, what, four hours after we land before I have to make my statement. I swear that summit will take years off me." She tried for a valiant chuckle. It sounded forced to him. Gutsy woman.

"I'm sorry." He was now sitting deep in the couch. And well away from her leg. "I only want to keep you safe. It's my job." More than his job, but this he left unsaid.

"Which you do perfectly well. I've never felt safer than when you were assigned to my team."

Yeah, the *team.*

He'd enjoy a private word with one of the players there, Raphael Sinon. Twice he'd caught that oily son of a bitch snooping around Selene's office when she wasn't there. Hector hadn't called it snooping, but Perseus sure did. That he disliked the rich mama's pretty boy would be the understatement of the year. There was something else going on, recent too, that made him twitchy. He couldn't put his finger on it, but he would, eventually. He always did. No, that was a lie. There'd always been one crease in his life he'd never been able to iron out.

"Perseus."

Her voice sounded closer. The heat of her breath—it smelled of apple, would it taste of it, too?—grazed his cheek and made him close his eyes. Ephemeral bliss. "Yes?"

"Do you think there's a chance we're going to have sex right now?"

Shit.

It took him a good ten seconds to recover from his shock. Like a golden apple, the offer sparkled in front of his eyes, tempting him, calling him, gradually seducing his psyche into compliance. His senses had long been won over. He wanted to. Hell knew he *wanted* to. To wrap her in his arms and press his face into her soft ampleness would make him the happiest bastard in the system.

And she'd almost died, for Christ's sake! He couldn't imagine life without her. An emptied chair. A house with no curtains. Nobody home.

So yeah, dammit, he did want to share himself with her. *Burned* for it, really. That was why he had to say no.

"That wouldn't be a good idea, Miss Delian. I'm really sorry." Pathetic. Painful.

"No," she replied in a subdued tone he'd never heard before. It broke his heart. "I guess it wouldn't be. I'm sorry, too, Agent Corinth. I thought...." She cleared her throat. "After today, I thought, if we don't...."

He reached into the darkness for her hand, but his fingers landed on her thigh. So hot and soft. Not helping. "I know what you're trying to say, Selene. But if I get fired, they'll assign another agent. I wouldn't trust your safety with anyone else. I wouldn't sleep a wink." Not that he did as it was.

"I wouldn't *accept* anyone else," she replied, her voice back to its normal strength. "Still, I'm sorry I put us both in this position. That wasn't very good judgment." A soft chuckle caressed his face. She'd turned toward him. So close. "But someday, we'll have to deal with this."

They might as well carve these words on his tombstone. "I know."

Saying more might open a dam he couldn't shut down again.

Chapter 3

What the hell had gotten into her? She'd never been shy or coy or even overly careful with her words. But she was wrong to say such a thing to him, for god's sake. "I'm sorry, Perseus. I never should've said that."

"It's okay. We'll forget everything."

How plausible was *that*?

Pain hardened his voice. What had she been thinking, inviting him inside? And asking if they would have sex! She'd only made it worse. Now he knew how she felt, what she wanted. He'd start acting differently around her. She'd ruined it all.

"I better go," he said.

And there he goes. Great going, Delian.

She felt a weight come off the couch. She stood as well, circumvented the table in small, cautious steps, her heart in her throat, her stomach in her heels. *Fool.*

The bulkhead felt cool against her palm when she ran a sweaty hand along the polymer on her way to the door, the way a blind woman would, timorous but proud, unsteady but resolute. Heartbroken but too stubborn to admit it.

A presence to her right preceded Perseus bumping against her. Instant fire. Blinding need.

Oh, god.

She gasped at the spike of arousal that had jabbed her in the belly. No other man had elicited such a strong and sudden reaction.

"Selene."

Her name sounded like a plea, his voice velvet against her skin. He hadn't yet put his helmet back on.

Something thudded against the floor. His helmet? She opened her mouth in a silent O when he gripped her hand, reversed it to expose the inside of her wrist and nipped her there. Marked her. His demanding mouth so hot against her skin, it burned.

When he abandoned her wrist, she stumbled forward. "Perseus." A harsh whisper.

Warm, forceful hands framed her face and pushed her back against the bulkhead, and as her nape connected, her heel struck the kick plate. He'd trapped her. In a red pulsating haze, she knew what he intended to do.

His mouth. A collision. Despair, lust, joy, the basest urges, a conquest.

God, it was good, so good.

The feral abandon with which he touched her felt so different from the stoic, guarded man she'd come to know. It left her buoyed and scattered, overwhelmed in the most delectable fashion. She wanted him to. Wanted him to make love to her, wanted to make him take her this way, up against the wall, fuck her hard and fast and without restraint. Screw decorum, inhibitions and security protocols. She'd waited long enough!

He didn't say a word as he wrestled his equipment and body armor off. Clatters and muffled thuds on the carpeted deck. She could feel his muscles bulging and cording in his haste to get rid of every barrier between their bodies. She helped as she could, oftentimes tugging when she should've been pushing, no doubt making a mess of things but just touching him—god, she was *touching* him! Her hands all over his face and neck, she felt him bite his gloves off before turning his attention to her sweatshirt, which he jerked over her head. She voiced her frustration when the damn thing trapped her arms above her head.

A gasp left her. Perseus had unceremoniously planted his hands on her breasts. Then he filled his face with them. Loving kisses turned into burning nips and languorous licks. Moisture gathered in her sex. The thrilling mix of aggressiveness and tenderness fired her every sense and reduced her mental processes to primal urges she couldn't control.

Her voice rose in the darkness, alien, discordant, as though it came from someone else. "Ahh."

Still partly trapped in her sweatshirt, she let him do to her what he'd been burning for. Let him mold and squeeze her breasts, tug at her nipples, and lick long passes up her sternum. The polymer buckled behind her when he crushed her against the bulkhead, his compact thigh jammed between hers, hips working hard to press a lump that had nothing to do with body armor into her belly, seemingly bent on meshing them into one person, one body, entwined and espoused. One.

"Selene," he breathed in her ear. Through the fabric covering most of her head, his voice had the ghostly quality of faraway whispers carried on a faint breeze. "Selene, Selene, Selene."

Each time he said her name, his tone carried a different edge. A plea, a threat, a demand. A gift. She hungered for things from him she wouldn't have tolerated from another man. Needs swelled from months of denial, of watching, of waiting for every small chance to touch him, be near him, smell him. Frustration. Urgency. Perseus had to take it. All. There might not be another chance. If they didn't act on it, this precious moment of discovery would pass and never come back again.

When she managed to get rid of the sweatshirt, Perseus caught her elbows from underneath, forced her arms up high against the bulkhead, and then kissed the tender skin along the underside. His thumbs dug into her flesh. He'd trapped her. She welcomed the pressure, arching against his pelvis to force him harder against her. After some fierce tugging, she felt him get rid of his top as well. This, she wouldn't miss for the world.

"I want to touch you," she demanded, pulling against his grip. He released her so she could fill her hands. Glorious. "Oh god," she whispered. "Just like I thought. Better."

Hard. Everything on him was hard. And so hot. She made explorers of her hands as she ran them all over his front and shoulders, his neck, his tight waist. Oh, that back! A delectable grid of corded muscles. Hair on his chest was soft against her chin as she ran it left to right in search of his nipples. When she found one, she sucked at it.

Perseus hissed a breath. "Do it again."

With enthusiasm bordering on frenzy, Selene trapped his nipple with her lips and proceeded to suck and tease the hard little point until she knew she was toeing the line of pain. He didn't seem to mind as he wrapped an arm around her head and kept her there against his chest. His scent filled her nose—god, she loved the clean smell of him. Every fiber in her body quivered for him, every sense stretched to its maximum for a mere taste. Young shoots straining toward light. She pressed her head against him to share a bit of his warmth. Feeling his heart pounding against her cheek proved the most sensuous and emotionally rewarding experience of her life, and in a strange and wonderful way, the most familiar as well. Somehow, she'd known this her whole life. The feeling of spotting one's front door after a hard and long journey. Home.

Perseus had never felt so torn between crushing a woman in his arms to lose himself in her, and cupping her beauty between tender hands to bask in it for as long as he could. The duality of her response shocked him. He'd made love to a few other women and had enjoyed a couple long-term relationships with smart and pleasant gals. And he'd also been intimate with women who'd wanted nothing less than for him to overpower them, which he could do. The physical release alone, for both parties, had appealed to him. But never before had he shaken with the urge to do it all at once and to the *same* woman. He hungered to bend Selene over the couch backrest, take her hard, make her moan his name—or just moan period—and he wanted her everywhere she'd take him. Yet in tandem with these animalistic visions floated some of a different sort altogether—tender moments of discovery and affection, taking their time exploring and tasting. Loving.

He'd long ago admitted to himself he had a crush on Selene Delian. A serious crush. He'd never let it impede his job. At thirty-seven, he'd developed the ability to separate work from pleasure. But then again, protecting her had turned from his job into the single most important thing in his life. That, and making love to her. Right now.

"Turn around," he growled in her ear.

He rolled her against the bulkhead so she faced it, plastered his front against her to pin her there, felt her breasts compress on either side, and bit his bottom lip as he filled his face with her hair. That gorgeous red mane. He didn't care that tabloids made fun of her frizzy hair. He liked it on her. Gave her character. Just like that slightly crooked canine tooth did. Sexy.

Her curvy backside provided the perfect anchors for his hands, filling them nicely. He squeezed for the sheer pleasure of feeling how her flesh molded to his palms, how he could dig the pads of his fingers in without fear of hitting a bone. Nothing killed the mood quicker than hitting bones on a woman.

The smooth fabric wrinkled under his touch. Those unflattering gray sweatpants had triggered a flurry of paparazzi activity as Selene came out of the gym, flushed with energy and adrenaline. Glowing. He had walked around with the stupidest hard-on. But when that moron had snapped badly angled pictures of her that had nothing to do with journalism and everything to do with humiliating her, Perseus had thoroughly lost it. Pounding the jerk into the pavement had felt so damn good, and the thankful look she'd given him had more than made up for the permanent mark on his file.

While the sweatpants felt soft against his coarse palms, what lay beneath would prove even softer. He kissed his way down her spine so he could tug her pants to her knees and feel her skin pebbling against his lips. He could die right now a happy man. He was *touching* Selene.

The skin of Perseus's hands felt rough against her butt. Delightfully so. He grabbed her cheeks, dug his fingers into her flesh, noisily kissed her before he rubbed his face side to side. She wanted to laugh but yelped when he bit her. Not hard enough to hurt, but enough to thrill.

"Do you know how long I've thought of doing that?" he murmured against her hip. "I would try to think of something else, *anything* else. But I couldn't."

All these months she'd been thinking about him, he'd been thinking about her? All that time? "It's happening now. I'm here now."

"I might be dreaming," he whispered.

She reached back to comb her fingers through his closely cropped hair. She wondered what color it was. "Reality starts with dreams." She felt him sigh against her lower back.

"Spread your legs for me." His imperious tone belied the gentle hand he wove in the space between her thighs, the deliberate pressure he applied so she'd part her legs for his attention, his touch.

A sense of abandon filled her, abandon to her senses, to his indulgence. No power struggle, no fragile equilibrium to maintain, only the senses. His. Hers. Satiation, months of anticipation. He could take her thus, in the dark, standing up and facing the wall. She wanted it.

Selene spread her legs for Perseus. Juices slicked her in a profusion that even she could smell, the scent of arousal, feminine and powerful. He seemed to notice and appreciate it, for he inhaled long and slowly while his fingers spread her wide. With her vulnerable flesh distended, she braced her hands on the bulkhead. Waited.

The first lick made her squeeze her eyes shut. Before she could voice her delight, Perseus rolled her against the polymer panel again and with forceful fingers, stretched her sex wide. She wanted to help. She reached to expose her clitoris to him but he grabbed her wrist, nipped it—to her thrilled gasp—and planted it against the bulkhead. Hard.

"Let me do it."

She felt his forehead against her belly as he dove for her distended pussy. Again, a second of anticipation both terrible and arousing preceded his tongue. He licked her in a straight and narrow pass and moaned against her mound. The noise alone would have been enough to trigger the spike of sexual energy that doubled her pulse and sharpened her need. But coupled with the heat of his tongue... sublime.

"That's my favorite spot," he whispered between licks. "Right here, where a woman's thighs rub together." A hand almost reverent pressed against the spot to which he referred. Perseus kissed her there. "It's so smooth."

"Kiss me there again," she said through a sigh.

He did.

"Again."

Another kiss, this one more proprietary. The precursor to a wave of pleasure, a tiny jolt piqued her belly. "Again. Please."

This time he didn't kiss her in that tender spot. He bit her.

Just as she gasped, he clamped his mouth against her sex and gave her the most enthusiastic, precise and relentless licking she'd ever received. He made a conqueror of his tongue and his lips, sucking, licking, almost whipping her hard little pearl until she started to shake, until she moaned for him to keep going, to *please* keep going. He did.

Implacable, he made love to her—*fucked* her—with his mouth. Moisture dribbled down her thighs, which cramped with the harbingers of climax. Inhibitions shredded. She placed her hand on the top of his head and gripped him, rolled her hips to his cadence so his mouth would press even harder. With a keenness that left her reeling, an orgasm flared from her vulva, spread to her thighs and up her belly, accelerated her heart rate and made painful points of her nipples. In its wake came heat like a fever.

Without relenting, Perseus kept his mouth against her sex while he began to rub her clitoris with a finger. She didn't know which one, didn't care as long as he never stopped circling.

Oh, god, oh.

Then into her he slipped a finger. Two. Rubbed and sank, twisted and retreated. Pushed back in. She abandoned his head so she could squeeze her fists behind her lower back for added pressure. She couldn't have spread her legs any wider without falling. She shook from head to toe. Sweat slicked her neck and back.

"That's it," he murmured between licks. "Show me how."

He thrust his fingers into her deep, claiming and stretching her. With his mouth, he made languorous passes followed by prolonged and incredibly noisy sucks that curled her toes. Hyperawareness. Her every muscle on fire. Her voice filled the cabin. The timbre and force of it surprised her because she'd never been a screamer.

Another wave hit. Hard. So close after the first that pain soon followed the overstimulation. Perseus must have felt the change, for he eased his licks and lightened his touch until only his lips, moth-light, grazed her flesh. So much honey and saliva coated her entire cleft that she could have received him without further stimulation. But if she wanted him inside her right now, he seemed to have other plans.

"Kneel for me," he said.

The heat of his breath traveled from her pulsating pussy to her belly. Then up further. Perseus was standing.

And she knew why.

Collision between her kneecaps and the deck. The pain should've made her grimace. It registered, but only on the surface. She had to have this man in her mouth right then and there. She had to taste Perseus, feast, gorge on his cock. Had to.

She touched him everywhere she could reach. With near despair—they had so little time together. Surely her hands had known him all her life, every angle, every curve and detail, bas-reliefs of flesh and bones and muscles honed into iron bands. Yet she rediscovered him on her way down. From head to toe. A straight nose. She loved noses. A sharp and well-defined jaw. A strong neck, thick shoulders. A cut chest without being striated. A firm and fit body. Shaking with foretaste, Selene focused her blind touch in the middle of him. Went on the hunt for his member, which she two-handed with impatience and greed. This was all hers. All this hot, hard cock.

Into her mouth she took Perseus. Deeply.

She heard his sharp intake of air. Reveled in what she could do to him, reduce this strong and lethal weapon to a man shaking with need for her. Her doing. She sucked him down again, deeper this time, all the way in. Smooth as silk, his shaft slid effortlessly. Working her jaw to accommodate his girth, she made a home of her throat while she kept his skin taut with both hands splayed around his groin. His pubic hair tickled the pads of her fingers while the mix of salty and sweet made her mewl deep in her chest. Liquid silk. Burning hot. She released him so she could lick her hands, gathered some pre-cum from his glans and spread it around for a perfect, lubricious rod. Around it she twisted her clenched hands, one clockwise, the other counterclockwise while she kept the head of his fine cock exposed so she could lick it to her heart's content. When he fisted her hair, she corkscrewed her hand down his shaft with renewed vigor.

"Selene," he warned, curling his hips away from her.

Her growl surprised even her. He wasn't going anywhere! She knew what was about to happen—and soon, judging by the muscles twitching on his thighs. She wanted this, too. Everything.

With every sense on the alert, she sucked him deep, licked his glans, and ran her thumb in circles over the tiny slit until faint pulsations heralded his peak. Just as the thick vein underneath his penis pulsated against the pads of her fingers, Selene sank on him. He shuddered. At the back of her mouth and along her velum, his cum surged in potent little jets. A gift she greedily appropriated. Precious ribbons of silk. Burning hot and tasting of man and tears.

While she swallowed, she heard a *plop* against the bulkhead, his hand landing on the polymer, then felt him start to sink down to the deck by her side. A hot thigh brushed against hers. She couldn't resist and squeezed it as she would a ripe melon. Good god, he had nice legs. Hair along his hard thigh made her sigh. So soft.

"Selene," he whispered. "You shouldn't have let me come in your mouth like this."

She grinned in the darkness. "Why not?"

"Because it's special. It means something. The guy should mean something."

With anyone else, she'd have suspected he was trying to tell her what to do or how to act—one of her flaws, her propensity to jump to conclusions. But Perseus was different. He only meant that he didn't feel "special" enough for her to receive him this way. But he *was*.

"Are you asking?"

His sigh lasted a long time. She could imagine him emptying of air. She patted forward until her hand touched his shoulder. "It does mean something special. The 'guy' as well."

"There were nights, Selene," he said in a tight voice. He gripped her hand so he could turn it over and kiss the inside of her wrist. She loved when he did that. "There were nights I couldn't sleep. Entire nights awake staring at the ceiling. And with the dumbest hard-on."

His laugh startled her—so deep and melodious, a singer's voice—and after a few seconds spent enjoying the sound of his voice, she joined him. "I've been busy too. Up here," she pointed to her temple, remembered he couldn't see her. "In my mind."

"What about down there?" he asked. She moaned unabashedly when he pressed his knuckles against her thigh and moved up to her sex. "Been busy down there, thinking of me?"

"Yes."

She had. Long hours alone in her bed, with her fingers in herself, all the while fantasizing they were his. Just thinking about it made her flush and tight with arousal.

Perseus rubbed the back of his fingers 'round and 'round against her vulva, parted her with his middle knuckle so he could stroke her clitoris, which hardened and began to pulsate. She bent a leg higher to give him more room and leaned her back against the cool polymer.

"I see two things happening," he began. He made a rumble similar to an engine's in his chest.

She loved it. Perseus could purr! "Yes?" She didn't care if she sounded breathless.

He took his time answering, rubbing with his knuckle before shifting his hand so he could cup her mons and slip fingers into her. She rolled her hips to deepen the penetration.

"Either we make love, slow and tender…." Perseus's fingers quickened.

She felt him kneel up, draw near. Heat signaled imminent contact. His mouth landed on her cheek, traveled back to her ear.

She swallowed. "Or?"

"Or," he whispered, "I bend you over that couch and take you. Hard."

She couldn't see it but knew which couch he spoke of. The ugly green one. It wasn't so ugly anymore. Not with what Perseus had just offered to her.

She cupped his strong jaw and let her fingers travel over his face to anchor his features into her psyche, trying to draw a mental picture of the man into her mind's eye. He must have been very, very handsome, with balanced proportions and hard, defined angles.

"So what will it be?" He kissed her neck, licked her under the ear. Trapped her lobe between his teeth. A hunter settling on a prey. Except she was no prey. But he was still a hunter.

"Time isn't something we have right now," she said against his mouth. He smelled of her nectar. She kissed him deeply. His tongue darted out and flicked her upper lip. That magnificent organ. "But I'll make sure we have plenty next time."

"Next time?"

Because she knew Perseus was a second away from turning his words into action—the split second of stillness before a thunder strike—Selene put all the clout, conviction and sang-froid she could into the one word that would start it all. "Yes."

With his other hand, he gripped her wrist and circled the small bone as if it were a clitoris. She drew in ragged breaths as she waited. Waited.

"Come with me," he said, standing with her in tow.

To her surprise, she didn't hit anything as she followed him a few paces away from the bulkhead and deeper into her cabin. Air left her in a great humph when he about-faced and wrapped an arm around her waist, and then bent her far back so he could get access to her breasts. He suckled with great gusto and noise.

A chime interrupted his vocal appreciation.

"Damn," he said. "The gravity alarm."

The ship had temporarily switched to dormant mode, shutting down gravity. Selene only had time to yelp before their environment changed drastically. She felt her feet slowly come off the carpeted deck.

"Hold on," Perseus murmured as he encircled her waist with an arm to keep them together.

Like a pair of teenagers, they chuckled and whooped as they lost contact with everything but each other. He was now truly her anchor. In every sense of the word.

"Come here, you." She wrapped her hand behind his nape to reel him in for a kiss, which he returned fervently. Their motions were slow, had to be slow, as they floated together in the center of the room.

Perseus pulled away. His hands found her butt, squeezed before slipping one along her cleft and rubbing her sex from behind. "Where was I?"

"R-right there," Selene pushed through her teeth. Fire accompanied his hand. In the weightlessness, she curled a leg around his thighs.

Before she could get her bearings, Perseus eased her around and plastered himself against her back by literally wrapping himself around her. She lost all spatial awareness. She no longer knew which way was the door or the couch or anything. She knew they floated upward, and rotated, too, because her hair tickled her face.

Perseus pulled her arms up, spinning her so he could kiss her lower back. Another rotation. Floating, the release, the sheer exhilaration. He stopped her twirling to kiss and suck her breasts. The combination of dizziness and darkness made her giddy, forced her to abandon herself to him.

"I want you," he murmured. "So bad."

"Take it."

She gasped when he spun her fast. Something connected against the back of her thighs. Oh god, he was getting ready to—

But instead of his cock, she received his mouth.

"Ahh," she moaned. Fire like a whip across her lower back.

He stretched her wide with merciless fingers. Tongue, teeth, sucking. Her flesh became his repast, her essence his wine. Like the roar of the ocean, her heartbeat filled her ears until all she could hear was her own pulse beating madly. Liquid war drums. Air replaced his burning mouth. Cool air. Perseus's hands gripped her by the hips. Fingers dug in. Anchors.

In the void that had become her world, only one thing mattered. Their union. And just as he said he would, he took her. Hard.

Her cry filled the cabin. With his feet he forced hers wider apart, nudged himself between her thighs and used the zero-g to angle himself right below her. By pulling on her hips, he brought her back hard and slow against him, matching their motions together. Then again. Then another penetration, as powerful as the first two but even quicker, tore a mangled gasp from her throat. The near brutality of his claiming called to her animal instincts, made the primeval female in her arch and claw behind her for any part of her lover's skin she could till. Her nails dug into his hip. He pushed in. Deeper. Made her his, unfurled her around his cock as they floated and spun in the primeval darkness. She urged him, taunted and begged, cajoled, threatened and implored for Perseus to take her, take it all. She was his. And he was hers.

Fine sweat made her palms slippery under his assault. After a series of vigorous thrusts that caused her thighs and breasts to tremble in their strange, blind, and weightless world, he snaked a hand around her waist and found a nipple, which he rolled pitilessly. But added with the hip work, the mix of pain-pleasure was too much to bear. Climax shot through her shaking body. Then again.

Behind her, Perseus kept rumbling the same word, over and over. Selene. Selene. *Selene.*

Without warning he pulled out and spun her to face him. She was ready, thighs wide and greedy hands searching for his magnificent cock when he locked them together again.

She cried out. Deliverance. Surfacing. Perseus moving inside her, so hot. So hot.

Cramps shot up her thighs but she pushed herself to remain wide for him so he could pump to his heart's content. Hard body and harder cock, she felt him working his way into another position. They had only minutes before the ship's systems rerouted the energy back to environmental controls, including gravity, and reached cruising speed.

She felt his hands close around her ankles. What was he doing? He raised her legs straight out in front of her and parted them into a wide V. Heat announced he'd placed himself at the junction of her thighs. He took her this way. Pumped. Tore moans of thrill from her. Together, finally. No time. Another deep penetration.

She only had time to cringe when the chime announced the return to one-atmosphere. With a harsh grunt, Perseus managed to put himself underneath as they hit the deck, his cock still encased in her flesh. She had no idea where they were. Didn't give a damn.

Out of the darkness exploded this kaleidoscope of ambers and reds, gold and white-hot. She came like a bomb dropping from the sky.

A violent shiver rocked him a split second before he pulled out halfway. She felt his hand gripping his cock and realized he'd kept himself from coming into her. After a few seconds, this time moving on top of her, he slid back in fully. It shocked her to realize no other man had ever bothered, especially in the middle of things. And with gravity not necessarily a certainty.

Panting, he collapsed onto her. The weight—the man weighed more than she'd expected—crushed her pleasantly against the deck. Still her anchor. For a moment, they stayed thus, coupled, him sheathed to the hilt. Remnants of her orgasm squeezed her vaginal muscles around his cock, which had grown slick with both their juices. From rock-hard, his member turned an enjoyable mix of firm yet pliable.

"Selene," he began, "you're—" She heard him gulping for breath. "You're everything, everything a man could ever want."

After she found his face, she framed it with her hands, kissed him on the forehead, the cheeks, and each eyelid. His glorious mouth.

When she felt him settle onto his side, she squeezed in front of him to spoon. Nothing better in the entire galaxy.

She smiled to herself. Peace settled over her like a comfortable blanket. After awhile, she couldn't help it and hugged the arm he'd draped over her shoulder, kissed the top of his hand and tucked it under her cheek with a contended sigh. To her undying joy, he returned the embrace.

"You know," she whispered in the crook of his arm. "I've been wanting this for so long. I would look at you and try to find every damn excuse just to touch you."

"I had noticed, yes."

"You did?"

"You think it was just good luck that you could sneak in a little pat here and there?"

She felt her cheeks warm. "And I thought I was subtle."

"You were. Are. I only noticed because I wanted it so hard, it hurt."

For some reason she couldn't explain, this remark made her sad. What sort of life had he lived before being assigned to her protection? Would he have to leave someday? The thought alone made her eyes sting.

"How long will you stay? With us—me, I mean."

"My regular contracts are four years, sometimes five when I ask for an extension and it's granted."

"Will you ask for one?"

"Yes."

"I'm glad."

Too soon, she felt him trying to squeeze out from behind her. "Yeah, I guess you should go back to your cabin. Hector would kick your ass if he found you here."

His quiet chuckles made her feel so good that she could've started to sing. Not a good idea for anyone caught too close.

She sat and listened to his quiet tread as he gathered his things. "Need help?"

"No, I got most of it."

"If I find bits of body armor, I'll know where they go."

"Yeah," he replied. She knew he was smiling. "Hector would rather you kept them."

"Oh, don't you start, too."

"He's right."

"Is everyone else in their pods?"

"Yes. I checked. Raphael was the last. I know because I waited." A snap and then a click indicated he'd put his helmet back on. She couldn't help the sigh swelling her chest.

"Don't trust Raphael, Selene," the robotic voice murmured.

She stood, blindly patting the way until she stood near the door. "Why not?"

"There's more to him than he let lets on."

"Raphael Sinon? Mister Personality? Voted Class of 65's Most Likely to be Planetary Commonwealth Chancellor?" She laughed. "I know you two aren't much alike, and I understand why, but I doubt the man is capable of causing real harm. That would mess his hair."

Perseus didn't laugh.

"That *was* kind of funny."

His hand found hers, squeezed. "Don't turn your back on him."

Her first instinct was to yank her hand away, but she aborted the reaction, took a deep breath and reminded herself it was Perseus's very protective instincts that made him so dear to her.

"I won't," she said.

He released her with a stroke of her arm. "If something were to happen to you...."

"Nothing will. You're there. And so is Hector. Plus it's only the transits that will be dangerous. The rest of the time, I'll be cooped up at the conference center, surrounded by other politicians and god knows how many Aegis agents and police officers. If I'm allowed to go to the ladies' room by myself, I'll consider it a treat."

"You don't need any, but good luck tomorrow. Your address is great, by the way. I like the last line."

"Reality starts with dreams," she quoted from her speech. "Not too over the top?"

"No. Just right. Like you."

At once filled with regret, hope and the most pleasant tingling of sexual satisfaction, she put her palm against the access panel, searched for the door trigger, and activated it. Soft amber light from the passageway widened on the carpeted floor of her cabin until it swallowed her feet and legs. She was naked and didn't care one bit.

"Now, you get some rest, Mister."

The Nod.

Perseus ran his index finger down her arm, stepped out of her cabin, and then turned and waited while she deactivated the access panel and locked it back. When the door slid closed and cut her view of him, she experienced a strange and irrational fear that someone had just snuffed out the light for good.

Chapter 4

15 June 2377, 1000 hours GMT
Planetary Commonwealth Headquarters
Reykjavik, Iceland

The noise from the crowd on the docking station outside sounded like the buzz of insects. As Selene waited for the door to open, she allowed herself a small sideways glance. Between her and Perseus stood Raphael, his impeccable hair combed back in a stylish wave, his gaze sparkling as he witnessed the historic scene through the rectangular porthole. As soon as she faced the door again, she caught him watching her, his blue eyes almost a physical thing touching her. Did he know? Even if he did, so what?

"There's more to him than he lets on. Don't trust him." Perseus's warning replayed over and over in her mind.

True, Raphael hadn't been his cool self lately, not since she'd forced her team and herself to take a four-day weekend. She'd even managed to make Hector convince Agent Corinth—Perseus—to take time off as well. Unprecedented victory.

Raphael had argued against it until the day before, when he'd unexpectedly changed his mind and couldn't wait to go planet-side. Probably to meet someone special. One more notch on his bedpost. One of many. Selene shook her head. He was allowed his downtime, just as she was. A pleasant tingle rippled up her spine. Perseus's hands....

She forced her expression to remain impassive when Hector nodded at someone through the porthole and then helped open the heavy exterior hatch. A loud *shh* followed by a *snap* indicated the ground crew had latched the mooring clamps onto the airlock. Air whistled as condensation formed around the rubber seal. Her ears popped painfully when Earth's atmosphere penetrated the cruiser's interior. Then came the noise.

The crowds. The handshakes. Faces all around, smiling. Dignitaries, interpreters, reporters trying to sneak in a question. The flashes of videocopters hovering like mad fireflies. People talking excitedly on their scriptexes. People smells, sweat, cologne, what they'd had for lunch. Machine smells, jet fuels, the acrid odor of her cruiser's hull as its temperature lowered. The crunch and clicks and shuffles of feet.

Lady Mayor Selene Delian straightened, smiled, and exchanged pleasantries as the living sea of people churned and channeled her team to a waiting motorcade of black hovercraft glistening in the pitiless Icelandic sun. All the while, she wanted only a bit of private time with *him*. She felt Perseus's presence behind her, ever vigilant, occasionally enjoining with the heel of his hand those who stood too close to her.

Then she spotted them, the two people who'd make the most trouble for her. Chancellor Marcus Ladon, the head of the supranational Planetary Commonwealth, and his Security Minister Philipa Rhodes. Both grinned and shook hands with her and then with Raphael and the staff, two teams facing off before the games.

"Lady Mayor," Rhodes said, her raspy voice barely audible above the crowd's drone. "Welcome. I look forward to hearing your address."

"And I look forward to giving it," Selene replied with a handshake. Not too strong, she had nothing to prove. Not too weak, she wouldn't let the older woman leave with the wrong impression.

Next came Chancellor Ladon with his long hand reaching her wrist bone in a damp, anemic handshake. Ugh. She'd rub her palm against her thigh at the first opportunity. The group of them smiled for the press and nodded agreeably before making a snail's progress toward the motorcade, stopping every third step to shake more hands, greet more people, and answer more questions. She let the other two proceed in front. Age before beauty, right? The irreverent thought made her smile. A real one.

Minister Rhodes said something, only a word, but Selene couldn't make it out in the din of the crowd. The older woman smiled and shook her head as if to indicate it didn't matter anyway.

They piled into the hovercraft, dignitaries and their respective staffs, close protection agents, and everyone else. In vortices of dust, the motorcade rose off the landing area, swerved into the sun, and sped toward its destination. Outside, sunlight hit the black rocky landscape. It reminded Selene of the moon, but darker.

The ride to the congress center proved short, thankfully, given that Selene sat right next to Minister Rhodes and her slim cigar with smoke the color of ashes rising to sting her eyes. Someone behind her seat coughed politely. Rhodes seemed neither to hear nor to care and kept puffing away.

Reykjavik sprawled beneath them in a black, gray and iceberg-blue labyrinth three hundred feet high and four miles long. One of the newest megalopolises, it was still fairly clean and safe, unlike older cities where crime was rampant and a can of water fetched half a month's salary. Yet most of Earth citizens wouldn't move off planet to one of the many colonies. As poor and miserable and sick as they were planet-side, they preferred such a fate to losing their Terran status and being called off-worlders. She'd been born on New Heraklion and couldn't understand the big deal of living on Earth. Sure, the wind was nice. Ventilation systems could never replicate a true breeze. But Terrans paid a high price for that natural air.

They approached a glass and tubular steel monolith that rose in the city center like a giant... well, a phallic symbol if she ever saw one. The mental image, so incongruous to the day's importance, made her grin behind her hand. She was due for some vacation.

From the corner of her eye she spotted Perseus near the door, facing her with several people separating them. He gave her that small nod on which she'd come to rely so much. It warmed her heart, and she replied in kind.

Across from her, Raphael seemed deep in conversation with Hector, who nodded, his face flushed and his mouth tight. At one point he shook his head, crossed his leg the other way, and then looked out the porthole while the motorcade landed.

Like overgrown teenagers about to attend a rock concert, they trooped out of the hovercraft excitedly talking to one another and into portable scriptexes, gesticulating, arguing and adjusting this or that.

More press. Hordes of them. The major news channels' videocopters swarmed overhead, robotic eyes and ears reporting in every known language the momentous event about to unfold. Surprisingly, she didn't feel nervous, only a little anxious. She'd long since learned her speech and its many variants to fit any sort of world events that could disrupt or affect the proceedings. She'd also worn her most boring suit so people wouldn't pay attention to her clothes but to her words. She'd done what little she could with her hair. That battle, she'd lost at birth.

"Lady Mayor," PC Chancellor Ladon said. His thick Scandinavian accent made the word sound like "mah-yohr". "We are very pleased to host this very important event. And allow me to extend...."

Flashes in her eyes. The drone of the videocopters. Selene paid attention to the man's words only enough to make sure she didn't lose the thread. Prosperity, independence, fate of humanity. It was all there.

The congress center's interior proved as impressive and ostentatious as the exterior. White marble floors, a cavernous lobby of stainless steel and granite with mahogany accents, and a ten-foot-wide burgundy runner that felt thick and luxurious under her feet. The urge to kick her shoes off and wriggle her toes in the silk and wool carpet made her sigh. At the end of the lobby, giant elaborately carved wooden doors that must have been harvested from a Chinese temple, complete with gold trim and copper brackets, stood in twin stoical sentinels to the assembly chamber itself. Nerves hit her then. Hard. Her first reaction was to turn to Perseus, who stood only two or three paces behind.

"Well, that's something else," Hector whispered close by.

She agreed with a nod.

"Lady Mayor," Minister Rhodes said, drawing near. She stood almost as tall as Raphael. But if her own assistant embodied suaveness and charisma, the older woman represented old-style autocracy. "We may have had our difference of opinions, but I think you were a gutsy adversary."

She turned on her heel. As she passed Hector and Perseus on her way to the assembly chamber, Selene saw the tall woman lean as if to speak with either man, but then she kept walking, apparently having changed her mind.

In her wake, Hector stood scowling while Perseus rubbed a hand behind his neck. Instant worry flared in Selene. But he straightened and everything was fine again. How fond she'd become of him.

"Let us proceed," Chancellor Ladon said, grinning a politician's oily smile as he extended his hand to lead Selene into the chamber where everything, even the hundreds of seats and ceiling, had been painted or upholstered in Prussian blue. Everyone waited for them before proceeding. Except Rhodes, who had already claimed her seat.

This is it, Delian. Mom and Dad died for this. Don't mess it up.

Selene smoothed her dark blue suit—she wouldn't win any fashion show with her boring suit and sensible pumps—before she posed by the chancellor and let the reporters capture the moment in a flurry of flashes. Then, with Raphael by her side, she entered the vast assembly chamber.

One last time before she made her address, she wanted to see Perseus, her anchor, her protector and silent confidante, if only to make herself feel better. She turned, expecting him to be standing near the doors, looking back at her. The one constant in her life.

Her heart skipped a beat.

No!

Just as the wall of people closed behind her, she spotted Hector's red face as he hurriedly flicked his scriptex open and yelled into it. She didn't hear his voice amidst the rest, only saw his mouth deform with rapid-fire orders.

At his feet lay Perseus, flat on his back.

Then the doors closed.

His ears kept popping. He couldn't clear them. Intracranial pressure made him squint against the daylight raping his brain. And against the word glowing behind his eyelids.

Chimera.

He could swear he'd heard it. Someone had said the word out loud a moment ago. But then again, it might have been the year before. He felt disjointed, pulled in every direction. For a moment he only stood there, his mind blank while his muscles screamed to react, to run, kick, or scream. Anything. There was something he should've done. Something important.

Then everything had turned red and black. He could hardly focus, and kept having to blink to clear his vision. His palms tingled.

Then *they* showed up. Misery loved company.

"Chimera, Chimera, Chimera," they whispered.

Would they shut the hell up already? His head hurt. So much.

But he knew how to stop the pain and the blinding word etched in his brain. All he had to do was kill Selene Delian. With her dead, everything would be better. The menace would be gone, the danger eliminated. Threat ID'd and neutralized. As simple as a bullet to the head.

"No." His voice sounded muffled in his ears.

He wouldn't kill her. He couldn't.

That murderous urge wasn't his. As much as it floated around his head, it hadn't been born there. It was something exterior. Something implanted.

"Fight it," he muttered under his breath. He didn't care if people turned to watch. Fuck them all.

When the pain hit the first time, he didn't know what to do except find a deep recess in his mind and try to weather the storm. But they found him, the monsters did. They pulled him out kicking and screaming and clawing at anything he could to hamper their progress—at the image of her, the quality of her noble character. She was a good person. Why should he kill her?

"She is the Chimera," they replied. "She *is* the monster."

More pain. He whimpered and would have ground his forehead against the concrete floor had he been able to reach it. Feverish heat wafted from his clothes. He was burning up! Jolts coursed through him, followed by violent shivers. As though he were being electrocuted. The taste of blood filled his mouth. He choked down metallic spit.

"Kill her."

He swung a fist but caught only air. "Fuck you! I won't!"

Chimera blazed bright. Blinding. Then pain. Wave after wave. He could barely stay conscious.

God, make it stop. Please.

"Only *you* can," they murmured.

So close he could smell them, closer than ever before. Fear, death, forgotten memories. Tentacles into his brain.

Pain rolled in waves. Blades of daylight in his eyes, the tiniest sound like a thunderclap. Nausea choked him. As did fear.

Make it stop.

Then he understood. It had been her all along. Somehow, she'd found a way inside his head and put the monsters there. If he killed her, they'd leave as well.

The agony racking his body and defiling his mind stopped instantly. Cool logic replaced confusion. He straightened.

Selene Delian *had* to die. Her complete schedule was a mere click away. It wouldn't be complicated. She wouldn't see it coming.

He knew just the way to do it.

Perseus woke to Hector yelling at someone.

"Go get some goddamn water before I get cranky!"

He smiled in spite of the pain in his neck. Damn, what the hell had happened? He'd been so hot under his helmet and tactical uniform. Although the stuff was built of breathable cloth and high tech body armor, it still made for a stifling experience in anything but controlled environments. Maybe he was getting too old for this.

With a hand that shook violently, he rubbed his neck, and then rolled into a seated position. He was so hot. The pitiless Icelandic sun had hit him hard as soon as they'd disembarked from the shuttle and then had grown even hotter while he'd stood on the tarmac, waiting for the press to run its circus. Selene had looked so at ease in the mayhem.

Hector crouched by Perseus's side. "Hey, there. What happened?"

"I don't know. I think I've got heat stroke or something." Other Aegis agents had come over and formed a circle facing outward, granting them some measure of privacy.

"No wonder. That thing is so damn hot. And a helmet, for crissake. Come on, I'll take you to the john. Cold water will do you some good. There's plenty of time while Selene makes her speech."

To hear the name out loud had a strange effect on him. Why had Hector made that face? As if the name tasted bad? Perseus stood, adjusted his helmet, and followed Hector into the bathrooms. They were bigger than his entire apartment. Much bigger.

Hector bent over one of the granite sinks along the wall and got the water going nice and strong.

Perseus looked at himself in the mirror, the antireflective face shield, the black uniform. Should he remove it? No one would ever recognize him. Not even his closest friends. Not that he had any. Except for one.

A word popped into his mind, a strange word he knew existed but to which he'd never paid attention. Until now. Everything was different.

Everything mattered, even strange ancient Greek words.

"Chimera."

"What was that?" Hector asked, straightening.

All it took was a quick little punch to the base of the skull and the Lady Mayor's chief of security crumbled in Perseus's arms.

"Sorry, old man." He gently lowered Hector to the floor.

The door opened. A young man gasped and would have turned around had Perseus not charged and tackled him to the unforgiving terrazzo floor.

Soon, Perseus had both unconscious men sitting on toilets with the stall doors locked from the inside. He donned the young man's clothes and slipped his gun beneath the shirt. Not a perfect fit, but close enough. It wouldn't matter anyway. After he did what he had to do—what did he have to do, anyway?—nothing would matter.

He came out of the bathroom feeling uneasy for some strange reason. Why should he? Yet another part of himself, a tiny nagging voice, remarked he shouldn't have done that to Hector, who was a good man. He'd always respected the chief, even enjoyed his dry personality. Hadn't he? But something moved him forward. In his skull the pressure intensified and gave him a headache. Fuck, his head hurt.

Rubbing his temple, he stepped onto an escalator but couldn't be bothered to pay attention to his surroundings—another weird feeling, he usually missed very little—as he climbed the moving stairs to the last floor. The one reserved for dignitaries. Like the Lady Mayor.

Avoiding the few security guards proved easy. Even the pair of Aegis agents never saw him as he crept from doorway to doorway before slipping onto a terrace that opened out on a pair of penthouses, each with a large bay window. Four hundred feet below, Reykjavik sprawled left and right and center.

Perseus padded around the penthouse to the left and moved a potted plant so he could punch through one of the glass panes. He cut his hand, didn't know why, but couldn't be bothered to care. What the hell was wrong with him? He was bleeding all over the goddamn floor, yet he didn't make a move as he stood inside the penthouse proper, breathing in the different scents and taking in the sounds.

It would be over soon. What? He didn't know. But he knew that soon, everything would be good. The nightmares would stop and the monsters would leave him alone. He had only one thing to do.

He might not have many virtues—they'd been beaten out of him by his tyrannical drunkard of a father—but patience was one of them. So he stood there, waiting, knowing he had several hours to go. Didn't care. Nothing mattered. Except that one thing. If only he could remember what it was.

How long did he remain this way, standing inside the penthouse's patio with four hundred feet of air a few inches behind his heels? Any-one who fell would scream for a long, long time.

When the door opened, he felt the change in the air. He slipped his hand under his shirt to retrieve his gun. He was ready.

Then that word surfaced again. Chimera. What the hell did it mean?

A sun blazed into his brain hard enough to make his sinuses burn and his eyes water. Pain jack-hammered his skull. Agony. In his head, gut, every limb. Liquid fire. Blades everywhere, slashing, stabbing.

Then brilliant clarity revealed his impending mission, an affront to everything in which he believed. A deed so dark, he'd rather die than commit it.

He had to kill Selene Delian.

"God, no," he whispered.

Chapter 5

Selene delivered her address with aplomb and personality, but her elation had been drowned in her worry for Perseus.

"You were good," Raphael remarked, smiling at someone before turning to her. His blue-eyed gaze bore into her. "Why didn't you mention the osmium processing? You were supposed to—"

"Because it's my address and I'll take it in the direction I choose," she snapped.

"Lady Mayor?" asked a young man with a scriptex on a platter.

She ignored Raphael's dirty looks—maybe she should've listened to Hector and fired the smug peacock a long time ago—and took the scriptex. "Delian here."

"Lady Mayor," Hector said.

From his voice, she knew he was nervous. He sounded subdued, her title forced. He usually called her Selene unless he was huffing and puffing about something, in which case he'd call her, "Ma'am, yes, ma'am."

"Agent Corinth? How is he?" She tried to modulate her voice but realized that anyone who knew her would be able to hear her concern. Things had changed. She couldn't hide it.

By her side, Raphael's eyebrow arched.

"Something happened, something bad. He's *gone.*"

A cold, clammy fist grabbed her stomach and squeezed. "What do you mean, Agent Corinth is gone? Be specific, for god's sake. Hector!"

"He was right with me." Hector's voice trailed through something she didn't hear. "Sorry, I'm trying to organize the search over here. He was there with me, then he collapsed. He said it was the heat. But when I took him to the men's room, he knocked me out and took off. He left his gear behind. He's gone. And he has his gun."

"*What?*"

She forced her brain into gear, but it kept slipping back to the *he-knocked-me-out-and-took-off* part. She replayed the words as though they'd eventually make sense. Except they didn't. Perseus would never,

ever do that.

"What happened?" Raphael leaned closer to listen in. "Who's gone?"

All strength left her. She pinched the bridge of her nose. Tears stung her eyes. *God, not here, not in public.*

"Selene?" Raphael slipped the scriptex from her deadened fingers. "Who's gone? Agent Corinth?"

She nodded, unable to say a word for several seconds. "He attacked Hector. Then he left and took his gun with him. No one knows where he is."

Or what he looks like.

"Keep yourself together, okay?" he murmured through a fake smile. "They're watching."

Selene nodded. Crazy scenarios played in her mind. But none of them made sense. Perseus would never leave, would he? Not this way.

"I need a break," she said between her teeth. "I'll be in my room."

She needed a pillow to cry into as well, but this, she left unsaid. She had to blow her nose. Her eyes welled with tears. She didn't wait for Raphael to follow—didn't care if he did or not, actually—as she rushed from the lounge and took the first elevator to the top floor. She met no one and was glad of it.

Her heart beat with the sustained roll of a war drum. Where was he? Why had he left? *Attacked* Hector? Why? That was so unlike the Perseus she'd come to know and trust. And love. She might as well admit it to herself now, in her darkest hour. She'd fallen in love with Agent Corinth, Perseus Samaras. Although to be fair to herself and to the spirit of what they'd shared, she'd known for a while that a special place in her heart had long been cordoned off for him. The revelation that she loved him felt similar to receiving a present. Until the very moment of the unwrapping, one knew there was something beautiful inside, something chosen. The present itself might be a secret, but one knew it was *there* under the wrappings. Or in her situation, under the uniform.

And now he was gone.

As soon as she stepped out of the elevator into the luxurious hallway, she could no longer hold the tears at bay. She rubbed them away as much as she could before walking by the pair of stoical Aegis agents. Neither of them hers, too tall, too big. One opened her door, and dazed, she stumbled into her suite, all seven thousand square feet of dark wood and frosted glass. The door closed behind her. For the first time in her life, Selene Delian allowed herself the luxury of bawling her eyes out.

She'd barely cried after her parents' deaths and subsequent funerals, not that an exploding shuttle left much for a proper send-off. Only once or twice had she let the stress affect her, leading her campaign as if her life would end if she failed. Now that she'd played her role and given the all-important address, now that she could at last find some peace, this nightmare assaulted her.

A soft knock at the door made her curse. Couldn't she get half a fucking minute of self-pity to herself?

"What?"

"It's Raphael," came the familiar voice. "I have news from Hector."

She'd turned and opened the door before the thought registered that she should've splashed some water on her face and tried to appear a bit more composed. She must have been a scary sight.

Raphael's eyes narrowed when he entered and closed the door behind him. "You look like crap, Selene. Why are you so upset over this? The address went well. Everyone is charmed."

"My bodyguard attacked my chief of security," she snapped too quickly to smooth the edge to her tone. It wasn't Raphael's fault. "I need a drink."

He nodded. "I think I'll join you this time."

She followed him deeper into the suite. Bright afternoon sun stabbed in at an acute angle through the massive bay window that occupied an entire wall of the penthouse. Potted trees aligned close together offered a bit of privacy. Not that anyone could see inside at this height. A circle of wet spots caught her eye. Against the dark floor, she couldn't tell what it was. Water from the gardener watering the trees, perhaps?

Chinks and *clinks* of glasses and bottles preceded Raphael joining her, crystal tumblers in hand.

"What is it?" She sniffed the amber liquid.

"I have no idea." He took a long swallow, unbuttoned his black jacket, and loosened his tie. It was the color of kiwi flesh. Raphael was ever ready for a photo shoot.

"You said you had news from Hector." The drink tasted the way perfume smelled. Ugh. But the welcome fire glided down her throat. The effect spread to her limbs. Potent stuff.

"Hector dispatched a security detail to look through Corinth's place, but they found nothing of interest. Did you know the guy sleeps on a mattress on the floor?" Another gulp. "Pathetic."

As much as Perseus's recent actions confused and frightened her, she wasn't about to let anyone call him pathetic. "I'm sure he has his reasons."

"Come on. What's up with you?" After a second or so, Raphael's blue eyes flared when he turned to her. "You two have something going on, don't you?" He shook his head. "The press will be all over that."

"What I do with my private life is none of your business. And if you have nothing else, you can get the hell out." The tumbler *thunked* when she set it on the glass table by the window. A faint breeze caressed her neck. One of the windows must have been open.

"Don't let his sad gray eyes fool you, Selene." Raphael's tone dripped with derision. "He's a stone-cold killer."

Selene backed to the middle of the room. Fear gripped her throat. And anger. "How would you know the color of his eyes?"

"A lucky guess."

"My ass. What are you talking about? When did you see him without his helmet?"

"A couple of weeks ago, when he was strapped to a gurney with a drill in his skull."

The words registered in her brain, but the meaning was so large, so vile, she could barely wrap her mind around it. "Strapped to a gurney? Why?" A drill in his skull? Good God!

A change came over Raphael, a change both terrible and all-encompassing. From debonair and fashionably arrogant, his expression turned darker, meaner, belied by the sparkling blue eyes and stylish blond hair combed back over his handsome brow. "I know a couple of things that have always escaped you, Selene. How to win is one of them."

"How to win?" she repeated, incredulous. Another step backward. "Win *what*?"

"Everything."

Movement at the edge of her vision alerted her to another presence. She jumped back, hit the table corner and had to use it for support as she watched a man step into the suite. He must have been waiting outside on the terrace.

No more than five-ten, handsome in a menacing way with a compact musculature. His close-cropped hair was dark and formed a widow's peak over his smooth, high brow. Thick shoulders pulled at the short-sleeved blue shirt while muscled thighs strained the faded jeans tight. He could have been pulled straight from an outdoors magazine, except for the dark, predatory glint in his eyes. He advanced with the precise and calculated walk of a hunter. Feral, primed, vigilant. Above blood-shot eyes the color of ashes, a thick scar ran down through an eyebrow and forked over the bridge of his elegant Grecian nose.

His well-formed lips murmured something she didn't hear. But she would have known that man among a thousand. "Perseus?" It never crossed her to mind call him by his Aegis designation. This was Perseus before her now. *Her* Perseus.

His eyes flared, blinked several times. He looked surprised, relieved, distraught, tried to say something but it came out garbled. He'd pushed the words through a snarl of pain. Perfectly aligned teeth flashed when he cringed.

What was wrong with him? An élan of empathy flared through her. The only time she'd ever experienced such a feverish heat wave had been in his arms, when they'd made love while everyone else slept in their stasis pods. Even gravity had left them alone together. The world had belonged only to them. The last two people in the universe. Nothing had mattered. As now, when nothing mattered but this man and his obvious plight.

"Perseus?" she repeated as gently as she could, given her voice's tendency to carry loud and far. She tamed it to a whisper for him. "Are you hurt?"

Chimera.

Inside Perseus's head, the word blazed. A planet about to go supernova. Cracks glowing, molten rock about to burst in incendiary spills.

Chimera.

The pain made him weak and lightheaded. He could hardly think. Through the agony, a notion kept surfacing. She'd known it was him. She'd called him by name. How could she have known, if she'd never seen his face? Yet Selene hadn't hesitated one second. And instead of the reaction one would expect—the horror of seeing a friend turning on a friend, an armed man in her room, for fuck's sake—her eyes had filled with compassion and relief. It made him feel a thousand times worse about what he had to do.

"Don't let her convince you," the monsters whispered behind him. He shook his head. Didn't want to listen. Fuck them.

Something clicked inside his skull and triggered pain of unimaginable intensity. Liquid fire being poured inside his head. He blinked to clear his troubled vision.

"She's the monster," the voices said.

Perseus swore the top of his skull would blow off for the pressure there. He had to do it. If only to stop the torture.

But he couldn't bear to harm her. He loved her, always had, always would. She was a friend, someone he trusted completely.

"Kill her."

Shaking his head didn't alleviate the pain or silence the whispers.

"*Kill* her!"

"No!"

Chimera.

Selene's heart was breaking as she watched him struggle against something only he could see. Or hear. He tilted his head as if listening to a conversation.

He shook his head emphatically. "No."

She turned to Raphael, who stood a bit in retreat, looking smug with his arms crossed. "What's going on?"

"He's here to kill you, Selene. Courtesy of PC and some very, very expensive nanotech. Biodegradable, of course. In a couple hours, the implant will be gone."

She felt as though she'd sat at a table where a game of cards was already in progress. Details floated around her, all of them out of reach. Meaning teased her with whispers she couldn't hear, like feathers against her nape, a broken tune on a breeze. Something big was going on. Much bigger than a former bodyguard turning on his employer. And Perseus wasn't just any close protection agent.

"Planetary Commonwealth did this?" She pointed at Perseus, who stood immobile, hands shaking at his sides, obviously prey to a terrible inner conflict. Anger bloomed in her chest. "PC and *you* did this to him? Hurt him this way, put that thing in his brain? You despicable monster! You'd better start running, Sinon, you hypocritical, backstabbing asshole!"

He waved airily. "Language, *language.* You're letting your roots show, Selene. But then, you've always been a peasant in a suit. Not even a good suit at that. When he's in jail for your assassination, I'll take New Heraklion back to the bargaining table, back under Earth's protection, where it has belonged this whole time. I'll fix all your mistakes, Selene. And your parents'."

"My only mistake was not letting Hector deal with you from day one," she snapped, her gaze never leaving Perseus. "I don't know what you're doing to him or how, but you're going to stop it."

"I can't. It's already been activated and can't be stopped. In fact, he should already have followed orders. My sponsor said the pain alone would motivate anyone to do anything. But I guess Aegis agents are a different breed." Raphael put his glass by hers, turned toward Perseus. "It's time. Chimera."

Perseus flinched as if someone had struck him. One hand went to his head while with the other, he pulled his gun from the back of his jeans to level it at her. The long, black matte weapon looked heavy in his shaking fist. The muzzle wavered back and forth. His hands *never* shook. He was Mr. Steady Hands. Her protector. Confidante. Friend.

"Perseus, please," she said slowly. "Don't listen to him. Fight it. You don't have to do this. We'll work it out. Okay?"

"He can't," Raphael said. "It's wired directly into his mental processes." Smiling, he turned to Perseus. "Chimera. Do you hear me, Agent Corinth? Chi-me-ra."

The smile died when Perseus took a step forward but froze in place. He quivered from head to feet. His breathing rattled in his chest.

Selene had no idea what he went through, only that it must have been excruciating to trigger such a strong reaction in the usually composed, stoical man. Sweat poured from his forehead and darkened his shirt. He panted hard.

"Perseus," she murmured. "Listen to me. They implanted you with this thought. It's not yours. It's theirs."

Chimera.

Perseus was shaking so hard he could swear everyone could hear his teeth chattering. He wrapped his index finger over the trigger.

And froze. Behind him, the whispers stopped. One second, two, ten. Time ticked away. Still he stood, immobile, fighting it with all he had.

That word. That fucking word!

He couldn't.

But Raphael kept saying the word, and each occurrence felt as if someone were whipping him with white-hot chains. He fought it. God, he fought it. That face he'd known for almost a year, those clear and sparkling eyes that had so appealed to him from the very start. He couldn't snuff that sort of light. She hadn't done anything wrong.

"Fight it," she implored him when he advanced by another excruciating step.

Perseus didn't know why, but he could tell she meant him. To fight it for himself, not for her sake. God, he loved her.

Dammit, he *loved* her! How could they ask such a thing! She'd shared herself with him in the most private, sensual and heartfelt way. Just imagining how her skin felt under his palms made him feel better.

The thought stopped him. For a split second, the pain abated. Like the howling wind changing directions and, for a short time, quieting. Perseus forced another detail of her body into his mind. Her skin.

Her perfect, smooth, soft flesh and how it felt around him.

His eyes cleared somewhat. He could almost breathe without wanting to puke from the pain. That was it. The key.

The sound of her voice as she'd whispered, moaned and cried his name, over and over. The heat of her sex clenched around his. Her breasts, two glorious handfuls of woman.

"That's it," Selene whispered. "Fight it, Perseus. Push it down."

Maybe there was a God after all. He fixed onto her gaze as he filled his mind with sensations of what they'd shared back in that dark cabin. It was working! Probably something about his sexual impulses ratcheting up his hormone levels, neurotransmitters, spikes in electrical activity or whatever. The fuckers hadn't thought about *that*, had they! And it worked.

Raphael Sinon abruptly grabbed Perseus by the shirt collar and reeled him up to his snarling face.

Any other time, Perseus would've sent Sinon home to his mama carrying his balls in one hand and his jaw in the other. But in his diminished state, he couldn't even lift a finger to stop the man from shaking the shit out of him. Alcohol overpowered Sinon's breath. Perseus *hated* the smell, let alone what it did to people.

"Chimera, Corinth!" he snarled. "Did you hear me? *Chimera!*"

Perseus felt himself slipping again into the black abyss that opened under his feet, one of white-hot fire licking his legs. Hell was waiting. His world became one of pain.

Chimera.

Selene's brittle self-control was unraveling fast. The sight of Raphael with a helpless Perseus by the shirt collar proved too much. "Leave him alone!" Selene threw herself at her assistant.

Everything happened at once.

Cursing, Raphael tried to wrestle the gun from Perseus's shaking hand.

Selene launched herself at him.

Like a team raising a trophy high above their heads, Raphael and Perseus struggled to find the trigger of the gun, now pointed at the ceiling. A third hand, her own, much lower, clawed at Raphael's wrist so he'd let go.

A gunshot exploded like a thunderclap.

It must have pulled Perseus from his trance. He snapped his knee hard into Raphael's groin. Raphael doubled over. Hand still over the gun, Perseus brought his other elbow hard against Raphael's nape, but not before the taller man had wrapped a long arm around Perseus's thighs. Struggling, backpedaling, they toppled sideways against the bay window. It shattered in a hail of diamonds as they tumbled onto the terrace.

A terrible struggle, strangely quiet. The spill of glass against concrete. The high wind whistling a plaintive tune.

"Perseus!" Selene jumped over the window-frame. Glass crunched under her soles as she rushed to the struggling men.

Dear god, the height!

Displaying incredible strength, Perseus dipped his shoulder into the much larger and taller Raphael, and with a powerful lift, sent him floundering back a pace or two.

"If you don't do it," Raphael snarled, wiping blood from his nose, "then we'll find someone else! There'll always be someone else willing and able!"

Before she could reach them, Raphael made a grab for the gun. Perseus pivoted, sidestepped, and at the last possible second, seized Raphael's wrist. Perseus used Raphael's momentum to bring him around in a complete circle, and with perfect balance, dipped, bunched his muscles, and sent Raphael up and over the handrail.

But Raphael had long arms.

Selene watched in horror. "No!"

Raphael gripped Perseus's shirt by the collar, which split down the front with a dry sound. The sudden tug was enough to destabilize Perseus's equilibrium. Windmilling with one arm, he leaned back over the railing. Far back. Too far.

Selene had never been good at sports. But now she charged forward quicker than she'd ever moved in her life. For a split second, she feared being too late, that she'd have to watch Perseus being dragged over the handrail by Raphael. That hateful son of a bitch!

"No!"

Flash forward. Sun in her eyes. Wind in her face and ears. Perseus's gray eyes, apologetic, loving, lost, fixed on her.

She was about to lose him. Lose the precious thing they shared.

The next moment, she had her hand around his wrist. Sweaty, shaking, but by god, she had him.

With a violent tug, the shirt collar gave and Raphael's scream reverberated as he plummeted out of sight.

The sudden release propelled her, hand still wrapped around Perseus's wrist, toward the middle of the terrace, towing him with her. He collapsed to his knees, panting, one hand pressed to his head. He still held the gun in a white-knuckled grip but had taken his index finger from the trigger.

From inside the suite came male voices. "Lady Mayor! Are you all right?"

"Run," she whispered as she grabbed him by the sleeve of his ruined shirt and hoisted him to his feet. "Run. *Now.*"

He turned bloodshot eyes to her. Tears streamed down his cheeks. "I'm sorry—I didn't—he wasn't alone."

"It's not important. We'll let the police sort it out. Please, Perseus." She checked back, saw heads bobbing inside the suite. "I love you. I'll cherish what we had, always. But go, *please.* Just go."

Haunted gray eyes bore into her soul.

She hadn't lied. She *would* cherish what they'd had. Turning away from Perseus was the hardest thing she'd ever had to do. Yet she did it. She turned her back to him. Had to.

Behind her, a whisper of motion told her he had disappeared. As silently as he'd come into her life, he left it.

Tears rolled down her cheeks. She waited as long as she could to give Perseus a few precious seconds before she faced the door.

The two Aegis agents assigned to hall duty burst onto the terrace with guns in hand.

"What happened?" asked a robotic voice that didn't sound half as pleasant as the one she'd been used to. "We heard a gunshot. Are you hurt?"

Soon, Hector joined them on the terrace to give her a situation report and a bear hug. Multi-tasking. Had the circumstances not been so dire, she might have laughed. As it was, she managed only silence and numbness. Everything else lay beyond her strength.

"Raphael," she began. Pinched the bridge of her nose to focus her thoughts. "He tried to kill me. He had an accomplice waiting up here." She looked over the handrail. Four hundred feet below, a tiny dark spot marred the concrete plaza. People had already begun to congregate. Little ants in suits. The height overwhelmed her and she shivered.

Hector swore. "That sack of shit." A satisfied sort of grimace tightened his face as he looked down, motioned for the agents to leave. "Do you think it could have been Corinth? Did you recognize him?"

She shook her head. "He was much too tall to be Corinth."

After a vague description that resembled almost anyone except Perseus, apart from gender and number of limbs, Selene collapsed on the sofa.

Hector rubbed his balding head. Flicked his scriptex closed. "I can make myself scarce if you want to be alone."

"No. I don't. Would you stay?"

He sat by her side, facing the broken window. Neither said a word.

✺⟨✌⟩✺

Selene's legs wrapped around his middle while he took her. So hot. So wet.

Perseus kept replaying their encounter, knowing if he let go for a single second he might start sliding again into the darkness, and he wasn't sure he could claw his way back up. So he fixated on their precious moment of intimacy. And while he did this, he ran. From something, or toward something? He wasn't sure anymore.

He'd almost done it. He'd come *that* close to pulling the trigger.

The pain still seared his body and inside his head—most of all inside his head—but he used it as fuel. They'd done something to him. He would find out what. But most important of all, they'd done something to Selene, and for this, he'd repay them accordingly. Not only had they conspired against the woman he loved, they'd tried to use him to kill her. And Raphael Sinon. That slimeball.

Selene's breasts, how heavy and soft and ample in his hands.

He squeezed his eyes shut. Focus, for Christ's sake.

At the last possible second, when he'd stood in front of Selene, trying with all his strength to concentrate on her voice and the memory of their lovemaking, with Sinon saying the damn word over and over, each instance a nail in his skull, he had remembered and recognized another voice.

From dark recesses of his mind, a scene kept replaying. Something being jammed into his nape. A click inside his skull. Then pressure, intense and painful. Two voices in the darkness, one he knew well, Sinon, and the other he had identified when he heard it again earlier that day.

A woman's voice, gravelly, older. A smoker's voice.

Minister Philipa Rhodes.

So she was in on this as well? No matter. He had plenty of rage to spare for all of them. He intended to get to the bottom of this conspiracy if it meant he'd die in the process. He didn't care. Selene was safe. Or as safe as she could be while he figured out who'd played a hand in the affair.

His anger dulled and confusion threatened him again.

Focus.

Skin so soft. That special place between her thighs, where they rubbed against one another. He'd kissed that spot. Licked it. Had rubbed his cock along the silk of her pussy.

The terrifying moment passed. He was in control again. Close.

Finding the older woman proved easy enough. Funny how civilians were allowed to roam the place unchecked and unchallenged. Except for Aegis personnel, and these he made sure to avoid. They weren't bound like police officers with complicated rules of engagement. If something didn't sit well with them, they were allowed and expected to deal with it using any means necessary, even the most lethal.

Death didn't scare him, but he had to get his hands on Rhodes. She'd tried to kill Selene. She would pay for that. He could not rest until she did.

Contrary to his training, he didn't intend to wait for the perfect opportunity. Time was of the essence. With that implant still in his head, there was no telling what else they'd programmed him for. The thing might make him try to kill Selene again. Or someone else. Or himself. Shivers raced up his back. He blinked the sweat out of his eyes, knowing he looked intoxicated at best and drugged at worst. That couldn't be helped right now.

Finally, he spotted Minister Rhodes's entourage. Not many people walked around with a retinue of staff and close protection agents. Not Aegis bodyguards, but hired thugs. He knew the kind. He'd dealt with them several times on his other assignments. Bullies who would shy away from nothing. Wannabes with fancy guns, no better than the crooks they fought.

His head throbbed, his ears buzzed. He was so thirsty. A general malaise made him shaky and disoriented. But through it all, through the pain and rage, he kept a steady grip on his focus. Selene's smile, the dimples on her Russian-doll face, the way her eyes flashed whenever something pissed her off. And how her flesh had felt around him, wet, so wet for him as he'd pounded himself in to the hilt. The taste of her honey.

He clung to that, the vision of what his life might have been had Rhodes and her puppets not decided to mess with him. He kept in his mind's eye what he'd lost. Fed off it, let it fuel his muscles and sharpen his mind.

Selene's lips around his cock. She'd swallowed his cum, for god's sake. That meant something to him. Picture it. Keep it there, on the surface.

Perseus crossed the crowded lobby and took a drink from the water fountain so he could keep the group in view without standing there and gawking like a slack-jawed moron. Soon they trooped into three elevators. Because she was so tall, Rhodes' silver head poked above the rest. Without running, but rushing nonetheless, he shouldered open the door to the closest stairwell and dashed up the levels, taking the steps four by four, then two by two when his heart began to hammer against his sternum. Nausea choked him. He stopped briefly, bent in half, caught his breath.

"I love you. I'll cherish what we had. Always."

Selene's parting words. The effect on him, balm on sunburn, a cool facecloth on a fevered brow. She hadn't judged him, though it would've been easy to do so. Why hadn't he spoken sooner? Why had he been weak enough to stand in front of her with his gun in his hand before he fought the programming down? Hadn't he loved her enough to try harder? Maybe he should have followed Sinon off the ledge….

I love you. He believed her. She didn't want to soothe him and then double-cross him. She'd meant it. Selene Delian never lied.

What gift they'd stolen from him. What light they'd taken. The best part of him, the protector and confidante. The man. Now only the killer remained. Even the monsters were silent. Maybe he'd dealt them a fatal blow when he'd fought the Chimera *thing* and won. Maybe hearing her saying these special words had destroyed the monsters.

But Rhodes and her accomplices had stolen it all. His hatred of them was proportional to his love for Selene. Scary.

From his excellent memory of Hector's security brief, he knew the Chancellor was housed in a nearby villa while the Security Minister would occupy the presidential suite. Level 133. When the white placard with black numbers bobbed into view, he paced himself and secured his gun in the back of his jeans. She was bound to have placed her thugs at every entry point. They'd have comms on them, relays to each other. He would break that link, and their necks as well.

When he reached the thick metal door, he waited to let his heart rate settle and his mind clear as much as possible before noiselessly clicking the handle lever up. Beyond the door, a shoulder occupied the thin embrasure. When he widened the gap, he saw another. Two men stood guard at this door. Pain in his head made him squeeze his eyes shut.

His thighs and lower back burning from hammering into her welcoming flesh. How good she'd felt, how right.

The throbbing receded. He could breathe again. God, would that thing ever leave him alone?

They never had time to turn around. He punched one in the nape. The man was still falling when Perseus wrapped his arm around the other's head and squeezed hard with a downward jerk. He felt more than heard the muffled crunch against his chest. He pulled both inert forms back into the stairwell with him. These two wouldn't wake again.

After a quick check, he rushed down the corridor with his peripheral vision on full alert and his hands shaking. So uncharacteristic for him. His hands *never* shook. His Aegis supervisor once said he should have been a surgeon. Ha.

Cushiony corridors, expensive brass and gold trim, carpet the color of blood. Everything had been built and decorated with Imperial China as the model, from copper brackets along the cedar timber walls to crushed oyster shell tiles worked into the mahogany floor. The hotel's presidential level proved even larger and more opulent than the penthouse in which they'd housed Selene.

He jogged to the end of the corridor, did the usual corner drill, then slipped onto the sort of interior courtyard linking the many sub-levels and pavilions. A water fountain gurgled by his side. Smells from cut flowers reached him. Then sweat.

A hand-chop aimed for his throat but never reached its mark. Perseus pivoted, sidestepped, grabbed the attacker's wrist and twisted it at an angle to which it hadn't been designed to bend. The bones cracked with a dry, brittle sound, like a small branch snapping underfoot. Perseus wrapped his other arm around the man's face just as he took a breath, no doubt to scream in pain.

At the very edge of his vision, he spotted someone else. Tall, skinny. Rhodes.

A punch to the temple downed the man. He'd hurt like a bitch when he woke. *If* he woke. Perseus was past caring.

Running, he reached the garden's corner just as a glass door closed. Beyond the thick greenish pane, Rhodes, wide-eyed, was frantically trying to lock it. She backpedaled at a furious pace when he aimed his gun to shoot through the thick door. He pulled the trigger as he leaped into midair. The door disintegrated into long shards. Some of it was still falling when he cleared the doorway, landed in a roll, and stood directly in front of Rhodes.

She flicked open a scriptex. He wrapped his hand over it to trap hers while he pressed the muzzle of his gun under her nose. "You won't need that, Minister Rhodes."

Her eyes, which he'd only seen narrowed in contempt or deep concentration, flared as wide as bridge tokens. "Agent Corinth. I didn't expect you to make it all the way up here. Remind me to fire my bodyguards. Those you let live, anyway."

"No games, Minister. You stole my life."

"You didn't have one to begin with, young man. I gave you purpose. A goal. An acquired target. And you still managed to miss it."

"I didn't *miss*. I fought it and won."

She opened her mouth, snapped it shut, tried again. "No one has ever been able to fight it. Not without putting a bullet through their brains." A mean smile twisted the old mouth. Lipstick marred a tooth. "Maybe you should consider it while you can, Corinth. Eating your gun would be a fitting end for a man like you."

A man like him. What was he, anyway?

Perseus took a step back. Selene's last words rang clear as crystal bells in his ear. She would cherish what they had. But if he killed the minister, what would there be to cherish? The memory of a man who'd gunned down an old lady, even one as deserving as Rhodes? What would Selene say to that? The throbbing in the back of his head impeded his ability to focus. He swallowed repeatedly. That thing, that fucking *thing* in his brain was trying to drag him back into the hole.

Selene's delectable wrist, which he'd bitten. The tender spot that tasted as silk felt. He'd almost come on the spot.

"Are you scared?" Rhodes asked, intruding into his mental struggle.

"Shut up!"

"It's understandable, Corinth. But you're Aegis. You have to suck it up, stand straight, and pull the trigger. It won't hurt. Not as much as you're hurting now—"

"I said, shut up!"

Take it all, Selene had urged while he thrust into her as hard as he'd ever dared. Take it. And Perseus had, knowing that as they clung to each other in the darkness and zero-g, nothing else mattered. He loved her with every last shred of his being. Also knew that life without her wouldn't be worth a damn.

Rhodes took a step forward. He watched her through the tears welling in his eyes.

"Is it throbbing?" she asked, seeming almost sincere in her concern. "Because if it is, it means the implant is decaying, and that my friend, will make it all much, much worse. Our researchers compare it to a brain embolism."

Selene's eyes, her smile. Three little words. I love you.

The pain relinquished its hold on his brain like an octopus letting go of a prey. A single clear thought pierced the fog.

The scriptex gleamed in the old woman's hand.

"Give me that," he said.

She must have heard the difference in his voice. "What are you doing?"

"Something a *man like me* wouldn't do. But I was lucky. A friend made me a better man. A friend I love."

Chapter 6

"That's him," Hector said, standing in the cruiser's hatch. "That's the new guy Aegis sent us."

Selene jumped to her feet to see for herself. A black helmet and then a pair of shoulders came out of the shuttle. The agent stepped onto the landing bay. Her heart skipped a beat. Could it be?

But as he straightened, she realized it wasn't Perseus. Too tall and lean. She'd been hoping against hope that somehow he'd be returned to her. Her heart sank back to its new home in the pit of her stomach. She doubted it would move from there for a long time.

For the flight home, Selene had taken the stasis aids. She wanted to sleep off the voyage—life in general, as much as possible. With everything that had gone on the day before, she didn't feel ready to face anything more stressful than choosing the day's clothes. And even that might be too much.

Yet as soon as they'd landed on New Heraklion, she could tell something momentous had happened, something apart from her bodyguard's disappearance and one of her staff trying to kill her. When the hatch opened, a staff member with his red tie askew rushed toward them through the security cordon. He made her new Aegis close protection guy, Agent Ancona, visibly nervous.

"Lady Mayor," he panted, waving a sheet of plastic film. "I'm so sorry for what happened! We should have seen it coming! So sorry. But you have to read this!" In his excitement, he shoved the sheet into the hand she'd extended to shake, apologized, and shifted foot to foot while she read the news report.

Noise from the spaceports dimmed as she read. The words collided, jumbled. Impossible....

"Oh. My. God. Hector, read this."

He took the sheet from her, squinting as he angled it for easier reading. "In light of recent events during the world summit held yesterday in Reykjavik... blah, blah... increased security and so on... an explosive communiqué involving the Planetary Commonwealth Commissions... whoa, now that's news... an anonymous tip has led to the arrest of Security Minister Rhodes and a handful of her staff members. PC Chancellor asked for his Security Minister's immediate resignation."

Hector looked at her, let out a vitriolic curse, and then resumed. "Charges range from fraud to treason. Minister Rhodes's trial is expected to last several months, with possible sentences ranging from ten years to life in prison." The translucent blue sheet was shaking by the time he looked up at Selene. "Treason. Well, she sure got it across the teeth, eh? And that picture says it all. Old bat."

It *had* to be Perseus's doing. That anonymous tip about the Planetary Commonwealth involvement had to have come from him. That meant he was safe. She chose to believe this theory because no other explanation was acceptable. Or bearable.

Hector had made sure to use a decoy shuttle this time, so Selene was afforded a quiet journey to the office right below her home. She'd long abandoned the pretense of separating her private life from her work, and reserved the top level of the building for her personal use.

Because they'd landed during the downshift, the main lights were still off, giving the empty building a sad, forlorn feel. Empty cubicles, tabletop communication relays flashing with unread messages, the ventilation units softly whirring. Selene stopped in front of her door and poked her head inside the darkened office. The relay flashed with messages. She stopped counting after twelve.

"Well, damn, some people don't have lives." Hector pulled a plastic sheet from under his mail slot by the counter. "Another candidate for my job." He flicked the polymer seal with a thumb. "And Aegis-approved, too. Finally, someone with some damn qualifications."

She couldn't help but laugh. "Back at the wheel with us." She felt like a hamster, running, running, not going anywhere.

"Want to interview him tomorrow? There's a number to call."

She shrugged. "Sure."

"What's wrong?"

"Nothing." She tried to look interested in the sheet Hector held in his hand. "What's his name?"

"Never mind his name, Selene. What's wrong? Aside from almost getting shot, the shuttle crash, the AWOL bodyguard, and Sinon turning out to be a snake of the first order—aside from all that, I mean." Despite the smile, Hector looked old and tired.

"I miss him."

"Not the ass-wipe Raphael, right?"

"No, not him."

"Yeah," Hector replied, nodding. "Me, too. But he'll do a good job, too, this new Aegis guy. They all do."

Down the hall, Agent Ancona stood with his back against the wall, his helmet-covered face angled away from them.

Selene sighed. It just wouldn't be the same.

By suppertime, a headache of cosmic proportion had established residence behind her eyeballs. She'd had to extinguish half a dozen fires, as Hector called them, and then gave two interviews, replied to dozens of messages of sympathy, and prepared for Julie's send-off. To say she was getting cranky would be the understatement of the year. She wanted to go home. Fifty paces away and up an elevator ride. So tempting. But there was so much yet to do.

Her relay chimed twice rapidly. An inside call. *"What?"*

"Well, good evening to you, too, ma'am," Hector huffed. "Sorry to disturb you, ma'am. The candidate, he's here, ma'am."

She sighed. Another thing on her list. Maybe he'd turn out to be qualified, compatible, and if she were very, very lucky, not as abrasive as Hector. Bless the old man's heart, but he needed to stop *saying* he'd retire and actually *do* it. Exactly as the countdown calendar on his door indicated.

"He's in your office right now?" Selene smoothed her shirt, tested her breath against her palm. Damn coffee.

"Yes. Send him in? Do you want me there, too?"

"No, just send him. You and Aegis have already cleared him. I'll call you if I need anything else. Thanks."

Raphael would've handled these things. He'd jealously guarded access to her office as he would a Great Wall of China from hordes of barbarians. They'd need to promote one of the staffers. That excited young man with the crooked red tie, Chris, perhaps. He needed to work on his etiquette, but decorum could be taught, unlike enthusiasm, which he seemed to have in abundance.

So many things to do.

She clicked the relay closed, donned her jacket, and walked around her desk—a flat surface struggling to support the massive piles of plastic sheets and various things that seemed to collect by themselves. *Leave two folders together for five minutes and this was what happened.* She moved a stack off the chair so the man could at least sit.

A subtle smell wafted to her. Aftershave and peppermint.

Her heart hammered once hard, then in a series of arrhythmic thuds. The file she was holding slipped to the floor. She didn't care. Her cheeks grew numb, and for a frantic moment she feared collapsing. But she forced herself to focus and slowly turn to face the door, hoping her heart wouldn't be crushed with bitter disappointment.

Then she saw him.

There in the doorway to her office stood a man dressed in a dark gray suit, which gave him a smart, businessman look despite the scarred eyebrow. Or perhaps because of it.

"Perseus."

She could say nothing else.

"Lady Mayor Delian." His eyes blazed like gray suns.

She'd missed that voice, that set of shoulders, the quiet strength. His presence.

Melting in a puddle on the floor would be easy. Not something she could afford to do in her position. She'd learned to keep emotions for private settings and situations. Her office wasn't part of that life. But inside, the woman in her rejoiced.

With a cautious smile, she clutched her hands behind her, stood straight. "I'm glad you applied for the position."

Such a strange voice was coming out of her mouth. Alien words, exotic notions. A chasm could open right under her feet, but she wouldn't even notice the fall. Numb. Surreal.

He filled her office with his quiet intensity and filled her with untold joy. She felt as if she'd stepped out of a cave into a brilliant spring morning. There was so much she wanted to tell this man. A million questions pushed and shoved to be asked. Her palms tingled for him.

"My file," he said simply, proffering a rhombus-shaped black plastic envelope with the Aegis logo embossed on the seal flap.

Selene took a step toward him, extended her hand and pinched the envelope by a corner. But at the last second, Perseus gripped it tight. Their gazes met.

"I've beaten the monsters." He pointed to his temple.

If she shook any harder, she'd slip right out of her pumps. She nodded because she couldn't say a damn word. So he'd dealt with what Rhodes had done to him, that thing they'd implanted in his brain. The monsters they put in his head. He'd prevailed. She'd never doubted he would. Even so, fear had continued to gnaw at her. What if? They could have killed him. A fresh wave of anger washed over her.

"What about those who sent them? Did you deal with them, too?"

A nod.

God, she'd missed it. Such a simple little motion, yet one that carried so much meaning to her.

Heat rose in her cheeks when he released the envelope and drew nearer. His smell became intoxicating, the depth of his gray eyes unfathomable. An alpine lake on a cloudy day.

"I'm back," he murmured. His lips glistened after he moistened them. She couldn't look at anything else. "If you're willing, we can try to glue the pieces back together."

"Are you?"

"I don't remember wanting anything else as much as I want this."

"Meet me at the elevator," she whispered, dropping the black envelope on the pile by her side.

Perseus nodded, turned and left her office. Only his scent remained with her. Almost a dream. It had been the strangest few moments she'd ever experienced. Two separate entities fought for control of her body. The first, the Lady Mayor, had to remain professional and detached for his and everybody else's sake. And the other, the woman in her, demanded that she throw her arms around his neck and hug him fiercely.

Not two seconds later, she stepped out of her office and slowed in front of Hector's door. "He's hired," she said over her shoulder as she marched on.

His questions—and Agent Ancona—followed her down the hall, but she neither answered nor stopped. She didn't pause until she rounded the corner and joined Perseus in front of the massive steel door—Hector's doing, with a hack-proof access panel showing an ascending sequence of numbers. So he'd already activated it. Excellent memory. He'd only been up to her place a couple of times during social events.

Agent Ancona stood directly in front of the door, facing her even though Perseus must have been the object of his attention and scrutiny.

"Thank you, Agent Ancona," she said, nodding. "He's an old friend. One I trust implicitly."

On the lapel of Perseus's jacket faintly glimmered a tiny black pin in the shape of a sword piercing a globe. Clearly, this meant something important. Ancona angled his head at the lapel pin and took a step back.

The door chimed and opened on a veritable steel safe of an elevator. Sometimes, Hector had too much fun tinkering with the building's schematics. She and Perseus entered, stood near enough to touch each other, but didn't. The door closed.

"When do you expect to know if the station will get nation-state status?" Matter-of-fact, life as usual.

Shivers raced up her back. She forced the elation down. "Tomorrow at the earliest. It depends if it's unanimous."

To stand so close to Perseus without touching him felt like the old days. Right there, yet so far. An awkward silence fell between them. She didn't dare turn to look at him. What had he expected? An effusive welcome, tears, laughter? Or had he feared coming to see her, on the chance she'd be angry and turn him away? Did he feel the way she did, torn between duty and love?

Sweat slicked her hands when the elevator stopped one level up to let them out onto the carpeted hallway of her home, which she'd furnished and decorated in rich burgundy and red tones. She loved red.

Behind her, the door slid shut with a hiss.

From the corner of her eye, she saw Perseus standing very still, looking at her, hands by his sides and head slightly tilted. She knew that stance, had seen it often. He was assessing a situation.

"Perseus, I'm—"

She turned in time to catch him raising a hand to cup her cheek. His kiss stole the breath from her.

A dam breached, and her heart surfaced from the deep for a long and avid intake of air. Elation. Glorious and dazzling. She let herself go. Completely. Trusting.

Their lips touched with a tenderness unmatched in any of their previous stolen moments.

Perseus had barely dared to breathe until this moment, this kiss. Earlier, while waiting for his interview, he'd been scared. Scared of her reaction. What if she kicked his ass to the spaceports and off the station? What if she greeted him with a cool handshake and a polite smile, recognizing him but unwilling to welcome him back into her heart? Or the very worst scenario of all, hiring him but granting him nothing more than platonic relationship, all business, a half-life working by her side without ever again being intimate.

The thought alone made him sweat. He would have understood and accepted her decision, of course, and never let the wound show. He was good at that, hiding his wounds. The devil knew he must have been scary back on that roof, waving his gun around like a fucking lunatic.

Despite everything that had happened—the assassination attempt, the near crash of her shuttle, Sinon turning out to be a backstabbing sack of shit—she'd still acted the cool, professional and composed woman he'd come to love so much. As if nothing had changed. Business as usual. No biggie. Hell, he knew some guys who liked to believe they were badass but wouldn't have been able to cope with half of what she'd had to go through in the last twenty-four hours. She embodied true strength to him. No bravado, no bullshit or posturing. And her reaction when she'd spotted him had instantly allayed his fears.

When, with her heart in her gaze, she'd reached out to retrieve his file, exposing that strong and feminine wrist bone he loved so much, the sight had almost unmade him. He'd had half a mind to wrap his arms around her and never let her go. But he controlled himself. They were in her office, where she worked, where she was his boss, not just the toughest, smartest, kindest and most beautiful woman in the world. Plus, he doubted Ancona—appointed by Aegis on his personal recommendation—would have appreciated that very much.

Selene pulled away so she could look up at him. He loved that he had her panting. Male pride.

"Was it you?" she asked, all gleaming eyes. "The anonymous source that brought Rhodes down?"

He nodded, running a thumb over her bottom lip. He loved the shine of it. "I had her, Selene, right at the end of my gun. But I couldn't kill her."

"I'm glad you didn't. That would have been too easy. What about that implant?" She ran a hand over his head, suddenly looking worried, and didn't that expression just make him want to lie on the couch, moan and grimace and let her minister to him all night. He pushed the ludicrous notion away.

"Sinon was right. The implant did decay and stopped functioning. But by that time, I'd already managed to reach Aegis HQ. They had their docs take a look at it and record the scans on data sheets. For proof, you know. And meanwhile, my bosses called their friends, who called their friends, and so on. We take care of our own."

Aegis's director had met him in person, a cool cucumber of a woman old enough to be his grandmother. They'd collectively *flipped* over what had been done to one of their agents. Aegis was sacrosanct, the one place where politics never dared put its oily finger. Through Aegis's inquiries, he discovered Rhodes had drugged his meal onboard the shuttle back to Earth—a forced vacation imposed by Selene on the entire staff—then taken him who-knew-where to have that thing put in his head. No one messed with Aegis. Not even Security Ministers.

Selene pressed her smiling face in the crook of his shoulder. The familiar smell of that cute, frizzy red mane made him sigh. Shampoo and a hint of perfume. Unbelievably erotic to him. Barely able to control himself, he crushed her against him. She returned the embrace with surprising force. Damn. She just might crack a rib.

"Thanks," he whispered. "For holding on. In every sense of the word." She'd saved his life back on that rooftop, but also in a myriad of other ways.

"Shh."

"I should've reported the first signs of illness when I started feeling weird and having nightmares." He shook his head. "Worse nightmares, anyway."

"What do you mean? You had trouble sleeping?"

"I always have."

When she leaned back against his arm to look into his face, he wasn't sure which expression he should let her see. That her concern touched him and made him feel special, valued, loved? Or that he was a tough guy who didn't need anyone's sympathy? Then again, he suspected she would see through any ruse. Truth would always supersede everything else with Selene. Nothing less than the truth.

Because he couldn't spill his guts and look at her at the same time—a guy had his pride, after all—he leaned his chin against her head and told her everything. He'd been an only child growing up in an abusive home, under the constant violence of an alcoholic father who chose the bottle to forget how much of an ass he'd been to Perseus's dead mother. As a boy, Perseus had recurring nightmares of monsters crawling out from under his bed. Even now, shameful as it was, he'd have the same nightmares, depending on his moods and the level of stress in his job. He slept on a mattress on the floor, for fuck's sake, because that usually ensured at least a couple hours of blissful oblivion.

He told her about stuff she probably didn't need—or want—to know. Things long past relevance. Petty details. Folks long dead. Missions gone awry, partners killed. As much as it cost him to share his baggage with her, as embarrassing as it was for a man to admit such frailty, he felt better doing it because, damn, it was Selene Delian who listened. That wasn't a small thing!

"Aren't you sorry you asked?" he finished, going for offhand but sounding lame. Christ.

She stood back from him, held his shoulders at arm's length so she could plant that gaze on him, the one that made grown men and women squirm for a place to hide. He didn't try to hide anything. She deserved the respect of a good, honest gaze. He owed her that. If she pushed him away, well, at least it would happen because of the truth, not because of lies. Lying to Selene was just not acceptable.

"No." Her tone was firm. "I'm *not* sorry. For anything. I'd do it all again—except for not letting Hector deal with Sinon right away. That, I'd change."

Her quick smile made him want to launch into a jig.

"But nothing else," she said. "And certainly not getting to know you better." Unshed tears made her eyes gleam. Precious gems. "That's been the best thing that happened since…." Sadness tightened her expression. "Well, in a long time."

She felt so right against him. He wanted her there and then. But he forced himself to wait so that when he leaned into her, she'd have plenty of time to see the love in his eyes and feel it on his lips. Later on, there would be countless occasions for blazing lust. Now, he wanted only to savor her. Take his time. Everything and everyone could go to hell and he wouldn't spare them a thought.

Their mouths drew closer as if drawn by unseen forces. Unseen, but not unfelt.

Selene stopped breathing when he was a scant few inches away. She couldn't help it. Perseus stole the breath from her. But she forced herself to look at him, to focus. The man's duality enthralled her, a mix of rugged good looks that contrasted with the gentle set of his mouth and loving expression in his gray eyes. She'd only seen his face twice, yet it felt familiar and comfortable, like looking into the face of a friend. Of the man she loved.

By raising her chin, she met him halfway, the symbolism not lost on her. When his lips pressed against hers, neither of them closed their eyes. The intimacy was a palpable thing.

This time, he didn't crush her to him—not that she'd object. Instead, he began to caress her with his lips and took his time discovering her mouth with his own. He brushed side to side while she parted her lips and waited. Each time he'd graze his way back over her mouth to caress the other side of her face, she would kiss him full on. He'd smile and keep going. She didn't know how long they stood in her foyer, simply kissing, hands idle on each other's backs.

Outside her bay window down the hall, station lights began to dim. Downshift was settling in. Behind her on the half-moon table against the wall, her relay chimed. She didn't answer. Unless her home went up in flames, she had no intention of coming out until at least the next day. And even then, it would be to make a quick appearance downstairs in time to get the newscasts from Earth before racing back up to him. Back home.

"I want us to make love in a bed this time," she said.

Nodding, he stood back and wrapped his hand around hers in a tight and comforting way. The man had some grip. "Lead on."

Selene slipped down the hall to her bedroom, the largest room because she needed a personal space away from everything and everyone. Her safe place. Her citadel and sanctuary. She'd splurged here, quite contrary to her usual frugal nature, and had created a look right out of Edo-period Japan. As soon as they entered her bedroom, he froze in the doorway.

"This means something to me," he began. Brought her wrist to his mouth and turned her arm to bare the tender skin on the inside. His teeth flashed against her wrist.

Her heart skipped a beat. At least one. Thrilling.

"You inviting me into your home this way. It means a lot."

"To me, too. This is the one place where I'm myself. No heels, no makeup. No bra."

"Good idea."

He eased her navy blue jacket off her shoulders and folded it neatly on the nearby lacquered trunk before undoing her top with precise and delicious-looking hands. She wanted to kiss them, rub them on her face, lick and nibble them. His fingers worked the knot on her wrap blouse with electrifying tenderness. Mr. Steady Hands. She intended to take her time, kiss and suck each of those perfect fingers. Scars covered knuckles the size of walnuts. She loved those too.

The blouse came loose to reveal her no-nonsense beige bra. She had nicer ones, but not as comfortable. Of course, she had to choose the ugliest to wear that morning. Typical.

After Perseus peeled the blouse from her body, he pressed a soft kiss to her ample cleavage. She shivered.

"You're beautiful," he said simply.

"Do you want to turn on the lights?"

"No. It's perfect this way."

"Just as well," she replied, looking down at herself.

"Why do you say that? You don't think you're beautiful?"

She smiled. "I'm all right. I was teasing."

He shrugged off his jacket and folded it, too. She loved watching him work, the way his hands moved economically, precisely.

"You like teasing?" The wicked lift at the corner of his mouth made her breath catch in her throat. Oh, the man could be bad. Bad in a good sense. In a *great* sense.

"Sometimes."

He nodded. "Good. I loved being teased. Sometimes."

Selene put her hands all over his chest as soon as he had his shirt open wide enough for her to touch skin. So hot. Dark hair parted his torso in perfectly symmetrical halves. Compact, sinewy muscles rippled under the skin. She pressed a reciprocal kiss between his pectorals.

The shirt followed the jackets on the trunk. "I wanted to do that," she said.

"Next time?"

"I'll remember."

"Good." Perseus looked over her shoulder to the bed and grinned. Such a gorgeous smile he had. It lit up his pale gray eyes. "I like your bed."

The single most expensive piece of furniture she'd ever bought, her bed was made of real wood, with a foot-thick mattress on a slat frame raised several inches from the floor. It weighed a *ton*. She should know. She'd hauled it back and forth enough times when she first moved into this apartment and tested each angle in the room. She'd finally—to the very vocal relief of her helper, Hector—settled for the middle of the room, facing the bay window but not too close to it.

"You're going to invite me in?" He drew near and leaned over to run a hand across the jade green satin cover.

Selene kicked off her shoes, smoothed her pants, and sat on the foot of the bed facing the window. She gave the mattress a quick double-pat. "You don't need an invitation into my bed."

With the lengthening shadows of the station lights dimming for the night, he seemed to tower in front of her. Strength emanated from his every pore, his widow's peak, arched eyebrows, and Grecian nose. She loved his nose! It gave him such character. His was proud and long, starting high between his brows and running in a narrow and straight bridge to a graceful flare of nostrils. His elegant mouth matched it well, providing a tantalizing contrast to his scarred eyebrow and knuckles.

Perseus knelt in front of her and reached around to unclasp her bra one-handed.

"You do this often?" she said.

His eyebrow quirked and a mocking grin lifted one side of his mouth. "No. But I'm good with my hands."

A frisson tingled down her spine when the bra came loose and released her breasts, which sagged and made her feel like taking a deep breath. Her skin tingled with the sudden release. She had an itch that wouldn't go away.

He dropped her bra on the bed and kissed the red straps' indentations on her skin before massaging gentle fingers along her shoulders. "I love your breasts. May I?"

She shivered in pleasure.

He smiled. "I'll take that as a yes."

When he splayed his hands and cupped her breasts, elevating them as godly offerings with a look of reverence on his face, Selene had to close her eyes for the sheer exhilaration. Heat heralded imminent contact. She *ahh*-ed when he closed his mouth over a nipple. Ran his tongue beneath the tender point, then around and around. Sublime.

She admired the tilt of his head as he leaned into her, and sent her hands to roam over his back and nape. She touched him to her heart's content. All that glorious skin and all those hard muscles. The diffuse light outside her window graced his flanks and illuminated the little bumps of muscles along his ribs and the play of corded biceps. Amber haloed his head and shoulders and the fine hairs on his muscled arms. She enjoyed watching him work. Relished the sounds he made deep in his throat. Loved how he made her feel.

"Make room for me," he murmured as he nudged her knees with his shoulders.

She sat with her thighs wide apart. The synthetic wool stretched with a faint rustling sound that seemed to delight him. He cocked his head near her knee and listened with his eyes closed.

"Sometimes," he whispered, "I'd tune my helmet audio feed just to hear you move. It's much better like this."

"And sometimes," she replied in kind, "I'd try to imagine what you looked like. It's much better like this."

They shared a smile. Quiet companionship. Comfortable intimacy so long sought.

Beyond the thermoplastic pane, dots of light from other habitats began to flicker. The hydroponics gardens across from her apartment blazed like a scintillating blue Milky Way, each tiny sapphire indicating a pod where vegetables and other plants grew. She loved walking in the moist shade, admiring the vibrant foliage.

"Do you think it'll go through?" he asked as he moved to the other breast.

She gasped when he sucked on it hard enough to curl her toes.

"I hope. New Heraklion deserves to be more than a labor camp for Earth."

"I agree. But I don't care."

She looked down at his intense gray eyes in the darkening shadows. "Why not? You live here. You're going to work here. It's our home."

He shrugged. "Even if you lived on one of the lunar colonies, I'd make it my home. It's not the place itself. It's where you happen to be. That's my home. Right here." He licked his lips and kissed his way up her chest to her neck.

Serious heat wafted to her cheeks. Because she didn't know what to do, she wrapped her arms around his shoulders and squeezed him as tightly as she could, the way she'd wanted to do for so long. He felt so good against her. Such a great mix of her softness and his solidity. In body but also in personality. She'd found a rock in this man, an anchor, a shield. While he organized the logistics involved in the station's security and her own personal safety, she'd take New Heraklion to the next step.

Unless Earth voted to push it back down to colony status. But she'd fight that decision! With Perseus at her side, she could fight any battle.

"Make love to me," she whispered in his ear.

With a gentle but firm hand, he pushed her onto her back. She sighed long and hard as he unzipped her pants and slid them off, panties included. These he didn't fold. They landed beside the bed, the scriptex in one of the pockets clinking when it hit the floor. She didn't care.

Selene opened her mouth in a silent "O" while Perseus licked his hand from the heel of the palm to fingertips and, his unwavering gaze on her, pressed it against her sex and began to rub in small, circular motions. Heat from his skin, coupled with his saliva, provided the perfect combination. A tingle spread to her thighs. She widened them a bit more.

But when he spread her with one hand and dampened the pad of his other thumb, she fisted the cover on either side. Oh, this would be good, so g—

"Ahh." She couldn't have kept it in had she wanted to.

Perseus put his wet thumb against her clitoris. She was already so fired that the simple gesture elicited a jab of pleasure down her belly and into her sex. Contractions, blissful and powerful, tightened her channel. In spite of herself, she clamped her thighs on his shoulders for the sheer delight of feeling him.

"You liked that?"

"Yes. Do it again."

He did, good man!

"Oh…. *Ohgodohgodohgod.*"

What began as a ripple intensified to a whole-body rush of heat and energy that left her quivering and gripping the cover so hard she heard the stitching give way. Between her thighs, Perseus licked his finger again and rubbed her hard little pearl. When she raised her head to watch him, he spared a hand to put his thumb under her chin and enjoined her to lie back down. Then he leaned over and licked her cleft in a pointed and blunt pass. She arched her back.

He *mmm*-ed to the rhythm of her hip rotations, the vibrato of his deep voice passing to her flesh. Each second of this sweet torment took her closer to the edge. It loomed in front of her, an abyss of carnal abandon. Red and gold oblivion.

With a powerful suck of her pussy, he pushed her beyond the threshold. An orgasm ripped through her. In her writhing, she'd raised a foot off the floor and used it to force his head harder against her. She let out a yelp of thrill when he grabbed her ankle, raised her leg straight and out. The grip, powerful and so incredibly hot, provided perfect escort to another wave of ecstasy. With his mouth, his forceful handling, he took her again and again. Juices mixed with his saliva and rendered her sex so slick, so hot, the sensation alone would have made her come. But his mouth....

He made love to her with it. Licked her delicately, then devoured her in long and greedy pulls. Kissed her lips and that spot on the insides of her thighs, the one he'd confessed was so dear to him, causing her body to arc off the mattress with the thrill of his fingers in her. Everywhere. His tongue and fingers. Taking turns. Claiming her.

When he stood, she meant to claw her way up his pants and force his cock out of them. He couldn't do it quickly enough to satisfy her need. But he took a step back and unclasped the waistband. He panted hard. His belly constricted and created delicious-looking muscle definition.

"Turn around," he murmured with a circular gesture of his finger.

She rolled over and sat up on her heels, watching him kick his shoes off, get rid of the socks and let his pants drop to his ankles. He stepped out of them as he advanced toward her. Compact muscles played on his thighs. God, he was magnificent! She'd always loved the man's legs.

But he didn't stand in front of her, as she'd expected—and *hoped*, because she wanted another taste of that glorious cock straining his abdominal muscles. Instead, he moved to the head of the bed and climbed onto it. Stood there.

"Don't move," she said. On her knees, she scooted up to him and planted a proprietary kiss on his thigh. Muscles twitched. Good. She liked him fired up.

He looked down at her and ran a gentle hand through her hair. Managed not to become entangled in her curls. That was something else. "If you want me to last—"

"There's plenty of time tonight." Her words belied her yearning impatience. She two-handed him and wrapped her lips around his cock. He tasted as good as she remembered.

His hand in her hair became a metronome to her work—the harder and quicker she'd go up and down his length, the more demanding his hand would become. Matching rhythm, synchronized intensity. Brutal sucks, and his fingers would curl into her scalp. Languorous licks on the underside of his glans, and his fingers became moth-light. A shudder began in his thighs, spread to his belly. From the tight set of his balls, which she squeezed in between rubbing his shaft back and forth, she knew he was close. But he abruptly pulled away.

"Not this time," he murmured. "This time, we're doing things *my* way."

"Oh?"

The wicked lift of his lips set her back on her butt. He sat near the edge of the bed, and then angled his scarred eyebrow and patted his lap in invitation. She couldn't scoot off the bed fast enough!

She was about to straddle his lap when he shook his head and made a circular gesture with his index finger as if stirring a pot. She turned her back to him, expectant, trusting.

"Mmm. You have the nicest butt."

She chuckled. "And there's enough for both of us."

"I know. I'm a lucky bastard." Perseus grabbed it with both hands, curled his fingers into her flesh, squeezed a few times in obvious delight. Was that a growl she heard deep in his chest?

It hit her then. They were together. Really together. No barrier, no distance, no obstacle over which to jump. Finally together. A shot of adrenaline made her giggle and shake her head. How long had she waited for this?

"What's funny?" He licked her cheek, rubbed it, licked again.

"We're together. In my *bed*."

She heard him sigh long and hard. "If it's a dream, I'll be mighty pissed when I wake up."

She reached back her to pinch his shoulder. "So? Dreaming, then?"

"Oh, you. Bend over. Right now. As far as you can."

Grinning wide, she planted her hands on her knees and curled her butt up at him. Not the most dignified position. As if she cared.

And she cared even less when his face pressed against her cleft, side to side, his tongue reducing it to throbbing nerve endings, fingers splayed to keep her put. Those hands, god, those hands. She bit her bottom lip when he sucked and nipped the inside of her thigh.

"That's all mine, this right here," he whispered while rubbing the special spot on her upper thigh. He kissed it gently.

She yelped when he bit her again, a tad harder this time. The mix of pleasure and near-pain accompanied her to one fine peak. Liquid heat gathered in her folds, which he spread wide so he could bury his face there once more.

Hips rolling, she pressed herself against his mouth, found a rhythm that he followed, accelerated. Oh dear god, it was so good. And it was Perseus. Her Perseus!

Fingers slipped inside her and pushed her beyond the edge. She fell in a chasm of brilliant light and dancing suns, of liquid fire and satin whips. His tongue, his fingers. Her voice, rising, rising. *Ah. Ah. Ah.* With Perseus gripping her tightly and forcing her back against his face, she came on a long moan.

Unrelenting, merciless, his fingers worked her, as did his mouth. Sucking, sucking, devouring. Again. She cried out her pleasure, implored for more, and demanded it. As burning needles started to poke her distended flesh, Perseus slowed and then stopped.

She panted, swallowed hard. "I want you. So much. In every way. On that bed, the wall...." She laughed. "The damn roof! Everywhere! You know how long I've wanted this?"

"The roof, huh?" he replied with a gentle caress of her thigh. "Would the window work for now?"

"What?"

She pivoted so she could wrap her arms around his head and force him to her chest. He didn't seem to mind one bit as he buried his face in her breasts. "With the light, Selene," he said, his voice muffled. He hooked his thumb at the window. "With the light, your hair looks on fire. Now *that's* a turn-on to me. It's always been."

"My hair?" She raked her fingers through it.

"Yeah."

He took her hand and escorted her to the window. Good thing for the antireflective coating. She'd have made quite a show for the neighbors across the station. Her apartment might be one of the highest on-station, but with the angle, folks below would've been able to see.

"Stay there."

He backed away, his gray gaze lost in the deepening shadow as he retreated all the way to the bed and slowly sat down, as if his entire being was concentrated on her instead of his own movements. He rested his elbows on his knees and planted his chin his hands.

"My god, Selene...." he murmured. He sounded awed. "My *god.*"

Instead of exposed and vulnerable—posing naked in a window that went from ceiling to floor, for Pete's sake—Selene felt powerful and sexy and to hell with everything else.

"Please touch yourself for me," he said softly in the gloom. "Because I don't think I can walk."

"Where?" Her nipples hardened into painful points.

"Everywhere. Your shoulders, there. Touch your shoulders."

She did, ran a hand from her shoulder down to her wrist. The other arm.

"Your hips, your thighs."

Hands shaking, she touched herself. Everywhere he directed, she sent her hands, but when he asked her to dip a finger in herself, she froze. Her hands hung by her sides. "You come do it, Perseus."

The challenge in her voice must have cured his temporary paralysis because he sprang from the mattress, all lethal grace and quiet intensity, and stalked up to her with his eyes narrowed to dark slits. The collision drove the air from her. She snarled as loudly as he did when they fed on each other's mouths, tilled each other's skin, fought against gravity and momentum, and stumbled their way back to the bed to fall onto it with muffled curses.

After a brief struggle, he easily pinned her hands above her head and nipped a necklace around her throat and neck.

"Take it!" she growled.

Sexual fury blazed in his eyes. Muscles twitched and bunched along his shoulders and biceps. Oh, he was going to. He was going to take it, take it all. She felt it coming, the storm, the explosion. But instead of pushing into her as she desired, he tucked his bottom lip behind his teeth and with a grunt, brought his face against the crook of her hips.

And there it was again, that magnetic pull, that almost tangible click as their parts came together.

She couldn't help the gasp. "Ah!"

Perseus was on fire. Someone had dumped him into a volcano for sure!

If he didn't get another taste of her fine, fine pussy, he'd have a heart attack. So instead of ramming himself inside her to the balls—something they both wanted—he dove for her glistening cleft and filled his face with her juices, rubbing them around her cheeks and thighs, licking her clean then starting all over again. Each time he sucked at her pussy, he felt the tremor of pleasure passing through her. He loved her reaction to him. Loved it! So he gave her more. More tongue, more finger, more growling—this, he simply couldn't stop. Tongue-fucking Selene Delian would be the apogee of his life. Well, then again, sinking into her would be hard to beat. Already, his cock throbbed with unspent release.

Both hands on her formidable breasts—god, he loved each and every curve on that woman—he straightened so he could press his cock all along her wet sex, back and forth, up and down, in teasing nudges and forceful rubs. Hands full of her ample beauty, he gave her sweet wet pussy a quick penetration but retreated right away. Her impotent buck made him lick his lips. He did it again. Same reaction. Another teasing thrust and hasty retreat.

"*Perseus.*"

The warning in her voice served as fuel on the inferno burning his resolve. *She* wanted it. The devil knew *he* wanted it, too.

When he curled his hips back, she must have felt he was getting ready for one epic round because she gripped her knees and arched wide and high for his taking. No gift more precious than this woman's trust.

The explosive penetration was like a kick in the gut. He grunted for the sheer tightness and wetness—the *rightness*—of her, the strong vaginal muscles contracting in a ring around his cock. Joined, one person. With her, in her. He was finally home. With each thrust he was banishing the monsters, each one, to hell with them. Selene loved him. There was nothing they could do to him anymore.

And he pushed, pulled, thrust back in. Into her. Into his home.

Selene's voice joined with Perseus's. To her rising, uninterrupted legato, he provided a tight, deep-throated bass. Each penetration unfurled her around him. Rubbed her in all the right places. Covers in each fist, she held on against the near-brutality tempered with the precise skill of a loving man. A series of thrusts lifted her knees. She cried out his name, always his name. The man she loved. Claiming and branding her. His fingers curled into her flesh. His cock pushed deep, to the end of her.

On a crystal-clear note, she came. With her eyes squeezed shut, a kaleidoscope of amber, red and gold swelled and twirled behind her eyelids, danced and roiled to the rhythm of her heartbeat, a feverish sarabande to carnality. Perseus pushed one last time with a tiny explosion deep in her womb. His seed filled her just as his voice filled the room.

"I love you," he panted in her ear before collapsing on his side, facing the window and taking her with him. "So much, so hard, it's scary."

"Not to me."

"I know. Nothing scares you." He sounded proud.

Sweat and their respective nectars linked them. Comfortably so. Languid and spent, she draped his arm around her so she could kiss his hand, each finger. They smelled of their love and union.

When their breathing normalized, Perseus pulled out, but not to leave, only to squeeze the covers from underneath their sated flesh and wrap the sheets over their forms. Nestled one against the other, she closed her eyes, smiling. No words were needed.

Outside, the station went to sleep.

❦ ⚬❀⚬ ❦

The scriptex's chime woke her. Grumbling, she lifted herself on an elbow. Daylight spilled into the room. "What time is it?"

Perseus rolled partly off the bed and dragged his pants to him to look at his scriptex. "Almost eleven. Ten fifty-four precisely."

She couldn't remember the last time she'd slept so long and woken this late. "Wow."

"I agree." He turned to her, raked a hand through his short hair. "Want me to hide in the closet?" His mouth laughed, but his eyes looked serious.

The scriptex chimed again. She had no doubt if she asked, he would conceal what they had together. That was the exact reason she didn't ask.

She leaped off the bed to retrieve the annoying item from the pocket of her pants. "No hiding. This is my home, my life. Up here, I'm Selene Delian, not the Lady Mayor." She thumbed the device on. "Yes, Hector?"

"How the hell did you know it was me?" came the gruff reply in the scriptex.

"I'm gifted that way."

She smiled when Perseus hid his grin and pretended to fluff a pillow. Discretion personified, that man. God, she loved him. For all these little reasons. Because he'd thought of retrieving her shoe after the near-crash of her shuttle, for squeezing her hand after that awful teledebate the month prior, for locking the shuttle door so she'd have some time to compose herself. Myriad, simple, little details.

"Got the news right here, hot off the telefeed."

She listened to Hector even though her complete attention rested on Perseus walking around the bed in his boxer briefs with one sock in his hand while he searched for the other. So normal.

Hector said the words she'd known he would, gave the full report in his brisk speech pattern. She thanked him, informed him she'd be a little late that morning, and then laughed when he replied she already *was* before he disconnected.

Perseus sat on the corner of the bed to put on his socks. But she knew by the tight set of his shoulders that he waited for the news, that he must have seen the effect on her face.

"They rejected it. Almost unanimously." The news should have deflated her. But this morning, with Perseus sitting on the corner of her bed, his attentive pale gray eyes on her, she honestly couldn't be bothered. In fact, it only galvanized her resolve. New Heraklion would become a nation-state. Not that day, but eventually. She was young. So was Perseus.

"Are you going to petition PC again?"

She nodded. "That's why I was elected. That's what I was raised to believe. If they think they broke my back, they have another think coming."

He grinned. "Damn, you're sexy when you're fired up like that." He curled his index finger at her.

Crossing the divide between them felt so good as she came to stand between his feet. He kissed her belly and each breast.

She ran a hand in his short hair and patted down a cute little cowlick that stuck out near his crown. "Did you have nightmares?"

He shook his head. "When do I start harassing Hector?"

"Do you have any plans for today?"

Perseus looked up at her. "Today, no. But tonight...."

Another pair of kisses to her breasts. Her nipples hardened.

"Then tomorrow night," he said, "and then the one after."

She grinned and turned her head to watch the station's life beyond her window. Bees in a hive. The queen bee now had her king. She found the analogy amusing.

"What is it?" he asked, standing by her side with her hand in his. "Did a news shuttle just crash?"

They shared a snort of laughter. "I don't think the media will like the station's new chief of security very much, huh?"

His expression turned darkly eager. "No."

"We need them. They have their fingers on the pulse. And we need that pulse."

Perseus nodded. "And I'll have *my* finger on *their* pulse. If they come within thirty feet of you—"

"I doubt they ever will again."

"Good."

He kissed the top of her hand and retrieved their clothes, which he distributed according to their owner.

"Do you enjoy cooking?" she asked, pulling her pantyhose from the pants. Another pair ruined. They needed to make these things studier, dammit.

Scarred eyebrow cocked, he turned to her, froze with his shirt partly on. "No. Why?"

"Me, neither. That should be fun."

"What will?"

She put her fists on her hips, which created a wicked, responsive lift on Perseus's lips.

"You're turning me on, Selene," he murmured, giving her a pronounced once-over. "We'll never get anywhere like this."

"Well, logistically, it would be better if you lived close to me. I mean, really, *really* close."

His expression sobered. Confusion, bewilderment, then hope washed over his sculpted face until joy illuminated his ash-colored eyes. "I'll learn to cook."

About the Author:

After a twelve-year career in the Canadian military (army), where I learned English and the many uses of parachute cord and gun tape, I decided to recycle my skills and become a writer. Of erotic romance. What can I say? I'm a late bloomer. To know more about my books, my real-life adventures or my opinions about nothing important, visit me at www.nathaliegray.com.

Edge

by Dominique Sinclair

To My Reader:

I've fallen in love with every hero I've written about and my, oh, my, Noah Tyler is no exception. Sexy, strong and packing more than just a powerful gun, Noah is a true hero. And every great hero needs a woman to complete him. I didn't make it easy on Noah; I gave him a beautiful hellion to test his patience, to challenge his mind, to arouse his body to point of madness. I love Catalina, her strengths, her weakness, her kick ass self. I see beauty in the love I have brought to her on a dangerous path.

I hope you, too, fall in love along Noah and Cat's journey.

Chapter 1

Catalina laved salt off the web of her thumb and finger, tossed back the shot, then bit into a wedge of lime. *Close enough to five o'clock*, she thought as the tequila went down smooth and warm with just a little shiver across her skin.

She nodded to the bartender. "*Uno mas.*" She needed another. The past three days she'd made herself as visible as possible in the dingy little Mexican town of Malto, and that meant a maelstrom of emotions suffocated her every breath.

Three days and she had yet to receive a reply.

The bartender tossed a bar towel over his shoulder, scratched his belly just under the hem of a grimy white A-frame tank riding his gut. Grisly black hairs scraped under his nails as he considered her a moment with beady eyes, a sneer forming under his handlebar moustache.

Laying an American twenty on the table, she shoved her empty glass the width of the bar. "*Por favor.*"

Lifting the tequila bottle by the neck, he made his way down the bar to scoop the bill into his baggy jean pocket and refill her shot in one fluid motion. "No change," he said, leaving the half-empty bottle and turning away.

A three-bladed fan whirred off balance overhead, doing very little to circulate the hot, humid air. An old man, ninety if a day, sat in the *cantina* doorway on a stool, one wooden leg, shorter than the other three, wobbling as he spit tobacco into a tin can. A trio of *banderos* played cards in a dark corner, the man on the far right glancing from beneath the brim of his weathered straw cowboy hat at random intervals.

She could only imagine what they must be thinking of her. Most women wouldn't dare step foot in a place like this, especially not a woman traveling alone in a foreign country.

Ah, but Catalina wasn't like most women.

Salting her hand, she downed a second shot. Sweat beaded between her breasts, between her shoulder blades, and dampened her forehead. Fisting her humidity-limp hair, she pulled the tired strands back into a ponytail and twisted a loose knot to cool her neck.

For a moment she considered giving up, driving back to the coast, returning to her fancy, air-conditioned hotel on the beach, ordering an icy coconut drink with a pink umbrella. Only Catalina never gave up.

Maybe the messenger wasn't able to make the delivery. Maybe her message wouldn't lure him out of hiding. Maybe her intel was wrong, maybe he wasn't here at all. *Maybe, maybe, maybe* played in her tequila fuzzy brain like a taunting drum, her finger echoing the beat on the scarred bar top.

Until *maybe* turned to a definite *no*, she wasn't giving up. She came for a man she'd never met. A man who clearly didn't want to be found.

Too damn bad.

Suddenly a blue-suited forearm snaked over her shoulder. "Been a long time, Cat," said a voice, deep and raw, just behind her ear.

Recognition hit hard and fast. Noah Tyler. The name sobered her like a plunge into an icy lake. She came to find a man, just not this particular one.

This one she'd hoped to never see again.

Closing her eyes, she forced her body to remain relaxed, inhaled a deep breath, nice and slow to disguise the lung-expanding fullness of it.

This couldn't be happening. Not now. She was so close. *So close.* And Noah would blow it all. Her fingers curled into her damp palm as she opened her eyes, not bothering to hope this was an alcohol-induced scenario—she could feel the cool band of Noah's Rolex pressed against her throat.

The bartender stepped forward, a wooden bat swung over his shoulder. One of the men at the table stood, scraping his chair on the chipped tiled floor. The old-timer in the doorway pinged a wad into the spittoon.

Catalina shaped a smile. *"No problema aqui,"* she warbled to them all. The last thing she needed was to draw more attention to her unexpected company. *How did he find her, and why now of all times?*

The bartender shrugged and went back to his business. The man at the table sat, lifted his cards. The old-timer pinged another wad.

Noah loosened the hold around her throat, cupped her jaw and angled her head to the side until her mouth hovered at the soft skin of his shaven chin. She didn't dare look up into his eyes, couldn't risk him seeing the emotions she needed another moment to conceal.

She swallowed to tame her vocal cords. "Miss me?" she finally asked, all sweet and innocent, as if her pulse wasn't stuttering, her mind racing toward a thousand possibilities for escape.

"I'd like to say I didn't miss you a bit." His other hand found her knee and swung her around. He stepped between her thighs, pressing her back into the rough edge of the bar. "Only it'd be a lie." He leaned forward and flicked her knotted ponytail, cascading her hair over her shoulder. The gun holstered beneath his jacket pressed against her shoulder, the spiced scent of his neck swirled at her nose as he poured himself a shot of tequila and tossed it back, no salt, no lime.

Her initial response to his unannounced arrival tucked away, Catalina lifted her lashes to gaze into his baby blues. "Why are you here?" she asked, knowing very well the answer to her own question, but stalling for time.

He thunked down the glass and twined a lock of her hair around his finger. "Time to go."

Scraping her teeth over her bottom lip, she slowly went for the .32 Tomcat tucked into the low-riding band of her denim shorts. "What if I said...?" Running her right hand over Noah's shoulder, she cupped his nape, slipping her fingers through the dark blonde strands neatly cut above the collar. She pulled him downward, her mouth brushing his ear, and expelled a soft, hot breath. His shoulders stiffened. "Said that I would be willing to discuss you walking away and pretending you didn't find me, somewhere more...." Pressing harder against him, her breasts flattening against his chest, she nipped his earlobe with teeth just hard enough to get attention, yet soft enough to distract.

"Private?" Noah whispered his hand down the thin cotton sleeve of her unbuttoned overshirt, moving toward her hand slowly bringing 'round the gun. "I'd tell you"—He gripped her wrist, forcing her to loosen her hold, and took the gun from her slack fingers—"nice try."

"Bastard," she whispered.

He dumped the magazine, slipped it in his suit pocket, and shoved the sub-compact in the back waistband of his pressed navy slacks. "Can't argue with you there." Noah shackled her gun hand, cinching the silver bracelet tight. He slapped the other handcuff to his own wrist. "Say *adios* to your friends, Cat."

She snarled, then turned to give the bartender a little wave. "You'll regret this, you know," she said to Noah as he hauled her out the door and onto the dirt street.

He slipped on a pair of sunglasses and flashed her the damned smile that tugged a dimple in his left cheek. "Yeah, I know."

A toddler wearing nothing but a soggy cloth diaper, chest stained red from a popsicle he mouthed, played stick with a mongrel dog outside the little motel Noah checked into upon arrival.

He slid the key in the lock while Cat dug a *peso* out of her pocket and handed it over to the tike.

Noah had witnessed poverty often enough that he should have developed a mental immunity to the sight of shoeless children with nothing more than sticks and stones to play with. Keeping himself at an emotional distance kept him alive, but children broke through his heart every time.

This explained why he'd already given a peso to the little tot when he checked in.

He kicked open the door with his loafer. "Here we go, home sweet home," he said over sounds of workers on the roof replacing missing tiles, hammering and calling in Spanish to one another.

Cat watched the toddler run away with his shiny *peso*, then planted her free hand on her hip and glared bullets at Noah with iridescent green eyes. "You know how to treat a woman right." She walked into the room, jerking her arm forward, yanking his chain both figuratively and actually.

He allowed himself an inward smile. *Same feisty Cat as always.* Not that he expected to find a complacent woman where a hellion had always been. "Won't be staying long." He elbowed the door closed and flipped the light switch. A single bulb hanging over a saggy twin bed flickered a moment before burning out, leaving the room in swirls of hot rays seeking entrance through a small cracked window.

His duffle lay where he'd dropped it on the unmade spread that smelled of a hundred years of dirt and odor woven into the fabric. It was a small pleasure he didn't have to sleep there that night after all. He had what he'd come for—Catalina.

"Look." Cat turned and raised her shackled wrist, taking his hand up for the ride. The skimpy little crocheted bikini number she wore beneath an unbuttoned overshirt slid up to reveal the bottom arc of her breast.

His grandmother knitted baby booties that covered more skin.

"May as well release me now," she said, "because I'm not going back with you."

Stubborn woman. Noah expected no less. He fisted his hand over hers, producing a tight knot, and jerked her arm behind her back. He pulled her forward, his thigh between her long, firm-legged stance, and flattened her against his chest. "Be a good girl, and make this easy on the both of us."

Tucking her bottom lip under her front teeth, Cat tilted her chin and nuzzled the underside of his jaw, a low purr vibrating from her throat. "If I recall, you prefer me bad."

Goddamn right, that was how he preferred her.

On a growl he hauled her backward, knocking her into the wall with its peeling terracotta colored paint, their cuffed wrists slamming above Cat's head. A framed picture of a bowl of fruit done in faded velvet and crusted oils crashed to the floor, shattering wedges of glass. Noah kicked Cat's feet apart, forced himself deep in the apex of her thighs. His body hardened as his hips nailed her to the wall, his erection instant and throbbing, demanding he bury himself deep inside her.

He crushed his hand over her small, taut breast, lifting the supple weight. Her nipple budded against his palm as he squeezed, his eyes closing as he shuddered. She arched her back and slid her hips in a slow circle, daring him to lose control.

He wouldn't take her dare, but did allow his thumb to stroke once, twice over her nipple before moving his finger upward beneath the soft yarn strap to trace a thin scar.

In a moment of fascination, he considered the little freckles sprinkled over her nose and cheeks, enjoyed her skin glowing warm bronze with a tinge of pink, no doubt compliments of the Mexican sun. Thoughts of suntan oil, sandy beaches and Cat naked and wet surged another pump against her.

He couldn't indulge in such fantasies. He wouldn't allow her beauty to beguile him, *again*.

And yet, when she smiled and snaked her leg around his calf, the heat of her moist juncture radiating through too goddamn many layers of clothes against his thigh, a greater pain throbbed.

Slipping her hand between them, Cat ran her palm the length of his pained erection. "Does this mean you'll reconsider my offer?" she asked, tone sultry.

He sucked in a deep breath as she slid her hand up his shaft, played her thumb over the sensitive tip in small circles. "Didn't even consider it twice," he said, jaw tight, body primed. He took a step back, dropped his hand from her breast, and snagged the phone off his belt. "Nice extraction," he said, nodding to the small incision scar as he rammed an AES encryption algorithm device to the cell's dataport.

She glanced downward to where she'd removed the global positioning device, gave a little shrug. "If you're calling Harris, remind him I'm out."

He nearly choked on a laugh. "You know better." He punched in the routing code to Harris's line. Cat might be a hellion, but she was one of the best agents ever trained by the Department of International Intelligence. Harris wouldn't cut her loose until he decided she was no longer an asset to the team.

"Damn." With a snap, he closed the phone. "No signal."

"Oh, pooh." She pouted her bottom lip and batted her thick eyelashes bare of mascara. "Guess you'll just have to let me go."

"Not a chance." He stepped away from her, moved toward his duffle on the bed, dragging her along. "Button up that damned shirt. You're damn near naked under there."

She glanced down at her bronzed globes loosely contained in the bikini top, then up at him with feigned innocence. "And the problem with that is?"

With a jerk, he pulled her in front of him, fisting the long strands of sugar brown hair kissed with sun streaks at her nape, and jerked her head back. If he startled her, she didn't show it. Instead, her eyes darkened and dilated. Challenged. He stared down at her a long moment, knowing she was playing games with him, games the raging hot blood still pumping through his body didn't mind one damn bit.

But he'd lost the last time they played, he reminded himself. He released her, giving her a shove. She stumbled a step, the corner of her mouth curving as she righted herself.

≈≷(GƆ)≶≈

Sitting next to Noah in a rented Toyota Highlander, her body coiled and achy, Catalina tried to despise him. He'd shown up out of nowhere, handcuffing and kidnapping her, jeopardizing what she'd come to Mexico to accomplish—finding the man who killed her biological mother.

Instead she dealt with tangled emotion and twisted desire. Her goal might have been to get Noah to leave without her, but the second she touched him and felt his familiar heat, the haunting want that never left her took possession. She'd wanted him inside her, wanted him to fill the void he'd left, even if only for a few crazed moments.

She'd never thought she'd see Noah Tyler again. And she'd never expected to want him with such intensity. Her breast still burned where he'd touched her; her lips still tingled for a kiss he didn't deliver.

Catalina drew in a long breath, reminding herself she had a job to complete. And to do that, she needed to rid herself of Noah. Tamping down the residual licentious quakes still vibrating in her body, she angled her head and glared at him. Anger felt better when it worked above the circulation of sheer physical want.

"How did you find me?" Her tracks over the past year were covered. She had left no crumbs for DII to follow, or more importantly, for Noah to follow. They'd lied to her by omission, so the farewell she bade them both was permanent.

Noah slowed the Highlander to allow a beat-up truck to pass. "Never been far behind you."

She shouldn't have been surprised. To believe she could stay a step ahead of those who'd trained her to hide was wishful thinking. And still, she had hoped. But another little part of her also hoped Noah would come for her, hoped he couldn't live without her, hoped he needed her as she'd needed him.

He'd kept tabs on her for the past year and never once let her know he was close. *So much for hopes.* "Why now?"

"Mexico's a little far for our comfort. It's time to come home. The agency cares about you, Cat." His cuffed hand wrapped over hers, squeezed. "Despite what you think of me, despite what's happened, *I* care."

The words, spoken with a soft sincerity she knew to be another lie, daggered the remnant of her heart. Her chin quivered. "So you let me believe I was out, free and clear." She turned her head to stare at the blanched trunks of trees with emerald green leafed tops blur by on the jungle side of the road. "How dare you come for me now? It's been a year."

He smoothed his thumb over her knuckles. "You know how the agency works."

Yeah, she knew how the agency worked. No one left without Harris's approval, and to her knowledge, no one had ever left the agency alive. She should have known there'd be no exception for her, especially if they'd broken the cardinal rule of *no fucking fellow agents*. If only they'd explained the unspoken clause of a life term before she signed on the dotted line.

Catalina glanced in the side mirror and saw a car approach from behind, increasing speed until it rode the Highlander's tail.

"Friends of yours?"

She shook her head. "Let 'em by."

The truck that had passed them earlier slowed. "Don't think they want to pass," Noah said, checking the review mirror.

The truck suddenly turned hard, angling across the road. Noah stood on the brake, twisting Catalina's arm upward so he could grip the steering wheel with both hands.

Even as she was thrown forward against the dash, Catalina thrust her hand in Noah's jacket, yanked the Glock from its shoulder holster, reacting on sheer instinct. The Highlander fishtailed to a stop. A cloud of red dust floated down, covering the windshield.

"Who the hell are these guys?" Noah asked, glancing between the vehicles.

Simultaneously the car and truck doors opened. The driver of the truck put a gray cowboy boot to the earth and lifted the nose of a revolver. The driver of the car rested the barrel of a sawed-off shotgun on the V of the door and hood.

Catalina took a quick assessment of each man, recognizing them from the card table. "Looks like my friends from the bar."

"Don't look too friendly. What'd you do, mark the deck?"

"Let's play twenty questions later." Something told her this was the moment she'd waited days for, the reply to her message. Noah's presence could ruin everything—if it had not done so already. "Right now, just get us the hell out of here. Your call." She'd do damage control later.

Noah didn't hesitate. He rammed his foot on the gas pedal, craned the steering wheel and accelerated the Highlander across the road, off the shoulder and over a ditch.

Catalina braced her palm against the dash, eyes wide as the vehicle slammed atop the pasture's barbed wire fence, crushing a wooden post, and hit the earth with a teeth-jarring thud, whipping her head forward.

Before the tires got traction, gunshots exploded from behind, pelting bullets into the back of the Highlander. "Son of a bitch," Noah said, his focus dead ahead. "These guys aren't looking for a friendly game of five-card draw." A shotgun blast blew out the back tire, deflating it on a long hiss. He fought to keep the SUV straight as he plunged onward. "Too bad I didn't opt for that extra rental insurance."

Catalina gave Noah a glance. "You should've been a comedian." She aimed the Glock over her shoulder and tried to hold steady, near impossible with Noah plowing through the bumpy field like a bulldozer. The *banderos* hopped back into their vehicles and tore into the field. Noah was right about one thing—they weren't interested in making friendly.

Noah yanked her cuffed hand, pulling her across his lap. "Stay down. Shot's too far." He jerked the Highlander for a hard turn.

She righted herself against his protest. "Might get lucky." Reaffirming her aim, she plugged a shot through the Highlander's back window, blasting out a chunk of glass. As he'd predicted, her bullet didn't meet its mark.

The Highlander broke the edge of the pasture and bounced onto a two-lane track leading into a tangle of vines and *zapóte* trees. The vegetation became denser, and flashes of brilliant blue sky penetrated the emerald overhang of jungle as branches slapped and scratched the front windshield.

"Any idea where this road heads?" Noah asked, forced to slow down, the back tire completely empty of air and large potholes digging the road.

Before she could answer, a bullet whizzed through the back, lodging into her headrest with a *poof.* She jumped forward, stomach sinking. If the car had been a few yards closer, if the bullet had been two inches higher—

"Goddamn it, I said stay down."

Catalina fought against his pull to safety. "Give me the key to these cuffs so I can handle this situation two-handed." *No more playing nice guy.*

Noah jerked his head toward the rear. "In the duffle."

She crawled over the seat and tried to reach for it. Shackled to Noah, she couldn't even clear the rear seat, let alone get hold of the bag. She took another aim at the car behind just as the Highlander began to climb a hill. Taking another wild shot, she clambered back into the front. The Highlander caught air, landing with a smack, tumbling her onto the floorboard.

Noah pulled the steering wheel hard, laid on the brake, spinning a one-eighty to a stop. "Shit."

Giving her head a moment to stop spinning, Catalina eased up and glanced out the back through tracers swarming her vision, struggling to hold steady aim. "Why'd you stop?"

Noah nodded forward as he slid her Tomcat from his waistband, dug in his pocket for the clip and rammed it home. Catalina slowly turned her head, not liking the look on Noah's face, and instantly knew why. She stared out into emptiness—no road, no ground, only an old, knotted tree growing like a hood ornament at the edge of a cliff.

"You've got to be kidding," she said, shaking her dazed head. They were at a dead end, literally.

The car roared up to the left, the truck to the right, trapping the Highlander in a wide V. Catalina had a split second to make a decision. If she were alone, she'd toss her weapon to the ground and take her chances. Certain assets got her far in sticky situations. She'd bet these men were sent to scare her away, not kill her. But she wasn't about to gamble Noah's life. *Damn sentiment.*

She switched the Glock to her cuffed hand and squeezed the door handle, knowing she risked everything she came to Mexico for to save the life of the man she'd never wanted to see again. *Ironic.* "Come on." She opened the door and jumped out, Noah smoothly sliding across the seat to follow.

The third *bandero*, who had yet to make his weapon known, did so now with a blasting of a machine gun set on a tripod in the back of the truck. Noah shoved Cat to the wheel well at the first rat-a-tat of fire. "Stay down!" he called. Bullets rained along the side of the Highlander, blasting out the windows.

Under the cover of Noah's body, sheltered from the spewing shards of glass falling like confetti, Catalina forced out the sound of shots echoing in her ears, ignored the sulfur heavy and thick in the afternoon heat, and willed herself to calm, to think, to plan as DII had trained her to do. She may have been wrong about that not-wanting-her- dead part. It seemed the men were hell-bent on leaving no chance of a heartbeat behind.

The machine gun suddenly paused, leaving a dull ringing in her ears. Noah seized the moment to ease up and fire off three rapid shots from her Tomcat. She used the brief advantage of cover to do a quick search for an escape route. No way could their firepower hold back three men and a machine gun for long, especially while she and Noah were cuffed together.

Through the wafting of gun discharge and settling dust she nearly missed it, a cable secured to the trunk of the tree, lining out over the gulf of emptiness. She could just barely hear the sound of a waterfall.

Noah let off two more shots, then hunkered down to shield her once again as the machine gun laid out a round, ripping apart the side of the Highlander with thunder rounds and metallic pings.

"Noah," she whispered, nudging him.

He eased back to look down at her, jaw tense, eyes dark, pulse surging in his neck. She nodded at the cable, and then spanned the width of the handcuffs to show the chain linking them.

"Remember?" she asked, referring to the time they'd lost communication with the pickup team after planting surveillance equipment at the plush ski-hideaway of a suspected drug lord and had to slide down a lift cable. They'd had a pulley then, but now the cuffs would have to improvise.

His jaw ticked several times, as he was no doubt estimating their chance of making it. He nodded. Without hesitating another moment, Noah lurched forward, his hand pumped into a tight hold over hers, pulling her along. They both righted to full height at the base of the tree, took two full, exposed strides. The machine gun repositioned its aim, spraying bullets as Catalina jumped off the edge of the cliff, Noah hurdling over the top of the cable before they both dropped downward.

The thunder of the waterfall cascading across the cliff drowned out her scream of absolute pain and Noah's "son of a bitch" as they came to an arm-jolting halt, the chain catching over the cable. As they began to glide over the river some hundred feet or so below, Catalina's arm felt like it was slowly ripping away.

The cable bowed with their weight and much too soon they began to slow. The *banderos* wasted no time in repositioning themselves and resuming fire, the shotgun booming a shell, reloading, booming another, the last just inches shy of Catalina's head. The revolver worked through its rounds, one catching Noah in the arm, sending a pulse of blood.

Swinging her legs around, Catalina returned a succession of fire, her aim off as her body spun, stopped, then swung back around. "You okay?"

He nodded, craning a look back and taking his own aim at the *banderos*. "We gotta jump. Can you pull yourself up and get over the line?"

She looked up the length of her arm, already burning with pain, to her hand twined with Noah's, both sporting a sickening shade of purple and red from the pressure, then glanced behind her to the cliff where the truck emerged and parked. The *bandero* jumped in the back, adjusted the machine gun.

Shoving the Glock into the front of her shorts, she swung her body to gain momentum. This caused a fierce growl from Noah, but she had no choice. Dangling out in the open, they'd be pulverized by the machine gun.

She swung her leg, thrusting every muscle upward and managing to link her foot around the cable. Snaking her leg over, she pulled the dead weight of her body to crest the line. Before she could steady herself, she rolled over the top and dropped down Noah's side, releasing them quick as if the line had been cut.

Chapter 2

Freefalling toward the water, Catalina and Noah angled forward, spread their arms and legs parachute-diver style and caught wind to slow descent, the roar of waterfall and tat of machine gun surrounding them.

The river below approaching fast, and it was too late for her to wonder if the pool was deep enough, or if jagged rocks lurked below the diamond surface. Catalina accepted the moment for what it was—possibly the last moment of her life. She'd faced that moment several times when working for DII, and just as then, she wouldn't give up until death claimed her.

She worked to right her body, tugging Noah to do the same so they'd plunge into the water feet first. Drawing in a breath, she tightened her hold on Noah's hand and tipped her face up to catch a ray of the sun's brilliance before breaking the surface, the soles of her feet slamming against what might as well have been concrete. Swallowed and pulled down by cool river, Catalina didn't fight the gravitational drag until they came to a deep water-bobbing stop.

Amazed to be alive, she pushed herself around to look at Noah, an aura of red from his wound effervescing in the dark greenish-brown water. He smiled at her with that damn grin pulling at the dimple in his cheek.

Reaching out, she cupped his jaw, wondering when their luck would run out and death would win. Noah always told her luck had little to do with anything, especially staying alive. Skill and training determined the outcome. Catalina wasn't so sure. Everyone had to die sometime.

Just not today. She slid her hand around to his nape and pressed her lips to his a long moment, feeling the firmness of his mouth, the confirmation of life, the same old high she always felt when they triumphed.

It was as if a day hadn't passed, as if they were still partners. But they weren't, she reminded herself, lungs aching for the need of air.

As one, they kicked toward the undercurrent and were swept along just below the churned surface, bobbing up only to catch a quick breath until they were far enough from the spree of bullets to emerge. The rush

of adrenaline washed away, Catalina drank in huge gulps of air, the
weight of the undertow threatening to pull her back down for another
turbulent ride.

"There," Noah called over the rampant river, nodding to a fallen
log coursing just ahead of them, jutting in and out of rapids. They dove
under, pushed forward, surfacing and reaching for the log with their
cuffed hands and summoning one last bit of strength to haul their chests
out of the water and flop their arms over the log, holding on for a free
ride through the jungle.

❧❀☙❀❧

Like a river rat, Noah staggered toward shore, picking his way over
jagged rocks slick with algae. *Bring Catalina home*, Harris had ordered. He should've known better than to believe the assignment would
be simple. Not a goddamn thing involving Cat had ever been simple.

He'd thought she'd be down here catching some R&R, working on
a tan, drinking Piña Coladas. But whatever the task on her agenda, it
wasn't pretty.

Cat stopped in the ankle-deep water. Dapples of sunlight coming
through the overhang of trees along the shore played like a halo over
her head. Ah, but she was no angel. Not in the hotel room, not back
there on that cliff.

"You're bleeding pretty bad," she said, touching his arm.

He was a little lightheaded from the loss of blood and altitude drop,
not to mention oxygen deprivation from being underwater. Now he
fought for steady orientation and looked at the rivulets of blood dripping from the bullet hole. Hard evidence she wasn't just on vacation.
"Didn't know you cared."

She cast him a glance to suggest she indeed did not. "I'd prefer not
to leave a trail of blood for those *banderos* to follow." She went down
on her haunches, ran her hand under his pant leg, and slowly slid out
the nine-inch blade strapped to his calf, all the while looking up at him
with river drops on her lashes.

Hard not to admire a woman who knew how to handle a man's own
weapon. Hell, he'd always admired her. Right from the start of her
training they'd formed a silent bond, learned each other's weapons as
well as their own, moved together as one. And that bond grew stronger
when they became lovers. They needed no words to know the other's
thoughts. In bed, words were lost in the ferocity of their coupling. The
need to feel, to claim, to become one was so strong the world seized to
exist. They were insatiable. They were invincible.

Damn shame things ended the way they did.

Cat noticeably favored her arm as she stood.

"You okay?" he asked, forcing away the regret trying to worm its way where it didn't belong. She'd walked away from both him and DII, and he'd be best off remembering it.

She bunched the front of his shirt with her hand still colored red and purple from the pressure and pulled the tails from his waistband. The knife in the same hand bladed dangerously close to his gut. "I'm more concerned with stopping your bleeding. Hold your shirt out."

Once she'd sawed off a hunk of the shirt he'd just had tailored in Milan, she lowered his jacket and cut off the shirtsleeve, using the bullet hole for a starting point. She checked the front of his arm and padded her fingers around to the exit wound. "Lucky you." She guided him to a large, flat rock in the shallow riverbed. "Sit."

He did as ordered. Cat knelt beside him, cupped water in her hands to rinse the blood away, then began to wrap the piece of cloth to staunch the flow. Though his arm burned like a bitch, he knew the situation could be worse than having a beautiful woman on her knees, hair slick off her forehead and dripping wet strands down her back, breasts damned near spilling out of the soggy little crochet number. Hell, it was the stuff fantasies were made of. Too bad he couldn't indulge.

Not this time.

Cat tied the final knot, holding one end of the swatch between her teeth. "There, that should hold." She stood, gave him her good hand and helped him up.

He withdrew the Glock from her waistband, the back of his hand brushing along the firmness of her abdomen. She'd stayed in shape—damn good thing. It had cost him weeks of matching her sit-up for sit-up, hours upon hours at the compound gym and miles of running hills to hone her body to perfection. The second woman allowed into the agency, she was determined to be as strong as any other operative, if not stronger.

"If you're taking yours, give me mine." She reached around him for the Tomcat.

He maneuvered out of her reach. "Sorry, no can do."

"Please?"

A sardonic plea if he ever heard one. "Nope."

"Fine." She flipped him a look and for a moment it felt like old times.

But old times were over. He already made it clear to Harris he wouldn't take her back as a partner. Partners didn't walk out on each other. Besides, he worked solo now and liked it that way. No room at the top for two.

They found a place to rest, then emptied their shoes and wrung their socks. The jungle loomed quietly at their backs save the occasional caw of a bird or the rustle of an unseen animal in the foliage. The heat of the sun felt good, the air a little drier now they were further from the gulf. But a tint of moisture, a tinge of salt, crawled the air.

"Now'd be a good time to tell me what those guys wanted."

Cat wiggled her toes, tinkling a silver chain with a lone sterling heart around her ankle. "Nope."

"Could've taken more than a bullet to the arm for you back there."

"Nobody asked you to."

He gathered her hand in his, cuffs clanging together. "Cat."

"Walk away, Noah," she whispered. "Just walk away and forget any of this happened."

"I never walk away from a job long as I'm alive to complete it."

"This isn't a job. This has nothing to do with you."

"You're right. My job is to bring you home."

She narrowed her eyes, cocked a brow. "Even *if* you manage to take me back to headquarters, you can't force me to stay."

Couldn't argue with her there. His job was to get her back to DII. Harris could deal with her after that. Cat would then no longer his problem.

Easy words to think, harder to live by. For a year she stayed put in the little flat she'd rented in Paris, then suddenly she pounced out of there like a kitten after a butterfly. Worse than an itch he couldn't reach to scratch, he wanted to know what brought her to Mexico. What was worth risking her life for?

But there was plenty of time to get her to talk. She wasn't going anywhere without him. "How's your arm?"

Working her shoulder and pumping her hand, she shrugged. He knew she'd endure whatever pain she felt without complaint. One of the first lessons he taught her—it'll stop hurting eventually. Hadn't been so easy for him to stop trying to protect her from the pain.

"Let's get moving. Need to put a little more distance between us and that machine gun," she said, slipping on her socks and shoes while he did the same.

White tennis shoes squishing, Cat led the way, sticking to the river shore, picking her way over rocks and knotted roots cutting out of the bank, forging on as if she knew exactly where she was headed, the ribbon of river endlessly winding through the jungle acting as tour guide.

"Any idea where we are?" Noah asked after a while as the sun slipped another degree behind the distant jagged mountaintop.

"You shouldn't be worried about getting lost. Harris knows where you are twenty-four seven. The cavalry will no doubt be riding to your rescue by dawn."

A completely accurate description of team members loaded with a GPD. Harris didn't like to lose men. He spent too much time and money training them. "Let's worry about the now. We can figure out tomorrow when it comes."

Cat paused and looked back at him with an arched brow. "I have no intention of still being with you when tomorrow comes."

She must not remember how she used to lie in his arms and wish tomorrow never came so they could stay in bed forever. Noah said curtly, "Long as I'm chained to your pretty little ass, you don't have a choice." He couldn't help himself. His gaze dropped to the wet denim pockets shaping the heart of her bottom as she marched away, yanking him along.

❧⊱⟨✦⟩⊰❧

Thunder roared from a mass of black clouds hovering above the mountain peak like a swarm of angry bees. A bolt of lightning exploded in a web of thin silver rays, momentarily lighting the emerald-shaded darkness draping over the jungle.

Just what they needed, Catalina thought. *A summer storm.* Her feet hurt, her legs ached from walking non-stop, and she was hungry.

Noah said, "Let's call it a night and head for shelter."

She turned to glare at him through the darkness inking the jungle. "Right. There's probably a Hilton just around the next bend."

"Hope room service is still open," he said back, matching her retort.

Catalina smiled. Few people got her dry humor, and fewer still matched her on it glib for glib. Noah never missed a beat.

He pulled the blade from his ankle strap and took the lead, moving them away from the river into the denseness of broad-leafed trees.

It was darker beneath the canopy of trees, and sounds of wildlife intensified, branches and vines taking shape of ominous menace. Catalina cautioned her steps, gaze darting to this sound and that. The closest she'd ever come to being in a jungle at night was the grove of trees behind the country home she grew up in. Her parents' house. The thought of those she knew now to be her adoptive parents evoked sudden and conflicting emotions, near suffocating her breath. The pendulum swung in a matter of seconds from love to abandonment with a whole lot other feelings blurred in between. At least she no longer blamed them for dying. That had been the response of a confused eighteen-year-old whose life had been ripped apart.

Blame in another form still lingered.

They never told her she'd been born to a dead woman.

They never told her the man who killed her biological mother would someday be released from prison and free to live his life. Twenty-five years in prison was a small price to pay for murdering a pregnant woman. If it took another twenty-five years, Catalina would look the murdering bastard in the eyes and demand to know how stolen diamonds could be more valuable than her mother's life. Then she'd shoot him right between those eyes.

And if she could get rid of Noah, that day would be soon.

Something reached from the dark, snagging her by the hair. Catalina whirled, forearm instantly whipping up and back to deliver a blow... to a low hanging branch.

Noah spun, drawing his Glock. "You okay?"

She expelled a breath, nice and slow, then nodded. "Branch." Another roar of thunder boomed ahead, vibrating the ground, shaking the trees. She'd rather be creeping through a suspected arms dealer's mansion planting surveillance equipment, or hacking into a corrupt government official's computer knowing any moment a goon armed with an Uzi could find them, than take another step into the twisted darkness. "Are you sure we're safe in here?"

Noah holstered the gun, touched her cheek briefly, softly, barely, his eyes midnight blue, shadows playing on the face that lived in her dreams. He grinned. That damned dimple.... "Hey, I trained in this kind of shit."

Catalina knew he'd done a stint with the SEALs, leaving when his time was up to join DII. He'd called Switzerland home ever since. Nothing waiting for him in Iowa, he'd once told her. She'd let it drop, though curiosity never left her. There was much she didn't know about Noah Tyler, much he clearly didn't want her to know. None of it mattered now.

"Right. Trained to survive in any circumstance." It should have made her feel better. "If you think I'm going to eat ants for protein and wring moisture from my socks for water, you're sorely mistaken."

Noah smiled and tugged her onward. "In a few moments we're going to have enough water pouring on us we could do a backstroke, not to mention the river is relatively clean. As for food, we're in the jungle, so there are plenty of edible fruits and plants."

"Great, Tarzan. We can scamper up a tree and pick coconuts. Later we'll invent fire. Sounds like fun."

"Look on the bright side."

She couldn't suppress a heavy sigh. She wasn't one to be melodramatic, but she couldn't deny she wanted a queen-size bed with satin sheets. At least her mind had left the past to focus on the unpleasant present. "Which would be?"

"Mosquitoes won't be out in full force tonight, long as the rain comes. But on the down side, the Hilton's booked. We'll bed down over there."

She followed his nod toward a small clearing with a lone tree growing huge roots out of the soft ground, creating a pocket of three-foot walls for protection, the trunk five feet or so wide at the back. "Lovely."

"Take up your complaints with the concierge. Come on, give me a hand."

Catalina sighed and grudgingly helped Noah gather fallen logs and thick, spade-shaped leaves, laying the foliage over the tree roots like a bundle of corn stalks. They finished the mini-hut just as the first raindrop splattered on her nose.

Before they crawled into the shelter, Noah knocked loose a bunch of short, fat, blackened bananas. Catalina gathered her knees up to her chest and wrapped her free arm around her legs, feeling as if the jungle had pressed down upon her with a giant foot. Before long, her cuffed hand found way into the hollow of Noah's palm. Without saying a word, he tightened his hand over her knuckles.

Rain pattered on the leaves, gaining intensity by the moment like a crescendo in a classical masterpiece. Thunder roared, applause to the concert. "At least we're in the jungle this time," Noah said, voice hushed. "The last time we were holed up together—"

"Yeah, I remember the last time we were stuck together in a storm." She'd had enough trips down memory lane for one day, she'd had enough of them over the past year. Instead she focused on the present, how much better off she would be with Noah Tyler out of her life. After all, if he hadn't shown up in Malto, handcuffed and kidnapped her, she'd be in her hotel room, nice and dry. Or better yet, on her way to meet with the man she'd come to Mexico to kill.

Noah leaned his back against the trunk and moved their shackled hands to rest on his leg. "Was just going to comment on how cold it was back then. But now that you mention it, I do recall a few creative ways we stayed warm. Banana?"

Her mouth opened, then clamped shut. She was not about to get pulled into discussing those *creative ways*. Lord, but they had been creative.

He wagged the thick, soft-yet-firm fruit in the air. "Last chance."

Though she was tempted to refuse, Catalina grabbed the banana. It made no sense to deny her body nourishment just to prove she didn't welcome his presence. Before she could stop him, he gripped the head of the banana, broke back the stem and peeled away the thick skin, his gaze meeting hers in the darkness, holding for each slow pull until the fruit revealed its sweetness.

It'd be easier to hate him if being with him weren't as natural as breathing. "Thank you."

"Any time."

She took a bite of the over-ripened fruit, the sweet, earthy meat melting in her mouth like pudding. "Hmm, not bad."

He broke away a banana from the bunch for himself. "Come a little closer," he said, tossing the peels away and taking half the fruit in one bite. "You're shivering."

Hesitating only a moment, Catalina inched over until her shoulder brushed Noah's, careful not to hurt his wound. And then she snuggled a little closer still, feeling safer now, warmer. Secure.

"Better?"

"Mmm." She leaned her head on his shoulder. "Thank you."

They sat listening to the rain and finished their fruit, then kicked off their shoes. In the silence and rhythm of the rain, Catalina grew sleepy and curled up on her side, resting her head on Noah's thigh for a pillow.

He loosely twined his hand through hers, along the length of her fingers, his other hand smoothing the hair off her forehead. "Comfy?"

"Hmm-mmm," she murmured and closed her eyes, allowing the pleasure of his soft strokes. His hands had always been strong, soothing, the gift of touch.

"Good night," she heard him whisper in the drum of the storm just before she dozed off.

❧☙

Some hours later, Catalina woke shivering to the sound of a faint beeping. The temperature had dropped in the passing hours and cool moisture clung to the air. Beads of rainwater dripped through the leaves, but the storm had passed. She glanced at Noah's Rolex announcing the hour against a soft background light. Four a.m. Looking up to the shadow of his face, she waved her hand slowly in front of his nose. No response.

Lifting her head from his lap, she inched her fingers up his pant leg and removed the knife without so much as a whisper against his calf. Laying her cuffed wrist on her leg, she blindly worked the lock with the tip of the blade. She had every intention of being rid of him by the first rays of dawn. No way would she be going back to DII with him.

Not tomorrow, not ever.

Noah shifted, lifted a knee and rolled partially to his side. Catalina held still, waiting patiently for him to fall back asleep, giving him a few more minutes before she worked on the lock again. The knife slipped and gouged into the pad of her thumb.

"Shit," she whispered, feeling blood seep to the surface of her skin.

"Keep that up and you'll chop your whole damned hand off," Noah said in the darkness as he grabbed the knife and stabbed it into the trunk of the tree just above her head. "Go back to sleep."

Catalina pursed her mouth tightly and slid downward onto her back.

She should have known he'd feel her movements and wake. Knowing Noah, he'd probably been aware of her since the watch alarm went off. He rarely fell into a deep sleep, even after they made love, and he barely closed his eyes when in the field.

His arm, wrapped around her, brought her body so close that her breasts flattened against the planes of his thick chest. "What do you think you're doing?" she choked out as he threw a leg over both of hers, pinning her in place.

"Like to wake up tomorrow with my hand in one piece." He yawned and snuggled her a little closer. "You're a shitty locksmith."

"Tell me about it." She thought about demanding he release her, only she never imagined she'd be lying in his arms again. The weight of him was so achingly familiar. His body, so much a reminder of what they once shared, kept her silent and taking comfort in what she swore she'd never allow herself to have again.

The hand pressing between her shoulders eased, and his thumb began to work small circles. His leg stretched out, his foot slipping between hers, massaging with the arch of his. She moved her head to rest in the crook of his shoulder and closed her eyes, telling herself it was just for tonight, just a small setback in her being over Noah Tyler.

She nuzzled her nose to his throat, nearly pressed her lips to his skin. Just for the rest of the night, maybe she wouldn't be quite over him. Still, she kept her mouth hovering just shy of contact. She knew to kiss him while so intimately entwined would be more than a temporary setback.

She steeled herself, and reminded herself. She shouldn't forget he'd played a part in Harris's lies, kept Harris's secrets. For that, she could never forgive him.

Slipping her hand under his jacket, she slowly glided over his shirt toward the holstered Glock.

"Don't even try it," he said in a soft, sleepy tone, bringing her closer still.

She relaxed her hand on his side. "Can't blame a girl for trying," she whispered, knowing Noah would expect no less of her.

And try again, she would.

Chapter 3

Noah lay motionless in the rays of morning light fingering through the branches and leaves of the shelter like rays of a green crystal reflection. A bird cawed; another chickered. His arm was numb beneath Cat's head, but he remained still, comparing the current situation to his first UTD training mission.

His team of six, called "tadpoles" by the instructors, were awakened at 0200 to their bunks being upturned by Chief Wilks. He ordered the men to gear up and head out. Noah was tossed out of his bed and onto his ass, and his mind snapped to alert before his aching body did. *Hooya.* This was what he'd joined the SEALS for. Training or not, it felt like the real goddamn thing.

Heart hammering a thousand taps a minute, adrenaline so high he could barely sit still in the boat, Noah drifted silently with his platoon through the black canopy of tree overhang lining the river. The other guys felt the excitement too, and they couldn't help flashing big, toothy grins that shone in the moonlight beneath their camo-painted faces.

Noah had still been wearing a big-ass grin himself when one of the instructors tossed him overboard in a fashion that took him by surprise and didn't make a splash.

He took in a lungful, emerged to the surface, containing the urge to hack out the water and drink in air. Under no circumstance would he make a sound. It may have been a training mission, but they completed all tasks as if it were the real thing, and silence was a survival mechanism.

One by one he saw the dark heads of his teammates bob to the surface. As team leader, Noah made sure all men were accounted for and aware of the boat already downstream. Treading water, with the weight of his boots, gun, pack and ammo belt weighing him down, he motioned his team to make for shore, gave the signal to rendezvous there come the next nightfall. He made his way into the swamp to bunk down for the next eighteen hours, where he sat motionless, silent save the sporadic birdcall to the other six men to check their position and well-being.

The hours of darkness weren't so bad. Come day, the temperature rose, the smell of the swamp intensified, alligators languidly passed by. His muscles cramped and ached like a bitch from holding his position. Dusk didn't bring much reprieve. The mosquitoes were thick and blood-hungry, despite the mud Noah slathered on his face and hands. The portion of c-rats and few sips of water he'd indulged in weren't doing much in keeping him fueled.

He'd never known such torture as that swamp endurance exercise.

Until now. Holding Cat while she slept, trying to ignore the feel of her curves pressed against his body, the rise and fall of her breasts against his chest, made that training mission seem like a stint in Disneyland by comparison. Hell, he could deal with her when she openly tried to seduce him to her advantage with more ease than when she was all cuddly, warm and sweet.

Shifting his weight slightly to put a little distance between them, he frowned as she snuggled up closer, hand sliding to his lower stomach. She gave a little moan from deep in her throat and Noah's muscles contracted. He sucked in a slow, deep breath, groin tightening.

How many mornings had he wakened to her hand slipping beneath the covers to cup him? Too goddamn many to forget the silk of her palm, the kisses on his shoulder, neck, jaw.

He clenched his molars on the memories of their mornings, their nights, afternoons and all the times in between.

It was all pleasure. Until she walked out on him without so much as a goodbye.

He wouldn't forget that little fact.

But his body, rock-hard and ready, seemed oblivious to the warnings his brain tried to send. "Damn," he muttered, raking his free hand through his hair.

"What's wrong?" Cat asked, her voice morning-dewed.

He glanced down at her face titling up to look at him with bedroom eyes, dark and sultry green in the low light. "Not a goddamn thing," he muttered. "Time to get up and get going."

She scooted up, rolling her shoulders and neck, the overshirt slipping down her right arm to expose the little crocheted number askew, uncovering enough flesh to reveal again she had no tan line. "I'm stiff."

Me too, he thought, pushing the shirt up her arm to her shoulder. "Took a *helluva* beating yesterday. Once you get up and moving, you'll feel better." His hand lingered at her collarbone, feeling the steady thrum of her pulse.

She looked down at his hand, shifted her shoulder to remove it. "How's the arm?"

He flexed his fingers. The wound burned like wildfire. He needed a patch job and a nice shot of antibiotics. But he'd taken worse hits and lived to tell about it. "Fine."

They sat in silence a few moments, their cuffed hands barely touching in the space between them, awkward as if they'd woken from a drunken one-night stand.

"I'm thirsty," she said, "and I-uh, need to, um...."

"Right." Shoes inspected for spiders and put on, Noah shoved aside the branches and leaves to let in a waft of morning air scented with fresh rain. "Let's move before it gets too damned hot to breathe."

He stood with his arm outstretched over a bush while Cat took care of morning business on the other side, then relieved himself behind a tree while she gave him her back. Heading to the river, they washed up and took a drink.

There Noah surveyed the river and the mountain range to the east. He should've done a thorough preliminary study of the area, memorized landmarks, distance to nearby villages, destination of the waterways. And he would have, had he known he would be ambushed and forced into the jungle instead of sitting first class on a jetliner headed for Amsterdam. "Any idea where we are?"

"Why don't you call Harris and ask him?"

He'd tried the cell numerous times since the trip down the river and once before Cat woke this morning. Still, he gave it another shot. The palm-sized phone didn't power on. "Still wet."

"Darn. Well, then. Let's blow these cuffs off and I'll be on my way. Harris is sure to have a rescue team here for you anytime, so help yourself to a banana or two while you wait." She batted her eyelashes and smiled curtly.

Apparently a night's rest—albeit one interrupted by her escape attempt—didn't make Cat any more reasonable. Not that he thought for a moment it would. "Sorry, baby, got orders."

"Too bad I don't take them anymore. And don't call me baby."

"Harris has a different opinion about that."

She raised a brow. "He's entitled to think whatever he likes. I'm not going back."

If her tongue weren't good for so very many other things, he'd be tempted to cut it out. But right now his focus needed to be getting out of the damn jungle, after which he'd worry about getting her home. "Where does this river lead?"

Cat gave him another one of her glares, then relented on a long exhale, smart enough to know he wasn't letting her go anywhere without him. "There should be a little town not too much farther downstream."

"What else?"

"That's it for the radius we can travel without supplies, as far as I know."

"We turn up there, we're pretty much guaranteed a not-so welcoming party by those friends of yours." The *banderos* had the entire evening, night and morning to anticipate their movements and get a head start, which Noah had no doubt was underway. They'd made their deadly intentions clear back on that cliff. "Let's head back to Malto."

"More than likely, both places are being watched."

Once again he cut off the desire to know what trouble Cat was knee-deep into. He'd rather have her en-route to headquarters in one piece as soon as possible than have his curiosity cured face-down in the jungle with a bullet to the back of his head. "Yeah, but we know the layout of Malto, which gives a little room for maneuverability." Always best to know the entrance and exit routes at all given times. He nodded to the jungle. "Let's take the scenic route."

"I don't get a vote?"

"Nope. We're walking targets on the riverbed in the daylight. We go for cover."

"But it'll be easier for the team to pick you up if you stick to a clearing."

"Harris has more on his plate than worrying about me."

"Other things than making sure his prized little agent in blue is secure?" Cat grunted. "Doubt that."

Noah tugged her along as he backtracked into the jungle, finding a path used by wild animals to walk. "Harris knows I can handle you on my own."

"Then perhaps he's not as smart as I thought he was."

Noah suppressed a smile. "Harris knows exactly what he's doing."

Hours later, with the sun blazing rays through the canopy of trees and foliage, sweat dripped down Catalina's back, beaded between her breasts, and filmed her forehead. She'd long since decided she preferred the jungle at night with all its creepy things and scary sounds to the scorching, unrelenting day. She couldn't remember ever being so incredibly, miserably, thoroughly hot.

With Noah's help, she'd pulled her hair back into a ponytail and tied it with a soft vine, and cut the sleeve off her shirt so she could remove it and tie it around her waist. Then she helped him remove his jacket and shirt, leaving only his gun holster above his jeans.

Now, narrowing her gaze, she watched the sweat glisten on Noah's back, his muscles flexing with each swing as he used the knife like a machete, his skin turning more golden by the hour. If he was half as miserable as she, he didn't show it. Of course, as he'd said, he trained in this shit.

Thirsty, achy and tired, Catalina found her thoughts wafting to the feel of his body during the night, the softness of his lips in her hair, the cocoon of his arms, leading her to spend mental energy damning him. Damn him for walking back into her life. Damn him for stirring up old feelings and memories she'd tried to forget. Damn him for still being sexy and strong and smiling that damned grin and touching her lightly, touching her rough. Damn him for making her still want him.

Damn him, damn him, *damn him.*

She bumped into his back, not realizing he'd stopped. "Sorry," she muttered, damning him for stopping unannounced.

He placed his foot on a fallen log. "Need a break?"

Did the ocean need water? "Sure." She sat, a leg on each side of the log, arm raised to dangle from Noah's. "We could make better time if we removed these cuffs."

"Sure would." He swiped his forehead. "But then I'd have to chase your sweet little ass down, wouldn't I?"

"We're in the middle of the jungle. I have no idea if we're going in the right direction. I'm dying of thirst. There's little chance of me running off." She gave him a kewpie doll look of pure innocence.

"Ah." He straddled the log and ran his hand over the abrasions on her leg from the slap of prickly vines and branches. "She admits to needing me."

"Hardly. I just don't want to be alone in the middle of nowhere."

He reached behind him and tore off a long, cone-shaped leaf from a plant. The faintest green-colored goo ran over his fingers. "Is that what scares you, Cat? Being alone?"

The question hit a little too close to home for comfort. She despised that about Noah. He seemed to be able to reach inside her and expose her weaknesses. Not that she'd ever give him the satisfaction of knowing it. "This isn't about me, or us. It's about survival."

With a squeeze, he dripped cool liquid from the plant onto her leg and set the leaf aside. "You sure about that?" he asked, smoothing the gel over her tiny cuts and scrapes.

Mentioning the word *us* had been a mistake, she knew immediately. "Whatever it was we had...." His strong hands kneaded her legs, fingers stroking. "Oh, that feels good."

His hand rounded to the back of her calf, massaging, soothing. "Aloe Vera. What were you saying?"

"Whatever it was we had...."

He moved to her other leg, starting on her knee and moving upward, his body leaning forward. "I'm listening."

"Is...."

His hand moved under the hem of her shorts, the cool extract contrasting with the heat of her skin.

"Over." Delicious sensations radiated to her toes, swirled around and made way through the rest of her body.

His knees pressed her legs outward as he moved forward, his body casting a shadow over her as he eased her to lean back against the smooth trunk of a tree. "Maybe what we had"—he inched closer still, his gaze on her mouth—"would be easier to understand if we talked about it."

"What is there to say?" Her eyelids fluttered to half-mast.

He lightly traced his mouth along her jaw to her ear. " 'Goodbye' would have nice," he said, voice low and deep, his bare chest, hot and sweaty, mating against her suddenly heavy breasts, erecting her nipples into steely, pleading points.

A part of her knew she needed to respond to his statement, a greater part just wanted to close her eyes and feel. When he nipped the lobe of her ear and delved his thumb beneath the elastic edge of her bikini bottom, she whimpered in time to the chicker of a small animal scampering in the branches above.

"Noah…." Her hips tilted upward for the stroke of his thumb over the swollen lobes concealing her valley. Her fingers slipped through his, the handcuffs jingling as her hand tightened. "Damn you, Noah, don't do this," she breathed, though her head tipped back, the crown of her hair pressing against the tree, her breasts slipping along the granite of his chest.

Even knowing she needed to be over him, she heard her breath shallow and deep with his next teasing stroke, this time parting her folds to dip through her valley, stopping to press her nubbin as it throbbed against the pad of his thumb.

Laving his tongue down her neck, between her breasts, Noah blazed a languid trail to her nipple as if he had all day to torture her. He sunk his teeth into the bud and suckled while working her nubbin in small circles, the heat and pulse of his erection between them. Her breath caught at the back of her throat. *So hot.* The air, her skin, her breath. Her free hand found way to his shoulder, nipping crescents into his scorching skin.

His mouth came upward, and she tilted her chin down to capture his kiss, but he hovered shy of contact, his darkened eyes lifting to meet her dazzled gaze for a moment. He slipped his hand from between them, ran his scented thumb along her bottom lip and stood, giving her a dimpled, cocky grin.

It took Catalina a moment to realize he'd just paid her back for the seduction game she'd attempted to play back in Malto. She narrowed her eyes and glared up at him, reorienting herself with all the reasons she had for hating him.

"I'd be happy to tell you goodbye right now," she said, swinging her leg over the log and standing. "All you have to do is blow these cuffs off."

"Sorry, that goodbye will have to wait until I dump your sweet ass off in Harris's office."

A four-foot long iguana with spikes that would make a punk rocker jealous stood guard atop the boulder. Catalina edged around to get a look down over Malto. The creature seemed harmless, though she wished it'd take a hike. But then, it was better up there than sinking his row of tiny, sharp teeth in her ankles for an afternoon snack.

The bluff provided a clear view of the town and she oriented herself briefly from their location, marking the *cantina*, the crumbling hotel, the rows of weathered houses lining the road leading out of town.

"Looks pretty quiet," she whispered. "Must have made it just in time for *siesta*." What she wouldn't do for an afternoon meal followed by a nap in a hammock beneath the shade of a palm.

Noah leaned over her to take his own assessment. "Let's make for that station wagon parked behind the pink house."

Cat pushed him out of the way to sit, back to the boulder. Her lips were dry, cracking, throat sandpaper. "Look, Noah, I know you're following orders, but I've got business to tend to."

He lowered himself beside her and slid her a long look, sweat gliding down his temple. They hadn't stopped for any more breaks since the fallen log, keeping a steady, unrelenting pace through the jungle. No water, no food, no conversation. "And what business would that be?"

"The kind that doesn't include DII." She held out her palm, face up. "I'll take my weapon and that goodbye."

He slipped her gun from his waistband, removed the clip, checked the cage, slammed it back in place and returned it to nestle at his back.

"Dammit," she said, "you can't expect me to go in empty-handed. The *banderos* could be lying in wait down there."

"Can't expect me to let you go at all. Now, tell me about this business." When she didn't respond, he stretched out his legs and surveyed his slacks, muddy, torn, and wrinkled. Then he leaned his head back on the rock. "Let me know when you're ready to talk." He closed his eyes.

The sun blared down like waves of sauna steam, yet the heat didn't compete with the irritation riding Catalina's nerve endings. She stewed for several minutes to the sound of the iguana's tongue swooping in and out of his mouth as he snatched flies, his thick tail thudding on the boulder now and then.

No way in hell would she allow Noah to worm his way into this. She'd had the situation handled until he showed up, and she would regain control again once he left. But getting him to leave without her was tantamount to making it snow in Mexico.

And yet she had to try.

"What if I promise to report into DII within the week?" Barely enough time to complete her mission. But it was better than no time.

Noah crossed his feet at the ankles.

"Oh, come on, Noah." She lifted her shackled hand and touched his thigh, feeling his muscle tighten beneath her hand, hoping the intimate contact would make him give a little. "One week. After all we've been through together, you owe me that."

He peeked open one eye and glanced at her, closed it, and yawned.

She said, "Damn it. Let me have this. Let me do this."

"Do what, Cat?"

She didn't respond.

"If you don't tell me, I can't help you."

Even if she convinced Noah to leave her, he'd already told her DII had been watching her for the past year. Harris would keep Noah or another operative on her tail, especially when he learned what happened with the *banderos* from the bar. Harris had a protective streak when it came to her. After her adoptive parents died in an automobile accident, he brought her into the agency, planning to sit her behind a desk and have her do part-time secretarial work while she finished college.

She didn't want to go to college.

She wanted excitement and danger to help her snuff the grief. So she'd fought and kicked and argued like a bad-tempered child until Harris relented, the way he had never been able to deny her wishes from the time she was a little girl. He assigned her to Noah for training, thinking she'd change her mind by the week's end. She hadn't quit. She'd thrived. So Harris put his trust in Noah to keep her safe and made them partners.

Partners, *hah*.

Minutes ticked by, with the sun roasting her face and shoulders and Noah languidly making it clear she wasn't going anywhere without him. The only place he intended for her to go was back to headquarters, Catalina had few choices. This shadow of protection would walk with her wherever she went, and with this cloak, she'd never get close to her mark.

She could go back to headquarters, look for another chance to escape, only she knew she would never again get this opportunity. It took quite a bit of digging through Harris' office, but she'd found the file and learned everything there was to know about the man who shot her pregnant mother and left her for dead in the middle of a snowstorm. Catalina had known everything about the bastard for the past year, except where he'd slithered to after his release from prison.

He didn't want to be found, that much was clear. He would disappear again, if he hadn't already. Catalina might not be able to get another locate. She couldn't let that happen. There was a bullet in her Tomcat with his name on it.

A bullet that would be wasted if Noah succeeded in hauling her back to headquarters. She had to escape. Now or never. She just hoped when Noah recovered, he wouldn't be too pissed at her for using his own technique to subdue him.

Without further hesitation, she bent her knuckles to form half a fist and swung her elbow in a semi-circle, aiming the *Tyler Special* straight for Noah's windpipe. One swift blow and he'd lose consciousness. Wouldn't be able to speak for a good week. She'd blow off the cuffs and be on her way.

His hand caught her wrist mere inches from impact, fingers constricting until her bent knuckles went lax. He opened his eyes, looked directly at her, jawbones flexing. He suddenly jerked her hand down, straddled her, pinning her hand beneath his knee. He pulled her Tomcat from his waistband and shoved the tip under her jaw, knocking her head against the rock. "I'm done being nice, Cat."

Eyes narrowed, pulse pounding, she glared at him. "Go to hell."

"Not without you. Tell me what's you're up to. *Now.*"

Catalina's gaze lowered to the gun tucked under her chin, up into Noah's fierce eyes. She knew at the first opportunity he would have her on a plane headed for headquarters. Now that they were out of the jungle, back to civilization with transportation and communication, her time was up. She had one shot left of staying in Mexico. One extremely long shot.

She hated being pinned into a corner where her only chance of moving was to beg for trust from the man she'd vowed to never trust again. "You said you couldn't help me if I didn't tell you what was going on. Would you help me?"

He considered her a long moment, clearly debating whether she was yanking his chain or trying to pull another fast one. "Talk."

She swallowed, hand numb beneath his weight, giving herself one last chance to change her mind. "I came to meet my *father.*" The word made her physically sick.

Noah's eyes flashed, darkened.

"Don't look so surprised. Why do you think I left DII? Did you and Harris really believe you could keep it a secret forever, the fact I was adopted, that my biological father killed my mother? Granted, twenty-five years was a good cover-up period, but the truth always comes out. Now I'm just asking for a couple days to meet with him, I want to hear from him how he could do it. Hold Harris off. Please. I need to do this. I need to speak to him. I've come this far, gotten this close." She wouldn't be close enough until he was dead.

He shoved the tip of the gun further into her jaw, near knocking into her molars. "There's no way in hell I'm letting you anywhere near that man."

"Damn you, Noah Tyler." She jerked her head away, pushed up her knee to toss Noah aside and scrambled from beneath him. The iguana inched forward, his bull legged stance firm on the rock. "Who the hell are you to decide if I meet with him or not?"

Noah pulled on the cuff, preventing her from standing and forcing her onto her knees. "Harris has kept you safe from that bastard your entire life."

"Safe from what, Noah? Huh?" She shoved at his chest. "He already killed my mother. He has no reason to kill me."

❦

Noah's lip twitched. Sweat trickled down his cheek as time ticked by, Cat glaring at him with venomous rage. He'd lost Cat as a partner, a lover, a friend, all to keep the information from Cat, so how the hell did she find out? Before he could ask, a barrage of voices and the barking of dogs came from the jungle. "Shit." Noah stood, heaved her up. "They've got our scent."

A dog looped into the clearing, dancing at the end of a chain, hungry to move on, the scent he tracked strong.

Noah grabbed Cat's hand and pulled her into a sprint across the pasture toward the station wagon they'd marked earlier, leaping over clumps of cow pies, tufts of grass, potholes. They rushed a half dozen chickens, sending them squawking into the air. A donkey went into a fit of hee-haws. The ox that'd been in the road the day before lifted his head and ambled after them, the bell around his neck bonging.

So much for a quiet getaway. The yips and barks of the dogs sounded closer. Noah glanced over his shoulder to see they'd been unleashed and were gaining ground. No German Shepherds, but those hounds would want blood.

Noah hurdled a small wooden fence. Cat cleared it a second behind him, stumbling as she landed. He whirled and caught her before she fell. "Come on," he said, righting her and moving around the little pink house to the station wagon.

Noah pulled open the driver-side door, Cat slid inside, he followed, frilly red balls hanging from the rim of the interior roof bouncing in his face. He slammed the door just as one of the dogs jumped against the window, big muddied paws clawing as it growled low and deep, jowls pulled back to show yellowed fangs. *Hello, Cujo.*

Noah slid his knife from under his pants and jimmied the ignition with the blade as rosary beads hanging from the review mirror swayed.

Antsy in her seat, Cat glanced out the back window. "They're right behind us."

He cranked the knife. The engine fired up with a blast of Mexican music from the speakers and a cloud of black exhaust exploding from the tailpipe into the *bandero's* faces. He rammed the gear into drive and floored the accelerator, spitting pebble and dirt into the wake of the exhaust.

"You good?" Noah asked over the blare of music.

Cat gave one last look behind them and slid down into her seat, her cuffed hand dangling from Noah's as he steered. She turned off the stereo. "Grand."

"We need to talk."

She took in a deep breath and exhaled it slowly. "Drive, Noah. Just drive."

And so he did, knowing the *banderos* would pick up a ride as easily as they'd acquired one. But he wasn't about to let the topic drop. He gave it several miles driving like he'd just been given ten seconds to flee hell before he asked, "Is he worth your life, Cat?"

She snapped her head his way, glared for several moments. "What life, Noah? The one that's been nothing but lies and deceit? The one where the people I trusted kept secrets from me? I don't call that a life."

The tremor in her voice riding the sarcasm hit him where it hurt, his heart. "Harris did what he thought was right."

"What about you, Noah? Did you think it was right denying me the truth? Hmmm? Did it ever occur to you I was strong enough to handle it on my own?"

"You've just spent the past twenty-four hours running from men who want you dead. Need I say more?"

Cat jerked her head around to stare out the window.

Let her be pissed. Let her take it out on him. If it kept her alive, Noah'd be the focal point of her anger. Hell, he'd paint a bulls-eye on his chest.

But he'd do anything to make it all go away. Erase time, go back to the way things were before, keep her in a place where the truth was unknown and she was safe, protected, instead of running halfway around the world to the man she needed to be as far away from as possible.

The station wagon gave a sputter, a jerk, and the engine cut. Ramming the gear into neutral, Noah glanced to the fuel tank dial beneath the dashboard covered with a mock-zebra striped spread and swore.

"What's wrong?" Cat asked.

After coasting up a small hill, Noah stopped the car at the top and cranked the ignition key, pumping the gas pedal, trying to fire the wagon up. If they could make it just a few more miles.

Cat rubbed her temples with two fingers. "Never mind, don't tell me. I don't want you tell me we're out of gas. I don't want you to tell me we have to walk again. I'm tired, Noah."

"Okay, I won't tell you." He watched the review mirror, knowing the *banderos* weren't far behind. They would be atop them sooner rather than later.

And right now, with no gas, sooner would be a whole hell of a lot sooner than Noah preferred. He tapped his fingers on the steering column, surveying the lay of the road and terrain ahead of him. They could head into the jungle again, but when the *banderos* found the car, they'd send out the hounds.

"We can't just sit here," Cat said, watching over her shoulder.

Noah squinted at the bottom of the hill. "How deep do you suppose that is?"

She turned around. "What, that?"

"Yeah, that." He put the car back into neutral and let it coast down the hill, gaining speed and heading off road. "Get ready to jump," Noah said, hand on the door handle, waiting to make sure the car would keep its course.

"You're kidding," Cat said, but she scooted up beside him, readying herself.

The car bounced over rock and tufts of bush, the swamp dead ahead. Noah pushed open the door and pulled Cat out as he leapt. He landed on his back, knocking the wind out of him. Cat landed atop him and they rolled several times, arms and legs twining, twisting. The car splashed into the water.

Noah lay for a moment with his eyes closed, the hard steel of the Tomcat jabbing into his back, lungs empty and Cat's soft breasts flattened against his bare chest.

"You okay?" she asked, pushing herself off him.

He drew in a deep breath and felt the sting of his bullet wound tear open, fresh blood seeping into the bandage. On a nod, he lifted himself onto one elbow and watched the hood of the car sink beneath the murky water.

Cat sighed. "Now what?"

He looked from the sunken car to Cat's sunburned face, the freckles creeping onto her cheeks and forehead. He pulled a twig from her hair. "We let them pass us up thinking they're still hot on our tail." He heaved himself off the ground, stretching his back. "Then we'll pull up a shade tree and wait to hitch a ride." He led the way to a patch of long grass and weed and lay on his stomach with Cat beside him. "Keep nice and still. I think I hear a car now."

Cat lay flat and motionless as he watched through the blades, verifying the *banderos* as they passed. "Let's give them ten, fifteen minutes to get on down the road before we move."

She rested her head on her forearm and looked at him a long moment.

"What?"

She smiled. "Nothing. It's just that sometimes... Never mind."

Sometimes it felt like old times, Noah silently finished for her. An air duct, a closet, standing on a ledge outside an window a hundred stories high, they'd often waited like this, motionless, breathing controlled, listening, bodies touching. Thoughts of the pleasures they would explore later made the eternal seconds bearable, and knowing that at any moment they could be discovered made the danger worth every minute.

Once upon a time, they were goddamn good together.

Chapter 4

Catalina never saw anything more fabulous than the double-decker bus bouncing down the road with a handwritten cardboard destination sign shoved in the front windshield.

But once Noah flagged it down, the fabulousness lost its sheen rather quickly. The bus was overcrowded, not air-conditioned, and smelly. Four hours later, Catalina was hot, sticky, irritated, and smelling slightly of the pig the woman in the seat next to her cradled like a baby during the trip. Catalina was ushered off the bus along with Noah and the other passengers like a herd of cows. She wondered if she'd ever been quite so miserable.

One glance over her shoulder at Noah ducking to step off the bus behind her and the answer resounded through her exhaustion. *Yes, she certainly had been.*

The morning she'd walked out on Noah and DII had been much, much worse. She suffered a personal storm, emotional hell. She left confused. Angry. Alone. Betrayed.

Stepping onto the street, she adjusted the shirt draped over the handcuffs linking her to Noah and put the lid on the memories trying to escape. "Gee, that was fun," she said, trying to keep her tone light when in fact the past weighed heavily, always there, never leaving her quite alone. The weight pulled harder when the source of the pain walked beside her.

Noah, jacket slung over his shoulder to conceal the gunshot wound, plucked a blade of grass from her hair. "Beat walking."

Catalina tried to ignore the brush of Noah's wrist against her ear as he scooped his fingers through her ratted hair to shake a leaf loose. Watching it tumble to the sidewalk, she closed her eyes a moment, took in a deep breath, then stepped backward, putting distance between them. She was too exhausted and hot to keep her defenses up any longer, and she wanted a hot bath and room service.

"Let's find a payphone, and I'll arrange us to be on the next flight," Noah said, giving the deserted street an assessment. The other passengers had already dispersed, walking up flights of stairs into apartments above shops that had closed for the day, or heading off down the road.

"Look, I've got a hotel room already paid for and waiting." Catalina gestured toward the harbor. "One more night isn't going to hurt. I'm tired. I want a bath. And I need food." When she read the hesitation and speculation on his face, she didn't give Noah a chance to tell her no. "Come on, Noah. They aren't going to find us tonight, and you're as tired as I am. Besides, your arm."

He said nothing for a long moment, then blew out a breath. "One night, Cat. I'm calling Harris in the morning."

She lightly touched his arm. "Thank you. It's just a few blocks from here."

Each step she took was slower than the last, the bottoms of her feet burning as if she were walking over hot coals. Catalina resisted the urge to twine her fingers in Noah's and lay her head on his shoulder as they headed for the hotel. Instead she closed her eyes for a few blind steps, allowed the evening air coming in off the ocean cool the sunburn blazing her face.

A few hours earlier, vendors would have been out in hordes selling their wares with tourists a-plenty congesting the sidewalks and streets. But now the streets were quiet. She stopped across the street from the hotel and blinked twice to make sure the building really stood, half expecting it to fade away like a mirage into the hues of sienna and magenta splayed across the backwash of sky as the sun hovered on the horizon.

"This it?" Noah asked.

To her relief the hotel remained solidly intact before her weary eyes. However, the relief turned out to be short-lived. Noah's kidnapping had happened before she could retrieve her wallet, and the wallet contained one truly important item. "My keycard."

Noah glanced at her. "You don't have it?"

She shook her head, not bothering to tell him she didn't have any identification with her either. No way would the front desk even let them in the front door all covered in sweat and dirt, their hair matted and clothes torn. Not to mention they were handcuffed together, Noah sporting a bullet wound. If they even tried, the odds of spending the night in a Mexican jail cell were high.

"What floor?"

"Twenty-one." She followed his gaze to the outside fire escape ladder. "Nu-uh, no way, I'm way too tired."

"Then I'm open to suggestions."

Her desire for a long hot bubble bath began gurgling down the drain-pipe. She couldn't do another night in the jungle with Noah, but more than that, she *needed* the bath. And food. A slow smile spread on her dry, cracked lips. "Actually, I do have an idea." Giving the chain a yank, she pulled him across the street, heading around the side of the hotel to the employees' entrance and into the service elevator.

Catalina motioned Noah to keep quiet as the elevator doors opened on the selected floor. She checked both ways, then led Noah down the hallway, stopping to peek through the fogged glass in the locked door of the sauna. She instantly jerked back.

"What?"

She didn't tell him what she saw—a big, hairy man belting a white robe under his bulging gut while a woman with a moon-like collection of cellulite on her derriere bent over to slip on a flip-flop. Catalina motioned Noah aside. "Nothing," she whispered back, moving him to stand at the back swing of the door.

"Wh—"

"Shhh."

The couple emerged and headed down the hall. The man gave the woman a generous squeeze on her ass and she slapped his shoulder playfully. Nothing like a trip to Mexico to rekindle a marriage. Catalina would've preferred not being witness to the first foreplay in possibly twenty years. She caught the door before it closed, slipped into the steam-filled room, and shut the door on a soft click behind Noah.

"Take off your clothes."

Noah raised a brow.

She could guess the thoughts flickering through his mind. "Do you want to get into the room or not?" She turned her back on him to wriggle off her top one-handed, then removed her shoes and socks, shorts and bikini bottoms, all the while with handcuffs jerking this way and that as Noah worked to strip as well. Gathering her clothes in a garbage can liner, she held her hand out for Noah's, still keeping her back to him. She tossed his items in the bag and reached back again. "Weapons."

"They stay with me."

"For God's sake, Noah. I'm not going to shoot you and leave you for dead in the sauna room." Her hand remained empty. "Your body's too big for me to move on my own without getting caught. And besides, I'm much too tired to try. Hand 'em over."

Cold steel slapped into her palm. She stuffed her .32 in the bag and reached back for his Glock.

"Promise."

"Okay, I promise I won't shoot you and leave you for dead in the sauna room."

Noah slid the Glock to her, his hand remaining over it for a moment before releasing.

She knotted the bag, pushed it aside and pressed her forearm over her breasts. Stepping into the open shower stall, keeping her back to him, she felt the heat of Noah's gaze slide down her spine. She glanced over her shoulder to see his gaze lingering on her bottom. "Stop look-ing," she demanded, refusing to allow her own gaze to drift down his naked body.

"Admiring, not looking," he said, reaching around her to twist on the water spigot, his bare chest pressing against her arm, the soft hair on his legs brushing her thigh. "Don't forget this is your plan, not mine."

The spray of warm water hit like needles against her sunburn. The sun's rays still seemed to still be working deep in her skin. Forcing herself to drench her hair and body, keeping her arm over her breasts, she took the shower's beating without complaint, then stepped aside. "Your turn."

Noah raised the showerhead to compensate for his height and stepped beneath the spray, letting out a low deep moan as the water ran smoothly over the tan the sun had given him. Water pooled over his broad shoulders and coursed through his chest hair, running down the thinning trail of dark hair over a muscled stomach, then continued past the line of tan where his slacks shadowed the sun. Catalina wouldn't glance lower. She knew even in softness his shaft was thick.

"Admiring?" Noah asked.

She angled her head away, heat flaming her already scorched cheeks. His body was made for looking, touching, tasting. She'd always pre-ferred keeping the lights on, wanting to see his complete maleness as well as feel it. She also liked it on top, but not for the control. He stole her control away the moment he touched her, kissed her, filled her. She liked to be atop him so she could splay her hands over the cut of his pecs, bend her knees around his lean hips, see his large, strong hands upon her breasts, the tips of his fingers pinching her nipples into plea-sure points of pain.

Her breasts suddenly weighed heavily and her nipples swelled against her forearm. Catalina damned him once again. Making love to Noah Tyler would forever be imprinted on her mind and her body, and no amount of denial and anger could dissipate the memories. She knew that very well, because in the past year she'd tried, willed, cried, screamed in the effort to rid him from her soul. Even her attempts to find another lover had failed. She couldn't touch another man without comparing him to Noah, and once the thought of Noah entered her mind, she couldn't laugh, couldn't smile, couldn't breathe. It was not exactly easy for another man to deal with.

So she stopped trying and just waited for the day when she'd wake up and not think about Noah, go to bed and not think about Noah. That time had yet to come, and now he was back in her life making certain it never would. A forever curse, a constant haunt. If only he'd go away and leave her alone….

His movements, as he worked loose the strip of fabric from his bullet wound, brought Catalina out of her thoughts. He moved his arm under the water to wash away the dried blood, rivulets of red running over the handcuff to wash down the drain. She realized suddenly that the bullet could have hit him anywhere, his heart, his stomach, straight into his forehead. He could have died out there.

"Noah—"

The sauna door bleeped. Noah snaked his arm around her lower back, bringing her flush against his slick body. "Shhhh... company," he whispered, his mouth beside her ear, the rough growth of his beard against her cheek. His heart beat against her, and warm water ran over his shoulder, sliding between them as the door handle moved down.

Noah slipped the pads of his fingers over the arch of her bottom, lifted, pushing her upward, her nipples slipping over the soft hair on his chest. Her mouth parted on a small gasp and her breath hitched. His mouth hovered over the shell of her ear. "Goddamn, you're beautiful," he whispered, his hot breath spraying delicious tingles down her nape. The door swung open. Noah's hand twined with hers, pressing it against his thigh to keep the shackles out of sight.

"Oh! Sorry, I-I'll, I'll come back later," a woman's voice said, followed by the whoosh of the door closing.

Noah didn't release Catalina. Instead, he held tighter, a shudder going through his body. "Cat...." He pulled his head back to look at her, his mouth slowly moving downward, the water beating against his neck.

She closed her eyes, knowing she needed to stop him before he kissed her. Once his mouth touched hers she would be lost, pulled into an abyss of pleasure so long denied. "No," she whispered, the word against his breath. "Don't." *Please.*

He leaned his face against hers, his mouth touching the corner of her mouth. She felt him struggle with his own desire in the flexing of his hand and the bunching of the muscles in his arm. He closed his eyes, and she felt his lashes butterfly against her cheek. "It's hard," he whispered, words feathering her cheek, "being over you."

She swallowed, nodded. "I know." *I know.* She finally pulled loose, unlocking her hand from his hold, and angled away from him, once again covering her breasts with her forearm. "Time to get us into the room."

Noah shut off the water and moved with her to the house phone by the door. She dialed the front desk, pressed the phone tight to her ear. "Um, hi, oh gosh, this is terribly embarrassing. This is Leslie Marks from 2102, and I, uh, well...." She held the phone away from her mouth, giggled like a school girl. "Yes, honey, another glass of wine." She brought the phone back to her mouth. "Oh, yes, as I was saying I'm in the sauna with, er, a friend and I just realized I left my key in the room.

Would you kindly send someone with a new one, along with, um, a couple robes?"

"*Si, Señora Marks, no problema.* I will have someone up, *uno momento.*"

"Thank you." She hung up the phone, keeping her back to Noah. "They're bringing a key."

He laid his hand on her shoulder. "Nice work."

"I was trained to lie by the best," she said, the jab low and dirty. "Once we get these cuffs off, I'll call down and see about getting you a room."

"No"—he leaned down, his lips brushing just behind her ear—"you won't. You're not taking a step out of my sight."

The last thing she wanted was to share a hotel room with Noah, inhabit the same space, breathe the same air. But she knew better than to argue with him.

✻҉⟡⟠⟡҉✻

Wrapped in a white robe a size too small, Noah considered Cat's hotel room, decorated in old world Mexican charm with splashes of vibrant color contrasting with the dark wood furniture. He nodded approval. Beat the hell out of the previous night's accommodations.

Cat set down the bundle of clothes, took out his Glock, and slapped her cuffed hand on the edge of the table. "Do you want to do the honors, or shall I?"

Noah shook his head, took the weapon from her. "Don't you think shooting inside the hotel might attract a bit of attention?"

She cocked her head to the side, squinting her eyes. "Fine, we'll go down to the beach."

"I don't think so—"

"I already have to suffer sharing my room with you. I'm certainly not staying cuffed to you as well."

"Promise you won't run."

She shoved back a fist of tangled wet hair from her cheek. "I'm too tired to run, Noah. I want a real shower alone, clean clothes, room service, and twelve hours in that bed. Also *alone*."

Damn if she wasn't cute all fired up and dignified. "If you even blink wrong—"

"I could always start screaming rape, and you could spend a few months in a Mexican dungeon. That is, if the police bother taking you to the jail. I hear trial and jury down here often happens in the middle of nowhere with a bullet to the back of the head. Got to keep the vultures fat and happy, after all."

Noah knew she wouldn't dare. He also knew he'd have her sweet little mouth shut before she got out the first word out if she tried. He moved to take his shoe from the pile of clothes.

"What are you doing?"

"Quieter and safer if we use this." He slid out the insole and removed a little silver key.

Red crept up her neck and brightened her already sun-kissed face. Her eyes narrowed to slits, and her lips pursed. He readied himself. So when her free hand swung upward, he caught her wrist.

"We can play rough later. I'm goddamn tired right now." He dropped her hand and used the key to free them from the cuffs. Then he rubbed the red band around his wrist and watched as Cat stormed into the bathroom, slamming the door behind her.

She had a right to be pissed, but when dealing with a woman like Cat, a man had to do what a man had to do. He called room service and added Aloe Vera to the order when he heard the shower turn on and her cry out. Despite the pain of her sunburn, she took a lengthy shower, no doubt attempting to use all the hot water just to piss him off.

Hell, after the way she'd pressed up against him in the sauna room, a cold shower wouldn't be a bad idea.

Skin aflame from shower needles, Catalina cursed as she dried off with what felt a fluffy towel to her hands but a scouring pad to her body. Tucking the towel around her and wrapping her hair toga style in another, she glanced in the mirror at the three thousand new freckles over her nose and cheeks, chest, and shoulders. Damn, she hated freckles. Wincing as she dabbed moisturizer onto her face, she decided to hold off slathering her body for the morning.

She was still good and mad at Noah for keeping them cuffed when he had the key all along, so she came out of the bathroom, prepared for a good fight. But the smell of food overrode her temper as she followed the scent to the table.

Noah moved past her into the bathroom and closed the door without saying a word. *Fine by me.* The fight could wait until morning as well. Forgetting to dress, she sat at the table and lifted the silver dome to a platter of sautéed shrimp in spicy pepper and cilantro butter with rice and beans. After she poured a glass of chilled white wine, she dug in to her meal, eating like a woman starved for weeks. She didn't stop until her entree and half of Noah's was gone.

Served him right, she decided, wiping her mouth with a linen napkin, the food and wine making her twice as tired as before and a little tipsy. His stunt with the cuffs could have gotten them both killed.

By the time Noah emerged from the bathroom, towel wrapped

around his waist, she was in bed, lying on her stomach, only the sheet draped softly over her scorching bare back. She drifted in a semi-coherent state, but when the bed dipped with his weight, she found the strength to murmur, "Sofa pulls out."

"Good to know," he said, his voice low and smooth from a dreamy distance.

She was vaguely aware of the sheet slowly peeling back from her shoulders and the feel of the air-conditioning whisking across her heated skin. She gave no argument. She snuggled deeper into her pillow, her hands crossed beneath it. Drifting a little deeper into sleep, she sighed at the feel of hands smoothing cool moisturizer over her blazing skin and achy muscles. So natural, so right to have Noah's hands on her body, his strong, callused fingers splaying before drawing in, melting away pain and defenses. A small whimper escaped her as he reached for the bottle of Aloe Vera, squeezed another dollop in the hollow of her lower back, his lips dropping to her shoulder as he smoothed his hand over the curve of her bottom, fingers reaching to the back of her leg, pressing deep into her sore muscles.

She lay there, her breath shallow, her bottom raised, her knees parted for his hand. His fingers rounded to her center, moistening a path to her soft folds engorging with his touch. A contraction deep in her womb moistened her core and sent a shivering wave through her belly into her chest, hitching her breath, drying the back of her throat. Her fingers dug into the sheets and her mouth parted, the warm breath against the fabric of her pillow swirling back heat against her cheek. Never had she the power to deny her body Noah's attentions. He gave her pleasure and satisfaction, a euphoric recall she couldn't deny herself. Better not even to try, better to allow her body the pleasure so long denied. She eased her hips back as his tongue drew along her ribcage, over her hip, his mouth taking tiny bites, licking to the slit of her ass, rounding to suckle over her opening, drawing her flavor and her heat from her body. His tongue played in her opening, tasting her while his finger found the insatiable point of her desire, softly at first, teasing before quickening his rotation, building tension, stroking fire. The hard muscle of his thigh and the soft hair on his leg brushed against her side. The sculpt of his chest pressed against her hip, his nipple hard, mimicking the ache in hers. His free hand reached under her to find her breast then her nipple between his thumb and forefinger to pinch, shooting glorious, glorious pain and pleasure downward to twine with the coils deep within her, stretching toward succulent release.

As the orgasm came, pulse upon pulse, contraction riding contraction, Catalina sank her teeth into her upper arm, suppressing Noah's name screaming inside her. Even in the crazed release, she refused to give him verbal confirmation of her body's response. She longed for him. She knew her pleasure could only be heightened by the feel of him inside her, riding her orgasm with powerful thrusts. Hard. Fast. Fierce. He knew how she liked it, knew how to leave her feeling she'd been thoroughly fucked, body aching and sated. She pushed back further, opening her legs wider, open and ready for him. Waiting for him. And Noah drank the last of her contraction, pulled his mouth from her, slicked over her sensitized clitoris one last time and drew to his knees. Instead of moving between her legs, gripping her hips and entering, he moved to lie beside her, giving her his back.

"Sleep tight, Cat."

"Bastard," she hissed, before collapsing onto her stomach, knowing damn well he was proving a point.

He still controlled her.

Chapter 5

The doctor left the hotel room looking quite satisfied, with good reason. Catalina had paid him four hundred American dollars from her stash in the room safe to patch up Noah and keep silent about the nature of the visit.

She twisted the dead bolt and crossed to the deck where Noah stood. He was wearing the outfit she'd bought while he slept the day away in a deep, fevered sleep, hoarding the entire bed. Considering his injury, she shouldn't begrudge him that, though she had to remember that she lay half the night craving the fulfillment he didn't deliver. She should have been satisfied with the orgasm he so easily gave her. But she'd wanted more.

Even as she damned him, she admitted he was impressive in the tan cargo pants with wide pockets and his orange-and-red tropical print shirt billowing in a sea-scented breeze coming up off the Gulf of Mexico. He did look great in his suits, but it was nice to see him a little less... serious. Noah Tyler wasn't one for the casual look, but they needed to blend with the other tourists, not stick out like B-rated FBI agents in a Hollywood film. Suppressing such thoughts, she cleared her throat. "Arm better?"

Noah turned, leaning against the wrought-iron railing. "Feels like I just got stitched together with a local."

She smiled, lifting the short sleeve of his shirt to check out the patch job. "He *did* think he was coming to treat an upset stomach. I'm sure he did the best he could. Want me to go get some codeine from the drug store?"

"Can't afford a foggy head. Doc left some aspirin and antibiotics. How's the sunburn?"

"Better," she said, knowing he was responsible for soothing away one pain and inflicting another.

With a kick off the rail, he passed by her into the hotel room. He was nonchalant, as if he hadn't played her needs as easily as a member of the orchestra. "I'll take some coffee."

On a nod, grateful for a mundane task, she headed to the mini-kitchenette. Setting cups of coffee on a tray along with sweet bread she'd brought back from the corner bakery, Catalina inhaled a deep breath, lifted the tray and carried it to the sofa table. So she might not be completely over Noah Tyler, but she was wiser this time around. She wouldn't allow him to break her heart again. She took his pleasure and wouldn't offer herself to more. And anyway, wasn't he the one who denied it?

Now as she sat across from him, hardening her resolve, one question nagged at her. Why hadn't she left? Opportunity galore presented itself all day while he slept through the onset of infection. Instead of running, she'd found him a doctor, bought him clothes, brought food. She was taking care of him as if he still mattered, as if she couldn't quite bring herself to turn from him again.

"Have you called Harris yet?"

Noah looked at her over the brim of his coffee cup, took a swallow. "Not yet."

"But you're going to."

"I have orders."

"To bring me back."

"Yes."

"And then what?"

"Talk to Harris. It's none of my business." He sounded unconcerned.

"Have you always known?"

"Known what?"

She raised an eyebrow.

"Yes."

"I hate you for that."

"I know."

But do you care? Catalina controlled a shiver of rage vibrating from her chest outward. Her fist balled. "It's my life."

"You gave your life to DII."

"I want it back."

"You've had time."

"I want more."

"What if you don't like what your father has to say?"

"I'll deal with it."

"How can you be so sure?"

"How can you be so sure I won't? What makes you and Harris believe I'm so weak? I'm not a little girl anymore. You know me, you know better than anyone my capabilities. Fuck you."

"I know there are some things you can never forget once you known them. They'll go to bed with you every night, wake with you every morning. Eat away at you like a goddamn rat in the cellar."

"That's exactly how not knowing feels. I've read the files, the reports. I want to understand why my mother had to die."

"Give Harris a chance to explain."

"He's had his chance to explain for twenty-five years."

"I think," Noah said, "you were never supposed to know."

"But I do. Damn it, I do."

"And you hate everyone for it. Yeah, I accept that. How did you find out?"

She wanted to throw something. Noah was sitting there, accepting her hate and anger as if they didn't bother him. "Doesn't matter who told me."

It'd been Jarrod, Harris's right-hand man and pilot since the beginning of DII. She found him alone in his office one night, looking like hell. She sat with him awhile as he spilled the story over several too many whiskeys and waters. He made her promise never to tell Harris what he'd revealed to her.

So Catalina had picked the lock to Harris's office and gone through his files with a fine-toothed comb. The files confirmed Jarrod's story. Her biological father, Jacques Kahn, was a criminal dubbed The Shadow. Her mother, Carina Bellfurce, was a beautiful young French woman beguiled by Jacques' charms, and soon she became pregnant. Then Kahn suddenly disappeared with a large number of stolen diamonds. Harris learned of Carina's plans to run away from them and gave chase. But he found her dying. Kahn, wanting the diamonds for himself, had shot her and left her and her unborn baby for dead.

That night of revelations had been long, and Catalina had passed it numbly, in a state of disbelief and horror and confusion. By dawn, feeling returned. She knew if she even looked at Harris she wouldn't be able to control her anger and her hurt. Somebody would pay for all she had lost.

And that someone would be Jacques Kahn, her biological father.

"I need air." She stood and turned to the door.

Noah snagged her by the wrist.

She didn't try and loose his hold. Instead, tears threatened to well. "Let go."

"No."

"Just a walk, Noah. A walk. I need to think. If I were going to run, I could've left already."

"Why didn't you?"

She averted her gaze. "I don't know."

"I think you do. Fifteen minutes. A second more and I will come after you, don't think I won't."

She didn't hesitate. As soon as he released her, she swung open the door and let it slam closed behind her.

Chapter 6

Noah stood on the balcony as he waited for the cell phone connection to route through the secure satellite. He watched Cat walk down the beach, wearing a pair of calf-length white pants and a light pink tank top showing a slice of skin on her midriff. The ends of her blonde hair lifted in the sea-salted breeze.

Harris answered the phone. A small blow of guilt punched Noah in the gut. All he'd ever wanted was for Cat to be happy. "Sorry it took so long to get back to you, Harris."

"So tell me quick. I'm too goddamn old to wait."

Cat disappeared behind a massive rock formation on the shoreline. Beyond her, the sun's brilliant rays reflected on the water. He didn't like her being out of his sight, and had only agreed to her demand so he could make this call. But if she didn't return within the fifteen minutes he gave her, he'd slap those cuffs back on in a heartbeat.

"I've located her."

"Is she well?"

"You'd better sit down."

"I'll take it straight up. What's happened?"

"She's here for Kahn."

The squeaking of Harris lowering himself into his a chair came through the line, followed by a long silence. "I don't understand."

"She knows."

Noah heard the unmistakable sound of a drink being poured.

Harris hissed, aftermath of a straight shot going down. "How?"

"She's not saying."

"Son of a bitch. I've had my best men looking for him. How did she…?"

"You know Cat when she's determined."

"Has she made contact with him?"

"Not yet."

"But he's there?"

"So I gather, from the events of the past couple of days. It hasn't been pretty. He's here, but I don't think she's got a solid locale on him yet. Best I can tell she has gotten a message to him, and he's responded. He's not happy about being found."

"I can imagine."

"His men tried to kill us."

"You, probably. Not her, not until he has answers."

"I'm not so sure. The quicker we get her out of here, the better."

"Hold your position."

"What are you saying?"

"I want Kahn."

Noah's gut fisted. "And you'll use Cat as bait?"

"She's the only lure that will bring him out of hiding."

"You're a son of a bitch."

Noah heard Harris's fist slam on his desktop. "I'm the director of this agency. Kahn is still an active file. Those diamonds need to be recovered. Twenty-five years, he hid them well. I have no doubt he has them in his possession now that he's out of prison."

"And you still want revenge. For a jewel theft."

"Not the jewels. He killed her. He killed Carina."

"And if he kills Cat as well?"

Harris was silent for a moment, then said, "I trust you to prevent the possibility."

Noah drew in a long, steadying breath. He couldn't refuse an order from Harris. He had no choice if he wanted to protect Cat. Still, he had to question if revenge made Harris call the wrong shot. "I'll get a locale on Kahn, but once he's found, you wait until Cat's out of country before you send in a team. That's the only way I'll work this. I need your word."

"You're still in love with her."

"I'm just not as cold-hearted a bastard as you are."

"Love will only crush your heart and bleed your soul."

Not the first time bitterness had seeped from the old man. "Your word."

"My word," Harris snapped. "Find Kahn. I'm in route, should be there by midnight."

Noah found Cat sitting on the beach, shoes kicked off, feet buried beneath the sand, arms wrapped around her legs, chin on her knees. She picked up a little seashell, held it in her palm. She looked up when he joined her.

"Nice beach," he said.

"My parents—I mean, my adoptive parents—it still seems so foreign to refer to them that way. Anyway, they took me to the beach once."

Her voice was soft and quiet, her gaze drifting out over the waves lapping to the shore. "I was maybe five or six. My dad put me up on his shoulders and walked into the water. I started screaming, calling for my mom, trying to get down, but he just held my legs tighter. 'It's okay, Cattie Kin,' he said. He spoke in this kind of melody that I can still hear sometimes. 'It's okay, Cattie Kin,' he said. 'Papa's got you. Just open your eyes, stretch out your arms, and trust me.' Trust me, he said, and I did. I stopped screaming and kicking and fighting and he waded into the water until the waves broke against my ankles. Then he lifted me from his shoulders and gently lowered me into the water, right up to my chin. 'See, Cattie Kin,' he said, 'all you have to do is trust.'"

The watery tone of Cat's words made Noah want to wrap his arm around her and hold her. He knew from her file that the couple who raised her were in their late forties when they adopted her. There was no other family, no aunts, uncles, cousins on either side. Harris hand-selected them to raise Cat, to be a couple with a new baby and no one to notice.

"I trusted him to keep me safe, trusted that he would always love me. I trusted him right up to the end." Cat's voice broke and her hand clenched the shell so tight the edge cut her hand, blood dripping onto the sand. She shook her head, blinked away tears. "You don't understand, do you?"

"Explain it to me."

Cat opened her palm and stared down at the red-stained shell. "My whole life, I trusted him to keep me safe." She hurled the shell into the ocean. "He wasn't even my blood. And even he was lying to me."

Before she got to her feet, Noah grabbed her around the waist, hauled her to his lap and cradled her. "Don't run, Cat."

"At the end of the day, there's no one I can trust but myself. Not you, not DII. Just me."

"You may not trust me, Cat, but you need me."

"Hah. You're the last person I need, Noah Tyler."

He hauled her upward and around. Then he lowered his head and kissed her, capturing the words she spat with his breath. He tangled his hand in her hair, sweeping his tongue to delve deep into the heat of her mouth, seeking to tame the fire in her soul. Her hand slid under his shirt and up his chest.

He pulled her head back, stared down at her swollen lips. "I may be the last person you think you need, but you do want me."

Cat glared at him. "All I want is you to go away and leave me alone."

"If I tell you I've changed my mind? That I've decided to help you?"

She didn't even pause to consider it. "I don't want your help."

"Accept it, or I'm calling Harris for pick-up, and don't think you won't be on a plane by nightfall."

She searched his eyes. He knew damn well what she sought. "Why?"

"Because I've played a part in this hurt consuming you. If you believe finding Kahn is the right thing to do, I want to help. I want to be there for you."

"Your being here has already caused problems."

"I'll keep a low profile." He pushed her onto her feet, stood and resisted the desire to take her hand in his. "Starting tomorrow. Right now I think we both need some down time."

"The last time you suggested down time…."

"I promise it won't last three days this go-round. Dinner, maybe a little dancing, that's all."

"Are you trying to seduce me, Noah Tyler?"

"Are you going to let me, Catalina?"

She bit the bottom corner of her mouth, suppressing a smile. "Maybe."

※〜(♡♡)〜※

"Oh, hell no," Noah said, as two beautiful *senoritas* pulled him from his chair. "Cat, help a man out."

Catalina raised her shot of tequila in a mocking toast. "You're on your own on this one!" She saluted with the glass, downed it and relaxed into her wooden chair as the women pulled Noah into a circle on the dance floor. The Chicken Dance in full swing, half the restaurant-full of tourists joining in the lively music, Noah had no choice. He flapped his arms, clapped his hands, all the while shooting Catalina a "come save me" glance.

She covered her mouth to stifle a fit of giggles, thinking she'd never seen anything so hilarious in her entire life. Who would ever thought to see Noah chicken-dancing. "Woot, woot!" she called out, leaning a little tipsily forward to sip a melon margarita, drawing the tip of her finger along the brim of the oversized glass for a lick of salt.

A waiter came and set down two steaming plates of rice, beans, and prawns. "Enjoy, *senora.*"

"*Gracias, amigo.*" Taking a prawn by the tail, she swished it in the cilantro butter and bit into it, dripping warm sauce on her chin. Barely noticing the change in music, she greedily ate three more before reaching for a napkin.

Noah grabbed her wrist, pulling her upward and into his arms. "As punishment for making me dance that hideous dance, it's your turn." He turned her in a semi-circle and pushed gently at her bare lower back toward the dance floor.

Finally getting her mouth of food down, she smiled to herself before shouting over the music, "If this is punishment, I'd love to find out what happens when I'm really bad!"

He pulled her back, her bottom firm against his pelvis, her shoulders against his chest. "I like you like this, Cat," he said behind the shell of her ear, the heat of his breath swirling, spraying tingles. "Unguarded. Smiling."

Eyes closing half-mast, she drew in a deep breath, trying to focus through the effects of alcohol and an admittedly fabulous time. "Don't get used to it. You're still on my shit list."

"Don't worry, I won't forget. But right now that's exactly what I'm going to do, and so are you." He spun her around, framed up in an exaggerated ballroom position and smiled that damn smile. "May I have this dance?"

Swiping the forgotten butter off her chin, she nodded curtly, liking Noah this way as well. "Why, *si, señor,* you may." She raised her palm to meet his, placed her hand on his shoulder and followed his lead. And if she wasn't mistaken…. "When the hell did you learn to salsa?"

"Bogotá. Don't ask. You're stepping on my toes. Back on your right. Forward left. Forward right, hold. There you go. Keep following my lead."

As he guided her through a double turn, she shot him a glare over her shoulder. "Who in Bogotá taught you to dance?"

He opened them up, pulled her across him, changing sides and picking back up the four-count rhythm. "Her name was Marisel. Had a body like a goddess."

"A goddess, huh?"

"Jealous?" His steps became closer, moving forward to the beat of the music.

"Never. Now you're on my toes. Did you break her heart?"

Noah drew her body closer, his chest solid against her shoulder, mouth brushing her temple. "No. Her brother's. Quite by accident. I would rather have brought him in alive."

"And Marisel?"

"Restoring her *familia's* plantation to its original harvest."

Catalina wouldn't ask if Noah slept with the Bogotán goddess. Some duties called for behavior she didn't want to know about. She'd promised herself to never ask when first assigned to Noah, when she first realized the depths of infiltration the jobs entailed. The woman in her would always wonder.

Noah lifted her chin with two fingers until she met his gaze. "There hasn't been anyone since you."

A small smile wavered on her mouth. "It's none of my business."

Even as she said the words nonchalantly, his admission flamed an old possession. He had always been hers.

He gathered her again in his arms, a soft brush of his lips behind her ear. They were moving now to a beat of their own, the music, the atmosphere, everything forgotten but the feel of bodies. Melding. Breathing. Warm. "Noah...."

"Shhh. They're playing our song."

She rested her head on his shoulder and allowed her fingers to push deep into the muscles below his shoulders. "We don't have a song."

"We do now."

How did he manage to make it so easy to forget how much she despised him? The song eventually changed, but they remained in union on the dance floor until finally the heat of his body, the fuel of the alcohol, and the never-ending want lightened her head and made her legs weak. She angled her head and whispered, careful not to make her want a plea. "Take me back to the hotel and make love to me."

His hand found hers and he led her to the table, snatching an orchid from a bouquet and tucking it behind her ear. "I'll go pay the bill."

She smiled as he walked away and reached for a cooling prawn. Midway, her hand stilled as she saw the folded paper tucked beneath her drink. Casting a glance in Noah's direction, she slipped the note across the table, held it on her lap, and unfolded it. The hotel key card she'd left in Malto fell out.

She read the words, then stood and wove through the crowd toward the ladies' room and out the back door.

Chapter 7

Noah slipped into the hotel room, deftly closed the door behind him and leaned against the frame to watch Cat search the in-room safe where they'd left the guns. She slammed the safe door closed and whirled around, seeking an alternate hiding spot before her gaze stopped on him.

"Shit. Noah. You startled me."

He moved into the low-lit room, aware of his own predatory posture.

All sweet and innocent, she smiled and ruffled a hand through her hair. "I thought I would freshen up and meet you here."

"Good. For a moment, I thought you were trying to run away from me again." He continued to walk toward her, backing her up until she met the wall. Amused, he watched her control her breath so that the roundness of her cleavage barely heaved. He delved his fingers through her hair, setting free the orchid he'd tucked behind her ear. Gripping the hair at the base of her neck, he fisted until her head pulled back. "You wouldn't do that, would you?"

Her eyes slanted.

"Would you—?" Hot, hard, angry, raw, he shoved his pelvis to her belly, bending at the knees to drag his erection into the apex between her legs. "Cat?"

She shook her head. "No. I—"

He pulled off his belt, lowered his zipper and freed his cock. He bit her lower lip, ending her opportunity to continue to lie. He adjusted her to settle across his thighs, opening her legs wider, releasing the fiery heat of her sex. He could take her now. End this aching need to fuck her in a few deep thrusts, release the pent-up frustration pounding at him for days.

"Not another word, Catalina." He forced the words against her mouth, erection raging too hard, too damn near painful not to take her now. "Not another goddamn word unless I ask something of you. Understand?"

She nodded, her nose nudging against his, her tongue moistening her upper lip.

"Good." He always enjoyed that about Cat. She might be a hellion, a handful, a pain in his ass. She might be trained and capable and strong. She might know how to give and receive pleasure. But when he demanded it of her, she knew when to succumb. She'd pushed his patience to the limits, and she'd pushed his libido past sanity. Being with her was like constantly being on the edge.

Now he was going to make her pay for it.

Sliding his hand down the front of her shirt, he cupped her breast, lifted the soft weight from beneath the fabric, pinched her nipple until she gasped, the little bud swelling into steel. Her back arched and her leg wrapped around his, foot anchoring his calf. Releasing her breast, he fisted her shirt at the hem and tore it off her. Palm flat against her back, he shoved her against the wall, teeth anchoring into her shoulder until a metallic sting of blood washed his mouth.

Laving the pain he'd inflicted, he slipped his hands around her waist, unfastened her pants and slid them down her legs, his tongue dragging along her spine to the hollow of her back, through the seam of her sweet ass, head moving between her legs as he knelt, lifting one foot, then the other, tossing the pants aside. Her bottom lifted, her stance widened as he tongue drew toward her center, finding the milky heat, tasting her desire.

His erection throbbed, orgasm pushing at his head. It took every ounce of self-control not to drive himself inside her, to allow himself the feel of her. Withdrawing his tongue, he nipped his teeth at her ass, the side of her waist, up her freckled shoulder blade. Heat still radiated from her sunburn, yet she shivered as he lifted her hair and drew his tongue up her nape.

"What do you need, Catalina?" He opened the face of his Rolex and extracted a small, clear tracking device, no bigger than the tip of his pinky finger, thin as paper. He pressed it below her hairline, kissing the spot to make sure it adhered.

Her shoulders rolled back, her abdomen pressed outward, her nipples thrust against the textured wall. "I need…." Her head dropped back to rest on his shoulder. Her dark eyelashes fanned closed against her cheek.

"Tell me," he whispered against the arch of her ear.

Biting her lower lip, a little moan caught in her throat. "I need you inside me."

Noah dropped his pants, stepped out of them, turned her around and lifted her astride his hips. The tip of his erection jutted along her wetness, and he could smell the sultry heat of her. "Where do you want my cock, baby?"

Her gaze, eyes so dark they neared midnight, lowered to his mouth as she drew her tongue beneath his upper lip. "In my mouth."

As she slowly circled her hips, the lobes of her sweetness worked his erection harder, bigger. Her fingers dug into his shoulder blades. "Between my breasts, my legs. I need you inside me, Noah. Now."

Holding Cat secure across his lap, Noah started for the bed, stopped midway at a table, set her ass on the edge and cleared the surface with a sweep of his arm. Kissing her, he lowered her backward, her blonde hair contrasting with the dark wood. Leaning down, he rolled a taut nipple between his teeth, flicking with his tongue. A tiny cry from Cat as she pushed her shoulders down to thrust her tit deeper into his mouth. He had to be the luckiest goddamn man alive.

Adjusting her knees around his waist, he stood, gripped her hips and pulled her forward, her ass barely on the edge of the table. The tip of his erection found her moist opening. Her face flushed, the freckles on her cheeks paling beneath her passion.

"Are you going to fuck me now, Noah?" she asked, lifting, pushing her hips forward to take his cock farther inside her.

Noah fought against the want to drive into her. Instead, he pushed forward, languidly entering her, stretching her. Pushing her knees apart like butterfly wings, he closed his eyes a long moment, drew air through his nose, exhaled through his mouth. "Not yet, baby. I want to feel you come on me."

Catalina slipped her middle finger into her mouth, drew it out slowly. "Are you sure, Agent Tyler"—her hand lowered between her breasts, brushed the back of her knuckles over her stomach, slid her fingers in her valley—"that you can handle such torture?" With her slick finger, she found her nubbin and worked a slow circle.

"Oh, I can handle it." He shoved deeper inside her still as Cat aroused herself, her walls tightening around him, her heat growing hotter. "That's it, baby, come for me. Come on my cock." Her breathing turned rapid, shallow, her eyes began to dilate as she worked herself, her hips jerking forward, her heels pressing into his lower back, trying to push him deeper inside her. He held his position. Reaching forward to toy with her nipple, he pinched lightly, harder as her knees began to tremble.

"Oh, Noah, I—I…." Her gaze seemed to implore him to help her control the sensations. Her free hand gripped the edge of the table, and the muscles in her arm bunched. "I'm going to come."

So hot, so wet, so incredibly tight around him, her inner walls now trembled with the rest of her body. If he released even one muscle now tightly under control, he would lose it, he would come inside her.

"Noah!" Suddenly she bucked upward, her hand stilling, cupping her mound. Her hand snaked around his neck, clawing his nape.

Her contractions came hard, one pulsing after another, her pussy gripping and releasing his cock like a fist pumping him. Still he didn't move, held deep inside her until her orgasm began to fade. She nipped at his neck, her sweaty forehead against his shoulder. Scooting backward, she moved until his cock came out of her. Pushing his belly, she moved him a step back and lowered herself to her knees.

Noah growled as she took his cock, dripping with her juice, into her mouth. Damn, he loved that about her.

※ঊৢৎ⁗

A traveling band played from the streets below, the sound of guitar and vocals barely drifting up to the balcony. Catalina stood wearing Noah's shirt. Holding it close with one hand, she breathed the pungent salty scent hanging in the thick air. Noah came up behind her, wrapped his arm around her, twined his fingers with hers, and with the other hand, produced a cup of tea.

Accepting the warm cup, she blew into the mug and took a swallow. "Hmmm, you remembered." Her adoptive mother swore drinking hot liquids on a hot day equalized the body's temperature.

"I don't forget much." He dropped a kiss on her shoulder.

A storm brewed. Dark, ominous clouds hung low in the sky, blocking the stars and moon. The wind seemed to pick up force with each passing moment. Catalina barely noticed. She had exactly two hours to be at the rendezvous spot. Two hours to somehow slip away from Noah. Problem was, she didn't want to leave him. Not yet. It'd been so long since she'd been touched, so long since she'd known pleasure, ecstasy.

Noah's hand slipped into his shirt, found her breast, brushed his thumb lightly over her raw nipple. On a sigh, she leaned against him, allowed him to be her strength. She could spend forever in that moment, in Noah Tyler's arms, her entire body aching, bruising, deliciously so. No one else had made love to her so thoroughly.

The street band began what Catalina imagined a love song with the strum of guitar, the singer's voice filled with emotion, rising over the crash of wind. Noah's hand smoothed over her ribcage, down her belly, slipped between her legs and delved gently into her valley, pulling upward the hood concealing her clitoris.

"Noah, we can't. There are people awake. I'm sore. I don't think I can take—"

He slipped his finger lower, curved into her vagina, slicking his finger with the deeply fragrant moisture.

"Any more...." Closing her eyes, she relaxed against him as he moistened her clitoris and began to masturbate her.

Setting the cup of tea on the balustrade, she slipped her hand into her shirt, found her breast, her fingers squeezing her nipple. Coils tightened deep in her belly, radiated outward on heat waves. Champagne-like bubbles spread across her skin. Moving his finger beneath her hood a little higher, Noah massaged a new erogenous spot, taking her higher, sending another crescendo of pleasure. Reaching back, she gripped Noah's firm buttock, her fingers pressing into his muscles, her bottom rotating against his hardening shaft. She couldn't believe he was ready again.

"Oh, *god*, Noah," she moaned, the back of her throat drying. Just as the orgasm tore through her, a raindrop struck her nose, dripped onto her lip. She laved it off, sighing, "I've missed you."

Noah lowered her to the balcony floor and opened the shirt to bare her breasts to the wind and rain. He entered her, his penis engorged as he filled her to the point of near pain. Her soreness from the previous encounters when he'd given it to her hot and hard relaxed with the gentleness he bestowed now. She stared deep into his eyes as he withdrew ever so slowly, and her inner walls quivered still with after-waves of her orgasm.

Rain began to beat down, cool drops pooling on her warm, sensitized skin. They found a rhythm uniquely theirs, the rain, the strum of guitar, the beat of their hearts. Noah pushed damp tangles of hair off her brow and kissed her forehead. The wet hair on his chest mated against her breast, brushing her nipples. Anchoring a foot against his lower back, she moved him over, changing positions so she was astride him. She traced the stitches on his arm with her finger, leaned to kiss the bullet wound. He'd chanced his life for her.

She tilted her head back, Noah coming forward to suckle her breast. Catalina sunk down deep upon him and rode him until he growled her name from deep within his gut. Her orgasm matched the power of his, ripping through them both. She collapsed atop him and smiled.

Chapter 8

The smell of over-ripened fruit had reeked when the burlap sack was brought down over Catalina's head. Now, a good two hours later, with the sun beating down, the stench reached a nauseating high point. The vehicle transporting her hit another pothole without slowing, jarring her upright and tumbling her onto her side. The assholes could've at least buckled her in. Shoving her elbow into the seat, she strained to right herself, her hands numb behind her back, the swelling in her wrists tightening the ropes.

Should she survive this, Noah would kill her. And she couldn't blame him. After their lovemaking and the drowsy hours afterwards, she should have awakened him, told him her plans, let him provide back-up. Too late now for regrets. Besides, informing Noah could've gotten them both dead. But this might not be the disaster she feared. After all, she was still alive, and each minute of the past hour lessened her doubt she'd stay that way. If these men had been ordered to kill her, they'd been driving long enough to have pulled over, hauled her out of the car and plugged one between her eyes—if that was their aim.

The car took a hard right turn, climbed up a small hill, and finally came to a stop. "This is it," she whispered into the dank darkness of the sack, slowly drawing in a deep breath.

The door opened and a large hand clasped around her forearm and dragged her across the seat. Her handler greeted one, two... three different men in Spanish. Catalina picked up a few words from the rapid dialect, nothing to indicate where she was or what to expect. Rain seeped in through the burlap sack and her feet stuck in soggy earth as her handler led her up a pyramid of steps. As a door opened, a man spoke in a soft voice, barely audible, so Catalina couldn't pick out a word to translate. Her handler moved her forward, releasing her as she stepped inside. The door closed behind her.

The man pushed her forward. "So you are the woman making fools of my men? I expected a Zena-type warrior princess!"

Catalina didn't respond. She wished she'd had more time to think this through.

"I do not believe you to be foolish. Brazen and bold, but not foolish. If I am wrong, I won't hesitate to kill you." He freed the noose from her neck. "Curiosity has always been a shortcoming of mine." He pulled the sack from over her head and turned her around to face him. "Curious with thoughts of how you found me, who sent you. Mostly, mostly." He paused.

Catalina blinked several times, adjusting to the golden glow of candles, focusing on the man standing before her. The man who killed her mother. *The man she would kill.* Jacques Kahn, the infamous Shadow.

He stood maybe two inches taller than she, his hair near white, lines clawed at the edges of his eyes. A hard man, the years in prison obvious. And yet, he was handsome and in his eyes were specks of brilliance, as if his mind held knowledge of the earth. His gray-green stare myopically searched her face, focusing for a moment here, there. He took a step closer as if he couldn't quite see enough.

She barely contained the urge to spit in his face.

His bushy eyebrows furrowed and lines creased his forehead. He raised an eagle talon-like hand toward her cheek. A tear shimmered at the corner of his eye, anchoring on a wrinkle. "Carina."

"No." Catalina took a step back, revolted by his touch. "Catalina. My name, it's Catalina." Let her name resound in his head as she took his life.

He scrubbed his hands over his face, shoving his fingertips into his eye sockets. "Forgive me," he whispered. "Forgive me."

❧⟨☙☙⟩❦

An old grandfather clock tolled four a.m., and Jacques Kahn still breathed. Catalina wished for her Tomcat to silence the damn noise.

Exhaustion seeped from every pore of her body. Tracers of light played around her vision; pins seemed to jab into her temples. Her hands were numb and swollen, still tied behind her back.

It seemed impossible, everything Jacques Kahn had told her over the past hours, and yet she believed him, this complete stranger, this man. Her father.

Or did she simply want to believe him?

Did she need ever so badly someone to trust after so many had betrayed her?

She'd come to kill him. Now...*now?* Nothing prepared her for this.

Noah. If Noah were here, he could help her sort through this.

Rain beat on the tiled roof in relentless pings, wind whipped palm branches against the dark windows. Catalina's mind spun in a thousand directions, a thousand questions swirled. She went back to the beginning of the story Jacques told her, piecing it together with what Jarrod told her that drunken night and what she'd found in Harris's files. "So you were working on satellite technology. And my mother was—a jewel thief? And in exchange for not pressing charges against you for satellite espionage and my mother for a jewel heist—"

"The Queen's jewels, no less." Despite a reminiscent smile, pain deeply etched Jacques' eyes and, she could see the toll of relieving the past in the sagging of his shoulders. "Your mother tended to enjoy the daring."

Maybe Catalina should have been angry to discover she'd been born the child of criminals. Somehow, it simply explained her daring enjoyment, her quest for adventure, her love of thrill. "Harris brought you both into DII."

"To catch a thief.… We were assigned together, your mother and I. I fell in love with Carina the moment I met her."

Catalina wanted to ask about her mother, to ask if she looked like her, sounded like her. Had her eyes, her nose, chin. She couldn't. Not yet. Facts now. She'd sort out the emotional entanglement later.

"I wish you could have met her," her father said as if reading her thoughts.

Catalina nodded, a lump in her throat. "Tell me again, about the job, about The Shadow."

Her father leaned forward as if to confide a secret. "Now that was some crazy son of a bitch. Worldwide heists, the most secure and guarded banks, Germany, Sweden, France, Japan, the US." He snatched his hand forward and back. "In and out without so much as a whisper. Ah, but we got close to him, had his hideout secured. You wouldn't believe the riches that SOB had stockpiled. It was like a lost temple."

Catalina scrubbed at her forehead with the pads of her fingers. "He was never caught."

"No."

"But my mother knew his identity. She never revealed him. Why?"

Jacques must have sensed her murderous edge had calmed. He came to her and released her hands. "She needed more time to get enough evidence. Then Harris received intel pointing the finger at me. He always wanted your mother, and I stood in his way. Arranging for life in prison would get me out of the way."

Catalina pumped circulation back into her hands, then walked to the window and stared out at the storm bashing the jungle. Tracing a raindrop down the fogged pane, she tried to imagine Harris with enough emotion to put an innocent man in prison. Her fist curled and pressed against the window. She just couldn't see it. Harris played by the book. And yet, he had kept this all a secret from her.

"So you and my mother planned to run away before Harris could fabricate a solid case against you."

"Understand, Catalina, we had nothing between the two of us, not a dime. I didn't know she planned on stealing the diamonds from The Shadow's stockpile, but I didn't ask that she replace them either. We were coming here, to Mexico. A new life for the three of us. Free of our past crimes, of DII. A family, that's all she wanted."

She didn't hear him stand or move behind her until his hand touched her shoulder. She jerked away. "A family? Damn you! Why weren't you there to meet her that night? Pregnant and alone! She must have been terrified waiting for you."

For a moment, he seemed a ghost walking through time, memory. Haunted. His lower jaw trembled. "I have lived twenty-five years imagining that night differently. Twenty-five years. I loved her. Dammit, I loved her and you, I loved you." Gripping his collar, he jerked away the top button. "As God is my witness, Catalina, I believed you died that night with her."

"Harris convicted you for the Shadow's crimes."

Head dropping into his palms, Jacques whispered, "I didn't care, stopped caring twenty-five years ago. Until tonight." Lifting his head, he reached a hand out as if beckoning her to him.

Everything inside her wanted to move forward, to take his hand. Instead, she rooted herself in place, her eyes narrowed. "Did you kill her? Did you kill my mother?"

Looking her directly in the eye, he made the smallest motion no with his head. "I loved her. I would never have harmed her."

"Liar," a voice hissed from behind Catalina.

Jacques' eyes narrowed as he turned. "You." He reached into the chair cushion and pulled out a gun. "You son of a bitch. You killed her."

Catalina whirled around as a gunshot reverberated through the room. The moment slowed. Images warped. Sound elongated. Harris stood there one moment, a split second later he jerked backward, the bullet catching him in the shoulder. Noah seemed to materialize from nowhere, his gun drawn. Catalina's fingertips dug into her scalp as she covered her ears and screamed as the second shot fired. Her father collapsed backward into the chair, the gun dropping from his hand, blood seeping through his shirt.

Catalina's throat thickened. She wanted to vomit as she stared numbly at Jacques. Slowly she moved her gaze to Noah. "What did you do?"

Noah holstered his gun, moved to kick Jacques' gun across the room. "Harris. You okay?"

Harris leaned against the wall and groaned as he slowly lowered himself to sit. "Still kicking. He alive?"

Noah glanced down at Jacques. "He's alive. Goddamn it, Cat. What were you thinking?"

Tears sprang to her eyes, her lower lip trembled. Could Harris really have killed her mother? The man who'd been a family friend, her boss? "We—we need to get my father to a hospital."

Noah said, "Jarrod's outside with the helicopter. Help me get Kahn loaded up."

Catalina nodded, frozen for another moment before she could move to help Noah. Draping Jacques' arms around their shoulders, they lifted him and carried him through the house, out into the storm.

"Son of a bitch, that hurts," Jacques muttered.

"You're okay, you're okay," Cat said. "We're getting you to help."

"Chopper is just beyond that grove of trees," Noah said.

"You're going to be okay," Catalina said again, angling her head against the sheets of rain as she trudged through the mud, vines snapping at her ankles.

Noah jerked open the side door to the helicopter and called to Jarrod, "Get on the radio, find the nearest hospital. Harris is down, too!"

Catalina jumped into the helicopter and pulled her father in, his body collapsing atop her. She stared at Noah a long moment, tears and rain blurring her vision. "Hurry, Noah. Please hurry."

On a nod, he slammed the door closed.

"What's going on out there?" Jarrod asked, starting the engines.

A numbness crept from her toes to her fingers. "Jacques shot Harris."

"Who—shot me?" Jacques asked, his voice barely above a gurgled whisper.

She smoothed his cold, sweaty forehead. "Noah. He's, he was... my partner. At DII. I'll explain it all later. Jarrod, have you contacted a hospital? Is it far?"

"Not getting through on the radio. Storm's bad." The blades began to whir.

None of this made any sense. Jacques had accused Harris of killing her mother. Harris had accused Jacques.

"Jacques, are you sure Harris killed my mother?" she asked, still smoothing his brow. "Jacques?" She tried to rouse him. "Did he?" she asked Jarrod. "You were there that night. Did Harris kill my mother?"

Jarrod turned around in his seat. "No, little girl." He smiled, his red goatee glowing in the lights of the dash. He took something from his pocket and lunged for her. She toppled back, her head knocking the wall. Jarrod jabbed her arm with a needle. "He didn't."

The sound of an engine loud and whirring echoed in Catalina's head.

Her eyelids felt like lead as she tried to open them. A long moment she stared through blurry vision at rain sheeting a fisheye window. With a thick, dry tongue, she licked her lips, tried to swallow. The ground beneath her dipped and bounced. Helicopter. She rolled her head to the side. "Jacques." She lifted a heavy hand toward his body, dropped her fingers at his neck, found his pulse. Vision doubling, she stared ahead again. "Jarrod?"

"Ah, you're waking up, Cattie Kin." The old nickname sounded strange in the pilot's voice.

Catalina wanted to ask where Noah and Harris were. But she couldn't find the energy to speak. Instead she willed her mind to clear the fogginess. Willed her system to cleanse itself. Jarrod had injected her...why? She wiggled her toes, her fingers. Counted to ten over and over until she no longer stumbled over the next number. Jarrod had been a staple in her life, always by Harris's side. Uncle Jarrod, she used to call him. He gave her a helicopter ride for her tenth birthday. "What is going on?" she asked, so tired, so confused.

Jarrod didn't respond.

The floor of the helicopter was rich with blood. Too much blood. Easing closer to Jacques, she laid her cheek to his. His skin felt cold, his breathing slowing more with each moment. "He's going to die."

The helicopter began to lower. Soon the bird bumped on the ground, landed. Jarrod cut the engine, swiveled in his seat, pointed the gun at Jacques head. "He better not die yet. I've waited too long for this."

Catalina heaved herself to sitting position. "For what?"

Jarrod gave her father a kick in the shoulder, rousing him. "My diamonds. Where are they, Jacques?"

Her father's eyes opened slowly and he rolled his head to the side to look at Jarrod. "You... Shadow."

Jarrod's finger tightened on the trigger and lifted the barrel at Catalina. "Tell me. Where are they?"

No words came out of her father's mouth, only a trickle of blood.

Catalina sat back on her haunches, her groggy mind connecting the dots. "You're the Shadow," she said.

Jarrod's corner lip lifted, almost as if suppressing a grin.

She shoved herself up onto her unstable feet. "You killed my mother." Hate and anger boiled inside her, giving her strength. "You used me to find Jacques."

"I only want what's mine. Because of your whore mother, everything else I fucking lost."

Rage clenched in Catalina's stomach. "What you stole."

"Touché. Don't look at me like that, Cattie. It was the perfect goddamn setup, working for the agency trying to find me. Carina was going to turn me over to Harris. I couldn't let her do that. "

"So you killed her. You let my father rot in a cell for twenty-five years." Her stomach knotted and bile rose in her throat. "You son of bitch." Gripping the overhead bar for support, she kicked the gun out of Jarrod's hand, then pulled her leg back and delivered a *Tyler Special* with her foot to his windpipe.

Jarrod's head snapped. He flew back and hit the dashboard. The gun clanged on the floorboard. Catalina snatched it up, shoved Jarrod's limp body aside, and found his cell phone. She didn't care about securing the line. Her father was out of time. She punched in Noah's number.

"Please, oh, please. Work. Noah." A sob clogged her throat as the phone rang and Noah's voice came on the line. Finally, holding back a flood of tears she spoke. "Hey, Tyler?"

"Cat. What the hell? Where are you?"

"In the copter. It was Jarrod. He's the Shadow. He killed my mother."

"Where is he now?"

"He's—he's out. I think. I may have killed him. I've got to get my father to the hospital."

"I've got a tracking device on you, but the signal is weak."

She climbed onto the pilot's seat, exhaled a deep breath. "Remember when you said you'd teach me how to fly?"

"Cat?"

"It's time, Noah. I trust you. Tell me what to do."

The phone was silent a long moment. "I love you, Cat."

She nodded, bit her bottom lip. "I know."

Chapter 9

Catalina rose from her chair and took her father's hand. "Hey, you're awake."

The monitors hummed, the IV bag dripped, and her father managed the smallest smile. "I'm sorry for everything."

Smoothing her thumb over the back of his hand, she returned the smile. "It's okay. Everything is going to be okay now."

As if his hand weighed heavily, he slowly lifted his arm, pointed out the window to the night sky. "Did you know"—he drew in a deep breath through the oxygen tube in his nose—"people often mistake satellites for stars?"

She sat on the edge of the bed, nodding. "I've heard that before. Harris tells me you were quite the pioneer of satellite technology in your day."

"Yes. My designs were… innovative." Jacques sighed. "I made terrible decisions. Paid for them, and the price too high."

"It's all in the past."

"That one. See there?"

She followed the direction of his finger. Framed in the window was the night, and she could see a star shaped and colored just a little differently than the rest. Her gaze swept to her father's face, and her eyes widened. "That's where you hid the diamonds."

His eyes closed. He nodded. "That's where I was… that night. I planned to bring them down… the satellite, the jewels, once I was safe, here, with Carina…. Your mother." He drifted out, a small smile on his weathered, pale face.

The door opened. Catalina turned and put her finger to her lips. Easing off the bed, she crossed the room and stepped into the hallway. Noah tucked a strand of hair behind her ear. "Harris is being released. I've booked us a flight. It leaves in an hour."

"You're sure it's okay for him to travel so soon?"

"Yeah. He's tough. He wanted to say goodbye himself."

"I understand."

"He, ah, accepts your resignation from the team. When you're ready, he's going to need a statement. You may have to come back for a formal inquiry."

"I'll keep myself available."

Noah brought his arm around her, his hand fisting in the back of her hair as he pulled her against him. He kissed her forehead. "I'm sorry, Cat. I only ever wanted to protect you."

Closing her eyes, she brushed her lips against his cheek. "I know. I needed to know, though, about my mother and my father. I just wish there could have been an easier way."

"I love you," he whispered, kissing her forehead once more.

"I know."

Noah released her, took a step back. "Call me if you need me. Anything, anytime. I'll be there."

Catalina nodded. "Thank you." She laughed out loud as his B-rated movie-agent loafers squeaked on the green tile floor as he walked away. "I love you, too," she whispered when he rounded the hallway corner.

Now she knew the truth of her past. Now she was free of DII. Now Noah was leaving for good. She had everything she thought she'd wanted when she left DII. Her stomach churned and her chest ached. She couldn't swallow because her tears wouldn't stop. "Damn you, Noah Tyler," she said, digging in her back pocket for Jarrod's cell phone. She pushed numbers as she started down the hallway.

He answered on the second ring.

"You said," she hurried her steps, "to call if I needed anything."

"Name it."

She began to run. "I need to be in your arms when I go to sleep and when I wake up. I need to touch you and kiss you and make love to you. I need a partner. I can't trust just anyone with my life. And we both know no one else would put up with my smart mouth. I need to be the one you salsa with, because if that Bogotán goddess comes near you again, so help me.... I need you in my life. I need you, Noah Tyler. I love you."

She pushed open the double doors leading outside the hospital. "Do you hear me, Noah Tyler? I love you." As she scanned the parking lot, her brows knitted together. "Damn it, where are you?"

A hand clasped her arm and pulled her hand behind her back, a handcuff snapped around her wrist. "You didn't really think I would go anywhere without you, did you, Cat?"

She turned and glared. Noah was grinning that damn grin, pulling the dimple in his cheek. "You're so lucky I love you, Noah Tyler. So damn lucky."

"I know." He snapped the other cuff around his wrist. "I love you too, Cat. And I'm not letting you go."

About the Author:

Having lived in Africa, Mexico and around the United States as a child, Dominique Sinclair once again calls eastern Washington State home. When not writing, you can find her on a never ending adventure of being a single parent to two teenage children. She loves to read, garden, and dance (everything from ballroom, two-stepping to Salsa). Dominique loves to hear from her readers. You can visit her on the web at www.dominiquesinclair.com.

Beast in a Kilt

by Nicole North

To My Reader:

I'm in love with Scotland and those hot hunks in kilts who are equally capable on the battlefield or in bed. Find out what happens when a virginal lady seduces the cursed Highlander she's been in love with since childhood. Will she claim his body as well as his heart and destroy the curse which imprisons him? I hope you enjoy *Beast in a Kilt*, the second in my kilted shape shifter series for Red Sage, the first being *Devil in a Kilt* in **Secrets, Volume 27**.

I dedicate this story and all the others to my wonderful husband, who endlessly supports and encourages me. I couldn't have done it without you.

Chapter 1

Scottish Highlands, 1621

"Aye, the lass will make a fine bride," John MacPeter, chieftain of the MacPeter clan said. His bug-eyed gaze raked Catriona MacCain head to toe. He near drooled, and his belly jiggled when he chuckled.

Catriona cringed, hoping the dim candlelight of Farspag Tower's great hall hid her expression. Unable to abide the sight of him, she lowered her gaze to the Turkish carpet covering the stone floor. She envied her selkie older brother, Brodie, at the moment. Even though he was cursed, at least he was free and frolicking with the other selkies in seal form. She was trapped here in hell.

"Splendid." Her mother clapped her hands once and gave an almost imperceptible bounce on her toes. "We shall hold the *rèiteach* on the morrow to determine the dowry and bride price, and if all goes well in the negotiations, the wedding a fortnight hence."

The MacCain clan elders stood behind her mother, smiling and nodding.

Were they all daft? The lecher before her had already buried three wives. Catriona wondered if they'd perished from the stench of him. She swallowed the disgust rising in her throat. Death would be preferable to bedding down with him.

Why, dear God, isn't Brodie here to prevent this?

After John MacPeter headed up the spiral stone staircase toward his guest room, her mother walked Catriona to her chamber.

"Please change your mind, Mother. I detest that beslubbering, claybrained horn-beast. His very nose is like an anvil. And by the size of his belly, you would think he is set to deliver twins. I do not believe he has bathed in more than a—"

"Catriona!" Her mother blanched, her skin contrasting sharply with her black hair. "Do not say such things about this noble man," she whispered, checking behind herself in the dim corridor. "What if he should hear? You have spent too much time with your grandfather."

"On the contrary, I have not spent enough time with him. Could I return to England?" *Please, God, anything but to be thrown to the swine-laird.*

"No." Her mother urged her into the bedchamber and closed the door. "You are old enough to marry and must do your duty for the clan. You will secure peace and protection. You will grow to love John MacPeter." She smiled as if Catriona were a silly child. "It takes time for affection to grow between a man and his wife. I detested your father when we first married, but soon I was mad about him."

"When you married Father, he was not as old as the MacPeter. Even were he alive now, Father would not be as *old* as the MacPeter. Perhaps you should marry him."

"Oh, no. That wouldn't do at all. He wants a young wife who will bear him many sons. Besides, as the daughter of a chieftain, you know you must marry someone of consequence. Since your father passed, the MacPeter is the most powerful chieftain in these parts and we need his protection. Not to mention that your ne'er-do-well brother has taken himself off somewhere."

"Brodie is a selfish lackwit," Catriona muttered.

"And you are fortunate John MacPeter found you to his liking. When first he heard you had red hair, he was displeased."

"What?" *Why, that bastard.* He objected to her red hair, when everything about him was revolting? What an arse.

"My darling, you know I love your red curls." Her mother kissed her cheek. "Sleep well, my child, and dream of your future husband."

"Ugh!" Catriona grimaced and slammed the door behind her.

"Your mother is right." Her maid, Aggie, approached from the corner to help her undress.

"What? You wish me to marry that swine?"

"Aye, and ye'll be lucky to have him. He's a powerful man with much land. If ye'd been a crofter's wife, ye'd ken what I mean—hard work, day in, day out."

"Surely there is a younger, less repulsive chieftain somewhere in the Highlands."

"A man is a man. Doesna make much difference his age."

Catriona doubted the truth of that. "If Brodie were here, he would prevent this. What must I do?"

"Obey your mother, that's what." Aggie hung up her clothes and left.

Catriona crawled between the featherbed and counterpane, but she was sure to get no sleep this night. She stared up at the rose velvet canopy held aloft by carved wooden posts. As the minutes passed, her desperate thoughts shifted into dreams. She held in her hand a missive with her brother's name scrawled on it. She turned it over, broke the red wax seal and opened the paper. But she couldn't read the words. Not enough light. The harder she strained to see them, the blurrier they became. *Blast!*

Waking slightly, Catriona turned onto her side and the dream changed. She lay naked in a strange, but very large, sumptuous bed with someone…a man. *Heavens! Torr Blackburn?*

The dim candlelight revealed the rugged masculine beauty of his familiar face. His darkened green eyes gleamed. A whiff of his clean musky male scent reached her, and she wanted to press her nose to his neck and breathe him in.

He skimmed his fingers over her arm, her stomach, sending swirls of pleasurable sensations through her. He should not touch her thus, should he?

Why not? It was only a dream. She had always secretly yearned for Torr's attention, but he didn't appear to know she existed beyond being the pesky little sister of his best friend.

His intent gaze searched her own. He rolled on top of her and kissed her, the bare skin of his hard chest and muscled abdomen near searing her with heat. His mouth demanded she focus solely on him. Was this what a real kiss from a real man felt like? Not a dry little peck, but a carnal feasting, his tongue tasting inside her mouth. Flicking, tempting, teasing. *Mmm. Mo chreach!* She yearned for something more.

And in the next instant, he gave it to her. Already lying between her legs, he slowly nudged his shaft inside her. She had watched animals mate and always wondered why the females didn't kick the males off and run away. Now she knew. Because of the pleasure and a burning, instinctive need for more. Scarcely able to breathe, she had never thought she would love having her body invaded in such a way. But this was Torr whom she'd always watched, craving something from him she didn't understand. With his well-honed, yet graceful warrior's body, he was a prime example of a stud in human terms and probably an expert with the tupping.

Yes, indeed. He was everywhere at once, his lips eating at her mouth, his hands stroking her, his shaft sliding deep. Faster and faster. Never had she imagined a feeling so overwhelming. So wicked. She spread her legs wider, arched her back and buried her fingers in his hair while he surged more urgently inside her.

She screamed and awoke, her thighs clenched tightly together. Shivers of pleasure spiraled through her. Oh heavens! What had her body done in response to Torr? In a *dream*? A feeling more intense than any she'd had in real life.

"I've lost my sanity," she whispered, remembering the shuddering hot pleasure that gripped her as he'd pumped himself into her. She wanted Torr for a lover? Why on earth would she dream of him? She had not seen him in several months. But indeed, she missed him.

Or was this a dream of the future? She sat upright in bed. "Faith!"

Had she dreamed of her future husband, as her mother had advised?

"What if I could marry Torr instead of the MacPeter?" she whispered. *And why not?* She refused to put her future in anyone's hands but her own.

She did not care that Torr, a third son, was not a chieftain. He held the respectable position of *bladair*, spokesman for his chieftain older brother. Torr was the most intelligent, well-read man she'd ever met, and a skilled warrior knight.

She leapt out of bed and in the meager dawn light, dressed as best she could without Aggie. Did the missive she'd opened in her dream hold some importance? Was it real? She slipped out the door and along the corridor to her brother's dim library. Once inside, she ran to the desk and shuffled among his dusty papers. Nothing.

Catriona skulked into the great hall, trying to make herself as unobtrusive as possible. The servants hustled about the large room preparing breakfast, the muted early light squeezing through the high narrow windows and a few candles the only illumination. The scent of baking bread and sizzling bacon wafting up from the kitchens made her mouth water.

Moments later, the outside door opened and the steward entered, whistling and carrying a folded parchment.

She scurried to him. "What is that, Drury?"

He bowed. "A missive for his lairdship, m'lady."

Dear heaven, her dream held some truth. "Let me have it."

He drew back, clutching the missive to his chest. "But, shouldna he open it?"

"He is not here, nor has he been for a fortnight."

"The elders or your mother, then?"

Catriona snatched the paper from his grip and fled up the stairs. Drury sputtered after her.

She burst into her room, slammed the door and barred it. Not recognizing the seal, she broke the red wax with shaking fingers, unfolded the paper and read.

Brodie, Chieftain of Clan MacCain,

There is hope. The curse that afflicts us can be broken, and in my case has been broken. I am now a man whole again with no remaining ill effects from Wilona MacRae's curse. The requirement is love given and received in equal parts, with complete trust and without reservation. Wilona and her accomplice, my cousin Alpin MacTavish, are headed in your direction. I am also sending this missive to Torr. If either of you can stop these two villains, please do.

Gavin MacTavish, Chief of Clan MacTavish.

"*Mo chreach!*" The curse could be broken? *Thank you, thank you, thank you!* Catriona danced on her toes. "I must tell Brodie."

She threw on her fur-trimmed, black woolen cloak, slipped down the back servants' stair and headed toward the rocky shore of the North Atlantic. She glanced back at the five-story tower house perched on a cliff above the sea, hoping no one saw her. The harsh sea wind yanked at her cloak and ankle-length, belted plaid *arisaid*. She tucked them tighter about her as she descended. Shivering, she inhaled the familiar scent of brine and fish. A touch of rain hissed through the air, wetting her face.

Gazing first north, then south along the jagged shoreline, she saw naught but gray boulders and seawater reflecting gray sky. Mist wreathed the mountains and islands in the distance. Nothing moved but the white-capping waves, thundering against the crags, and the screeching birds, darting this way and that. No seals to be found lounging on rocks.

"Brodie!" She picked her way among the large stones and called out again. Nothing. "Blast!" He was no doubt having a grand old time. And she was being bartered off to a barbaric beast. She stumbled along the narrow trail to the cave her brother sometimes used and stepped inside.

"Brodie?" Her voice echoed, but no response. Empty, dark and dank. Less appealing than the unfriendly weather. She returned outside. "Brodie, get your arse back here, damn you! And take responsibility for the clan. I need your help!" Wind tore at her clothing and chilled her to the bone. The rain fell harder, stinging her eyes. It was turning into a gale.

Scrunched and shivering, she scuttled back up the path to Farspag. In her bedchamber, Aggie helped her change into dry clothing.

"Impulsive lass, running out in a gale that way," Aggie grumbled. "Ye'll catch your death."

"I must find Brodie. He will tell MacPeter to go to Hades."

"Catriona!"

"I refuse to marry that beast!"

"'Tis too late to prevent it now. The negotiations for your *tochar* are underway."

Catriona's stomach ached. "I wonder how many cattle my clan is paying him to take me off their hands?"

"Let's hope 'tis no' too many. The feast will be held tonight. I shall fix your hair in a lovely twist."

"How can my own family, my own mother, treat me with such coldness?"

Aggie snorted. "'Tis the way of the world."

"I am naught but a pawn, a piece of property, something to be used to buy protection."

"Aye. Ye're a woman. Get used to it."

"I've never belonged here. I wish I'd stayed in England." She'd always felt at home with her grandparents the three years she'd lived with them as part of her *education* to learn refined English manners. Ha. Her outspoken grandfather wasn't exactly an expert on that.

"Your father was Scottish, as ye are. And ye'd best start acting it," Aggie said on her way out the door.

"Hmph." Catriona sat on her bed, slid the missive from beneath her pillow and re-read it. "*...love given and received in equal parts, with complete trust and without reservation.*" The solution rushed to her. "Elspeth MacBeal!" She leapt off the bed. "Yes, that's it." She would wager near anything that Brodie still loved his former betrothed, and likely, she loved him. "How will I find her?"

The answer came to her—the beloved image of the man from her sexual dream. *Torr!*

～)(ᘓᘓ)(～

Sir Torrquil Blackburn stared out the tower window. The orange-yellow sun hung over the Western Highlands and reflected off the loch below, but the rest of the sky was gray. He did not look forward to this night. He smelled a storm in the air, a violent storm.

"Here, lad. Drink this!" Finnian trotted into the chamber, his plaid robes flapping, and presented the vial with a flourish.

Torr eyed the violet-colored liquid. "What's in it?"

"Dinna be asking that." Finnian shook a gnarled finger. "I never reveal my formulas. Do ye wish to be cured of the curse?"

"Aye, but I dinna want to die."

But Finnian had already closed his eyes and begun chanting in Gaelic, his long white beard swaying.

Torr sniffed at the open top of the vial. It smelled like mint and some other familiar herb. Lavender? Thus far, none of Finnian's elixirs had worked any magic. But he was willing to try one more time.

Torr threw the liquid to the back of his throat and swallowed. It burned all the way to his stomach. He coughed and flung the empty vial onto the table. His stomach rumbled. Nausea welled up, growing intense. He ran to the open window, hung his head out and vomited into the garden. When his aching stomach muscles finally unclenched, the nausea was gone and a cold sweat covered his body. He washed his face and rinsed his mouth with water.

Finnian gaped at him. He might be a mediocre physician, but he sure as the devil was no conjurer.

"Ye're trying to kill me, Finnian. No more!"

"Pray pardon, lad. I didna ken 'twould make ye ill."

"I'll never be able to resume my duties as spokesman for Angus at this rate."

"Your brother loves and respects ye."

"That doesna matter. Plenty in Clan Blackburn would accuse me of sorcery or possession and kill me for it when their chief isna looking."

"Sir, I shall keep trying to discover the magic formula." Finnian bowed and shuffled from the room.

Torr regretted snapping at the old man, but dealing with this damned curse, he was near his wit's end. Should he be resigned to the fact his life was over and he would never have anything beyond what he had now? He stalked from the tower into the cool evening air. Thunder rumbled in the far distance.

He strode into the trees by the loch and removed his kilt and shirt. Daylight grew dim. The cool wind raised gooseflesh across his skin. When the sun dropped behind the high *ben* to the west, a whirlwind of rage and power spun through Torr. His body transformed into that of a white horse. Incredible strength infused his muscles. He galloped through the gloaming toward the loch. At the water's edge, he held his breath and dove for the depths. The icy water soothed his temper as he swam.

A while later, he waded onto the bank and shook himself. Lightning flashed nearby, followed seconds later by a crack of thunder. Rain pelted him. His muscles exhausted, he took what little comfort he could from this nightly ritual, the cool wind on his wet skin, the fresh flavor of the grass, much more tasty than the dried barley he'd eaten all winter. As for the cold, he did not feel it. He sometimes suspected he was numb in this form, both inside and out. After all, kelpies were heartless water demons.

※)(ʊʊ)(※

"And where do ye think ye're going, m'lady?" Aggie asked.

"Oh, blast." Catriona pressed her lips tightly together and scrunched back into the corner of the narrow servants' stairway.

The maid brought the candle closer and eyed her. "What's that on your face, then? Did ye tumble down a chimney?"

Catriona put up a hand to shield her face and the soot "wrinkles" she'd made. "I was cleaning the hearth. Could you have a bath brought up to my chamber?"

Aggie cocked her head. "And since when do ye clean hearths?" Her perceptive, beady-eyed gaze dropped. "What's that under your bodice and your skirts? Ye havena become that fleshy. Nay, this morn ye were still lean as a pike. Ye're trying to sneak out before the feast, aye?"

Catriona huffed. *Blast!* She hoped strangers wouldn't see through her disguise as easily as her maid had. Maybe she should take Aggie on the journey to find Torr. She was planning to convince one of the older stable lads to accompany her, but on second thought, Aggie would probably be a better choice. She knew how to wield a dagger.

"Oh, very well, you've found me out," Catriona said. "You must come with me."

"Where? And what's that on your teeth? They look rotten."

"Soot. 'Tis part of my disguise." Catriona carried extra in a tin box so she could reapply it when needed.

Her maid grabbed her sleeve and tugged her up the stairs to her bedchamber.

"Aggie!"

"Hush." She closed the door and barred it. "Now, what is it ye're about? Ye best speak quickly before I tell your mother."

"I must find Torr Blackburn for the sake of our clan." *And my own future.* "He will know where to find Elspeth. She must come back to Brodie, beg his forgiveness and rekindle their love."

"That whore what broke Laird Brodie's heart?" Aggie spat the words. "Why would ye wish them back together?"

"She's not a whore. He loves her, and she still loves him. I know it. And love is what breaks the curse that has imprisoned Brodie and his two friends since last year."

"The curse? Your mother demands such evil not be spoken of. Ye know naught of it."

"Yes, I do. The knave Alpin MacTavish wished his cousin Gavin dead so he could take over as chief of Clan MacTavish. Alpin and his four friends ambushed Brodie, Torr, and Gavin. Laird James MacRae died in the skirmish, and his mother, Wilona, took her revenge by placing a curse on Brodie, Torr and Gavin."

"Who told ye all that?" Aggie asked.

"Brodie. 'Twas only the curse that parted Brodie and Elspeth and caused her to run away with another man. But I heard that Elspeth was back with her clan. She is a relative of Torr's mother, so likely Torr will know where to find her."

"But ye dinna ken where to find *him*."

"I've been to Castle Dubhuisge three times. 'Tis only some twenty miles distant."

Aggie gasped. "Ye're daft! Ye canna travel that far. Your mother and the clan elders will forbid it."

"I'll not be asking permission and neither will you. If I don't do this—if I don't find a way to help Brodie break the curse so he can take over his chieftain duties again, the clan will go down the garderobe chute fast."

Aggie planted fists on her wide hips. "We'll go nowhere without asking your mother and taking several armed guards for protection."

"You will be my armed guard."

Aggie shook her head, her white kerch flapping over her brown curls.

"And if you don't—" Catriona paused, searching her memory for something she might hold over her maid's head. "I shall tell Mother about how you slip comfits and fine foods out for the villagers."

She pressed a hand to her throat. "Och! Ye wouldna tell her, m'lady."

"I most certainly would. And I ken you and Drury are lovers."

Aggie's mouth dropped open and snapped closed a few times. "Ye're a wicked lass," she hissed. "Naught but a hoyden."

"Indeed, you have the right of it." She pulled her brother's weapons from her pockets. "Do you think three daggers and a pistol will be enough?"

The next night, Catriona shivered as the squat, round man named Hamish paddled his little boat along the length of dark Loch Mirich. Thankfully, no storm raged this night as it had the previous night when she and Aggie bedded down in an empty cattle byre for wont of a more suitable shelter. Well, empty except for the dung. Now her aroma matched her grimy face—all the better for her disguise.

Despite the cold, she could not help but admire the full moon and millions of stars that glowed down from a midnight blue sky. She focused on the splash of the oars leaving the water and plunging in again. Catriona prayed no giant loch monsters lurked beneath, waiting to rise up and devour them. She forced herself to take a deep breath of air scented with fish and peat bog.

Aggie gripped her hand and scooted closer.

"'Tis all right, Aggie," she whispered. "We shall be there forthwith." She had not suspected her maid would turn out so fearful while away from home.

Hamish huffed as his arms pumped the oars. She'd told him she wanted to arrive quickly and would pay well for this service.

When they arrived an hour later, Hamish jumped into the shallows and tugged the boat toward the bank. He held a hand up and helped her alight. Icy-cold water splashed onto her shins and filled her shoes.

She released a short scream. "Blast! I didn't want to get wet."

"Pray pardon, m'lady. 'Twas as close as I could get."

"Grrr." *Gnarly little weasel.* Catriona dug into her pocket for the coin and pressed it into his palm.

"My thanks."

While he helped Aggie off, Catriona lifted the bottom edge of her skirt and squished onto dry land. She convulsed into shivers.

"Hurry, Aggie. My feet are so blasted cold now—"

Aggie grabbed her arm, stopping her. "What is that?" she whispered.

Catriona followed her gaze to a large white horse standing in the moonlight.

Hamish cried out a prayer and paddled away quickly.

The horse snorted, then pranced before them, showing off his long mane.

"How lovely!" Catriona clapped her hands.

"M'lady," Aggie whispered, her eyes big as saucers. "Is that a kelpie?"

"Nay. 'Tis but a beautiful horse. Someone's prized stallion who's escaped his stall. 'Haps he belongs to Laird Blackburn."

"And what do ye think kelpies appear as? Bonny horses. Look, his eyes are glowing green. 'Tis a kelpie, I swear. Come, lass! He will eat you alive."

Chapter 2

Aggie dragged Catriona away from the loch shore and toward a path that led to Castle Dubhuisge.

"Are kelpies real?" She glanced back at the white horse, now calmly nibbling grass.

"Aye." Aggie gasped for breath and slowed a bit. "Selkie's are real, are they no'? So why wouldna kelpies be?"

"But selkies are not a threat to people."

"'Tis how they differ. A kelpie will lure ye onto his back with his beauty and friendliness, then he'll dive into the loch and eat ye! Doesna matter to him if ye're alive or drowned when he has his meal."

"But horses do not eat meat or live in lochs."

"He isna a horse, lass. He only looks like one. Ye canna apply logic to the world of magic."

A stick snapped behind them. Catriona jerked around. The white horse stood close, watching them, his sleek coat glowing in the moonlight. His head held high, he sniffed the air and switched his tail. His breath fogged the chill night air.

"He's following us," Catriona whispered, now a bit uneasy because she hadn't heard him approach.

"Run!" Aggie grasped her sleeve and took off.

Catriona had no choice but to trot alongside Aggie if she wanted to keep her sleeve. "We cannot outdistance a horse!"

"If 'twas only a horse, I wouldna be running." She huffed.

"I ken that. But he seems biddable."

"Kelpies are unpredictable. One minute they can be sweet and charming, the next, in a violent, killing rage."

She shot a quick glance back but didn't see him. She slowed, then stopped, her eyes searching the darkness for his white form. A chill coursed down her back. "He's gone."

"We are here to see Sir Torrquil Blackburn," Catriona told the guard through the fifteen-foot iron gates of Castle Dubhuisge. Thank the heavens, dawn had broken as they arrived and now illuminated the massive beige sandstone castle.

"He doesna reside here," the man said in a harsh voice. He wore a belted plaid and leather armor, his hand on a sheathed sword at his side.

Catriona's hopes fell. Surely she hadn't come all this way for naught. "Where is he?"

"In old Blacktower, there. Beyond the wood." He pointed toward the remains of an ancient castle in the distance.

What? Why was Torr living there and not with his clan? She faced the guard again. "I thank you."

He bowed.

"I dinna like the wood," Aggie whispered when they neared the trees. "The kelpie could be hiding in here."

"Which is why we should make haste." Catriona tugged her maid into the dimness beneath the dense canopy of limbs. She shivered at the drop in temperature and inhaled the pungent smell of pine needles and moldy rotten leaves. They followed a well-worn path across the mossy, leaf-strewn ground and emerged a short time later close to what must have once been a large castle. It now lay in crumbled ruins but for one black stone tower left standing. Had his brother cast him out?

Catriona ran ahead of Aggie across a wide flagstone courtyard and up the steps to the wooden door. She lifted the heavy iron knocker and let it fall. Several times. Nothing.

"Oh, blast. Torr Blackburn! Are you here? Anyone?"

Moments later, the door screeched open and an ancient man with a white beard peered out. "Aye?"

Surely he couldn't be—"Torr?" *Please, God, no. Torr can't have been cursed into the form of an old man.*

He cackled. "I wish, but nay. I'm Finnian. Wait a moment." He slammed the door, almost hitting her nose.

"How rude." She turned to Aggie. "Don't you think?"

Her maid nodded, her eyes still round as she surveyed the area around and behind them.

"Stop worrying about the kelpie. We are safe here."

A distant bell rang inside the tower. A few minutes later, the door swung open again, revealing a lean but muscular man in a kilt.

"Sir Torr. Thank the saints!" She wanted to fling herself into his arms but curtseyed instead.

He looked no different than the last time she'd seen him almost a year ago, long chestnut-brown hair, intense pale green eyes that cut through a person, sensual lips, and beard stubble covering a strong square jaw. Her dream of him flooded her mind and heat rose to her face.

He frowned. "Who the devil are ye?"

Torr had seen these two women last night when they'd arrived by boat, but he didn't know them. The woman closest to him smiled, revealing blackened rotten teeth. Aside from that, he'd never before seen a wench with such a dirty face. And she smelled as if she'd been sleeping with cattle.

"I'm glad you didn't recognize me."

"Should I recognize ye?"

"I'm Catriona."

"Catriona?" Who in blazes was Catriona? The only one he knew was Brodie's bairn of a sister, and this hag certainly wasn't her.

"Brodie's sister!"

He drew back. "'Tis no' possible. She's but a wee lass."

She placed a hand upon her wide, lumpy hip and glared at him. "Do you have some water I could bathe my face in?"

"I dinna have time for this, mistress. I'm busy."

"Please. I have important news."

"Very well. Enter." Waving them forward, he gave her a scathing glare and pointed her in the direction of a pitcher of water. She was a lunatic, certain sure.

Once she'd washed her face and wiped her teeth, the woman faced Torr again. By the saints, she did look like Catriona, but a bit older, like a woman now instead of a wee lass. Surely she was not old enough to be grown. She lowered her cowl, revealing bright red hair, and pulled sacks of something from beneath her worn, belted-plaid *arisaid*. Holy mother Mary, she was good with a disguise.

He frowned, coming closer to examine her because she was lovelier than he remembered, her blue eyes multifaceted as sapphires and her skin smooth and creamy. "Catriona?"

"Ah, you remember." She smiled, her teeth now white.

"Are ye daft coming here alone?"

"I'm not alone. Aggie is with me."

"She's but a maid. Is she no'?" He eyed her, wondering if she too wore a disguise.

"Yes, but she only appears weak. She once fought in a battle alongside her late husband."

"Still. The danger. Outlaws roam about. They'd be overjoyed to find a tasty morsel such as yourself."

"Indeed?" Catriona's voice squeaked before she smiled. A flush crept up her neck and over her face. Mischief and interest lurked in her eyes, the kind that brought Torr's body to life and made him hard. Saints! He had been too long without a good swiving.

Catriona represented the kind of trouble a man liked. Och! But as a wee lass, eight years his junior, she had always followed him around, staring at him and asking silly questions when he'd visited Brodie. She was supposed to be a child, not this breathtaking woman. He could hardly reconcile the two.

"'Tis naught to be pleased about." He turned away, trying to smother his lust.

"Did you receive a missive from Chief Gavin MacTavish?"

"Nay. Would ye care for refreshment? Molly!" he yelled down the servant's stair. "Bring bread, cheese and ale if ye please." He again faced Catriona. "What kind of missive?"

"He sent it to Brodie, but since he'd been gone a fortnight, I read it." She held out a piece of folded parchment. "Gavin said he sent you one."

Torr took the paper and read. *The curse can be broken...love given and received....* "Is this genuine?" He examined the broken red wax seal. Indeed 'twas Gavin's seal and this appeared to be his handwriting. He had not seen his good friend in a year or more. The curse had come between them and sent them their separate ways.

"I couldn't find Brodie to show it to him," Catriona said. "He's off with the other selkies, at Ròncreag or lord knows where. We must find a way to break the curse. Brodie simply must come back and lead our clan. We grow weaker each day. And he can prevent me from having to marry the horrible MacPeter chieftain."

Something sickening and painful rose up within Torr at this news. "MacPeter? Ye mean Long Nose John MacPeter?"

"Indeed, my mother and the clan elders are forcing me to marry him a fortnight hence unless something can be done. I hate the toad. He is vile and probably a murderer."

"Ye ken him well, I see. But, according to this—" He rattled the paper. "—stopping Wilona MacRae and Alpin will no' break Brodie's curse."

"No. We must find him someone to love."

Torr snorted and shook his head. "And how are ye proposing we do that?"

"You will help me find Elspeth MacBeal and convince her to come back to Brodie."

"Are ye daft, then? He would string us both up. Last I saw him, he said he'd just as soon see her die as to have her touch him again, after her betrayal. Besides she doesna love him, or she wouldna have treated him thus."

"I heard that her lover sent her back home, so she is free." Catriona looked too eager by far. "She is related to your mother's clan, is she not? So you must know where she resides."

Torr shrugged. "Still, Brodie willna want to see her."

"'Tis worth a try. Our clan's future is at stake. My future is at stake." Catriona's blue eyes burned into him.

He had never met a lass with so much fire in her veins. He had to admit, over the past year he had lost much of his own enthusiasm and joy for living.

"Why dinna ye just steal Brodie's seal skin when he takes it off? That's the way to trap a selkie on land."

"I've tried to find it, but he hides it well. Anyway, he's not happy as a human, not so long as the curse is in force. He told me he yearns for the sea desperately and cannot stop obsessing over it when he's in human form and on land." Catriona eyed him curiously. "I understand you are cursed, too."

Torr nodded, hating the direction this conversation was going.

"How?" She lowered her voice. "Are you a selkie?"

"Nay. Ye dinna want to ken." And he would not discuss it in front of her servant.

"I do. We need to find a way to break your curse, too."

Torr turned away and paced to the large, cold stone hearth. Could he believe what Gavin said in this missive? Why had he not received a copy yet? And if what he said was true, by the saints, how would he find someone to love him that much? Love was for bards and poets and rarely came to pass in the harsh reality of life.

Molly, his bone-thin, middle-aged housekeeper, came up the stairs, carrying food and drink on a large wooden platter.

"Won't you eat, sir?" Catriona asked, her voice echoing in the high-ceilinged room.

"Nay, I already have. Refresh yourselves. Molly will help ye with whatever ye need. I shall return forthwith." He closed the door on the way out and strode toward the wooden stables he'd constructed a year ago. Inside, the stable lad was mucking out a stall.

"Billie, go to Castle Dubhuisge and ask Laird Blackburn if a missive arrived for me. If so, please bring it back."

"Aye, sir." The tall, gangly youth loped away.

Iosa is Muire Mhàthair. Was there hope? Could it be possible he wouldn't have to live out his life as a kelpie?

An hour later, Torr sat on a bench inside the stables, reading the missive Billie had brought back from the castle. *Love.* How would he find a love such as this? And why on earth would love break a curse that no other spell or magic formula would break?

"Torr?" called a female voice.

He stiffened, hoping she wouldn't find him. He needed more time alone to think.

Catriona stuck her head inside the door, her gaze locking with his.

"Aye." He held up the missive. "Here is mine. 'Twas at Dubhuisge."
She entered. "So you will help me, then?"

He blew out a breath. "Seems a fool's errand and impossible. We canna simply make Brodie fall in love with Elspeth. Or anyone, for that matter."

"I know, but I think he still has feelings for Elspeth. Perhaps he could forgive her. Even if we have to parade half the women in the Highlands before him, we must find someone he can love, who will love him back."

"'Twill be like trying to find a certain pebble in the loch."

She came forward, sat beside him and grasped his hand in both hers. "We must try."

Her voice was like silk, so feminine and light. He imagined she'd be able to sing beautifully. And her hands, so soft and cool…. He wished to feel them around something else. Desire flickered to life yet again in her presence and grew hotter with each second that passed. She had bathed within the last hour and changed her clothing. Her clean fragrance lured him.

She licked her full, pink lips even as she watched him. She had never been a demure lass who lowered her eyes before him. The strength and confidence, the challenge, in that bold stare made him want to see how far he could push her before she'd blush or run away. What went through Catriona MacCain's mind? Was that really lust he glimpsed in her eyes? She should be an innocent and not look at him thus. Would her mouth taste as delicious at it looked?

He leaned toward her, getting a deeper whiff of her sweet woman-scent. Her lips right below his, he brushed his mouth across hers. A lightning-intense frisson of arousal struck him.

"'Slud." He tore himself away, rose and stalked across the straw-softened floor. *By the saints, I canna do this.* Too many reasons—

His chest tightened. He swallowed hard, unable to believe how he yearned for her, his cock hard as stone. He should lay her upon this floor and fuck her long and hard. He knew she would not protest. Her eyes said as much. His hands itched to feel her soft skin and even softer curves. Breasts, hips…. It had been too long since he'd squeezed a woman's arse or slid his cock between wet, hot nether lips. He clenched his teeth to keep from groaning aloud.

Catriona didn't know what to make of Torr's behavior. He had almost kissed her. Or was that an actual kiss, that brief whisper of touch that made her heart race. Even now, she could not tamp down her excitement. *Why did he stop?*

He stood before one of the stall doors, his back to her. He was at once lonely and tormented, yet intense. As if he wished to tell her something. Wished to do something to her. Perhaps kiss her forcefully, or more.

Could it be possible he wanted what she'd seen in her dream, to bed her, to slide his shaft deep into her and give her that magical pleasure? She could not imagine denying him anything he desired. She now fully realized why she had been half in love with him for as long as she could remember. He possessed some mysterious quality that fascinated her, captured her mind, her soul. She did not know what. Those intelligent, expressive eyes that always carefully watched what was going on around him, but also held secrets. The edge of danger he exuded that dared anyone to challenge him, though she knew him to be honorable.

The memory of him sparring with Brodie a few years ago invaded her mind. The swordplay that had gone on for half an hour, much to the amusement of the clan. The way they had grinned viscously as they tried to slice each other limb from limb, neither succeeding or really wanting to. And the other competitions they and the whole clan relished in proving their strength or battle skills. She hadn't been able to take her eyes off Torr and his shirtless, muscled torso, glazed in sweat and dust. She kept waiting for some movement that would make his kilt flip up too high and reveal what he hid beneath it, but it never happened.

She forced herself to forget her own needs and focus on the true reason she'd come. But how could she convince Torr that finding a love-match for Brodie was worth a try? To do nothing meant certain disaster.

"You won't mind if Aggie and I stay here a few days, will you?"

Torr turned abruptly. "Stay here? At Blacktower?" The intensity of his darkened eyes remained wicked and a bit dangerous.

"Um, that is unless—"

He glanced away. "Aye, until I figure out what we shall do."

"You will help me, yes?" She wished she knew what tormented him so, what made that danger rise to the surface, and what form his curse took. Perhaps if he learned to trust her, he would tell her.

"I havena yet decided," he growled.

The next day, Catriona eyed Torr's rumpled clothing as he arrived through the front door of the great hall while she and Finnian were breaking their fast. Had Torr been out all night with a woman? Her heart ached. She dropped her gaze to the bowl of cold, runny porridge before her.

"A good morn." He bowed. "I shall take breakfast in my chamber, Molly." He disappeared up the stairs.

She noticed Finnian raise a white brow, his gaze flitting to her, then away. Hmm. Perhaps Torr's disappearance last night had to do with his curse.

Deciding to ask him, she rose abruptly. "Pray pardon." She ran down the stone steps to the kitchen. Tightly laid dark gray stone made up the floor, walls and ceiling of the large room. Heat emanated from the oven and cooking pit. She was thankful Aggie was occupied at the moment with laundry, for she would not like Catriona going to a man's room alone.

"Molly, I will take Torr's tray to him."

The maid set down the pitcher of ale. "Nay, m'lady, I can do it. Surely, ye have no' finished eating."

"I insist."

"Very well." She motioned to the tray holding porridge, bread, bacon and ale.

Feeling a surge of giddiness, Catriona grinned and came forward. Balancing the tray's contents, she climbed two flights of steps.

"Torr?" She waited in the open doorway to his chamber.

"Aye." His back to her, he wrote furiously at the desk before the window that looked out over the Highlands toward the west. His open books, scattered papers and ink sat before him. Abruptly, he glanced around at her.

"I have your breakfast." Catriona entered and set the tray on a bedside table.

"I thank you." For a few blissful seconds, his gaze held her in sensual bonds. His pale green eyes reflected a timeless, mystical quality. He returned his attention to his papers but didn't write.

She forced herself to breathe deeply. "What are you working on?"

"'Tis only translations of an ancient Celtic text."

Heavens. That sounded difficult. "Why?"

He waited a long moment before answering. "It interests me." He shot her a sharp, potent glance that stunned her for several seconds after he looked away again. His expression had been half warning, half anguish. Why could she not fill Torr's needs?

She was falling for him. Nay, had already fallen for him. Any time she'd been in his presence during the last few years, her heart rate and breathing had accelerated. Sometimes she grew lightheaded, as though she might faint. Even now, her whole body felt feverish, hot and cold at once.

She moved toward him, this man she'd loved even before she knew what love was. Tentatively, she touched his hair. Silky and soft.

He stiffened but said naught. Her hands shook with reverence and the thirst to explore him. She brushed her fingertips over his ear, the upper part of his cheek, the stubble covering his square masculine jaw.

His breath caught. "Catriona? Nay," he whispered, but remained still. He would not meet her gaze.

Look at me. She trailed her fingers down to his strong chin, the short whiskers scraping the pads of her fingers. Touching his lips snatched her strength.

Torr, I have loved you—

No, she could not say it. Instead she bent and pressed her lips to his. She knew not how to kiss properly, the way a man would like, but she wished to.

His lips pushed against hers a bit, then parted, his breath warming her. She kissed him again and did what she'd seen others do when kissing. She flicked her tongue against his upper lip. *Oh, that feels nice.* She yearned to taste him all over.

He groaned. "God's bones, lass. Ye're playing with fire." He tugged her to him and returned the kiss with more force, sliding his tongue between her lips. And then she knew what he'd meant. Her body was on fire, her lower belly, between her legs, an aching burning need. So overwhelming she knew not what to do next except hold onto him. They would become lovers. He would marry her. It had to be.

He surged upward, taking her with him to his tall height, and pinned her to the wall by the window. Her heart raced. He wrapped her legs about his waist and filled her mouth with eager and sinful tongue kisses. Oh good heavens, what would he do next?

Chapter 3

Torr pulled back a breath, breaking the kiss. "Ye dinna ken what ye do, lass." Warning gleamed in his eyes. Danger, daring.

Catriona felt him then, his hard, engorged shaft pressed against her sensitized crotch, their clothes preventing any direct contact. She felt inexplicably wet between her thighs again, just as she had after the arousing dream.

"Have ye been with a man afore?" Torr stared directly into her eyes, his gone dark.

Oh dear God! "You mean, in bed?"

His lips held the slightest smirk. "Aye. A bed can be used, but 'tis no' necessary."

She shook her head.

"A virgin, then." He lifted a brow, his look turning a bit scathing. "The virgin little sister of my best friend. A woman who is promised as bride to the chieftain of the MacPeter Clan. Are ye thinking I'm daft?"

She shook her head. All he said was true, but none of it mattered. She was his. He simply didn't know it yet.

His gaze bored into hers, then drifted to her mouth. "Saints! Ye tempt me," he rasped, and stroked that aroused male part of his anatomy against her crotch. "Ye feel that?"

She let out a breath and nodded. Oh yes, she felt him. Though she knew not why, her body craved him. Instinct told her he would give her the pleasure she had only dreamed about.

"I'm wanting to drive into ye to the hilt and fuck ye until neither of us can stand. I havena had a woman in months."

He wanted her? Heavens, she'd never imagined he would want her so badly. She slid her hands around his neck, into his hair.

"I want you to do that," she whispered against his lips.

He set her down then, roughly, and swung away to pace the room. She held onto the rough stone wall at her back, hoping her weak legs would not collapse beneath her. *No, come back.*

"Ye may have nay problem with my head being lopped off, but I do."

"No, Torr. I would not want to put you in danger. I—"

"No' one word more, lass. Ye shouldna have come here. 'Slud! Brodie will challenge me to a duel. I'm certain of it. I canna kill my best friend."

"He won't know. We have to find a way to help him, and you. That's why I had to come."

"Taking your virginity isna going to help either of us in the long term. 'Twill but drive a wedge in our lifelong friendship."

"I will not marry the MacPeter. I hate him. He is a stinking brute. You are the one…"

I should marry.

"Swiving me willna prevent a marriage to him. 'Twill only make your eventual marriage hell on earth when he finds out about it."

He said that as if it were already fact, an inevitable destiny. As if he would do naught to prevent it. As if he didn't want her. Of course he didn't. He saw her only as a daft, naive child. Not the woman who loved him.

She shook her head, tears stinging her eyes. "Nay. I will die before I'll marry him and be slaughtered at his hand." She approached the window. "I'd rather throw myself from this tower now."

Torr yanked her into his arms, her back to him. "Ye've gone mad. Ye're but having a fit of temper, aye? Trying to bend me to your will."

"I am not a child. And I do *not* have fits of temper." Why couldn't he understand? She couldn't even enjoy being held in his arms at the moment. She wanted to elbow him, but restrained the impulse. "Is it too much to ask that I wish to be happy?"

"Nay. Ye deserve happiness. But rarely does anyone get to choose the life they want, whether rich or poor."

"You wanted to be a knight and your brother's spokesman, and so you are."

"I'm neither at the moment. And I didna want to be cursed."

She turned, looking into his eyes. "Don't you see? We can help each other. I can help you break the curse, and you can keep me from having to marry MacPeter."

"'Tis no that simple." Torr guided her to a chair and made her sit. "Stay away from the window."

She wasn't going to throw herself out, but she was glad he cared enough to prevent it. She couldn't get enough of watching him, the way his body moved, sleek and graceful. And when she looked into his eyes, she saw his thoughts shifting and changing, a turmoil of emotions.

Each time she saw him she fell more and more in love with him. 'Twas not that she chose to feel this way. Something in him wrapped around her soul, binding her tightly, making her unaware any other man existed. Yet he was beyond her reach. How could she capture his heart, the heart of a brave, brilliant knight?

Torr avoided Catriona the rest of the day, saying he had work to do before they started their fool's journey to find Elspeth.

'Twas not a fool's journey at all, and she hated his pessimistic outlook. She would change his mind about her, and about the mission.

Finnian stayed locked away in his workroom for many hours, concocting a love potion they were to give to Elspeth. She and Brodie had been in love once upon a time, but now the magical potion couldn't hurt.

The next morning, Catriona waited outside Torr's bedchamber door. He'd been out all night again, doing lord knew what. Through the crack in the door, she heard sounds of bathing and changing clothes. If she wished to seduce him, this was as good a time as any. Drawing a deep breath to calm her racing heart, she entered his chamber without knocking and closed the door behind her.

He stood by his bed, naked but for holding the plaid before him, hiding his most masculine parts. *Heavens*, his body was glorious, the muscles of his chest and arms even larger and more defined than a few years ago.

"Catriona. Go," he commanded, his frown fierce.

Though defying his order took more strength than she knew she possessed, she shook her head and moved toward him. His sculpted arms, chest and abdomen mesmerized her. What a magnificent sight. She lifted her gaze to find him glaring at her, his jaw clenched hard.

"*Iosa is Muire Mhàthair*. Go now, lass, or ye shall regret much."

She swallowed hard. Her trembling hands clutched at her sides, she approached him. "Torr, I have loved you since I was a girl of but ten summers."

"Och. Damnation, Catriona, ye dinna ken what love is. 'Tis no' all flowers, kisses and sweets."

"I know that."

"Ye are an overprotected, spoiled, half-English bairn. Ye live in a dream world and ken naught of what is real."

His words pricked at her pride. Why could he not see she was a woman grown now? A woman who knew exactly what she wanted.

"Have you been in love before?" she asked, fearing his answer. What if he even now loved another?

"'Tis none of your concern."

"I don't think you have." *At least I hope you haven't.* She stroked unsteady fingertips over the hard, warm planes and muscled ridges of his chest. The dusting of hair and his male nipples fascinated her. A man's chest was so different from a woman's.

"Dinna challenge me this day, lass. I havena the patience for it."

"You said that you wanted to, well, you know." She could not make herself say that naughty word he'd said yesterday when he had her pinned to the wall.

"As I also said, I havena had a woman in months, and at the moment near any wench would do."

His words had the effect of a slap. Could he be so cold and heartless as to not care whom he made love with? Too late, she realized he looked into her eyes, easily reading her thoughts and emotions.

"'Tis the way of men. We are no' so selective as women."

'Haps that was true. Certainly her brother had a reputation for having lots of lovers.

"But I'm the only woman here at the moment."

He let out a long breath. "Ye want your brother or that damned Mac-Peter to kill me, is that it?"

"No. Never. Were he himself, Brodie would want me to be happy."

"I canna make ye happy, lass." His voice softened, as did his gaze. "I am cursed."

"Not if you—" She broke off. *Not if you love me.* But mayhap he couldn't. He did not care for her that much. "I will not go to the MacPeter without knowing what it would be like with you. I have wanted you, Torr, for a long time."

His jaw muscle flexed. "Ye dinna ken what wanting is."

"I do." She yanked his plaid away when he was least expecting it, exposing him to her view. Goodness, she had not seen a grown man's erect shaft before. His was long and thick and pointing up at her. It might have scared her, had she not loved him so much.

She swallowed hard again and glanced into his eyes.

"No' so sure now, aye? I didna think ye would be."

"Yes, I'm sure." Though terrified, she moved her hand slowly toward him and brushed it along his shaft. Hot, silky skin. She hadn't expected it to feel so hard.

He sucked in a hissing breath and almost closed his eyes.

She stroked her hand up, curling her fingers around him until she reached the velvety sensual-shaped head. It jumped. She jerked back.

He watched her, daring her, beneath half-mast lashes. "*Muire Mhàthair.* Ye torture me, lass," he said through clenched teeth.

"Does it hurt?"

"Nay! 'Slud!" He grasped her hand, tightened it around his shaft and stroked up and down. His eyes slid closed and he growled. He squeezed her fingers over the head, so tightly it must have hurt. But he moaned as if it felt good.

Moisture gathered between her legs. "I ache. Between my legs."

He cursed again, picked her up and laid her on the bed. "'Tis the ache of wanting."

"Yes, I want you." She stroked a palm against his cheek, his stubble rasping her skin. How she wished to kiss every inch of his face.

"Ye're a virgin, Catriona, the daughter and sister of lairds. Ye're an important lady, no' some tavern wench. Your destiny is to wed a chieftain or someone with a title."

"I don't care. I only want you, Torr. No one else. And I thought you wanted me."

"Aye. Of course I want ye. Ye've tempted and teased me without mercy."

"You like me, do you not?"

"Catriona—God help me—ye're so naive." He seemed at once exasperated with her, yet understanding.

"You can teach me. I wish to learn everything about making love with you."

"I have ne'er taken a virgin. I have a bit more honor than that."

"But I'm asking you to. I won't tell anyone. 'Twill be a secret." She wrapped her fingers around his shaft again, hard as stone. Her finger and thumb would not meet. She stroked around the base of the head over and over, loving the texture of him there and the way his breathing grew ragged. His gaze on her darkened, turned even more wicked and hot. His hips flexed once and he cursed.

Restraining his movements, he dragged her skirts up in a fist, then spread a hot, gentle hand over her upper thigh and hip. Brushing his lips against her forehead, he squeezed her bare derriere in a strong hand and moaned.

Her heartbeat sped up. He would do it. She saw a small glimpse of victory.

"I shouldna be touching ye, but God help me, I canna stop."

She explored the fascinating ridges of muscle in his chest and abdomen and inhaled his arousing musky male scent. "I want you to touch me. Make the pain stop."

"Och, lass. For a virgin, there is much pain."

She could not draw in enough air. "Why?"

"Because for my cock to fit inside ye, your maidenhead must be broken. This will be painful and ye will bleed."

"When will the pain stop?" Surely it wouldn't last long. In her dream, she'd felt no pain with the joining.

"I dinna ken."

"I can endure it." She squeezed his shaft again just the way he liked, noting his response.

He rolled her backwards, lay over her and kissed her. He nibbled at her lips, then explored deep, patiently teaching her what he liked. With his tongue inside her mouth, giving, taking and tasting, she craved another part of him inside her. Her ache intensified. She whimpered.

He was so delicious he made her dizzy. He tugged the neck of her smock down and brushed his lips over her nipple. A bolt of arousal shot through her and she arched to him. Her nipples beaded harder, protruding toward him. He rolled one between his lips, licked and suckled gently. Oh the pleasure of it! He treated her other nipple to the same bliss. She threaded her fingers into his hair, holding his head in place, the better to feel his stubbled jaw rasping against her sensitive skin, his demanding lips plucking at her nipple.

He raised his head slightly against the pressure of her hands, his eyes dark with need. "Ye are better than a bowl full of comfits."

"Make love to me, Torr." *Oh God, please now.*

"Patience, lass." He returned to suck at her other nipple, but this only made the hollow ache worse.

"You are too slow."

He lifted her leg onto his hip and slid his fingers further down her derriere, between her legs to the very center of her, where she yearned so badly. She held her breath, hoping he would end this sensuous torture. Oh, his fingers, stroking…. She could scarce think with the sensations ricocheting through her. One part pleasure, one part desperation.

"Mmm, ye're so wet."

"Is that bad?" She did not understand the moisture and was a bit embarrassed by it.

"Nay, 'tis vera, vera good," he breathed. "'Tis what a man likes."

"Why is that happening?"

"I think ye want me."

"I already told you that."

A small grin appeared on his face and disappeared. "'Tis a lubrication. Your body is preparing for me to slide inside."

She wished she were a worldly woman, someone Torr would want to seduce. "You wish to laugh at me and my stupidity."

"Nay. Ye are a joy, Catriona. Though ye dinna ken it, ye offer me a treasure. Ye humble me with your trust. I am no' deserving to teach ye these things."

"Yes, you are." She struggled out of her clothing and yanked her smock over her head. She had purposely not put on a corset this day.

Torr's dark gaze dropped to her breasts and stroked the length of her body. Though she was naked before him, she did not wish to hide. He tugged her closer his chest. Her breasts pressed against his hard chest. His fingers slicked between her legs, sliding along places no man had ever seen or touched. A burning madness came over her, possession, and she ground her pelvis against his. His enormous shaft pressed hard against her belly. She wanted him inside her so badly. She whimpered as she kissed his chest. "Torr?"

"Shh." He pushed her onto her back, spreading her legs, and crawled between them. He moved down so that he was looking between her legs, pressing her thighs wide apart. He spread her feminine folds with sure, gentle fingertips. "Mmm, beautiful." He lowered his head and put his mouth on her. His tongue, licking. She jerked with the shock of it.

"Torr?" she gasped. Oh dear heavens, what was he doing? Surely this was not part of mating.

"Ye taste like ambrosia." He sent a wicked glance up into her eyes just before he locked his lips around some especially sensitive part and sucked.

She cried out, not understanding the overwhelming sensations, yet craving something more.

He licked and ate at her as if she were a strawberry tart. He moaned and flicked his tongue into her just a little. Her hips flexed and she could not control them. She pushed herself toward him, yearning for something deeper. She wanted him to use his cock on her.

Her back arched and she clung to his pillow with her fists. God in heaven, she had not thought such intensity existed. She knew she loved him but this, this was more than she had ever imagined, even in her erotic dream. He licked at the sensitive spot, over and over, relentlessly, the sensations building higher and higher. She did not recognize her own body. It bowed up and some overwhelming, pleasurable sensation latched onto her and shook her. She screamed into the pillow, her body convulsing over and over. The pleasure would not let her go. She shuddered with it, all the muscles in her body contracting without her knowing how to control them.

Moments later, her breath returned in great gasps. And she was shocked at herself, shocked at how he could control her in such a way.

"Torr, what…? What happened?"

He raised up, smiling, and wiped the moisture from his mouth. "The pleasure. *Le petit mort.*"

"I thought you said it would hurt." *Liar.*

"The climax is most pleasurable. What will hurt ye, lass, is if I slide my cock inside your wee, tight hole. Ye have a maidenhead. I touched it with my tongue."

Heat burned over her face. Surely he was not supposed to say such things. Though she did not even know why that statement bothered her when nothing else did. "But that's what making love is. I am not sure what you just did."

He grinned and kissed her knee. "There are many ways men and women can pleasure each other. Did ye like it?"

"Yes. I never dreamed…." *Not about this.*

"And I never ate a virgin for breakfast before."

"Oh, you are awful!" The scalding heat returned to her face.

He chuckled and lay down beside her.

How she loved his smile. "Why did you stop? You have not yet—" She glanced down at his still engorged shaft.

"Believe me, I ken it."

"So why, then?" She stroked fingertips over him and found moisture on the tip.

"I'm trying to be honorable, but 'tis beyond that now, aye?"

"Indeed." She rose over him and kissed his chest. She did not understand why his scent hypnotized her, made her want to eat him up. He was scrumptious and she yearned to kiss every inch of him. Slowly she followed the line of dark hair that trailed down his stomach to his navel. She stared at his cock a long moment. His sensual musky scent was stronger here, and it compelled her to do something shocking. She kissed his cock.

Torr made a low sound in his throat. "Lass, ye are too bold by far."

The silky heat felt divine on her lips and she kissed it again. It was no more than he'd done to her. In fact, she wondered if she could do more. "I would give you pleasure, as you did me."

"Saints preserve me." Stiffening, he blew out a breath and pressed his eyes closed.

"Can a woman pleasure a man this way?"

"Aye, of course."

"Tell me what to do."

Torr sighed. 'Slud, how he wished she had not come here. How he wished she were not a virgin. How he wished many things. He had never seen or tasted anything as sublimely sweet as Catriona. If only he weren't cursed. If only he were a laird who could truly offer for her. But he had naught enough to give her a good life. And her promised to another.

If he took her, there would be no turning back. He could not fathom all the horrendous consequences of such an act.

After watching him a long moment, Catriona licked his cock, up along the length. The sight of her mouth on him made him want to come, but he couldn't. He closed his eyes and pushed the intense arousal away.

"Teach me what to do, Torr."

Saints! He had never seen such a hot innocent lass before. Clearly she already knew by instinct what to do. She licked the tip and the drop of liquid that had trickled out. He found that incredibly erotic.

He shouldn't allow her to do this, but he couldn't bring himself to make her stop. "Take the head into your mouth," he murmured. "Slide it in and out."

He braced himself for this. And when she did it perfectly—her warm, wet tongue caressing him, her teeth gently scraping the head—

the waves of pleasure almost ripped away his control. *"Mo dia!"* He groaned, took her arms and dragged her upward. His breathing harsh, he couldn't believe it when he felt his body tremble.

"You didn't like that?"

"Aye, too much." 'Twould not do to come in the mouth of a virgin.

Catriona crawled atop him. She straddled his lower abdomen and sat up, her sweet juices wetting his skin, her perfect plump breasts swaying over him. Och! He was near dying already.

"I once saw a woman sitting on a man, in much this way," she said. "But they were clothed. She moved up and down on him. At the time I didn't know what they were doing, but now I do. He was sliding his cock in and out of her."

"Naughty lass."

Maybe they could both have pleasure without him taking her virginity. "Slide down a wee bit." He pushed her lower, so that she hovered over him. "Now sit." The side of his cock slid along her wet slit and the head rubbed her swollen lips and clit. 'Twas almost like being inside. His rutting instincts were in a rage. But he couldn't ruin her life and endanger his own.

"Is this right?" she asked, thrusting her hips.

"Press down harder." When she did, he moaned. "Oh, aye. How does that feel?"

"Good," she breathed.

Just watching her was incredibly arousing, the feel of her. Her slick pussy lips sliding along his cock. 'Twas almost more than he could tolerate without driving himself inside her.

Pleasure built within him quickly, but he wished for her to climax again first. He licked his thumb and stroked that sweet sensitive bud of flesh.

"Oh, Torr," she whispered, her eyes closing. How he loved making her weak and giving her pleasure.

She cried out, threw her head back and shuddered even as she kept riding the side of his shaft harder and faster. He grasped her hips, holding her in place. His balls ached and he could delay no longer. His release rocked him so hard he could do naught to control his words or actions. Pleasure rushed over him like a burning wave of fire, consuming his thoughts.

When he opened his eyes and sucked in a great gasp of air, his seed had splashed over his chest. Catriona stared down at him, wide-eyed and slack-jawed.

One last aftershock of pleasure shook him. "Are ye well, then?"

She nodded.

"Did I frighten ye?"

"No, I just didn't know...." She stared down at the pearly white liquid.

"'Tis but my seed and naught to fear, especially since 'tis no' inside ye."

"Oh."

"Lie down." He urged her aside, rose and cleaned himself off at the water basin.

He returned to the bed moments later and tugged the sheet up to his waist.

"We didn't truly make love, did we?" she asked.

How could the lass be so innocent, yet so eager for carnal pleasures? "In a sense. But ye are still a virgin."

"But I don't want to be. If I am not a virgin, maybe MacPeter will no longer want me."

"Ye dinna wish to start a feud between your clan and his, now do ye?"

"No. But why must I be given to him? He is worse than a wild boar. I do not wish to lie with him as I do with you."

"Och." Torr stroked a finger along her face. How could he want to sink to the depths of pleasure with her again already? "Ye're beautiful, Catriona. Lovely. Sweet."

She took his face between his palms, stroked him with affection, searched his eyes. "Torr, will you be my husband?"

Chapter 4

"What?" Torr could scarce breathe.

"Will you marry me?" A hint of mist lurked in Catriona's eyes.

"Saints preserve us, lass. I canna do that." He pulled away and lay on his back, staring at the ceiling. Why did she not just thrust a blade into his gut? Offering him something he found he wanted to the depths of his soul, though he would've never suspected it before today. 'Haps her flights of fancy were rubbing off on him. He was ever a practical man.

She sat up and tucked the sheet around her breasts and under her arms. "You are a knight. Would you not rescue me from that brute?" Her eyes lured and persuaded.

What a wee manipulator she was. But since she was so transparent about it, he found it charming. Still, she needed to face reality. "When I say I am cursed, do you ken what that means?"

"No. You wouldn't tell me. Are you a selkie like Brodie?"

"Worse. I am a kelpie." His voice came out harsher than he'd intended. 'Twas not often he even said the damnable word for what he was. "I change form at dusk. At dawn, I shift back into a man."

Eyes wide, she drew in a quick breath. "When Aggie and I first arrived…." She swallowed hard, her gaze searching his.

"Aye, I was the white horse ye encountered on this side of the loch. Aggie was right."

"But kelpies are water demons who kill people."

"I have ne'er murdered anyone, and have only killed in battle or in self defense."

She frowned. "What do you do if someone leaps onto your back when you're in kelpie form? Do you eat them or jump into the loch to drown them?"

Such questions she asked. He shook his head. She had the same curious mind she'd had ten years ago. "No one has ever leapt onto my back. They ken better."

"Don't like to be ridden, huh?"

The teasing, playful look she gave him stirred his carnal urges back to life. He lifted a brow, wondering if he could resist her should she decide she wanted more sexual play. "Depends on who the rider is."

"Suppose 'twas me."

"And how would ye ride?"

"Gently. I would not dig in my heels nor use the whip."

He grinned at her silliness. "I would let ye, then."

"M'lady!" Aggie's voice echoed from the corridor and a knock sounded on the door.

Catriona hid beneath his bedcovers. He rose naked to stand by the bed in front of her.

"No' in here!" he called back and faced the door. "I havena seen her."

The door opened anyway and the maid thrust her head inside. "Oh, heavens!" She disappeared just as quickly.

⁂

"Be vera, vera careful with this, lass. Dinna break it." Finnian placed a vial of love potion into Catriona's hands.

She held up the glass container to inspect the clear liquid inside. "What must I do with it?"

"When you want the lady to fall in love with your brother, sneak a large dollop into her drink. I have seen it work its magic quickly. 'Tis potent. And if your brother needs any convincing, slip some into his drink as well. When both parties are given the drug, nothing can keep them apart."

"Sounds perfect." Catriona wrapped a short strip of cloth around the vial and placed it in the pouch tied at her waist.

"And dinna let it fall into the wrong hands or it could spell danger." Finnian pointed a finger at her.

"I shall be careful. I thank you for your help."

"I wish ye luck." The older man bowed and smiled.

She ran outside to join Torr and the stable lad who had just finished saddling two horses. Molly and Aggie followed with a satchel of supplies.

Aggie dragged her aside. "M'lady," she whispered. "I dinna approve of ye goin' off alone with Sir Torrquil. Ye must let me come along as chaperone."

"I'm sorry, Aggie. We can travel faster without you."

Aggie narrowed her eyes. "I ken how ye feel about him."

She hoped Aggie didn't know she and Torr had been naked together in bed yesterday. "Then you know I've loved him for years and I trust him with my life. He is a good man, the best and most noble I've ever met." *And the most delicious.*

"No man is *that* noble. Remember, ye are promised to wed another."

"Not if I can help it."

Though Torr didn't want to stop, the sun hung low in the orange-pink sky. He would shift to kelpie form soon. He glanced around at Catriona. Her eyes kept drifting closed and she'd swayed forward a few times. 'Haps he had ridden too hard and fast all day with few breaks, but he wanted this ridiculous trip over. There was no chance in Hades that Lady Elspeth would go back to Brodie. Not if she valued her life.

Torr dismounted and approached Catriona. "Tired?"

She nodded.

Clasping her narrow waist between his hands, he helped her from the saddle. When her feet touched ground, she stumbled, groaned and rubbed her derriere. He wished he could do that for her. She had the most firm, succulent arse he'd ever touched. And what she'd let him do yesterday…Saints! He still could not believe it.

She now gazed up into his eyes, her expression dark with wanting. With need. Arousal curled through him, and his cock sprang to attention.

I canna have her. I canna have her. He turned his attention to taking the saddle from her horse, and then his own, still trying to ignore her. But she watched him in a way no woman ever had. Except maybe her, when she was a younger lass. Far too young to think of in that way. She had irritated him back then with her legions of questions and useless comments. Not so now. She was beyond alluring, but out of his reach.

Though he was full aware of her every moment, he kept himself busy for the next half hour building a fire and unpacking supplies, including her bedroll.

She took out the food—bread, cheese and wine—and set it upon a plaid on the ground. She knelt and cut a slice of bread. Once he had bread and cheese, he seated himself on a rock on the opposite side of the fire. He would not trust himself near her. Simply watching her eat aroused him in a way no woman ever had. He loved the fullness of her dark pink lips and her tongue when she licked them. His thoughts drifted unbidden to when she'd licked his cock, taken it into her mouth. *Saints!* His cock hardened. He'd never before had so many erections in one day.

'Twould be so easy to take her right now. Certainly, she would not protest. He would but ask her to mount him where he sat on this rock, and she would ride him like a magical fairy-nymph from the wood, her long red curls glowing like flame in the sunset.

'Slud! He tore his gaze from her and fastened it on the horizon. Not long before he shifted, maybe thirty minutes. Then how would she view him? A beast. Would she fear him? Indeed she kenned what he was, but he didn't think she fully grasped it.

Catriona rose, came forward and sat beside him on the knee-high stone. Surely, she had not read his mind about how he wanted her.

Her sweet woman-scent reached him. He had memorized it yesterday, when he'd kissed, licked and sucked every luscious inch of her full, perky breasts. Nothing smelled or felt better. And even now he remembered the firmness of her beaded nipple against his lips, his tongue.

Feeling he was burning from the inside out, he swallowed a long swig of wine, remembered his manners, and offered her the bottle. She drank and handed it back.

Her eyes said things he wished she would keep to herself. She was so damned naive, she did not even realize he saw every emotion, desire and yearning skipping through her mind. When she rose and moved behind him, he tensed. She wrapped her arms around him and hugged him to her, her breasts pressing against his back. Though she wore a corset, he felt the roundness and wanted to rub his face against them. She kissed his cheek, her soft wet lips caressing his skin.

God help me.

He tried to remain still, but his head turned without his permission and his lips met hers in a half-sideways kiss. The feel of her mouth on his was delicious, sensual torment. She took his face between her hands and kissed him more fervently, flicked her tongue against his lips. His body was fully ready to make love to her for hours, but they had no time.

He pulled away and stood, trying to regain his normal breathing pattern. "'Twill no' be long 'til I change form. Ye should get into your bedroll and sleep. I'll go into the wood, and when I come out, I'll look much different. I shall stand guard tonight and protect ye. At daybreak, I'll shift back into a man."

She clenched her hands tightly and glanced about. "But when will you sleep?"

"I'm a light sleeper and I can stand up while doing so." He observed her jittery movements. "Ye dinna fear me in kelpie form, do ye?"

"Of course not." But her eyes said something else.

"I willna hurt ye."

She nodded.

"The time grows late. I'll be back forthwith. Sleep well."

"Wait." She ran forward and embraced him. "I thank you for coming along and helping me."

"Ye're welcome." He didn't have time to tell her how useless this trip was. "Stay here." He released her and strode into the wood, hating this damnable curse. If not for it, he might have had a chance of offering for her. But not with her promised to another. Regardless, were he not cursed, he could even now be kissing her and stripping the clothing from her body.

He removed his kilt, shirt and boots and waited for the time when day became night, the start of the gloaming. The cool breeze slid across his skin.

A scream echoed from back at the campsite.

"What the devil? Catriona?" He ran toward her but felt himself beginning to shift. He stopped and dropped to his knees.

Do not let anyone hurt her.

His transformation shot power and aggression through him. In kelpie form, he charged through the trees, his hooves kicking up leaves and digging into the soft black dirt. Seconds later, he emerged near the tent.

Two outlaws, one holding their horses' reins. Catriona swung a long dagger at the other. He dodged out of the way.

"Would ye look what a horse! That's the one we want."

Torr ran at the man attacking Catriona, reared up and flung a front hoof at him. He would kick the whoreson down and trample him if he had half a chance. The man screamed and fled. The other man already sat atop Catriona's horse. The attacker swung onto Torr's mount and they galloped away. Torr followed and easily caught up. Thirsting for revenge, he readied himself to clamp his teeth onto the man's clothing and yank him to the ground, but the bastard turned and struck out with a sword, missing Torr's neck by a hair's breadth.

He'd hoped the frightened horses would throw the men, but they sped up instead.

Torr could not leave Catriona alone long because another outlaw might be hiding nearby, awaiting an opportunity to attack her. He turned and galloped back to camp.

"Torr?" Catriona inched toward him, her eyes wide and curious.

He stopped and nickered.

"They stole our horses? Could you not get them back?"

Nay, I am but a kelpie. No' a worker of miracles, and no' invincible.

"What are we to do now?"

Are ye expecting me to talk, then? With his head, he pushed her toward the bedroll. *Go to sleep. We shall walk the rest of the way tomorrow.*

He was simply thankful the brute had not hurt her.

"You want me to sleep now? Are you daft?"

If he could've shrugged, he would have. *Sleep or no', I dinna care. Maddening lass.*

"That man attacked me. I shudder to think what he might have done if I didn't have this dagger." She pulled the long knife from a hidden pocket in the folds of her skirt. "I am fortunate Brodie showed me how to use it years ago to defend myself against men who would force themselves on me."

Indeed, I'm glad too.

Catriona kept up her nonstop blathering for several long minutes. Apparently she felt a companionship with horses, for he'd never heard her speak so many words all at one time. Or maybe her nerves had gotten the better of her. She told him how she felt about the damnable Mac-Peter, her mother and the clan trying to force her to marry the beast.

Funny, but Torr supposed he was actually the beast, especially at the moment. Forcing himself to listen patiently, he ate tough grass while she talked. At least he could get to know her better, considering how she bared her soul. She lay down on the rock where they'd sat earlier and stared up at the stars.

"Torr is the complete opposite of MacPeter. Torr is sweet and handsome and noble."

He perked his ears toward her. *What? Has she forgotten she's talking to me?*

"I could just eat him up like pudding."

She closed her eyes. Her words came out breathy whispers and somewhat indistinct, but he had better hearing than the average horse, and certainly far better than any human.

"Torr, you will love me, I swear it. I shall make you fall in love with me if 'tis the last thing I do on this earth."

Her words sounded so determined, they could've scared the wits out of a kelpie.

※⁜(ᗒᗕ)⁜※

The thick black iron gates that protected Kincreag Castle sent a chill of foreboding through Catriona the next afternoon as they approached. The top finials of the gates were fashioned like dozens of small battle-axes. She shivered. A heavy mist enshrouded the topmost towers of the castle.

"Is Cousin Elspeth at home?" Torr asked the warder. "Lady Catriona is an old friend of hers and wishes to see her."

Catriona forced a smile, hoping the guard didn't know how nervous she was. What Torr had said was almost the truth. She and Elspeth had always gotten along well when they'd seen each other.

The heavily armed man allowed Catriona and Torr inside the gates. Another escorted them into the large gloomy great hall to announce them. The scent of roast meats made her stomach rumble. The gentlemen of the house, chief's body guards and henchmen, turned from their discussion at the opposite end of the long room.

One of the kilted gentlemen came forward, smiling. "Cousin Torr! It has been a long time." They shook hands and walked away together conversing, leaving Catriona alone to mull over what she would say to her brother's former betrothed. What if she said the wrong thing?

A moment later Lady Elspeth, looking elegant as always in a finely woven red and green plaid *arisaid* over silken ivory skirts, descended the staircase. Catriona tried to assess the other woman's mood or thoughts, but her expression remained polite and blank.

"Lady Catriona." The blond woman curtseyed. "'Tis a pleasure to see ye again."

Catriona returned the curtsey. "You are looking well." She had always thought Elspeth incredibly beautiful with her platinum hair and snowy skin. She and Brodie had made a striking couple, her light to his dark.

Elspeth swallowed hard, motioned to a servant, and escorted Catriona to a private corner within the great hall. They sat in a grouping of chairs flanked on two sides by tapestries.

"What brings ye here? Is aught amiss?" Elspeth asked in a soft tone, glancing toward the men talking at the other end of the room. Her dilated pupils revealed a bit of her disquiet in spite of her great control.

"You are going to think this an odd question, but I wondered if you are still free to marry?"

"What?" Elspeth drew back.

Catriona rushed ahead. "If you are free, would you journey to Farspag with me?"

Her eyes widened. "Why? What of Brodie?"

"His health is well, but…." Catriona hesitated as she tried to find the best way to broach the subject. "He must marry right away. Rather, he must find someone to love. In order to break the curse."

Elspeth blinked rapidly and shook her head. "But he doesna love me any longer, I am certain. Not after what I did." Tears formed in her eyes. She dropped her gaze to her lap. "Heavens. I had so much. I dinna know what came over me to destroy it."

"'Twas the curse that caused you to go astray." Catriona patted her hand. "And now we need to break it. I'm guessing you are the only woman Brodie has ever loved."

Elspeth drew in a sharp breath and seemed to hold it as a kitchen maid brought wine on a tray and served it, along with tarts.

"My thanks," Catriona said, taking the goblet.

When the servant left, Elspeth shook her head and exhaled a choppy breath. "The last time I saw Brodie, he said that should he ever see me again, he would kill me."

"He would not do that. He loved you with all his heart."

"But no longer. I left with one of his enemies. I fell desperately in love with the man, but he tired of me during the handfasting, before the wedding ceremony was to take place, and sent me away from him. And I love him still. I couldna feel the same about Brodie now."

Blast! Catriona had to figure out a way to slip the elixir into Elspeth's wine or she would never agree to come along.

"Are you certain you won't try to love Brodie again? Love can break the curse. And I believe he would make a good husband."

"Nay. I'm sorry to disappoint ye," Elspeth said in a firm voice. She rose and avoided Catriona's gaze. "Will ye sup with us this eve and stay the night?"

"Yes. I thank you."

After Elspeth quickly strode away and up the stairs, Catriona searched the hall for Torr. He talked with the laird and his men on the other end of the great hall, their boisterous laughter echoing. When Torr's gaze caught hers, he excused himself and came toward her.

"What was the outcome, then?" he asked.

"She hasn't agreed to come with us yet. She has asked us to stay for evening meal and spend the night."

"I canna stay the night," Torr said in a low voice. "We need to leave right away."

"Nay. I will slip her the potion and she will fall in love with Brodie again."

He blew out a breath, appearing irritated beyond belief. "I will leave, then return for ye in the morn."

She nodded.

"Ye will be safe here. But dinna let anyone see the potion. If they catch ye, I'm no' sure I can get ye out of trouble."

※〜(ᚷᚢ)〜※

"Might I sit by you at evening meal?" Catriona asked Elspeth as everyone settled themselves around the hall full of tables. The bottle of potion felt heavy in her pocket. She tried to decide whether she needed to sit on Elspeth's left or right. Heavens! This was her only opportunity.

"Aye. I was sorry to hear Cousin Torr couldna stay."

"Indeed. He had business in the village." Catriona scrambled onto the bench at Elspeth's right elbow.

Thank God they were not seated at high table with Elspeth's brother. That would have made her mission much harder, considering the way the henchmen always closely watched anyone near the chieftain.

During grace, Catriona opened her eyes a crack and glanced around to see if anyone watched. Every head bowed and every eye closed. With trembling hand, she drew the vial from her pocket and dribbled a few drops of the love potion into Elspeth's wine. *Oh, what if that isn't enough? Just a bit more. A dollop. Blast! Too much.* She quickly recorked the vial and slid it into her pocket. Her stomach ached and she tried to calm herself. The hard part was over.

As the meal proceeded, the other clan members at their table, mostly women, observed Catriona with suspicion. She prayed they hadn't seen what she'd done.

The more wine Elspeth drank, the more her face and neck flushed. She glanced around, her blue eyes growing darker. Her breathing became erratic and she fanned herself.

"'Tis hot in here of a sudden, is it not?" she whispered.

Catriona nodded. "A bit." Though in truth, she didn't notice a change in temperature. Good heavens, how would the potion work? Would Elspeth have a sudden craving to see Brodie? Would she demand to be taken to him immediately? Catriona nibbled at her fish while secretly watching the other woman. *Please let everything work properly.*

Elspeth kept glancing back at the guard who stood by the door, a robust, kilted man. Why was she doing that? He didn't resemble Brodie in the least.

"Pray pardon." Elspeth rose from the bench, approached the guard and whispered something to him. Everyone at their table watched her, but no one else in the hall appeared to notice.

The guard cleared his throat. His rugged yet attractive face flushing, he signaled another guard to take his place. He followed Elspeth down the stairway that led to the kitchens.

Oh no! What is she doing? Catriona excused herself and hurried down the spiral stone staircase to the kitchen. She did not see them in the busy, cluttered room. Several servants worked, not noticing her. "Did Lady Elspeth pass through here?" she asked the woman nearest her.

"Aye." She pointed down a corridor beyond the far end of the overheated room.

Catriona did not want to venture in that direction. But she had to find out what the elixir was doing to Elspeth and why she'd asked a guard to come down here. Surely she hadn't fallen in love with him instead of with Brodie!

Catriona crept along the empty corridor. Hearing a sound, she paused outside a closed wooden door. Sounds of gasping came from inside. A woman crying out. Good heavens, was the guard murdering her?

She pushed the door open a crack and the cries and gasps came louder. She poked her head inside. By the dusky light from a tiny window, she saw Elspeth sitting atop the prone guard, his kilt hiked and his thighs bare.

Still fully clothed, Elspeth rode the man like someone possessed. "Mmm, aye," she gasped.

Oh no! Catriona's plan had backfired. How would she get Elspeth to love Brodie now?

The guard yanked up her skirts and caressed her bare arse. He bent his knees and put his heels to the floor and increased the speed of his thrusting. The guard's wet shaft slid in and out of Elspeth and his testicles bounced.

What have I done? Though Catriona knew she should not watch, she could not look away from the erotic sight.

"Oh, James, I love you," Elspeth said, and screamed.

Catriona jerked back and eased the door closed. *Blast!* Now she'd gone and done it. Her brilliant plan was ruined. Why hadn't Finnian told her how the potion worked? Damn the man.

I have to get out of here. She searched for the back exit of the kitchen and finally found it farther along the stone corridor. Twilight obscuring the details around her, she ran through the muddy kitchen garden, through the barmkin and toward the gate.

"Is something amiss?" a nearby warder asked.

She paused. "Nay. I but wish to leave."

"'Tisna safe for a woman to travel alone at night hereabouts."

"My traveling companion—Torr Blackburn—awaits me in the village."

The guard stood obstinate, scrutinizing her, his hand on the hilt of his sword sheathed at his side. Behind him, villagers passed through a small door in the wall.

"Stop her! She has cast a spell upon Elspeth!" a woman called from the tower entrance.

Oh dear God! Catriona dodged the guard and ran through the narrow doorway in the massive rock wall.

Murkiness settled over the land as she sprinted past the servants trudging toward the village. Shouting men followed. She glanced back to see clansmen with torches. Her heart raced and her throat burned. She hurried toward the wood behind the village. "Torr?" she screamed. "Where are you? Torr?"

A white horse emerged from the trees and galloped toward her, carrying something in his mouth. He halted and dropped a large bag at her feet. Their clothing and leftover supplies?

She picked up the satchel and looped it over her neck. "We must hurry! They are chasing me. They think I cast a spell on Elspeth."

He grunted and nudged her with his nose.

"You're too tall. I can't get on your back."

He trotted to a boulder and waited. Thankful he'd understood, she climbed astride his back and grasped handfuls of his long, white mane. He launched forward into a swift gallop, his hooves pounding across the earth. The wind snatched the cowl from her head and her hair came loose.

She glanced back, seeing the torches. "They're following!"

Chapter 5

The shouts of Elspeth's clansmen echoed from behind. *Hurry, Torr!*

In kelpie form, he flicked his ears and kept his gallop steady through the gloaming.

Catriona lowered herself over his neck, the cold early fall wind biting her skin. Torr veered off the road. She feared his hooves would tangle in the heather and gorse of the spongy moor. "Where are you going?"

She didn't expect him to answer, but when a large loch gleamed in the moonlight ahead, she understood.

"You're not going to jump in there!"

He made no noise, nor did he change his speed. The yells grew louder behind them.

"Blast! I can't swim!" She wished he could talk to her. Did he even understand what she said? Had he gone mad?

He launched himself from the bank. She held her breath as they dove into the depths. The icy water enveloped her. She locked her fingers onto Torr's mane, but the water lifted her off his back. Needing more security, she wrapped her arms around his neck and prayed he was a good swimmer.

The water roared in her ears, then drained away. Their heads rose above the water and she dragged in a great gulp of air.

Torr swam, his legs paddling wildly, toward the opposite bank in the distance. They moved swiftly across the surface. She didn't want to imagine the depth of the water beneath them. When they'd journeyed here earlier in the day, they'd taken a large ferry across this loch.

Moments later, Torr's feet touched bottom and he climbed the bank. She was too busy thanking God for her life to bother looking back or to wonder why she wasn't freezing to death. Torr continued his breakneck pace, galloping across fields of oat stubble and soggy heathered moors that stretched between craggy mountains. He jumped stone walls and thundered past startled herds of cattle.

Finally, when she glanced back through the darkness, she saw no torches.

Heavens, she had never ridden a horse that could run so fast. But then he wasn't a horse. He was a mythical creature. Kelpie legends said they were as strong as ten horses.

He slowed to a trot. Why didn't she feel chilled after going under that icy water? The heat from Torr's overworked body radiated upward, but that couldn't account for how she felt comfortably warm, though still wet.

Torr stopped at a stream for a drink of water, then continued on for many miles.

She woke sometime later, shocked she'd fallen asleep. What if she'd fallen off? Her hands ached from gripping his mane so tightly.

Through blurry eyes, she noticed dawn shimmering on the horizon.

Torr headed for a copse of trees and stopped. She dismounted. Her arse, back and legs ached. When she stepped away from him, she felt she'd suddenly slipped through a crack in the ice of a frozen loch. A huge shiver convulsed her body. She shrieked from the cold.

Torr moved his head toward her as if he wanted to be petted. When she touched him, the bitter cold evaporated. "Dear God, Torr. What magic do you hold?"

She stroked his muzzle and his forehead. He watched her, his green eyes glowing in the dim predawn light.

The wind that had passed swiftly over them dried his mane and coat. Her own hair was dry, but her clothing remained damp.

Torr nickered and trotted away from her.

She sucked in a hissing breath at the sudden chill. "Where are you going? I'm cold."

He stopped a short distance away and shook himself, then reared and neighed. Green light glowed around him, growing brighter, so intense she squinted, then closed her eyes against it.

At the sound of a man's groan, she opened her eyes. Where once the horse had stood, Torr sat back on his knees, human and naked.

Glancing around at her, he slowly pushed himself to his feet. He was glorious naked, with all those honed muscles. She couldn't stop staring.

"Well, I hope they didna follow us or figure out which way we came. Though if they show up at my brother's, I dinna ken what he will tell them. We may both be arrested for sorcery." Torr took the satchel from her shoulders and dug inside.

Pulling out his plaid and shirt, he flicked a glance at her. "Is aught amiss? Why are ye no' speaking?"

She cleared her throat. "I am, well…um…just trying to figure out how I feel about your being a horse all night and using you for transportation."

"Kelpie." With a dry smile, he yanked the white linen shirt over his head, covering his impressive muscles—and other parts—from her view.

"Yes, kelpie. But a kelpie is a horse, right?"

"If you say so." He belted his plaid about his waist.

"Did your clothing get wet in the satchel?"

"Damp, but 'twill suffice. Come, there is an inn nearby." He snatched the bag and took her hand.

She immediately felt warmer.

"How do you do that? Keep me warm?"

He shrugged. "I didna ken I could, until now. In kelpie form, I never get cold. Even in the midst of winter, whether wet or dry."

"You astonish me."

He lifted a brow but said naught. They walked a short distance to the old stone inn at the edge of a village. In Gaelic, the sign read, The Cock's Crow.

"Are ye hungry?" he asked as they crossed the rocky yard.

She nodded, loving the way his hand felt around hers, cozy and secure. She'd missed Torr—his human form—and she wished he'd kiss her. But he seemed impatient.

Inside the inn's dim common room, they ordered bacon, eggs, bread and ale from a serving wench. The scents of cooking made her stomach ache. She claimed a table at the edge of the almost empty room. Their ale arrived while Torr made arrangements for a room from the owner.

She sipped and the image of Elspeth riding the guard sprang to her mind. Such a forbidden sight. What had Elspeth been feeling? Catriona wished Torr would show her. Simply looking at him made her want him. Completely. Not just in sexual play. She wanted Torr to be hers in every way. And she wanted him to feel possessive about her, not send her off still a virgin to be married to someone else. He had to want her beyond all reason and she had to make him fall in love with her.

Catriona slipped the vial of potion from her pocket and poured a small amount in Torr's ale. She gave herself a wee bit too. Not that she needed any help falling in love with him, but she wanted the full magical effect. She plugged it with the cork stopper and dropped it in her pouch. A minute later, Torr returned and the serving wench brought their meal.

Near starved, she ate quickly, as did Torr. The more ale she drank, the more her blood heated like a fever from deep inside. She wanted to fan herself, but restrained the impulse. She glanced aside and found Torr watching her, his eyes dark. He had not looked at her thus since the last time they were naked together in his bed. The potion was working.

"I wish to go to our room now," she said.

"Your room," he corrected. "I have a separate one."

Not for long. "Would you escort me?"

"Aye." He stood abruptly and held out his hand to her.

They bypassed the chamberlain on the stair. "The bath has been delivered, sir. Chamber five."

"My thanks."

"Bath?" she asked as they continued on toward the room.

"I was thinking ye might enjoy one," he murmured.

"Indeed, I would."

He opened the door for her but remained in the hall.

Nervousness seized her. How on earth could she make a gorgeous, experienced and powerful man like Torr want her, love her? He saw her as naught but a silly lass. But she was more, so much more. His future wife.

"Please come in, Torr."

Giving her a longsuffering look, he entered and closed the door behind him. She sensed an undercurrent of arousal in him, but also caution.

Her hands trembled as she removed each item of clothing. Because of her overheated skin, she was glad to be rid of them, but still wondered what he thought of her. Would he find her tempting? Naked, she stepped into the tub of hot water, pretending she was an experienced courtesan.

Sitting and sinking into the heated bliss, she sighed. "Oooh, this feels so good." Her skin was far more sensitive than usual.

Torr observed her with dark intent but stood unmoving, still as a statue. He blew out a breath and tore his gaze away. The sound of his harsh breathing reached her. Was the potion affecting him as it was her? She ached for him. Sharp tingles covered her skin.

"Torr, would you wash my back?"

He turned then, a tortured look in his eyes, his face flushed and the front of his kilt noticeably tented despite the sporran. "'Tis hot as Hades in here." Glaring at the smoldering fire in the hearth, he removed his doublet. Sweat dotted his brow. He went on to remove his shirt.

"Are you well?" she asked.

"Aye." He opened the bottle of wine on the table, poured a glass and downed it in one swallow. "By the saints."

She bit her lip to keep from grinning.

He approached her, knelt behind her and stroked the soap over her back with his bare hands. "Mmm, ye have a lovely back."

Catriona smiled. "I've never considered it my best feature."

"Ye have many bonny features." He deeply massaged her shoulders and arms. Kissed her neck.

"Ah." She tilted her head aside.

He licked her neck, scraped his teeth across it gently. He washed underneath her arms and slipped his soapy hands forward to caress her breasts.

She leaned her head back against his chest and looked up at him. She kissed his chin.

He caught her mouth with his and kissed her, thorough and deep, with more passion than ever before.

After another kiss, Torr pulled back, frowning. "What have ye done to me?" He had never wanted a woman more than he wanted Catriona now. Arousal seethed through him and tensed all his muscles. He was nigh onto selfishly dragging her from that tub and taking her fast and hard.

She smiled up at him, deviously.

"What did...?" He stood. "The potion!"

"Aye," Catriona breathed, her skin rosy.

"Ye gave it to me?"

"And me."

"Damn ye, woman. Are ye a lunatic?" He stalked toward the door. "I shall find a wench." *I canna have her. I canna have her.*

"No!" Catriona jumped from the tub and caught the back of his kilt before he made it out the door. "If you do, so help me, Torr—"

He slammed the door and leaned against it, unable to close his eyes against the luscious temptation of her wet, nude form. *'Slud!* He could not draw in enough breath. His body felt on fire and covered with shivery tingles. With much pleasure, his cock yearned to slide inside her. Deep, hard, fast. Yet, he could not. What were the reasons? Virgin. And...what else?

"I should throttle ye!"

She unclasped his belt and let his plaid drop to the floor.

Saints! Touch me, lass. Touch me.

She patiently led him to the tub. "Get in."

"I dinna want to bathe. I want to fuck."

She climbed in after and straddled him. "You are a naughty lad."

"Aye." He devoured her mouth. Lifted her and sucked hard at her nipple. "Ye are a virgin and a lady. I canna have ye." He switched to her other breast. "I canna."

"You can. I give you permission."

She stroked his cock and the pleasure near suffocated him. He groaned, his whole body tensing with restraint.

"It seems even larger than before," she said.

"Ye gave me a damned potion. Ye shall pay for this, lass. We both shall."

She rose to her knees, kissing him. Her sweet taste, her soft skin obsessed him. Next thing he knew, she was pressing down on him, his cock prodding into the entrance of her virgin pussy. The heat. He mustered all his strength and tried not to thrust his hips. Such a battle with himself. But she pushed down on him, holding his face between her palms. He opened his eyes to glare at her. What strength and determination he saw in her eyes. The lass was bent on stealing his soul. Aye, she could do it.

"Catriona!"

"Mmm." She kissed him and tried to force his cock inside her wee passage.

"Ye're going to hurt yourself. No' to mention ruining your life."

"I don't care. It hurts not having you."

When her warm, wet nether lips surrounded his cock head, instinct took over. He grasped her hips and surged upward, lodging himself a few inches into her. He ground his teeth and groaned. God—the hot, tight feel of her! Surely this was heaven on earth.

She screamed and whimpered, locking down on him.

Saints, I shouldna have done that. "I told ye 'twould hurt."

She nodded, eyes filled with tears. "More. Do it, Torr." She clenched her jaw as if bracing for the pain.

"Och, lass." Heart aching, he pressed his eyes closed and tried to control his instinctive movements. "'Tis no' the way to do it." And especially, 'twas not the way to do it with her. Rising, he picked her up and carried her to the edge of the bed. "I shall try to make it easier on ye. Lie back. Relax."

She nodded and wiped at her eyes.

He withdrew, knelt by the bed and gently parted her sex lips, dark pink and wet. He had already caused her injury. Though he hated to see her bleed, such a sight awoke his possessiveness and made him want to do naught but thrust between those swollen nether lips again. *Ye are mine,* his primal side roared. And he was too aroused to consider any other side now. He licked his finger and stroked that wee sensitive nub of flesh that was swollen much larger than last time.

She squirmed and writhed on the bed, calling out his name. Moisture trickled from her opening. He rose and positioned his cock again to enter her. He regretted that this time would not be pleasure-filled for her, but next time.... He shoved into her quickly while she was relaxed and before she knew he would. Oh sweet heaven—her wet, tight heat— he wanted to ejaculate and fill her with his seed. He ground his teeth.

She cried out, her muscles squeezing him harder. Deep inside her, he held still and suckled at her nipples, teasing and taunting the little rosy tips. Nay, he'd never had a virgin, never had a lass so sweet and luscious.

A lass who loves you.

Did he love that idea or hate it? 'Twas foolish beyond measure, but he feared she was wrapping him around her wee finger. He withdrew and thrust in again. *Aye.*

Her breath caught and she moaned. He looked into her eyes, turned dark as night. Desire shone there, and more tender emotions as well. He tried to push deeper. She arched her back and though she was tight, her inner muscles relaxed a bit more. And the moisture, ahh, she was so aroused he glided smoothly. Though he tried to control his movements, they grew faster. The pleasure climbed. Her nipples poked against his chest, teasing him.

"Torr!"

"How does that feel?" he asked against her lips, between kisses.

"Wonderful."

"Does it no' hurt?"

"No. It feels...I don't know how to describe it. Like nothing else on earth."

Aye, he knew.

He increased his pace and she grasped his arse, digging her fingers into his flexing muscles, arching her back further, her head tossed side to side. He well knew what she felt. The same thing he did. A desire that was more insanity than anything. Lunacy and passion blended. And though he wanted to come, his body seemed resistant. The pleasure built and built. Faster and faster he thrust. He had never fucked a woman so hard before, and here she'd been a virgin, but now loving every second, crying out his name, begging him for more. His cock felt hard as an iron rod but incredibly sensitive. And every inch of her luscious passage caressed him, licked at him like an erotic flame.

He devoured her lips. Tears trailed from her eyes and he slowed.

I've hurt her. I'm sorry.

She buried her hands in his hair, holding his head. "I was made for you, Torr. I have always loved you."

Och! When she said those words to him, something he did not understand grabbed hold of him and punched him in the gut. Too many things he could not think of now, reasons he never should've touched her. But at the moment, he could not imagine resisting. Desire for her obsessed him.

"Catriona." Torr scraped his teeth over her neck and gently bit her earlobe.

"Yes." Catriona couldn't believe the strength of the sensations surging through her or that a part of his body was actually inside hers, bringing this magnitude of bliss.

That overwhelming pleasure claimed her again. And with him inside her, it was even more intense than the last time. She screamed.

The weight of his hard body upon hers, the way he held her down, his flexing hips, the strength and force—she loved it all. She was his now, and he was hers.

But one thing remained. He had not said he loved her.

He lifted himself up, pulled out and his hot seed shot onto her breasts. The way he groaned and stroked himself inflamed her arousal all over again. His breathing hard, he met her eyes and lifted her into his arms.

He set her in the tub once again and bathed her with soap and gentle hands. How sweet he was. But now he seemed reluctant to meet her eyes.

"I'm sorry I hurt you," he murmured.

"You didn't. I loved every second. I never realized the mating could be so...." What word did she search for? She had none.

"Aye, well. 'Tis no' always like that. The potion intensified it."

She closed her eyes. Why the potion? Why could it not be their special bond that fueled the intensity?

His wet hands stroking her breasts, her stomach and between her legs aroused her senses once again. A small moan slipped out.

Torr's wicked green gaze met hers, assessing. His interest appeared renewed as well.

He rinsed the soap from her body. She arose and pulled him into the tub. When he sat, she stepped out, knelt by the tub and bathed him. What an indulgence to touch any and every part of him. He watched her and his shaft hardened once again. Was that the effect of the potion too, or her? She slicked her soapy hand over it, washing her blood away.

"Mmm. Damned potion," he muttered. "I'm wanting ye again already."

"'Haps 'tis not the potion, but simply that you want me."

He lifted a brow. "If that be the case, ye shall ne'er see rest again."

Heat and happiness spread over her face. She grinned as she rinsed the suds from his body.

"Like that, aye?"

She nodded.

He tugged her forward and kissed her, his tongue flicking over her lips and into her mouth. He moaned and made the tongue play even more erotic. Once he released her from this sensual spell, she stood, took his hand and urged him up. Water drained from his hard-angled body, and she blotted it away with a strip of linen cloth. She led him to the bed.

"'Tis too soon. Ye must be sore."

She shook her head, unable to imagine stopping now. She wished to enjoy him for the rest of the day.

Hours later, the noise of the door opening and closing awoke Catriona. She peered out from under the covers.

"Good eve, m'lady." Torr set a tray of steaming food on the bedside table. "'Tis almost sundown and I must return to the wood. After ye eat, dress and meet me there and we shall travel on to Blacktower tonight."

She sat up. "You wish me to ride you again?"

A grin appeared on his face and vanished just as quickly. He handed her a cup of ale. "Aye. Turns out 'tis the fastest way to travel since we have no horses."

"You need to wear a bridle."

He frowned.

"In horse form."

"Nay, I dinna like bridles."

"But I feared I'd hurt you holding onto your mane so tightly."

"It didna hurt. In fact, as a kelpie I dinna feel much pain, cold or anything unpleasant."

"Very well, then. Whatever you wish." The sheet wrapped around her, she slid to the edge of the bed and took a bite of the mutton stew. Delicious. She hadn't realized she was so hungry.

She glanced up to find Torr watching her intently with that slight frown. "Why do bridles disturb you so much?"

"'Tis something no kelpie likes."

"Hmm. Do you know many other kelpies?"

"Nay. None. But I have read stories of others."

She had a feeling he wasn't telling her everything. She wished he would sit by her on the bed, kiss her sweetly, make love to her. But he seemed far away.

She sighed and forced her mind to their mission. "Well, Elspeth is not the one to break Brodie's curse."

"Did I no' tell ye?"

Torr looked so superior she wanted to throw a bannock at him. "Indeed, oh wise one. Not only is she in love with *James*, the guard, but she said she still has feelings for the man she left Brodie for." Catriona took a big bite of tough oat bannock and chewed while she tried to think of women who had come to Farspag that Brodie might have liked. "Where shall we find him a woman?"

Torr shook his head, looking irritable again.

"You and Brodie used to travel about together. Surely there was a woman somewhere he showed interest in."

"Brodie showed interest in every wench we encountered between the ages of fifteen and fifty."

She snorted. "You jest."

"No' by much." He glanced out the window. "The gloamin' is drawing close. In a half hour, meet me in the wood where I shifted this morn."

She nodded, wondering why he seemed displeased about something. She waited for him to kiss her, but he abruptly turned and slammed out the door.

"Hmph." What had his plaid in a twist?

Chapter 6

Torr woke slowly, realizing he was not in his bed alone. A warm, tempting female—Catriona, of course—pressed her plump breasts against him and placed kisses on his chest. Her red hair gleamed in the sunlight beaming through the window. Thankfully, last night's travel had passed smoothly. They arrived at Blacktower, ate and went to bed in separate rooms only hours earlier. How had Catriona eluded Aggie's watchful eye and slipped into his chamber?

"Mmm." He drifted, half dozing, enjoying the feel of her while his erection grew. He had not wakened so pleasantly in ages. He smoothed his hand down her naked back to her derriere and squeezed. He would definitely have sweet dreams with something so luscious cradled in his hand.

The door burst open. "Torr!"

Catriona let out a yelp and covered her head.

Saints! Torr lifted his head and glared toward Finnian.

The old man's mouth gaped within his white beard. He pushed the door closed. "What have ye done, lad?" he asked in a loud whisper.

"'Slud," Torr muttered. "She gave me your damned potion." *Yesterday.* The effects should have worn off by now, but he could not stop tupping her. Especially when she seduced him at every turn.

"Ah." Finnian grinned. "The potion works, aye?"

"It arouses lust, if that's what ye mean. Did ye need something?"

"Aye. I've had a vision."

Torr frowned. "More than half your visions amount to naught."

"But this one is real. I feel it in me auld bones. Wilona MacRae and her minion have taken over a manor house and killed the owner. She has a *keek-stane* that ye must steal."

"What the devil is a *keek-stane*?"

"'Tis a scrying-stone, much like a crystal ball, except 'tis almost flat. In this *stane*, I shall see the faces of the two women who will break the curse for ye and for Brodie." Finnian sent him a proud, toothless grin.

"I dinna—"

An unintelligible exclamation came from beneath the counterpane.

Catriona uncovered her head and sat up, her long red curls tousled over her face. "Indeed?" she demanded, shoving her hair back. "We must retrieve it!"

Torr snorted. "She may no' even have a scrying-stone."

"Aye, she does. I tell ye true, lad," Finnian said.

"And what's to stop her from cursing me worse than I already am, or Catriona?"

"I shall place a spell of protection upon ye both."

Torr scowled. Finnian had been trying to break Wilona's spell for a year and had not succeeded yet.

"I'll let ye dress now so ye may prepare for your trip." Finnian bowed and left.

Torr growled and rubbed his face. Catriona sprang from the bed, flinging on clothes in a blur.

"Ye put too much stock in the auld man's visions. Half the time they are so far off the mark—"

"I don't care. I must use any opportunity to break Brodie's curse. If you don't care that you are yourself cursed, so be it."

"I care that I'm cursed, believe me. But naught Finnian has done for the last year has worked. Why should this?"

"Because I'm involved now."

"Och! Ye think ye're the magic ingredient then?"

Her eyes lit up. "I know I am."

He let out a breath and shook his head. A woman of much confidence. How irritating.

Though he could not get excited about the coming trip, he dragged himself from the bed and washed his face in the basin.

"Why are you always speaking gloom and darkness? Why can you not see the good side of things?" Catriona stood at his back and stroked his bare arse while he dried his face. "Gavin's curse is broken and so may yours and Brodie's be."

"Aye. I just dinna wish to have high hopes only to be disappointed again."

"Believe." She walked away from him and began packing a bag.

That word was easy to say. Harder to carry out.

"Finnian, what does the *keek-stane* look like?" Catriona asked, standing in his cluttered workroom an hour later. She didn't see how he found anything in here. She had no inkling what half the devices and tools were. One wall of the room appeared to be a disorganized apothecary with jars of different colors of powders, leaves and roots.

Finnian turned from his task and eyed her through his spectacles.

"'Tis an almost clear, glass-like stone shaped like a very shallow bowl. The back of it is black. 'Tis about five inches in width and stored in a carved wooden box lined with red velvet. I saw it in my vision. Wilona calls it her crystal ball, but it is no' ball-shaped. Once ye take the *keek-stane*, Wilona's powers will be weakened. She willna be able to see into the future or locate people."

"We will bring it back for you. I'm determined."

"I've no doubt. I've already given Torr directions. Ye must be most careful." He handed her a coil of strong brown rope. "Tie Wilona Mac-Rae up with this. 'Tis a special rope. And before ye leave, I'll place a spell of protection upon both ye and Torr."

"My thanks." She turned to leave.

"So...ye gave Torr some of the love potion, eh?"

Heat suffused her cheeks, but she again faced him. "Aye, and myself."

He lifted a bushy white brow and waited. He had removed his spectacles and his piercing blue eyes surveyed her.

"If Torr would but love me, his curse would be broken too," she whispered.

"Ye already love him, lass?"

"I have for years."

He grinned. "Well, then. I shall help ye. When ye return, if 'tis your visage I see in the *keek-stane* as Torr's mate, he won't have a chance of escaping ye or his destiny."

A thrill shot through her. "You'll give me more of the potion?"

"If ye want it. But I dinna think ye'll be needing it."

※ ᘓ(ʊ̈)ᘔ ※

The next day, Torr waited with Catriona outside the two-story stone manor house, gazing toward the wooden gate and high rock wall. Finnian's directions had been flawless. Amazing. Torr had rarely if ever known him to be so accurate. But it remained to be seen whether the rest of his prophecy proved true. They had left at sunset, him in kelpie form and Catriona mounted upon his back. He'd found it the most effective way of traveling with her, but he was now in need of sleep.

"How do we get inside?" Catriona asked.

"Ye are good at asking questions," Torr said. Indeed she had not ceased her questions since he had shifted that morn. He was tired of one useless errand after another. As of yet, naught had led one step closer to breaking the curse, for him nor for Brodie.

"And you are good at not answering them. Why are you angry with me?"

"I'm no'." He glanced at her displeased expression, her blue eyes slightly hurt. Maybe he was unusually surly today. He would try to be nicer. In truth, he'd rarely been in a good mood since being turned into a kelpie.

"You simply enjoy being a horse's arse?" she asked.

"Interesting choice of words."

"Seemed to fit." She shrugged and flipped her hair over her shoulder.

He wanted to run his fingers through those fiery silken curls. He'd gone against his own rationality and succumbed to his lust for her. He was angry with himself, irritated beyond measure. He'd ruined her life and likely struck his own deathblow. When this was over and the dust cleared, at least two people would hunt him down with swords.

"Wilona doesn't know who I am, so maybe I could pretend to be a maid in need of work."

He shook his head. "She will see past the facade."

"Then what do you suggest, oh wise one?"

He gave her a sidelong glance. She had one impertinent little mouth. One he'd like to spend the day exploring...or watching her use on him. Sliding his cock inside her mouth, watching her lick the head. He hardened fully and covered his moan with a cough.

"Ye must stay out here," he said, trying to focus on the issue at hand. "I'll slip inside through a window or back door, tie them up and take the stone. If I have to kill Alpin MacTavish, so be it. I owe him anyway. He tried to kill me last year. The whoreson left me for dead."

"Did he, in truth?"

"Aye. When he and his five friends ambushed Gavin, Brodie and me, they fired pistols at us first. Then came out with swords. Alpin cut my left arm deep." Torr motioned toward the upper part of his arm. "I lost much blood. If no' for Finnian, I would've surely died."

"Why did they attack?"

"Brodie didna tell ye?"

"Well, yes, but I'd like your side of the story."

"Alpin is Gavin's cousin and next in line to be chief of the MacTavish clan. So he wished to remove the obstacle."

"They must be stopped. I'm going in with you. We're a team." She pulled one of Brodie's daggers from a sheath on her belt. It did not look right in her hand. She was too soft and delicate to fight with weapons.

"Very well, ye can go, but let me do the fighting. Wilona must be gagged so she canna speak any more spells upon us while we're here. Stay away from Alpin at all costs. He is dangerous, especially to beautiful young lasses."

Catriona smiled, all sweet and blushing. "You think me beautiful?"

"Aye. Now, let's go." Torr strode forward and kicked the latch of the small door in the wall. The wood splintered, apparently half rotten. He checked inside before motioning her forward. She was ever standing too close, brushing up against him. Even her female, floral scent distracted him. Not good in this dangerous situation. He found a window low to the ground, broke it, climbed inside, and helped Catriona inside.

"We find Wilona first, tie her up and gag her," he whispered. "I shall deal with Alpin after."

All was silent on the ground floor. He motioned her to follow him up the wooden staircase. The doors to the rooms they passed stood open, but the door at the end of the narrow corridor was closed. He turned the knob, eased the door open, and stuck his head inside. The scent of stale wine was thick in the air.

Two forms lay upon the bed. Torr crept closer, sword in hand, and could not believe what he saw. Wearing only a long, red wine-stained shirt, Alpin lay asleep on the bed, his wrists and ankles tied to the headboard and footboard, a gag in his mouth. Perfect. Torr grinned, wondering what on earth Wilona had done to him.

Wearing a smock and half covered with a blanket, Wilona snored beside him. Two empty wine bottles sat on the bedside table. Now they had to but tie her up.

After motioning to Catriona, who carried the rope, Torr laid his sword on the floor at the foot of the bed. In a swift motion, he flung Wilona onto her stomach, imprisoned her legs between his, and dragged her hands behind her back. She screamed, but he pressed her face into the pillow while he tied her wrists with a length of the magical rope. He wadded a piece of cloth, crammed it into her mouth, then tied another strip of cloth over it and behind her head.

Catriona tied her ankles with the remaining rope. He checked to make sure it was tight enough.

Wilona moaned and twisted about. Alpin mumbled and thrashed.

Catriona searched the room, throwing clothing out of her way.

"Where is the scrying-stone?" Torr asked Wilona. "Look in the direction of it."

She merely glared at him, evil emanating from her eyes.

"I dinna fear ye, bitch. I ken Gavin bested ye and broke the curse."

She squirmed like a snake. Even her very skin seemed to crawl. Her face contorted and she made a vile guttural, groaning sound. Her eyes turned black. Damnation, maybe he should fear her. He snatched his sword, moved across the room and started searching in a chest. He was tempted to kill her while he could, but according to the curse, if Wilona died, he'd remain a kelpie forever. He did not know the truth of that, but he would not chance it.

A puff of smoke burst from the bed. Only the ropes remained.

'Slud! Where had she gone? Something black swooped toward his head. He ducked and peered about the ceiling. A damned bat. "Catriona, hurry. Wilona has shifted."

"Here it is!" She held up the scrying-stone inside an open carved box. She closed it back and crammed it into her satchel.

"Good. Come!" He ushered her down the stairs and along the corridor toward the broken window. Catriona climbed out first, her skirts snagging on the remaining glass shards. He released the material and followed. The bat fluttered out the window and dove toward his head. He flung a hand up and knocked the varmint into a bush. Once through the broken door, he grabbed Catriona's hand and they raced toward the wood.

Several hundred yards distant, he slowed and looked back. "I dinna see them following yet, but they will."

Catriona breathed hard and held a hand to her side. Her eyes shown with excitement and a small grin appeared. "That was fun."

Was the lass daft? "I can tell ye've ne'er been the target of a witch of the Dark Arts. 'Tis no' always so much fun. And I dinna ken why I trusted Finnian's damnable ropes to work."

Her smile vanished and he regretted his harsh words to her. Indeed, he loved her smile and wanted to see it more often. "Come. 'Tis several hours yet before sunset. We dinna want them to catch up to us before then."

❦

"Wilona can shift into a bat, as ye saw, or any sort of flying creature she wishes—a raven, a hawk," Torr said hours later. He strode quickly along the rocky trail, dragging Catriona behind him. "She can also turn Alpin into anything she wants. Which means they could find us at any time."

"But I'm starving!" Catriona yanked at his hand. "Just give me a crust of bread, an old bannock. Anything. Even if the witch doesn't kill me, my hunger will."

Could a lass be any more spoiled than she was? He doubted it intensely.

"Torr, you knotty-pated varlet, do you want me to starve to death?"

He snorted, trying not to laugh at her ridiculous insults. "Very well." He paused and turned. "We shall stop for a few minutes." They had crossed onto his clan's land a short time ago, though that was no guarantee of safety.

"Thank God!" Sighing dramatically, she plopped onto the ground beneath a tree.

Torr dug into the satchel he carried and withdrew food—day-old bannocks, hard yellow cheese wrapped in cloth, and a flask of wine. He sat opposite her on the grass.

After they'd eaten in silence a few minutes, Catriona slid him a lusty glance. 'Twas not food she was starved for now.

Beneath his plaid, Torr's cock rose to the occasion but—he glanced about—this was not the place in the wide open, not far from a well-traveled trail. His eyes sought out the bushes close by. They would provide sufficient privacy for swiving.

'Slud, he should not be planning such a thing. A witch was on their tail. He glanced back at Catriona, meeting her dark, interested eyes.

"I am still feeling the aftereffects of the potion," she said in a husky voice.

"Wait a minute—the wine! Was it drugged?" he demanded.

Frowning, she shook her head. "I don't know. I didn't do it."

He shoved to his feet. "Finnian. Damn his weather-bitten hide. He is plotting against me."

Aye, now his body's heated, lusty response was more evident, just as it had been two days before when she'd slipped him the potion.

Catriona rose and joined him. She slid her hand around his neck, brought his head down and kissed him.

"'Tis no' safe here," he muttered between kisses.

"We have Wilona's *keek-stane*. She will not know where to find us. Finnian said taking it from her would weaken her powers and blind her to the future and the location of people."

"'Haps ye're right. Just a wee tumble." Torr tugged her toward the dense bushes a short distance away.

Catriona wanted him in every way. Holding her, he kissed her while snatching his sword from its sheath and the pistol from his belt. He lowered her to the ground, appearing near out of control. Muttering curses, he pushed up her skirts along with his kilt. He stroked his cock between her sex lips.

"Mmm. Ye're wet," he whispered.

"I want you. Now."

He pushed in gently.

Nothing in her life had ever felt so good as him inside her. Finally, she felt she belonged somewhere. When Torr was loving her, she belonged with him.

He flexed his hips, forcing his cock deeper.

"Yes," she hissed and arched her back off the rocky ground. His invasion, though still not comfortable, was nevertheless exquisitely erotic. She was becoming addicted to him.

He withdrew slightly and pushed back in, sparking pleasurable yearning.

"Oooh, feels so good," she breathed.

"Catriona," he moaned.

She whimpered and squirmed. "Yes, give me a good swiving and do it quick."

He pinned her to the ground and thrust in long strokes. She kissed his face and encouraged him.

Deep inside her, he stopped abruptly and turned his head. "Shh."

"What?" she whispered.

"I tell ye, mon, I heard somethin' o'er here. A woman crying out." The male voice came from beyond the bush.

She froze. Good heavens, who was that?

Torr snatched his pistol from the ground and pointed it toward the sound of footsteps.

Chapter 7

Catriona tried to wriggle from underneath Torr, but he held her in place with a hand to her shoulder.

"Be still," he whispered.

"But...." Was he daft? They couldn't continue, could they? The footsteps drew closer. *Saints!* She covered her face with her hands and peeped between her fingers.

"Well, if it ain't a—" The shabbily dressed young man cursed in Gaelic and froze, looking down the barrel of Torr's pistol. "Sir Torr?"

"I suggest ye walk away and forget ye saw us if ye wish to keep your head," Torr said.

The youth backed up, slamming into his friend. They turned and ran.

Her face burned so hot it ached. "Are they gone? Do you know them?"

"Aye. Members of our clan. Sons of crofters." Torr watched through the leaves, his eyes narrowed. Danger emanated from him.

She again tried to move from beneath him.

"Where are ye going then?" He returned his attention to her and flexed his hips.

"Surely we cannot. Is the mood not ruined?"

"Apparently no'." His firm cock still deep inside her moved only slightly, just a twitch, growing harder. "Naught stops that damned potion. Or 'haps 'tis a kelpie trait I was ne'er aware of."

His brief thrust set all her nerve endings ablaze. "Oh." She wiggled her hips, wanting more.

He laid his pistol aside and focused on her intently. At first his strokes were long and slow. Gradually he increased the pace, so fast she could only hang on and enjoy the ride. Convulsions of pleasure latched onto her several times. Though sure she could take no more, she wanted more when he gave it.

When it seemed he could thrust no harder, he paused deep, threw his head back and groaned as if in pain. But she knew it was pleasure, despite his frown.

He had released his seed inside her. He had said before that he shouldn't do that, but strangely she was glad he had. He would be her husband, and this was the first step.

After a few seconds, he muttered Gaelic curses and gave her a brief look of regret. "I should no' have—"

She placed a finger over his lips and kissed him. "I want you, Torr, and everything you have to give."

He pressed his eyes closed and kissed her, but withdrew. When he opened his eyes, the look in them was tortured. He pressed a quick kiss to her lips and lowered their clothing into place as he rose. "Ye're too good for me. Far too good."

How could he say such a thing? She had to convince him they were made for each other.

⚜

When Catriona and Torr arrived back at Blacktower the next morn after sunrise, Finnian met them at the door. "Did ye get the *keek-stane*?"

"Yes, but I cannot see anything in it," Catriona said.

"Maybe ye are no' meant to." He held out his hand and she gave it to him. Cradling the box like a fragile treasure, he scurried into his private lair.

"Finnian!" She tried to follow but he closed and barred the door. "I want to know what you see."

"Aye, lass. Give me some time." His voice sounded muffled through the thick oak door.

"The motley-minded haggard," she muttered and joined Torr at the pitted oak table. Aggie and Molly served fresh bannocks, bacon and eggs. Her stomach rumbled. She threw off her cape and dug into her food. Chewing, she glanced up. How she loved sitting across the table from Torr. This was home. She swallowed and smiled.

Torr eyed the cup of ale suspiciously and shifted his gaze to her.

She sighed. "I didn't drug it. Nor the wine yesterday."

"'Haps no', but ye have been known to."

"Was it so bad?"

"Nay, indeed. 'Twas one of the most enjoyable days I've had, ever."

Her heart warmed. She didn't think the wine was drugged at all. Her need for him had been her own, not potion-induced. Which meant his desire for her had been natural as well.

When she looked into his eyes, he glanced up at the ceiling.

"What are you looking at?" She followed his gaze, hoping Wilona hadn't tracked them in bat form.

"Naught. I was but thinking. Never mind."

"What? Please tell me."

He shrugged and looked a bit uncomfortable. "I have always loved this tower. One of my ancestors oversaw the construction of the castle three hundred years ago. Since I was a lad, I've wanted to have the ruined parts rebuilt just as they were before the English army knocked them down. My brother Angus might even give it to me, but only if I earn it serving at his side as his spokesman."

Catriona nodded, studying the old yet skillfully done construction. "Did you enjoy your position with your clan?"

"Aye."

"And you lost it because of the curse?"

"Indeed. The clan couldna trust me." Pain glinted in his eyes. "Angus is all that keeps them from coming after me. They think me a sorcerer."

She wanted to take Torr into her arms and hold him, but Finnian yanked the door open. He trotted into the great hall, a mysterious expression on his wizened face. Heavens! Had he seen something good or something terrible in the stone?

"What is it?" Torr demanded.

"Canna tell ye, lad."

"Can you tell me?" Catriona said.

He grimaced. "I'm no' sure ye'll like it."

Oh no. Had he not seen her face in the scrying-stone as the one who'd break Torr's curse? She rose, dread weighing her. "I must know."

"Come, come." Finnian waved her forward.

"Wait a minute!" Torr shot to his feet as she scurried toward Finnian's room. "'Tis my future ye're talking about. I deserve to ken what ye're saying!"

"Ye'll know soon enough, lad." Finnian slammed the door after Catriona and barred it.

"What did you see?"

"'Tis hard to explain. At first I did indeed see your face...."

A thrill shot through her.

Finnian grimaced. "But then your image became blurry and indistinct."

Her emotions shifted so quickly pain gripped her. "What does that mean?"

He shrugged. "I dinna ken. I am a physician, no' a wizard or conjurer. I but inherited a bit of 'the sight' from my mother. What I think it means is that ye could break the curse for Torr but there are obstacles. Ye both must overcome these in order to be happy."

She nodded and released her held breath. "And why do you not want Torr to know?"

"Because he'll fight against it, trying to control his own destiny. He's a rebel to the core. And stubborn." Finnian headed toward his work table.

Catriona followed. "What else did you see? What of the woman who will break Brodie's curse?"

"Aye! I have seen her image in the stone, but there is something unusual about her."

"What? Is she disfigured?"

"Nay, she is vera beautiful, tall, with light-colored hair, like sunlight. She doesna look like a Scottish lady."

"English? Irish?"

He frowned and shook his head. "It seems she comes from the sea."

"The sea? Like a selkie?"

Finnian shrugged, but his expression showed concern. "Mayhap I will see more later."

"But there is a woman for him?"

"Aye, if she will accept him. Ye must understand, people have free will. Fate and destiny exist, but if the people do no' make the right choices, 'tis all for naught."

Blast. Catriona had hoped for more definite answers. Was this what she and Torr had risked their lives for? "How do we find her and bring her to Farspag Tower?"

"Another mystery I dinna ken the answer to yet, but I shall cast a spell to help with it. I've had another vision. The spirits of your and Torr's ancestors are helping because they want the curse broken. Did ye have any dreams afore coming here?"

"Yes, I dreamed of Torr and the missive from the MacTavish."

Finnian nodded as if he'd known the answer beforehand. She hoped he hadn't seen her sensual dream of Torr. Heat rose up within her.

"One of your ancestors communicated to ye through that dream. I'm thinking 'twas your grandmother. Your father's mother."

"But she died before I was born."

"Aye. Doesna matter. Your ancestors are still concerned about the fate of your clan."

She glanced about the room, hoping not to see spirits. "Are they following me?"

"The world of spirit exists alongside our own. Merely on different planes."

What the devil did that mean? What if her ancestors had seen her and Torr making love? Ack!

Well, in truth, that wasn't the worst of her problems. She had to make sure Torr fell in love with her. Without him realizing what was happening.

In kelpie form, Torr stood by the loch that night, munching grass from a tender patch. He wished Catriona were out here with him. He enjoyed her companionship and, during their journeys, had grown accustomed to her light weight on his back. What he would love most of all was to be a man, beside her in bed right now. She would be warm and drowsy. He wanted to see the candlelight glowing upon her naked curves. But he was realistic, not a dreamer. Breaking the curse still seemed too far out of reach for him to fantasize about.

A noise caught his sensitive ears. He perked them and paused in his chewing. He sniffed the air. Aye, definitely an unusual scent for this area, human strangers. He snorted, trying to rid himself of the odor. He stared through the dim night but saw no movements.

He finished chewing and swallowed. The scent came to him again and he quietly moved toward it. He liked giving humans a rare glimpse of a real kelpie. He found it amusing to see who figured out he was a kelpie, and who thought he was a regular horse.

Something hit his neck and he jerked aside. A rope? *Around my neck?* He reared. Bolted. Something, or someone, was attached to the other end of the rope. Human shouts further assaulted his ears. Bastards. He'd show them the kelpie legends were true. But he could not free himself from the damned rope. He slung his head, trying to dislodge it. Pawed at it with a hoof. The rope end trailed the ground.

He stopped and turned to stare back at the humans. *Alpin MacTavish?* The daft man approached on horseback. Wilona MacRae sat on a smaller horse in the shadows. Saints! He had known they'd follow. But he didn't expect them at night.

Alpin drew near and extended his arm. A shot rang out. Torr bolted again and didn't feel the sting of a bullet. But then, as a kelpie, he rarely felt pain.

He hid behind a stand of bushes, pawed the ground and readied himself. If they wanted violence, he'd give them exactly that.

The other horse's hooves approached on the rocky ground. When they passed, Torr charged out in pursuit. He reared and thrust his hooves toward the horse's flank and Alpin in the saddle, missing by inches. The horse lunged into a gallop. Torr followed, gained ground and when he was beside the horse, he kicked with his back hooves toward Alpin, connecting with his thigh. The man cried out. His horse bucked and threw him off. He landed on the rocks with a thud, his horse galloping away.

Dinna mess with a kelpie.

Torr circled back and waited a short distance from Alpin. The disturbing tang of blood thickened the air. The man didn't move or make a sound.

Torr eyed him. Was the bastard dead? Hearing footsteps approaching, Torr hid behind another group of bushes, waited and watched.

A voice reached him. "Alpin! Where are you?"

Wilona crept into view, found Alpin on the rocks and bent over him. She stood back, muttering words and glanced about.

"Ye killed him, Torr! Do ye hear me?"

'Twas no more than the bastard deserved. This was the second time Alpin had tried to kill him.

Wilona raised her arms and began chanting, a mixture of Gaelic and English.

A spell. Another curse? Torr needed to get as far away from her as possible. He would go back to Blacktower. Except he felt very sleepy of a sudden. A sleep spell? *Nay!*

The darkness beckoned and he was helpless to resist it.

"Aye, that's a good lad, Torr." The words reached into his sleep and bizarre dreams. "Ye just sleep as long as ye want."

The scent of this human he now recognized. Wilona.

He snorted and opened his eyes.

"Ye're awake?" Her expression was overly bright and pleased with herself. Damn her evil hide. "Ye killed my friend, therefore, ye will take his place." She tugged him forward with a bridle. This was what he'd read about in the old manuscripts, a magical bridle that every kelpie feared most. The bridle caused a tingling cold anywhere it touched. He felt nauseous.

Dear God, he was doomed. Come to think of it—the morning sun shone brightly. He'd never been in horse form in daytime. The bridle must have kept him from shifting.

Wilona grasped the reins and pulled him forward. He felt sluggish, as if he had no will of his own.

"Ye are my servant now, kelpie."

I shall never be your servant.

"And ye'll never turn back into human form, unless I allow it." She smiled.

Bitch.

"Whoa." She stopped him beside her horse and set about removing the saddle. She then placed the saddle upon his back. He would see her pay for this someday.

After climbing onto a rock, she hoisted herself upon his back and led the other two horses behind.

"Be a nice pony and take me to my home. I'd hate to have to use my whip on you." She chuckled.

God's teeth. He wanted to buck and toss her into the loch, but his body would not obey such a thought.

"Come now, quicken your pace, Torr. I wish to arrive home by sundown."

Catriona searched the tower for Torr—his bedchamber, the kitchens. Already it was two hours after sunrise. Saints! He never arrived this late.

"Where the devil is he, Finnian?" Catriona raced across the great hall, trying to keep her feet from tangling in the rushes.

The old man frowned and returned to his chamber.

"Finnian?"

"A moment, lass."

"Blast!" What had happened to him? Catriona opened the tower's entry door and scanned the barmkin's broken walls and cobbled floor. She rushed out to the stables. All was quiet and calm, the stable lad gone since the outlaws had stolen their horses.

"Something's happened. He would be here by now," she muttered, going outside again. "Torr?" she called several times, scanning the heaps of broken rocks of the ruins. She ran forth and gazed down at the loch. Nothing moved except the water gently lapping the shore.

Thinking she heard Finnian yelling, she dashed back into the great hall.

"Lass!" Finnian yelled, trotting from his chamber.

"What is it?"

"Wilona MacRae has him. Enslaved."

Catriona felt as if someone had dropped a giant rock onto her stomach. "What? How?"

"She put a magical bridle on him while he was in kelpie form last night. He is completely under her control."

"Are you certain?" *Please, God, no.*

"I saw this in the *keek-stane*."

"We must rescue him!"

"But...."

"Do not tell me you are afraid, Finnian."

"Nay!"

"You're white as a specter. But you, dear sir, are a powerful wizard, whether you admit it or not. Surely you have spells that we could use against Wilona." Catriona's gaze landed on a broadsword displayed on the wall. *That's it. I shall kill her.* She climbed onto a table and took the sword from the wall. "And if not, I shall take care of her myself."

"Nay, lass. If Wilona dies before Torr's and Brodie's curses are broken, they will never be free of them."

"Oh." Drained of power and ideas, she tossed the sword onto the table. "Then what shall we do? When Torr and I broke into the manor house, we tied her up and gagged her so that she could not speak her spells. But she shifted anyway and escaped the magical ropes. She turned into a bat."

"She is a very powerful dark witch, lass. And now she's seeking her revenge."

Chapter 8

Torr awoke to cold water splashing in his face. He blew it away and slung his head. His arms ached from being stretched taut over his head. He was in human form, inside a bedchamber—the same house he and Catriona had broken into when they'd taken the scrying-stone. He glanced around at the sunlight spilling through the windows. How much time had passed? His stomach gnawed from hunger, but most of all he craved drink.

Wilona stood smirking before him. Never in his life had he wanted to strike a woman, but he wished he could knock her to the floor. With all his strength, he yanked at the ropes. The pain blinded him but naught budged. He tried to move his feet. Glancing down, he found them tied with ropes as well. And he was completely naked. *"Iosa is Muire Mhàthair."*

"Remember when ye tied me up, Torr? No' very nice."

"What are ye wanting from me?"

"Hmm." She glanced down his body. "I can think of a few things."

Taking the rope into his hand, he focused all his strength on pulling with his right arm, the strongest, his sword arm. The damnable rope was too thick, tied too tightly. "Bitch," he growled.

"Aye. Call me what ye wish. And I shall do to you what I wish." Her eyes alight, she stepped forward and grasped his balls in her hand. She squeezed. He ground his teeth and braced for the pain. But it never came.

"Disobey and these will be permanently mine, kelpie slave."

While he remained still and rigid, his mind scrambled for an escape, a way to lash out. *I will kill ye, that is a promise.*

"I see the hatred and lust for vengeance in your eyes. But I shall teach ye that what ye want means naught. I own ye now."

She released his balls and stroked a hand up his stomach, across his chest, her lustful gaze following. His skin crawled.

"Are ye thirsty?" She swung away and returned with a goblet. She tipped it to his lips. His thirst overrode all else for the moment. She'd deprived him of food and drink, and had forced him to run all night.

He drank a long swallow and before he knew it, emptied the goblet. The wine dribbled from his mouth and down his body.

"Oh no. Ye've spilled it," she cooed and licked the wine from his chest.

He jerked back, hating her tongue on him.

She took the bottle and trickled more wine down his body.

"Dinna touch me!"

"I thought ye understood that *ye're* the slave and I am the master."

"Understand this, oh daughter of evil, I shall kill ye! Your day will come."

She laughed. "I'm glad ye ken who I am. And violence arouses me."

He turned his face away and felt her tongue flick into his navel. And lower. *Nay!*

She grasped his cock in her hand and licked the tip. He remembered when Catriona had done that. *Oh God, Catriona. I miss ye, lass.* When would he see her again, if ever? His chest ached with yearning. His skin grew hot by slow degrees and desire prickled along his nerves. Against his will, he tingled with arousal, his cock growing and lengthening. What the devil? Not another damned aphrodisiac.

"Mmm. That's a good lad."

He yanked harder on his bonds. "What did ye put in the wine?"

"From what I've seen in my other *keek-stane*, ye should be familiar with the drug." Wilona took his cock into her mouth and sucked hard. Drew him to the back of her throat and stroked his shaft.

He could not help the intense arousal he felt. If he didn't look at her, he could pretend she was Catriona kneeling before him, giving him erotic pleasure.

"Oooh. What a nice big cock ye have. Hard as stone."

If only she would stop talking, the fantasy would be complete and her method of torture wouldn't be half as bad.

She fondled his balls, sucked them into her mouth, one by one, then went at his cock again fiercely. The potion intensified his arousal and his whole body felt on fire. His cock felt extra sensitive and engorged to the limit. She bit the head gently, her teeth scraping. "Look at me," she demanded.

When he didn't, she bit harder. Pain shot through him.

"I said look at me!"

He swallowed his disgust and did as she bid. His stomach roiled.

Her eyes were dark. Clearly she'd imbibed the potion as well. "I dinna want ye imagining I'm your sweet little whore. Catriona? Is that her name?"

When he didn't answer, she pulled sharply at his pubic hair. "Is it?"

"She is no whore, damn you!"

"Ah, but ye have fucked her, I know. I saw you."

"Where?"

Wilona laughed again, the sound vibrating his cock and only adding to the stimulation.

The faster he could come, the faster this mess would be over. When she went back to pleasuring him mercilessly, he closed his eyes and imagined Catriona. It was the only way to keep his sanity. Catriona's tongue swirling round the sensitive head. Catriona's wet mouth sucking and her hand stroking his shaft.

His climax rushed upon him and he let it go, thankful it was finally over.

When he glanced down, he saw that Wilona had caught his seed in a vial.

"What the hell?"

"Kelpie semen has many magical properties. Very good for potent spells, which I plan to make good use of." She smiled, licking a drop from her lip. "And it tastes delicious."

Bitch. Your day will come.

The potion's effects dissipated and he felt used and violated. How could he have been so aroused? He cringed, the clammy sweat drying on his skin. Instead, he focused on the pain in his arms and the ache in his stomach—nausea and hunger.

"I don't know why I didn't think of this sooner." She chuckled. "I'm glad ye killed Alpin. Already ye're a better love slave than he ever was. Easier to control. More tasty. I shall never let ye go."

Catriona and Finnian waited outside the walls of Wilona's stolen estate, Ferncraig. Finnian gazed into the scrying-stone silently for many long minutes. She hesitated to break his trance, but they needed to do something. She could not tolerate the thought Wilona might, even now, be hurting Torr.

First of all, it had taken some time that morning to borrow horses from Laird Blackburn without revealing why they needed them. Finnian had insisted Torr's abduction not be revealed. The laird might have wanted to rescue him and kill Wilona in the process.

Finnian came out of his trance with a giant shiver.

"What is it, Finnian? What did you see?"

"We must rescue him as soon as possible."

Why had he evaded her question? Was Torr well? Her skin chilled at the thought Wilona might already have tortured him horribly.

She headed through the doorway in the wall Torr had broken down last time, but she slammed against a barrier, hitting her forehead and knee.

"Blast!"

"Shh," Finnian hissed. "She will hear ye."

"What is that, glass?" she whispered and put her hand out. The substance felt like ice but was completely invisible. "Is this magic?"

Finnian approached, touched the clear barrier with his fingertips and narrowed his eyes.

This would take all day. She looked about for another way in.

Masses of vines covered the stone wall in places. Upon examination, she found a rusty metal trellis beneath and some of the vines were thick as her arm. She climbed the network much like a ladder. Good thing she hadn't outgrown the climbing tendencies she'd had as a child. She hoisted herself onto the top of the wall, scooted forward and dropped to her feet. "Ow!" That stung. She proceeded to the solid wood gate and unbarred it. Finnian crept through.

"I couldna figure out the clear barricade."

"'Tis naught to worry over. Come, we'll see if we can enter through the same window Torr and I did last time."

They crept around the side of the manor house, skirting piles of dried leaves.

The window was indeed still broken. She approached it. When she tried to stick her foot through the opening, something propelled her backward onto the ground.

"'Slud. That bitch," she said in a loud whisper. "Another damned invisible barricade." Her hip ached from the impact.

Finnian eyed her. "Such salty language coming from a lass? I can tell ye've been around Torr too long." Finnian neared the window, hands outstretched. He trembled. "Aye. She's placed a strong protection spell upon it."

Catriona rose. "There must be another way in." She threw a rock at another glass window, but it bounced back and hit her on the shin with much force.

Ouch! That thrice-cursed bitch. Clenching her teeth and hopping on one foot, she forced herself not to scream from the pain.

Finnian held his hands out before him and, with eyes closed, shuffled farther around the side of the manor house.

"What are you doing?" she whispered.

He ignored her, but stopped some distance away and stared at the ground. He swiped his foot back and forth. She ran to catch up. He'd uncovered a rusty metal latch on the ground.

"What is that?"

"A door to a cellar." He placed his staff through a ring and lifted. The hinges screeched.

"Shh. Saints! She will hear us."

He laid the door backward, flat upon the ground, and she peered into the black dungeon-like hole.

"Let me go first, lass. I shall detect any danger."

"Very well." Indeed, she did not want to go into that hell pit first nor second. Surely spiders of all shapes and sizes lived down there. *I must do this for Torr. I must do this for Torr. Ack! Torr, I'll kill you for this.* Chills covering her arms and trailing to her legs, she followed Finnian down the stone stairs. "'Tis creepy, like a cave. We need a candle," she whispered. "It stinks. Is something dead down here?"

"Shh."

After a time, her eyes adjusted to the darkness. They moved to another set of steps that traveled upward. But would they be able to get through that door once they reached it?

Holding to the back of Finnian's woolen robes, she climbed the steps.

He pushed at the door. "There is no knob or latch here. 'Tis on the other side."

"Maybe it will give way if you push harder."

"A moment."

She watched him in silence and his hands started glowing. Seconds later, something popped, the door swung forward and light flooded the stairway. He poked his head out and motioned her forward.

They emerged in a corridor beneath another stair. "Whew." Well then, mayhap he did know some magic. They stopped to listen in the entry hall before climbing the wide curving staircase to the floor above.

Laughter reached them from down the corridor. *Wilona.* Catriona had never wanted to hurt, nay *kill,* someone so badly in her life.

"I will draw her away from Torr and keep her distracted while ye go free him, lass."

Catriona nodded and hid inside a nearby room. Finnian returned to the entry hall and a loud crash sounded. Seconds later, footsteps rushed past Catriona's hiding place. She emerged and slipped farther along the corridor, checking inside each room.

Torr, where are you?

In the last room, she found him, tied naked in a standing position, his arms stretched far above his head.

"Dear God! Torr?" She ran to him and took his face between her palms. "Are you hurt?"

"Catriona." He stiffened. "Ye shouldna be here. 'Tis too dangerous."

"Finnian is here, too, keeping Wilona distracted." She took her dagger and cut the ropes that bound his wrists.

Jaw clenched, he groaned and lowered his arms.

She severed the ropes tying his ankles and removed them. His skin was raw and bloody with rope burns. She rose. "I shall kill her for hurting you so."

"No' yet, my wee warrior. I get that privilege when the time is right." He kissed her forehead. "Come."

"Where are your clothes?" Catriona tried to shut out the vision of Wilona looking at Torr naked for the many hours he'd been here. But most of all she hated the thought Wilona had touched him sexually. Any way she wished, and Torr could do naught to defend himself.

"I dinna have clothes. Did you bring some?"

"I didn't know you needed any." Trying to focus on escape and removing Torr from Wilona's clutches, she searched the cluttered room for something he might wear. Wilona's clothing and possessions lay everywhere. She dug through a pile while he searched elsewhere.

"Here is a plaid, belt, shirt and doublet. Must be Alpin's." She dragged the items from the bottom of a heap.

"Och. I hate wearing the whoreson's clothing, but 'twill suffice." Torr slipped the shirt over his head.

"Where is Alpin?"

"Dead. He had an unfortunate *accident* when they attacked me."

"Accident?"

Torr lifted a brow and belted the plaid into place. "He should've known better than to antagonize a kelpie." Finished dressing, he picked up a basket-hilted broadsword from a nearby table and tested the weapon's strength. "I'll explain later. Come. Stay behind me." He led the way along the corridor.

Loud crashes and shouts echoed from the entry hall.

"I pray Finnian is not hurt," she whispered, following Torr down the stairway.

When they arrived in the entry, Wilona was pinned high on the wall with invisible bonds. Her mouth was closed but she slung her head about and mumbled as if trying to open it.

"Saints!" Finnian was a more powerful wizard than she'd suspected.

"There ye are, lad. Are ye well?" Finnian asked.

"Aye." Torr glared up at Wilona, his expression darkening by the second, his fist white on the sword grip.

Fearing he might fly into a rage, Catriona slipped a hand around his elbow.

"Off with ye both, then." Finnian motioned. "And I shall hold her here as long as I can. Go."

Wishing he could kill Wilona now, Torr led Catriona outside where they headed toward the wood hand-in-hand. Two horses he recognized from his brother's stable grazed farther along.

Torr tugged her behind a group of tall bushes. "We shall wait on Finnian here. If Wilona hurts him, I swear…." The old man had become almost like a father to him over the last year.

"Torr, I was so afraid when I learned she had captured you." Catriona clutched him in her arms, stroked a hand over his face. "Are you well, in truth? Did she hurt you?"

"I am fine." God help him, he could scarce look into Catriona's eyes. In some bizarre way, he felt he'd been unfaithful. He hadn't, in truth, but he felt unworthy of her cherishing touch. Too dirty to touch sweet Catriona and her near purity. She did not know the ugly side of life.

"I love you with all my heart," she said. Tears glistened in her eyes. Her earnestness ripped at him inside.

He wrapped his arms around her and pressed his face to hers. "I dinna deserve your love."

"How can you say that? Of course you do." She pulled back and gazed into his eyes.

He met her gaze only briefly before looking away.

"What is it? You're holding something back."

"I canna tell ye."

"Why not? Did she abuse you?"

"I willna talk about it." He stared at the manor house and gate, willing Finnian to come through.

"Did she force you to have sex with her?"

He pressed his eyes closed. "No' exactly, but something similar." No use to lie. Catriona would figure it out if he did.

"What? Tell me. It wasn't your fault, Torr. You were tied up and forced to do her bidding. You should not feel guilty."

"Aye, but I do." When he met her eyes, his chest ached. "She gave me a lust potion and then used her mouth on me."

"And you enjoyed it?"

Och, such vulnerability shown in Catriona's eyes when she asked that. He would rather die than hurt her, but neither would he lie to her. "I didna want to enjoy it, but the potion was very strong. I couldna resist the arousal and I had no will of my own." Damn, how he hated his own weakness. "I shall kill her, I swear it," he rasped.

"You cannot until both your curse and Brodie's are broken."

"Aye. 'Tis the only thing that stops me. When she was having her way with me, I was thinking of you and how you'd pleasured me with your mouth. I imagined 'twas you there with me."

"I'm glad. You see, this is why I love you so much. You have a beautiful heart and soul."

He shook his head. "Ye deserve a far better man than I am." 'Twas true, but even so, imagining her with that better man was like someone slicing him to ribbons. Enduring Wilona's torture was naught compared to the pain losing Catriona would cause.

"No, I want only you. How can you let her continue to control you?"

"I am no'! What a damned absurd notion."

"You cannot love me, is that it?"

"Nay, I do." Torr pressed his eyes closed. "Saints, I do love you," he said in a fierce whisper. Why had he only now realized it?

She kissed him, and he accepted. He brushed away her tears with his thumbs, wishing she'd stop crying, but at the same time, cherishing the reason for them.

"I love you, Catriona. Never doubt it." He trailed kisses toward her neck. "The thought of you, the hope that I would see ye again is what kept me sane while I was bound."

"I want to erase her and her evil from your memory. Make love to me."

"The gloamin' is nigh upon us. I shall shift to a kelpie soon."

"We have time. Hurry."

She tugged up his kilt and took his shaft, already halfway hard and tingling for her touch, and stroked up and down. Arousal blazed a trail through his veins, down his belly to his groin. It had naught to do with any potion, and everything to do with his love for Catriona.

Looking into her eyes, he laid her upon the leaves, pushed her skirts up and stroked her wet slit with his fingers.

She breathed out a sigh and tugged gently at his cock. "Please."

He wished he could have bathed before taking her again, but what lived between them was not only the physical. His soul needed her healing touch. His heart needed her love.

Positioning himself, he pushed into her. Nothing had ever felt so good as Catriona. He belonged right here, with her, inside her. She locked her legs around his, and her arms around his shoulders, holding tight. Her love emanated from within her and wrapped around him in a warmth he had never felt in his whole life. He found himself whispering words of awe and he knew not what. Words of love and devotion. But they fell short, for he could not express the overwhelming storm of feeling inside him. She was the focus of his existence.

A tree branch cracked nearby. What the devil? Sensing a presence, he covertly turned his head to look but did not stop his actions, not while she was in the throes of passion. He saw naught anywhere around them.

Torr licked a finger and stroked Catriona's sweet little nub of pleasure. He fantasized about licking it again and increased his thrusting. With her climax, she tightened around him, squeezing and cried out. Aye, giving her pleasure was his main concern at the moment, second only to protecting her.

With the overcast sky, 'twas hard to tell whether sunset had already occurred or not. He assumed not, for he remained in human form and did not feel a shifting was imminent.

Wilona materialized before him.

He picked up the sword and pointed it at the bitch. Catriona didn't appear to notice her presence.

Wilona stepped back a few paces, lifted her arms and murmured a chant. He ignored her and focused on his profound love for Catriona. He did not know why, but he could not stop making love to her.

"I love you and I will protect you always," he whispered in her ear.

She held him tight, kissing his face. Feeling her love to the depths of his soul, he let the pleasure claim him and climaxed inside her. She was his now and he would not be letting her go, not for anyone.

He slowly became aware of strong, chill winds twisting the trees, swirling dried leaves, and Wilona's louder chanting. Behind them, a man's voice rose over the wind.

Lowering Catriona's skirts, Torr lifted himself off her. He turned and saw Finnian facing off against Wilona.

Catriona glanced around, frowning. "What—?"

"Come." Torr helped her up and tugged her away from the two, safe from their magical battle.

Lightening split the sky. A short distance away, Torr knelt behind a boulder and pulled Catriona to him. He held her tightly, her face pressed against his chest, and watched Finnian and Wilona. The air was heavy and oppressive, the sky thick with low, black clouds. Something fell around them, not rain. Black objects. Black creatures. He frowned. Dead bats and ravens. *Saints preserve us.*

The chanting swelled louder. Wilona's arms shook with the power she wielded. A great wind swept through, sucked all the dried leaves from the ground and lifted them through the tree limbs into the sky. A moment later they dropped again. Hail followed. The coin-sized pieces of ice bounced off everything, including his head. "Ow, 'slud." He tried to shelter Catriona from the worst of it.

The hail gradually turned to giant snowflakes, falling thick, blanketing the ground quickly. The temperature plummeted like mid-winter.

Finnian dropped to his knees, his arms lowering and trembling. *Nay! Get up, Finnian! Get up!*

Chapter 9

Torr refused to let Wilona defeat Finnian.

Rising to his feet, Torr removed his doublet and covered Catriona's head with it. "Stay here." He drew his sword.

"No! Come back! Don't kill her."

Focusing his thoughts fully on his greatest strength—his love for Catriona—Torr charged Wilona. He couldn't run her through, but he must do something to break her concentration. The basket hilt of his sword, which protected his hand and fingers in a cage-like structure, was durable silver. He bashed it into the back of Wilona's head. With a shriek, she toppled to the ground. Spitting leaves, she tried to push herself up. He held her face down, her mouth to the ground, preventing her chants.

She jerked and kicked at him.

"Finnian! Are ye well?" he yelled.

The old conjurer rose to his feet, lifting his arms higher. His voice echoed toward the clouds.

"Here!" Catriona knelt beside him. "Gag her with this." She held a piece of material that looked like the doublet sleeve.

"Put it in her mouth." He lifted Wilona's face from the ground.

"*Cruthaich…a' chomhachag!*" Wilona yelled. Her body vanished from beneath his hands and, amid a cloud of smoke, an owl flapped toward the tree tops.

Torr leapt to his feet. "Damnation!"

"She's gone." Shivering, Catriona wrapped her arms around his waist.

"Finnian, are ye well?" Torr called.

"Aye."

The wind died and eerie quiet descended. Torr glanced around the forest, up through the tree branches. The moon in a dark blue sky?

"What the devil?" Could it be so? It was too much to hope for. "The moon. 'Tis after sunset and I didna shift into a kelpie."

Catriona grasped his shirt in her fists. "The curse is broken!" She jumped up and down, looping her arms around his neck.

Though he was almost afraid to believe it, he smiled. "Aye." He picked her up, whirled her around and kissed her. Saints! The lass had saved his life and given him happiness untold.

The air warmed slowly to an autumn temperature again.

Finnian ambled forward, relying on his staff for support, his breathing labored. He paused, eyes wide. "Torr? Lad, ye're human and 'tis night!"

"Aye. Because of Catriona, the curse is broken." He hugged her to him and kissed her cheek.

Catriona returned his embrace. "We must go to Farspag Tower and help Brodie."

"Aye." Finnian leaned heavily against a thick tree trunk and sighed. "But first, I must rest."

"That battle of magic must have taken a lot out of you," Catriona said.

"Indeed."

They found the two black horses wandering about the wood. After Torr helped Finnian into the saddle, he and Catriona shared a horse for the ride to Blacktower. She sat behind him, her arms tight around his waist, her love secure around his heart. 'Twas the sweetest bondage he could imagine. He smiled, lifted her hand and kissed it, wishing he could tell her the depth and width of how he adored her. But no words existed. *I must find a way to show her.*

As well, he couldn't wait to tell his brother and his clan about the curse being broken. But first he had to help Brodie.

※≈((◡))≈

Torr, will you marry me? No, no, I can't say it like that again. Catriona sighed and watched Torr eating on the other side of the table at Blacktower. She even found the way he ate venison stew fascinating and sensual, the way he licked his lips, his square jaw clenching when he chewed.

His eyes met hers and he quirked a brow.

Would you do me the honor of becoming my husband? Hmm, that sounded a bit better, but it still lacked something.

"Is aught amiss?" he asked. "No' hungry?"

She shook her head. Why couldn't he ask her this time? *Grr!*

They'd made love during the night and also at dawn. He'd said he loved her. Surely she wouldn't have to propose again.

"We shall set off to Farspag in the morn," Torr said. "Are ye well-rested enough for it, Finnian?"

"Aye."

Now that the time had come to return to her clan, panic tightened

Catriona's throat. "I'm afraid to go back. What if they still try to make me marry the MacPeter?"

"I willna allow the whoreson to take my future wife from me." Torr's eyes glinted with malicious intent.

Oh dear heavens! *Future wife?*

A laugh burst from her mouth. "Torr!" She jumped up, skirted the table and hugged him from behind. "Are you proposing?" she murmured next to his ear.

"Indeed, I am. Will ye marry me?"

Lightness filled her. She felt she'd float away. "Yes! A thousand times, yes."

Smiling, he turned and gave her a kiss. "Now, we only need Brodie's blessing."

A bit of the air left her sails. She stood back. "But what if we cannot find him?"

"I shall, even if I have to take a galley to every tiny isle on the west coast."

She trudged back to her seat at the table. "What of MacPeter, my clan and Mother in the meantime?"

"We will find Brodie first."

"But we can marry without his blessing."

"Aye, but I wouldna want to make an enemy of my good friend. I want our union to be honorable and accepted by both our clans."

Aggie cleared her throat. "How will she get out of her promise to Chief MacPeter?"

Catriona turned and found a scowl on Aggie's face. She didn't care if her maid disapproved. "I cannot believe you would wish me to marry that brute. I thought you cared about me. I didn't agree to a marriage verbally nor on paper. Nor did Brodie. Only my mother and the clan elders."

"'Tis good," Torr said. "No matter what happens, we must not let the MacPeter nor your clan know we wish to marry until Brodie comes back. If we have to confront them, we must pretend to be only acquaintances. Else violence may erupt and your clan will be on the side of MacPeter."

Catriona's stomach knotted and ached, making her wish she hadn't eaten. She clenched her fists, wanting to hold onto Torr with all her might. He was her husband in body and spirit, even if not legally yet. What if they ripped him from her grasp?

Catriona hated each step they took toward Farspag Tower the next day. Indeed, they had to go help Brodie. But the queasy feeling in her stomach told her things would not go smoothly. The thick clouds blanketing the sky further darkened her mood.

After the four of them got off the ferry, they mounted horses. She rode pillion on a cushion behind Torr. Aggie rode behind Finnian.

When they were as yet a mile from Farspag, Torr turned. "A trail ahead leads down to a cave at the shore. Ye and Aggie can wait there while I go to Farspag and ask if Brodie has returned. I'll pretend I havena seen ye nor Aggie."

"You know about Brodie's cave?"

"Aye, we used to play there as lads."

"I think 'tis a sound plan." She would endure anything, even bat-infested caves, if it kept her away from MacPeter.

Before Farspag came into view, they directed the horses off the trail and across the moor, through knee-high shrub heaths and grasses. Waves crashing onto the shore grew louder and the wind lashed Cartiona's hair against her cheeks. She pressed the side of her face to Torr's back and tightened her arms around his broad chest, savoring the strong, vital feel of him. She wanted him again, wished to lie with him as her husband. But that might not happen for a while yet—days, weeks. She groaned.

Torr turned. "What is it?"

"Naught, except I want you."

"I want ye too, lass. 'Twill no' be much longer."

After a difficult trek down the bank to the rocky shore, they reached the cave, dismounted and entered. The scent of smoke emanated from the rough walls, but no sign remained that Brodie had been there recently. On a rock ledge she found his plaid, shirt, belt and boots still in the leather sack, as she'd expected.

"If he were at Farspag, his clothes wouldn't be here," she said.

"Still, I want to find out for certain." Torr glanced about, his head near reaching the low ceiling.

Standing by the entrance, Aggie cringed. "'Tis a home for bats. I pray ye will hurry, sir, so that we dinna have to stay here the night."

"Indeed I will," Torr said.

"I shall stay here and protect the women," Finnian said, poking about the cave with his staff.

Torr lifted a brow.

"Besides, I need to gaze into the *keek-stane* a wee bit. If Laird Brodie isna at the tower, 'haps I shall see his whereabouts afore ye return."

"Very well." Torr turned to make his way outside.

Emptiness gaping inside her, Catriona followed. What if she never saw him again? What if he never held her or loved her again? Her throat constricting, she clasped a hand onto Torr's plaid at his back when he neared his horse. His questioning gaze met hers and softened. He bent and placed a brief kiss upon her lips. "Dinna worry, lass. All will be well."

"I don't know that." She traced her fingertips over his face. "You are mine." She sucked in a deep breath of cold wind to still her fluttering heart. "You are my husband in every way but on paper."

Emotion gleamed in his green eyes. "Aye, and ye are the wife of my heart. Soon, 'twill be legal and all the world will know."

"Well, probably not the whole world."

He grinned. "They willna take ye from me. Ye have my word on that. Before ye know it, we shall be married and sharing a warm soft bed."

She sighed, imagining Torr in her own bed at Farspag, his warm, muscular body snuggled next to hers.

A yell echoed. Torr jerked around. Catriona glanced up at the cliffs and found a dozen arrows pointed at them. She gasped. "My clan."

Torr muttered a string of Gaelic curses.

She moved in front of him. He grasped her shoulders and tried to put her behind him again. A wee struggle ensued. "'Tis me. Catriona," she called out. "This is Torr Blackburn, a good friend of Brodie's."

"Where have ye been?" one of her clansmen asked. "Were ye taken hostage?"

"No! I will explain later. Do not harm my friends. Have the men put their weapons away. We are here to help Brodie."

The clansman she spoke to, one of Brodie's bodyguards, drew back and conversed with someone. All the armed men held their places.

"Damn the man," she muttered. "Why does he not tell them to lower their bows?"

"They dinna trust me," Torr said.

"Ye must come to the castle, m'lady!" the bodyguard shouted. "Your mother awaits. If ye dinna, we'll assume these two men stole ye away and took ye hostage."

Imbecile. "No, they haven't! This is Torrquil Blackburn. Brodie's best friend. You have seen him many times before. And this—" She glanced back at the cave entrance. "—is Torr's kinsman, Finnian."

"Come to the tower at once, m'lady!" Whose voice was that? Dear God, no. Not the MacPeter. His hateful, bloated form came into view.

"I willna let that whoreson have ye," Torr promised in a rough voice.

"Remain calm," she said. "I'll go to the tower and talk to Mother. I'll convince her to cancel her deal with MacPeter."

"Nay. He will no' back down. I heard it in his voice."

"I'm sending two of my men down to fetch ye," MacPeter said. "Ye alone come with them."

"No. I don't trust you."

"I dinna require your trust. But ye were promised to me as my wife and I intend to collect."

Torr reached to unsheathe his sword.

Catriona put a hand on his arm. "No bloodshed." With her eyes she begged him to understand. "I cannot lose you in this way. You must find Brodie."

On foot, two men with swords moved along the rocky shore toward them, wind blowing their plaids.

"I cannot marry you!" she yelled up at MacPeter.

"Ye can and ye will!"

"The Chief of the MacCain clan will not allow it."

"I dinna see your brother anywhere about."

"Bastard," she muttered quietly while the two MacPeter clansmen stumbled closer and closer.

"If ye dinna come with these men, we shall fill your friends full of arrows." MacPeter lofted a pistol over his head. "And lead balls."

"Only if you take me to my family."

"Indeed, I will."

"And you will let my friends go. Do not harm them in any way."

"Aye, of course, if ye cooperate."

"I'll go up," she whispered to Torr.

"*Iosa is Muire Mhàthair.* If he harms ye, upon my honor, I shall kill him."

"He will not harm me. I wish I could welcome you into my home, but it wouldn't be safe. Please try to find Brodie."

"Aye." Torr's gaze burned into hers. "I love ye, Catriona. Dinna forget that."

"Of course I won't forget. I love you."

"Come with my men!" the MacPeter commanded.

She wanted to give Torr one last kiss but could not with so many watching. For his safety, she had to pretend he was only a friend. But had MacPeter already seen them embracing earlier?

Hand still clenched on his sword hilt, Torr scowled as she headed toward the approaching members of the MacPeter clan. She wanted them to keep their distance from Torr.

They made their way up the narrow rough trail to where the swine laird awaited, smirking. The cold, shifting wind brought his stench to her. Her stomach near revolted.

She glanced back to see Torr standing with Finnian and Aggie. *May God protect them.* She headed past MacPeter and toward the castle. He and his men followed.

The MacCain guards opened the gates, stood aside and bowed. Her pulse drummed in her ears as she crossed the cobbled barmkin, the hooves of the MacPeter clan's mounts clomping behind her. Their gazes bored into her back and she shivered.

How could she convince her mother to understand her love for Torr? How would she get MacPeter to leave her be? *Please God, let them find Brodie.*

Inside the dim great hall, Catriona squinted, trying to recognize the occupants. Her mother sucked in a breath and swayed in a dramatic near-swoon before running to her and drawing her into a tight embrace. "Oh, Catriona, my darling. I was so afraid you were dead. Thank the heavens."

"I am well, Mother. But I must talk to you in private."

"Of course." She turned to the MacPeter and his men who had just entered. "Please refresh yourselves while I converse with my daughter."

MacPeter gave a brief nod, but his hard expression made Catriona wish she were anywhere but here. She tugged her mother up to her bed-chamber and barred the door behind them.

Her mother's face was pale. "What happened, daughter? Where have you been?"

"I ran away."

Her mother gasped. "Why?"

Catriona placed her hands on her hips. "I cannot and I will not marry the MacPeter."

"But you are promised."

"I didn't promise. You did."

"Parents arrange the marriages of their children. You know that. I have been preparing you to do your duty as a chieftain's wife your whole life."

Catriona swallowed hard. "I am already betrothed." *Halfway.* It wasn't legal and binding yet, but Torr had asked her to marry him.

"What? No! To whom?"

"Torr Blackburn."

Her mother's mouth hung open. "It cannot be. How did this happen? He is not a chieftain. He holds no land, property or titles, does he? He is a younger son."

"It doesn't matter to me. I love him beyond anything you can imagine. I have loved him for years. And he loves me."

"You ran away to him? How could you? You have ruined your life. Have you consummated the betrothal?"

"You ask too many questions, Mother."

"Have you?"

"Yes, and I will marry him as soon as it can be legally done. I may even now be carrying his child."

Her mother shook her head, a hand covering her mouth. "You have just brought untold wrath down upon our clan. The MacPeter will be furious with us."

"Once Brodie returns, he will clear all this up. He would not make me marry that swine. In the meantime, can you not put MacPeter off another fortnight? Tell him I require more time. By then maybe Brodie will have returned."

"I have lost all faith in Brodie." She shook her head. "I cannot even bear to think of him. His father would be so disappointed in him."

"He is cursed, Mother. He cannot help it. But Torr and Finnian are here to help him. The curse can be broken. Both Gavin and Torr are no longer cursed. We have to find a wife for Brodie, someone who will love him."

"We don't have time for this. Matchmaking your brother with someone is a waste of time. He is a scoundrel, a rake and a rogue. And worst of all, a selkie. No woman will want him. You saw how Elspeth departed in haste."

"She was not the right woman for him."

A fist pounded on the door. "M'ladies?" MacPeter's voice boomed through the thick wood.

Catriona glared at the door. "Yes?"

"I have waited long enough. Either the wedding takes place now or I start slitting the throats of MacCains."

"Oh, dear God." Nausea washed over Catriona. He truly was a murderer. "You see? He's a monster."

Her mother turned pale as snow and grabbed hold of the bedpost.

"Now! I mean what I say," MacPeter yelled.

Catriona inhaled a fortifying breath and opened the door. She would kill him in his sleep. The hated bastard glared down at her in the dimness of the corridor.

"Threatening me will not make me love you," she said.

MacPeter laughed. "I dinna want ye to love me. I want ye under me in bed and my bairn in your belly."

Catriona cringed. *I shall kill you, bastard.* She remembered one of Brodie's daggers still in her skirt pocket.

MacPeter grabbed her arm and dragged her down the stairs to the great hall. She barely stayed on her feet. Pain shot through her shoulder. Her clan stood in silence, even the emaciated, wide-eyed priest. Why didn't someone come to her aid? Defend her? Brodie's guards and henchmen stood along the walls in silence. Their swords were gone. *Sweet mother Mary.*

"Begin!" MacPeter commanded.

With a dry shaking voice, the slight priest began the ceremony.

Should she try to use the dagger? Even should she deliver a killing blow to MacPeter, his men would likely slay her and her whole clan in retaliation. No bloodshed.

God help me, she prayed in a mantra, her eyes closed. *I am sorry for my sins, but I love Torr. I love him beyond all reason. He is the husband of my heart.* Though silent, she prayed harder than she had in her entire life. Tears dripped from her chin.

"M'lady!" MacPeter elbowed her.

What did he want?

"Answer, damn ye, wench."

"No," she said, hoping that was the right answer.

The entry door burst open and booted feet entered.

"What the devil?" MacPeter said.

Catriona turned.

Brodie stood in the open doorway, large and commanding, his long dark hair still wet with seawater, his plaid askew and his shirt hanging loose. Torr waited beside him.

Thank you, God!

"What goes on here?" Brodie strode forward, sword in hand. His dark gaze skimmed over her and landed like a dagger point on the MacPeter. Torr followed, his sword also unsheathed. *Yes!*

"A wedding, as ye can see." MacPeter drew himself up, trying to be as tall as Brodie and Torr.

"She canna marry you. She is already legally betrothed to someone else."

"Who?" MacPeter growled through clenched teeth.

"Me." Torr's deadly grin hid untold danger.

"She was promised to me first."

"Nay," Brodie said in a cheerful tone. "She was promised to Torr when she was but a decade old. I have the contract in my library if ye require it."

What was Brodie talking about? Was this true?

The MacPeter's gaze sought out her mother. "Ye lied to me, madam."

She gawked, wide-eyed, mouth hanging open.

"And how do ye propose to appease me for taking back the bride your mother promised me, MacCain?"

Brodie shrugged. "Half a dozen cattle."

MacPeter glared. "Nay, I have plenty of cattle. What I dinna have is a wife."

"Sorry, I canna help ye there. Ye must find your own wife." Brodie lifted a brow and waited. "I'm thinking we're done here, unless ye'd like to go outside and have a pissing contest."

MacPeter snarled. "Ye'll be hearing from me again, MacCain." He motioned to his men and they followed him out.

Catriona grasped Torr's hand and inched closer to him. She wanted to dance and shout and hug her brother, then Torr, for saving the day.

Once the hall was quiet, Brodie's unnaturally dark, intimidating gaze slid from Catriona to Torr. "I would see ye both in the library."

Catriona knew she should've been afraid of what Brodie might say, but she could not believe her brother would be too harsh on them. Thrilled to be free of MacPeter, she smiled as she and Torr followed Brodie upstairs. She cherished the warmth of Torr's hand in her own.

"What is the damned meaning of this, Cat?" His gaze locked on his friend. "And you. How could ye take advantage of my little sister?"

"I have nay excuse, Brodie." Torr's gaze landed on Catriona with much affection and intensity. "But I love her."

"Oh, is that so? Ye *love* her. Ye think *love* means anything?" He dropped into the chair behind his desk. "Believe me, I have seen what love can do and how sincere and long-lasting 'tis."

"Torr's curse is broken," Catriona said.

Brodie frowned. "What? How?"

"Love. Because we love each other."

Brodie snorted. "Aye, I'm certain that explains it all."

"Gavin wrote missives saying his curse was broken as well, because of love." She withdrew the paper from her pocket and handed it to him.

"This has my name on it," Brodie said. "Why are ye reading my missives?"

"'Twas important. This is why I went to Torr in the first place, to enlist his help in breaking your curse so you would come back and lead the clan."

Brodie clenched his jaw, shoved to his feet and read the missive near the window. He lowered it and tossed it to the desk. "'Twill ne'er happen."

"Why not? Of course it will."

"I canna love someone I canna trust."

"Not Elspeth. Someone else."

"What makes ye think a different woman would be trustworthy?"

"I'm a woman and Torr trusts me."

"Aye, but that's Torr. He trusts everyone."

"Bah! Ye've gone daft," Torr said. "Ye should think about overcoming the curse, Brodie. As long as 'tis in effect, Wilona MacRae controls your life. I hated being a kelpie and am a hundred times happier now."

"I like being a selkie."

Catriona rolled her eyes. "We know that. You care more about your selkie friends than you do your family."

"Nay, I just feel more at home with them. And I met a beautiful new selkie right before I heard Finnian calling me with his mind."

"Grr! If you had been here all along, Mother wouldn't have tried to marry me to that swine MacPeter."

"So marry Torr. Ye have my blessing and I wish ye both much happiness." He rose and headed toward the door. "I must be going."

"Brodie!" Catriona couldn't believe how blithely he would throw off his responsibility.

"'Twas nice seeing ye again." He came back and shook Torr's hand.

"Likewise. Your clan needs ye, my friend. Ye are their leader and they look up to ye like a father."

Brodie sighed. "Very well. I shall come back here thrice a week to assure the well-being of the clan." He opened the door.

"Brodie!" Catriona said. "Get your arse back here! I'm not finished talking to you."

"Do something about your future wife, would ye, Torr? She doesna speak like a lady." Grinning, Brodie slammed the door on the way out.

Three weeks later, Catriona and Torr lay in bed at Castle Dubhuisge, his clan's main keep. Warm pleasure simmered within her from their recent lovemaking. The candles beside the canopied bed provided a cozy atmosphere, as did the fire in the hearth.

"Canna be a good omen if ye're frowning on our wedding night," Torr said. "Are ye unhappy with me already?"

Catriona smiled and placed a quick kiss on his lips. "No. You know I'm not. 'Tis Brodie I worry about now. My clan needs him. His absence makes all MacCains weaker. What if MacPeter should come back with a large force of men?"

"Brodie promised he would check on Farspag and the clan thrice a week. His men at arms ken well how to defend the castle against MacPeter or anyone else. Finnian will find Brodie when he needs to."

She blew out a tired breath. "But how will we find the woman to love Brodie and break his curse, especially this far away?"

"We shall go back to Farspag when needed. Are ye no' happy here?"

"Of course I am. I love your clan. Your brothers have been most welcoming, as has everyone." When Torr's oldest brother Angus learned the curse was broken, he shook Torr's hand and clasped him in a hug. 'Twas like two bears embracing and, amid much laughter, near turned into a wrestling match. Angus and his other brothers had teased Torr terribly about his future wife. The happy expression on Torr's face had brought tears to her eyes. This was indeed where he belonged, and she was thrilled his brother had returned the spokesman position to him.

"In a year, 'haps we will be sleeping in the newly restored Blacktower," Torr said, his eyes alight with energy and excitement.

"'Twill be lovely. I grew to love Blacktower while Aggie and I stayed there." Catriona admired his dream and wished to help him achieve it as she had attained hers by marrying him. Her dowry would help with that. But with Torr she would be content to live almost anywhere. He was so dear to her that even now, her heart ached when she looked into his eyes.

But every time she realized the magnitude of her own happiness, her mind drifted to her less fortunate clan and Brodie. "I keep wondering. Who is this new selkie Brodie met? Is this the woman who will break his curse, or someone who will keep him away from the clan forever? What if it's Wilona who's transformed from an owl into a selkie?"

"He said *beautiful*, did he no'? Wilona isna beautiful. 'Tis a wonder ye dinna have apoplexy with the way ye fash yourself."

"But—"

"If Brodie is meant to fall in love with a human woman and have a good marriage, he will. We canna force him." Torr stroked a warm fingertip over her face. "If someone had tried to force ye to love me, 'twould no' have worked. Ye would've rebelled and run the other way."

She kissed his hand. "No one need force me to love you. I have always, since the first time I saw you."

He studied her, then rolled on top of her, between her legs, holding his weight off her with his elbows. He kissed her and spread her legs with his own.

Heavens! This was the dream she'd had all those weeks ago. She had indeed dreamed of her future husband making love to her on their wedding night. Tears filled her eyes. She could not believe how lucky and blessed she was.

"What is it?" Torr murmured.

She shook her head. "I know we were destined to be together. I dreamed of this moment before I came to you and asked for help. This bed, the candles, *you* making love to me like this." She stroked his face, his beard stubble prickling her palms, and combed his hair through her fingers. In her dream, he'd had the same expression, his intense green eyes staring into hers. Into her soul. His body pressing down into hers, giving her untold pleasure. "I saw it all."

"I thank ye for bringing me a love so strong it destroyed a curse. Ye are my life now, Catriona," he whispered against her lips.

"And you are mine."

About the Author:

Nicole North lives with her husband in the beautiful Blue Ridge Mountains, but wishes she lived in the Scottish Highlands at least half the year. Though she holds a degree in psychology, writing romance is her first love. Beast in a Kilt *is her second novella for Red Sage* **Secrets**.

Check out our hot eBook titles available online at eRedSage.com!

Visit the site regularly as we're always adding new eBook titles.

Here's just some of what you'll find:

A Christmas Cara by Bethany Michaels

A Damsel in Distress by Brenda Williamson

Blood Game by Rae Monet

Fires Within by Roxana Blaze

Forbidden Fruit by Anne Rainey

High Voltage by Calista Fox

Master of the Elements by Alice Gaines

One Wish by Calista Fox

Quinn's Curse by Natasha Moore

Rock My World by Caitlyn Willows

The Doctor Next Door by Catherine Berlin

Unclaimed by Nathalie Gray

Men you've been dreaming about!

Secrets

Satisfy your desire for more.

*F*eel the wild adventure, fierce passion and the power of love in every *Secrets* Collection story. Red Sage Publishing's romance authors create richly crafted, sexy, sensual, novella-length stories. Each one is just the right length for reading after a long and hectic day.

Each volume in the *Secrets* Collection has four diverse, ultra-sexy, romantic novellas brimming with adventure, passion and love. More adventurous tales for the adventurous reader. The *Secrets* Collection are a glorious mix of romance genre; numerous historical settings, contemporary, paranormal, science fiction and suspense. We are always looking for new adventures.

Reader response to the *Secrets* volumes has been great! Here's just a small sample:

> *"I loved the variety of settings. Four completely wonderful time periods, give you four completely wonderful reads."*

> *"Each story was a page-turning tale I hated to put down."*

> *"I love **Secrets**! When is the next volume coming out? This one was Hot! Loved the heroes!"*

Secrets have won raves and awards. We could go on, but why don't you find out for yourself—order your set of **Secrets** today! See the back for details.

Secrets, Volume 1

A Lady's Quest by Bonnie Hamre
Widowed Lady Antonia Blair-Sutworth searches for a lover to save her from the handsome Duke of Sutherland. The "auditions" may be shocking but utterly tantalizing.

The Spinner's Dream by Alice Gaines
A seductive fantasy that leaves every woman wishing for her own private love slave, desperate and running for his life.

The Proposal by Ivy Landon
This tale is a walk on the wild side of love. *The Proposal* will taunt you, tease you, and shock you. A contemporary erotica for the adventurous woman.

The Gift by Jeanie LeGendre
Immerse yourself in this historic tale of exotic seduction, bondage and a concubine's surrender to the Sultan's desire. Can Alessandra live the life and give the gift the Sultan demands of her?

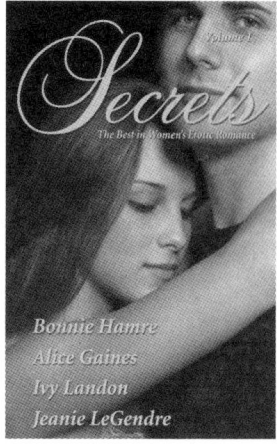

Secrets, Volume 2

Surrogate Lover by Doreen DeSalvo
Adrian Ross is a surrogate sex therapist who has all the answers and control. He thought he'd seen and done it all, but he'd never met Sarah.

Snowbound by Bonnie Hamre
A delicious, sensuous regency tale. The marriage-shy Earl of Howden is teased and tortured by his own desires and finds there is a woman who can equal his overpowering sensuality.

Roarke's Prisoner by Angela Knight
Elise, a starship captain, remembers the eager animal submission she'd known before at her captor's hands and refuses to become his toy again. However, she has no idea of the delights he's planned for her this time.

Savage Garden by Susan Paul
Raine's been captured by a mysterious and dangerous revolutionary leader in Mexico. At first her only concern is survival, but she quickly finds lush erotic nights in her captor's arms.

Winner of the Fallot Literary Award for Fiction!

Secrets, Volume 3

The Spy Who Loved Me by Jeanie Cesarini
Undercover FBI agent Paige Ellison's sexual appetites
rise to new levels when she works with leading man
Christopher Sharp, the cunning agent who uses all his
training to capture her body and heart.

The Barbarian by Ann Jacobs
Lady Brianna vows not to surrender to the barbaric
Giles, Earl of Harrow. He must use sexual arts
learned in the infidels' harem to conquer his bride. A
word of caution—this is not for the faint of heart.

Blood and Kisses by Angela Knight
A vampire assassin is after Beryl St. Cloud. Her only
hope lies with Decker, another vampire and ex-merce-
nary. Broke, she offers herself as payment for his services. Will his seductive powers
take her very soul?

Love Undercover by B.J. McCall
Amanda Forbes is the bait in a strip joint sting operation. While she performs, fellow
detective "Cowboy" Cooper gets to watch. Though he excites her, she must fight the
temptation to surrender to the passion.

Winner of the 1997 Under the Covers Readers Favorite Award

Secrets, Volume 4

An Act of Love by Jeanie Cesarini
Shelby Moran's past left her terrified of sex. International film star Jason Gage must gently coach the young
starlet in the ways of love. He wants more than an act—
he wants Shelby to feel true passion in his arms.

Enslaved by Desirée Lindsey
Lord Nicholas Summer's air of danger, dark passions,
and irresistible charm have brought Lady Crystal's
long-hidden desires to the surface. Will he be able to
give her the one thing she desires before it's too late?

The Bodyguard by Betsy Morgan & Susan Paul
Kaki York is a bodyguard, but watching the wild,
erotic romps of her client's sexual conquests on the
security cameras is getting to her—and her partner, the ruggedly handsome James
Kulick. Can she resist his insistent desire to have her?

The Love Slave by Emma Holly
A woman's ultimate fantasy. For one year, Princess Lily will be attended to by three
delicious men of her choice. While she delights in playing with the first two, it's the
reluctant Grae, with his powerful chest, black eyes and hair, that stirs her desires.

Secrets, Volume 5

Beneath Two Moons by Sandy Fraser
Step into the future and find Conor, rough and masculine like frontiermen of old, on the prowl for a new conquest. In his sights, Dr. Eva Kelsey. She got away before, but this time Conor makes sure she begs for more.

Insatiable by Chevon Gael
Marcus Remington photographs beautiful models for a living, but it's Ashlyn Fraser, a young exec having some glamour shots done, who has stolen his heart. It's up to Marcus to help her discover her inner sexual self.

Strictly Business by Shannon Hollis
Elizabeth Forrester knows it's tough enough for a woman to make it to the top in the corporate world. Garrett Hill, the most beautiful man in Silicon Valley, has to come along to stir up her wildest fantasies. Dare she give in to both their desires?

Alias Smith and Jones by B.J. McCall
Meredith Collins finds herself stranded at the airport. A handsome stranger by the name of Smith offers her sanctuary for the evening and she finds those mesmerizing, green-flecked eyes hard to resist. Are they to be just two ships passing in the night?

Secrets, Volume 6

Flint's Fuse by Sandy Fraser
Dana Madison's father has her "kidnapped" for her own safety. Flint, the tall, dark and dangerous mercenary, is hired for the job. But just which one is the prisoner—Dana will try *anything* to get away.

Love's Prisoner by MaryJanice Davidson
Trapped in an elevator, Jeannie Lawrence experienced unwilling rapture at Michael Windham's hands. She never expected the devilishly handsome man to show back up in her life—or turn out to be a werewolf!

The Education of Miss Felicity Wells by Alice Gaines
Felicity Wells wants to be sure she'll satisfy her soon-to-be husband but she needs a teacher. Dr. Marcus Slade, an experienced lover, agrees to take her on as a student, but can he stop short of taking her completely?

A Candidate for the Kiss by Angela Knight
Working on a story, reporter Dana Ivory stumbles onto a more amazing one—a sexy, secret agent who happens to be a vampire. She wants her story but Gabriel Archer wants more from her than just sex and blood.

Secrets, Volume 7

Amelia's Innocence by Julia Welles
Amelia didn't know her father bet her in a card game
with Captain Quentin Hawke, so honor demands a
compromise—three days of erotic foreplay, leaving
her virginity and future intact.

The Woman of His Dreams by Jade Lawless
From the day artist Gray Avonaco moves in next door,
Joanna Morgan is plagued by provocative dreams.
But what she believes is unrequited lust, Gray sees
as another chance to be with the woman he loves. He
must persuade her that even death can't stop true love.

Surrender by Kathryn Anne Dubois
Free-spirited Lady Johanna wants no part of the bind-
ing strictures society imposes with her marriage to the powerful Duke. She doesn't
know the dark Duke wants sensual adventure, and sexual satisfaction.

Kissing the Hunter by Angela Knight
Navy Seal Logan McLean hunts the vampires who murdered his wife. Virginia Hart
is a sexy vampire searching for her lost soul-mate only to find him in a man determined to kill her. She must convince him all vampires aren't created equally.

Winner of the Venus Book Club Best Book of the Year

Secrets, Volume 8

Taming Kate by Jeanie Cesarini
Kathryn Roman inherits a legal brothel. Little does
this city girl know the town wants her to be their new
madam so they've charged Trey Holliday, one very
dominant cowboy, with taming her.

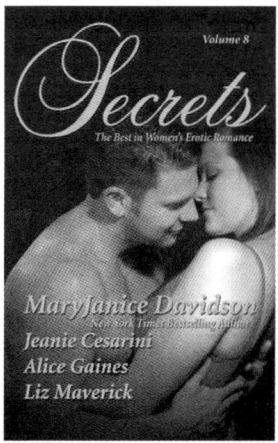

Jared's Wolf by MaryJanice Davidson
Jared Rocke will do anything to avenge his sister's
death, but ends up attracted to Moira Wolfbauer, the
she-wolf sworn to protect her pack. Joining forces to
stop a killer, they learn love defies all boundaries.

My Champion, My Lover by Alice Gaines
Celeste Broder is a woman committed for having a sexy
appetite. Mayor Robert Albright may be her champion—
if she can convince him her freedom will mean they can indulge their appetites together.

Kiss or Kill by Liz Maverick
In this post-apocalyptic world, Camille Kazinsky's military career rides on her ability to make a choice—whether the robo called Meat should live or die. Can he prove
he's human enough to live, man enough… to make her feel like a woman.

Winner of the Venus Book Club Best Book of the Year

Secrets, Volume 9

Wild For You by Kathryn Anne Dubois
When college intern, Georgie, gets captured by a
Congo wildman, she discovers this specimen of male
virility has never seen a woman. The research possibilities are endless!

Wanted by Kimberly Dean
FBI Special Agent Jeff Reno wants Danielle Carver.
There's her body, brains—and that charge of treason
on her head. Dani goes on the run, but the sexy Fed is
hot on her trail.

Secluded by Lisa Marie Rice
Nicholas Lee's wealth and power came with a price—
his enemies will kill anyone he loves. When Isabelle
steals his heart, Nicholas secludes her in his palace for a lifetime of desire in only a
few days.

Flights of Fantasy by Bonnie Hamre
Chloe taught others to see the realities of life but she's never shared the intimate
world of her sensual yearnings. Given the chance, will she be woman enough to
fulfill her most secret erotic fantasy?

Secrets, Volume 10

Private Eyes by Dominique Sinclair
When a mystery man captivates P.I. Nicolla Black
during a stakeout, she discovers her no-seduction rule
bending under the pressure of long denied passion.
She agrees to the seduction, but he demands her total
surrender.

The Ruination of Lady Jane by Bonnie Hamre
To avoid her upcoming marriage, Lady Jane Ponson-
by-Maitland flees into the arms of Havyn Attercliffe.
She begs him to ruin her rather than turn her over to
her odious fiancé.

Code Name: Kiss by Jeanie Cesarini
Agent Lily Justiss is on a mission to defend her country
against terrorists that requires giving up her virginity as a sex slave. As her master
takes her body, desire for her commanding officer Seth Blackthorn fuels her mind.

The Sacrifice by Kathryn Anne Dubois
Lady Anastasia Bedovier is days from taking her vows as a Nun. Before she denies
her sensuality forever, she wants to experience pleasure. Count Maxwell is the perfect man to initiate her into erotic delight.

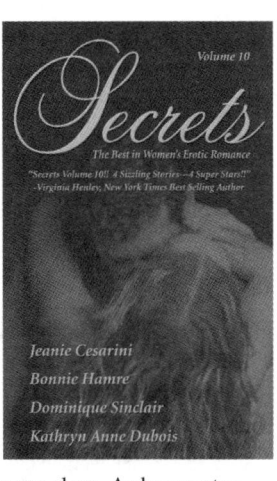

Secrets, Volume 11

Masquerade by Jennifer Probst
Hailey Ashton is determined to free herself from her
sexual restrictions. Four nights of erotic pleasures
without revealing her identity. A chance to explore her
secret desires without the fear of unmasking.

Ancient Pleasures by Jess Michaels
Isabella Winslow is obsessed with finding out what
caused her husband's death, but trapped in an Egyp-
tian concubine's tomb with a sexy American raider,
succumbing to the mummy's sensual curse takes over.

Manhunt by Kimberly Dean
Framed for murder, Michael Tucker takes Taryn
Swanson hostage—the one woman who can clear him.

Despite the evidence against him, the attraction is strong. Tucker resorts to uncon-
ventional, yet effective methods of persuasion to change the sexy ADA's mind.

Wake Me by Angela Knight
Chloe Hart received a sexy painting of a sleeping knight. Radolf of Varik has been
trapped there for centuries, cursed by a witch. His only hope is to visit the dreams of
women and make one of them fall in love with him so she can free him with a kiss.

Secrets, Volume 12

Good Girl Gone Bad by Dominique Sinclair
Setting out to do research for an article, nothing could
have prepared Reagan for Luke, or his offer to teach
her everything she needs to know about sex. Licentious pleasures, forbidden desires… inspiring the best
writing she's ever done.

Aphrodite's Passion by Jess Michaels
When Selena flees Victorian London before her evil
stepchildren can institutionalize her for hysteria,
Gavin is asked to bring her back home. But when he
finds her living on the island of Cyprus, his need to
have her begins to block out every other impulse.

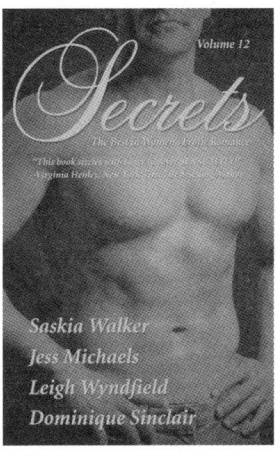

White Heat by Leigh Wyndfield
Raine is hiding in an icehouse in the middle of nowhere from one of the scariest men
in the universes. Walker escaped from a burning prison. Imagine their surprise when
they find out they have the same man to blame for their miseries. Passion, revenge
and love are in their future.

Summer Lightning by Saskia Walker
Sculptress Sally is enjoying an idyllic getaway on a secluded cove when she spots a
gorgeous man walking naked on the beach. When Julian finds an attractive woman
shacked up in his cove, he has to check her out. But what will he do when he finds
she's secretly been using him as a model?

Secrets, Volume 13

Out of Control by Rachelle Chase
Astrid's world revolves around her business and she's
hoping to pick up wealthy Erik Santos as a client. He's
hoping to pick up something entirely different. Will
she give in to the seductive pull of his proposition?

Hawkmoor by Amber Green
Shape-shifters answer to Darien as he acts in the name
of long-missing Lady Hawkmoor, their ruler. When
she unexpectedly surfaces, Darien must deal with a
scrappy individual whose wary eyes hold the other half
of his soul, but who has the power to destroy his world.

Lessons in Pleasure by Charlotte Featherstone
A wicked bargain has Lily vowing never to yield to the

demands of the rake she once loved and lost. Unfortunately, Damian, the Earl of St.
Croix, or Saint as he is infamously known, will not take 'no' for an answer.

In the Heat of the Night by Calista Fox
Haunted by a curse, Molina fears she won't live to see her 30th birthday. Nick, her for-
mer bodyguard, is re-hired to protect her from the fatal accidents that plague her family.
Will his passion and love be enough to convince Molina they have a future together?

Secrets, Volume 14

Soul Kisses by Angela Knight
Beth's been kidnapped by Joaquin Ramirez, a sadistic
vampire. Handsome vampire cousins, Morgan and
Garret Axton, come to her rescue. Can she find happiness with two vampires?

Temptation in Time by Alexa Aames
Ariana escaped the Middle Ages after stealing a kiss
of magic from sexy sorcerer, Marcus de Grey. When
he brings her back, they begin a battle of wills and a
sexual odyssey that could spell disaster for them both.

Ailis and the Beast by Jennifer Barlowe
When Ailis agreed to be her village's sacrifice to the
mysterious Beast she was prepared to sacrifice her vir-

tue, and possibly her life. But some things aren't what they seem. Ailis and the Beast
are about to discover the greatest sacrifice may be the human heart.

Night Heat by Leigh Wynfield
When Rip Bowhite leads a revolt on the prison planet, he ends up struggling to
survive against monsters that rule the night. Jemma, the prison's Healer, won't allow
herself to be distracted by the instant attraction she feels for Rip. As the stakes are
raised and death draws near, love seems doomed in the heat of the night.

Secrets, Volume 15

Simon Says by Jane Thompson
Simon Campbell is a newspaper columnist who panders to male fantasies. Georgina Kennedy is a respectable librarian. On the surface, these two have nothing in common... but don't judge a book by its cover.

Bite of the Wolf by Cynthia Eden
Gareth Morlet, alpha werewolf, has finally found his mate. All he has to do is convince Trinity to join with him, to give in to the pleasure of a werewolf's mating, and then she will be his... forever.

Falling for Trouble by Saskia Walker
With 48 hours to clear her brother's name, Sonia Harmond finds help from irresistible bad boy, Oliver Eaglestone. When the erotic tension between them hits fever pitch, securing evidence to thwart an international arms dealer isn't the only danger they face.

The Disciplinarian by Leigh Court
Headstrong Clarissa Babcock is sent for instruction in proper wifely obedience. Disciplinarian Jared Ashworth uses the tools of seduction to show her how to control a demanding husband, but her beauty, spirit, and uninhibited passion make Jared hunger to keep her—and their darkly erotic nights—all for himself!

Secrets, Volume 16

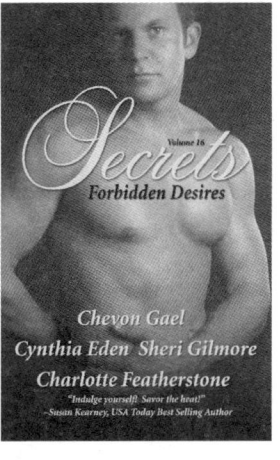

Never Enough by Cynthia Eden
Abby McGill has been playing with fire. Bad-boy Jake taught her the true meaning of desire, but she knows she has to end her relationship with him. But Jake isn't about to let the woman he wants walk away from him.

Bunko by Sheri Gilmoore
Tu Tran must decide between Jack, who promises to share every aspect of his life with her, or Dev, who hides behind a mask and only offers nights of erotic sex. Will she gamble on the man who can see behind her own mask and expose her true desires?

Hide and Seek by Chevon Gael
Kyle DeLaurier ditches his trophy-fiance in favor of a tropical paradise full of tall, tanned, topless females. Private eye, Darcy McLeod, is on the trail of this runaway groom. Together they sizzle while playing Hide and Seek with their true identities.

Seduction of the Muse by Charlotte Featherstone
He's the Dark Lord, the mysterious author who pens the erotic tales of an innocent woman's seduction. She is his muse, the woman he watches from the dark shadows, the woman whose dreams he invades at night.

Secrets, Volume 17

Rock Hard Candy by Kathy Kaye
Jessica Hennessy, descendent of a Voodoo priestess, decides it's time for the man of her dreams. A dose of her ancestor's aphrodisiac slipped into the gooey center of her homemade bon bons ought to do the trick.

Fatal Error by Kathleen Scott
Jesse Storm must make amends to humanity by destroying the software he helped design that's taken the government hostage. But he must also protect the woman he's loved in secret for nearly a decade.

Birthday by Ellie Marvel
Jasmine Templeton's been celibate long enough. Will a wild night at a hot new club with her two best friends ease the ache or just make it worse? Considering one is Charlie and she's been having strange notions about their relationship of late… It's definitely a birthday neither she nor Charlie will ever forget.

Intimate Rendezvous by Calista Fox
A thief causes trouble at Cassandra Kensington's nightclub and sexy P.I. Dean Hewitt arrives to help. One look at her sends his blood boiling, despite the fact that his keen instincts have him questioning the legitimacy of her business.

Secrets, Volume 18

Lone Wolf Three by Rae Monet
Planetary politics and squabbling drain former rebel leader Taban Zias. But his anger quickly turns to desire when he meets, Lakota Blackson. She's Taban's perfect mate—now if he can just convince her.

Flesh to Fantasy by Larissa Ione
Kelsa Bradshaw is a loner happily immersed in a world of virtual reality. Trent Jordan is a paramedic who experiences the harsh realities of life. When their worlds collide in an erotic eruption can Trent convince Kelsa to turn the fantasy into something real?

Heart Full of Stars by Linda Gayle
Singer Fanta Rae finds herself stranded on a lonely Mars outpost with the first human male she's seen in years. Ex-Marine Alex Decker lost his family and guilt drove him into isolation, but when alien assassins come to enslave Fanta, she and Decker come together to fight for their lives.

The Wolf's Mate by Cynthia Eden
When Michael Morlet finds "Kat" Hardy fighting for her life, he instantly recognizes her as the mate he's been seeking all of his life, but someone's trying to kill her. With danger stalking them, will Kat trust him enough to become his mate?

Secrets, Volume 19

Affliction by Elisa Adams
Holly Aronson finally believes she's safe with sweet Andrew. But when his life long friend, Shane, arrives, events begin to spiral out of control. She's inexplicably drawn to Shane. As she runs for her life, which one will protect her?

Falling Stars by Kathleen Scott
Daria is both a Primon fighter pilot and a Primon princess. As a deadly new enemy faces appears, she must choose between her duty to the fleet and the desperate need to forge an alliance through her marriage to the enemy's General Raven.

Toy in the Attic by R. Ellen Ferare
Gabrielle discovers a life-sized statue of a nude man. Her unexpected roommate reveals himself to be a talented lover caught by a witch's curse. Can she help him break free of the spell that holds him, without losing her heart along the way?

What You Wish For by Saskia Walker
Lucy Chambers is renovating her historic house. As her dreams about a stranger become more intense, she wishes he were with her. Two hundred years in the past, the man wishes for companionship. Suddenly they find themselves together—in his time.

Secrets, Volume 20

The Subject by Amber Green
One week Tyler is a game designer, signing the deal of her life. The next, she's running for her life. Who can she trust? Certainly not sexy, mysterious Esau, who keeps showing up after the hoo-hah hits the fan!

Surrender by Dominique Sinclair
Agent Madeline Carter is in too deep. She's slipped into Sebastian Maiocco's life to investigate his Sicilian mafia family. He unearths desires Madeline's unable to deny, conflicting the duty that honors her. Madeline must surrender to Sebastian or risk being exposed, leaving her target for a ruthless clan.

Stasis by Leigh Wyndfield
Morgann Right's Commanding Officer's been drugged with Stasis, turning him into a living statue she's forced to take care of for ten long days. As her hands tend to him, she sees her CO in a totally different light. She wants him and, while she can tell he wants her, touching him intimately might come back to haunt them both.

A Woman's Pleasure by Charlotte Featherstone
Widowed Isabella, Lady Langdon is yearning to discover all the pleasures denied her in her marriage, she finds herself falling hard for the magnetic charms of the mysterious and exotic Julian Gresham—a man skilled in pleasures of the flesh.

Secrets, Volume 21

Caged Wolf by Cynthia Eden
Alerac La Morte has been drugged and kidnapped.
He realizes his captor, Madison Langley, is actually
his destined mate, but she hates his kind. Will Alerac
convince her he's not the monster she thinks?

Wet Dreams by Larissa Ione
Injured and on the run, agent Brent Logan needs a
miracle. What he gets is a boat owned by Marina
Summers. Pursued by killers, ravaged by a storm,
and plagued by engine troubles, they can do little but
spend their final hours immersed in sensual pleasure.

Good Vibrations by Kate St. James
Lexi O'Brien vows to swear off sex while she attends

grad school, so when her favorite out-of-town customer asks her out, she decides to
indulge in an erotic fling. Little does she realize Gage Templeton is moving home, to
her city, and has no intention of settling for a short-term affair..

Virgin of the Amazon by Mia Varano
Librarian Anna Winter gets lost on the Amazon and stumbles upon a tribe whose
shaman wants a pale-skinned virgin to deflower. British adventurer Coop Daventry,
the tribe's self-styled chief, wants to save her, but which man poses a greater threat?

Secrets, Volume 22

Heat by Ellie Marvel
Mild-mannered alien Tarkin is in heat and the only
compatible female is a Terran. He courts her the old
fashioned Terran way. Because if he can't seduce her
before his cycle ends, he won't get a second chance.

Breathless by Rachel Carrington
Lark Hogan is a martial arts expert seeking vengeance for the death of her sister. She seeks help
from Zac, a mercenary wizard. Confronting a common enemy, they battle their own demons as well as
their powerful attraction, and will fight to the death
to protect what they've found.

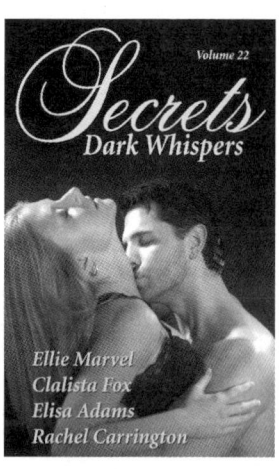

Midnight Rendezvous by Calista Fox
From New York to Cabo to Paris to Tokyo, Cat Hewitt and David Essex share
decadent midnight rendezvous. But when the real world presses in on their erotic
fantasies, and Cat's life is in danger, will their whirlwind romance stand a chance?

Birthday Wish by Elisa Adams
Anna Kelly had many goals before turning 30 and only one is left—to spend one
night with sexy Dean Harrison. When Dean asks her what she wants for her birthday, she grabs at the opportunity to ask him for an experience she'll never forget.

Secrets, Volume 23

The Sex Slave by Roxi Romano
Jaci Coe needs a hero and the hard bodied man in black meets all the criteria. Opportunistic Jaci takes advantage of Lazarus Stone's commandingly protective nature, but together, they learn how to live free... and love freely.

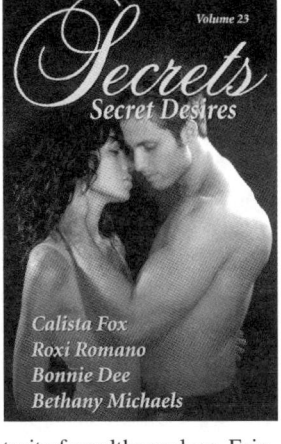

Forever My Love by Calista Fox
Professor Aja Woods is a 16th century witch... only she doesn't know it. Christian St. James, her vampire lover, has watched over her spirit for 500 years. When her powers are recovered, so too are her memories of Christian—and the love they once shared.

Reflection of Beauty by Bonnie Dee
Artist Christine Dawson is commissioned to paint a portrait of wealthy recluse, Eric Leroux. It's up to her to reach the heart of this physically and emotionally scarred man. Can love rescue Eric from isolation and restore his life?

Educating Eva by Bethany Lynn
Eva Blakely attends the infamous Ivy Hill houseparty to gather research for her book *Mating Rituals of the Human Male*. But when she enlists the help of research "specimen" and notorious rake, Aidan Worthington, she gets some unexpected results.

Secrets, Volume 24

Hot on Her Heels by Mia Varano
Private investigator Jack Slater dons a g-string to investigate the Lollipop Lounge, a male strip club. He's not sure if the club's sexy owner, Vivica Steele, is involved in the scam, but Jack figures he's just the Lollipop to sweeten her life.

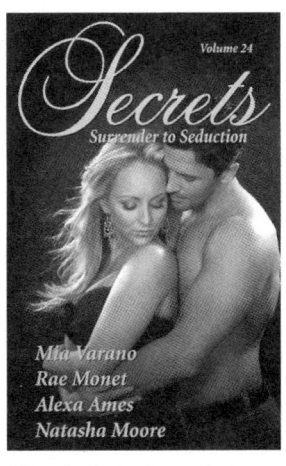

Shadow Wolf by Rae Monet
A half-breed Lupine challenges a high-ranking Solarian Wolf Warrior. When Dia Nahiutras tries to steal Roark D'Reincolt's wolf, does she get an enemy forever or a mate for life?

Bad to the Bone by Natasha Moore
At her class reunion, Annie Shane sheds her good girl reputation through one wild weekend with Luke Kendall. But Luke is done playing the field and wants to settle down. What would a bad girl do?

War God by Alexa Ames
Estella Eaton, a lovely graduate student, is the unwitting carrier of the essence of Aphrodite. But Ares, god of war, the ultimate alpha male, knows the truth and becomes obsessed with Estelle, pursuing her relentlessly. Can her modern sensibilities and his ancient power coexist, or will their battle of wills destroy what matters most?

Secrets, Volume 25

Blood Hunt by Cynthia Eden
Vampiress Nema Alexander has a taste for bad boys.
Slade Brion has just been charged with tracking her
down. He won't stop until he catches her, and Nema
won't stop until she claims him, forever.

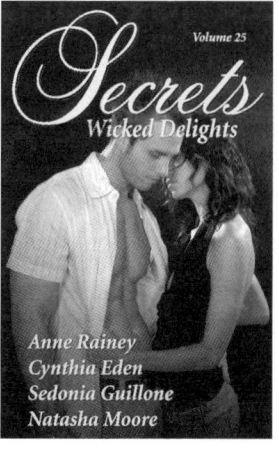

Scandalous Behavior by Anne Rainey
Tess Marley wants to take a walk on the wild side.
Who better to teach her about carnal pleasures than
her intriguing boss, Kevin Haines? But Tess makes
a major miscalculation when she crosses the line
between lust and love.

Enter the Hero by Sedonia Guillone
Kass and Lian are sentenced to sex slavery in the
Confederation's pleasure district. Forced to make love for an audience, their hearts
are with each other while their bodies are on display. Now, in the midst of sexual
slavery, they have one more chance to escape to Paradise.

Up to No Good by Natasha Moore
Former syndicated columnist Simon "Mac" MacKenzie hides a tragic secret. When
freelance writer Alison Chandler tracks him down, he knows she's up to no good. Is
their attraction merely a distraction or the key to surviving their war of wills?

Secrets, Volume 26

Secret Rendezvous by Calista Fox
McCarthy Portman has seen enough happily-
ever-afters to long for one of her own, but when her
renowned matchmaking software pairs her with the
wild and wicked Josh Kensington, everything she's
always believed about love is turned upside down.

Enchanted Spell by Rachel Carrington
Witches and wizards don't mix. Every magical being
knows that. Yet, when a little mischievous magic
thrusts Ella and Kevlin together, they do so much
more than mix—they combust.

Exes and Ahhhs by Kate St. James
Former lovers Risa Haber and Eric Lange are partners
in a catering business, but Eric can't seem to remain a silent partner. Risa offers one
night of carnal delights if he'll sell her his share then disappear forever.

The Spy's Surrender by Juliet Burns
The famous courtesan Eva Werner is England's secret weapon against Napoleon. Her
orders are to attend a sadistic marquis' depraved house party and rescue a British spy
being held prisoner. As the weekend orgy begins, she's forced to make the spy her
love slave for the marquis' pleasure. But who is slave and who is master?

Secrets, Volume 27

Heart Storm by Liane Gentry Skye
Sirenia must mate with the only merman who can save
her kind, but when she rescues Navy SEAL Byron
Burke, she seals herself into his life debt. Will her
heart stand in the way of the last hope for her kind?

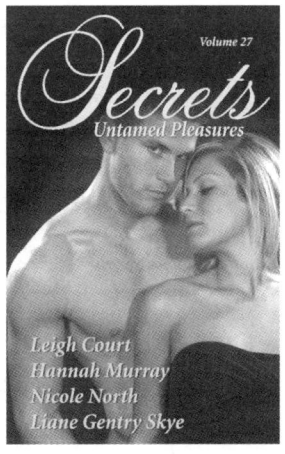

The Boy Next Door by Hannah Murray
Isabella Carelli isn't just looking for Mr. Right, she's
looking for Mr. Tie Me Up And Do Me Right. In all
the wrong places. Fortunately, the boy next door is just
about ready to make his move...

Devil in a Kilt by Nicole North
A trip to the Highland Games turns into a trip to the
past when modern day Shauna MacRae touches Gavin
MacTavish's 400-year-old claymore. Can she break the curse imprisoning this *Devil
in a Kilt* before an evil witch sends her back and takes Gavin as her sex slave?

The Bet by Leigh Court
A very drunk Damian Hunt claims he can make a woman come with just words. He
bets his prized racehorse that he can do it while George Beringer gambles his London townhouse that he can't. George chooses his virginal sister, Claire, for the bet.
Once Damian lays eyes on her, the stakes escalate in the most unpredictable way...

Secrets, Volume 28

Kiss Me at Midnight by Kate St. James
Callie Hutchins and Marc Shaw fake an on-air
romance to top the sweeps. Callie thinks Marc is a
womanizer, but as the month progresses, she realizes
he's funny, kind, and too sexy for words, damn it.

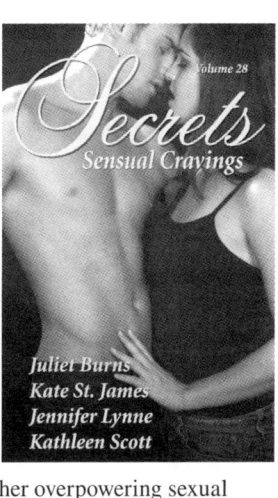

Mind Games by Kathleen Scott
Damien Storm is a Varti—a psychic who can com-
municate telepathically to one special person. Fear
has kept his Vartek partner, Jade, from acknowledging
their link. He must save her from the forces who wish
to see all Varti destroyed.

Seducing Serena by Jennifer Lynne
Serena Hewitt has given up on love, but when she
interviews for a potential partner she's not prepared for her overpowering sexual
attraction to Nicholas Wade, a fun-loving bachelor with bad-boy good looks and a
determination to prove her wrong.

Pirate's Possession by Juliet Burns
When Lady Gertrude Fitzpatrick bargains with a fierce pirate for escape, but unwit-
tingly becomes the possession of a fierce privateer. Ewan MacGowan has been
betrayed and mistakenly exacts revenge on this proud noblewoman. He may have
stolen the lady's innocence, but he also finds the true woman of his heart.

Secrets, Volume 29

Sweet-Talking the Opposition by Saskia Walker
Journalist Eliza Jameson is on assignment when she
finds the perfect distraction on board—old flame,
Marcus Weston.

Chimera by Nathalie Gray
From the overcrowded slums of a future Earth, he rose
as the perfect tool of lethal justice and deception. But
when his next assignment involves a popular politician
who's as smart as she's attractive, the greatest betrayal
would be to deny his heart.

Edge by Dominique Sinclair
Catlina Demarco has left the agency and Noah Tyler,
her former partner and lover, is intent on bringing her
back. Forced into the jungle by armed banderos, they end up working as partners,
their thoughts as one, their bodies craving, their goals conflicting.

Beast in a Kilt by Nicole North
Lady Catriona MacCain has loved Torr Blackburn since she was a young lass. When
Catriona's family promises her in marriage to a detestable chieftain, she needs Torr
to save her. But he's been cursed by a witch and doesn't believe himself worthy of
the virginal Catriona. However, she's determined to seduce Torr and claim him.

*Check out our
hot eBook titles
available online
at eRedSage.com!*

The Forever Kiss
by Angela Knight

Listen to what reviewers say:

"*The Forever Kiss* flows well with good characters and an interesting plot. ... If you enjoy vampires and a lot of hot sex, you are sure to enjoy *The Forever Kiss*."

—*The Best Reviews*

"Battling vampires, a protective ghost and the ever present battle of good and evil keep excellent pace with the erotic delights in Angela Knight's *The Forever Kiss*—a book that absolutely bites with refreshing paranormal humor." **4½ Stars, Top Pick**

—*Romantic Times BOOKclub*

"I found *The Forever Kiss* to be an exceptionally written, refreshing book. ... I really enjoyed this book by Angela Knight. ... 5 angels!"

—*Fallen Angel Reviews*

"*The Forever Kiss* is the first single title released from Red Sage and if this is any indication of what we can expect, it won't be the last. ... The love scenes are hot enough to give a vampire a sunburn and the fight scenes will have you cheering for the good guys."

—*Really Bad Barb Reviews*

In *The Forever Kiss*:

For years, Valerie Chase has been haunted by dreams of a Texas Ranger she knows only as "Cowboy." As a child, he rescued her from the nightmare vampires who murdered her parents. As an adult, she still dreams of him—but now he's her seductive lover in nights of erotic pleasure.

Yet "Cowboy" is more than a dream—he's the real Cade McKinnon—and a vampire! For years, he's protected Valerie from Edward Ridgemont, the sadistic vampire who turned him. Now, Ridgmont wants Valerie for his own and Cade is the only one who can protect her.

When Val finds herself abducted by her handsome dream man, she's appalled to discover he's one of the vampires she fears. Now, caught in a web of fear and passion, she and Cade must learn to trust each other, even as an immortal monster stalks their every move.

Their only hope of survival is... *The Forever Kiss*.

Romantic Times Best Erotic Novel of the Year

Object of Desire
by *Calista Fox*

Listen to what reviewers say:

"*Object of Desire* was a very good book! The
plot was fast paced, the adventure was thrilling,
and the espionage angle added a whole new edge
to the book. The developing relationship between
Devon and Laurel was fun to watch, and the romance between them was intense! ... I loved it!"
— Romance Junkies

"James Bond move over! Calista Fox is romanc-
ing the stone with a sexy new spy and a sizzling
hot story. With enough glitz for Jackie Collins and intrigue for Ian Fleming
fans, Fox blazes a new brand of the sexy spy."
—Erin Quinn, author of *Haunting Beauty*

"*Object of Desire* delivers sizzling sensuality, emotional complexity, and an
intriguing story—everything I've come to expect from Calista Fox!"
—Rachelle Chase, author of *The Sin Club* and *The Sex Lounge*

"A roller coaster of action and romance—you'll barely have time to
breathe!"
—Leigh Court, author of the award-winning novella, *The Disciplinarian*
(***Secrets Volume 15***)

In *Object of Desire*:

When treasure hunter and spy Laurel Blackwood raids Victoria Peak in Belize to
recover a rare Mexican fire opal rumored to evoke dark desires and passions, she un-
wittingly sets off a sequence of dangerous events—and finds herself in the midst of a
battle between good and evil... and lust and love. Being chased through the Yucatan
jungle is perilous enough, but Laurel must also keep the opal from falling into the
hands of a deadly terrorist cell, a greedy Belizean dignitary, and one particularly hot
and scandalous treasure hunter named Devon Mallory.

For ten years, Devon has had his eye on the thirty-million-dollar prized opal
and his heart set on winning Laurel for keeps. But her web of secrecy and now her
betrayal over recovering the legendary stone without him has Devon hell-bent on
stealing the opal from her and collecting on the massive pay-out. Unfortunately for
Devon, there is much more to Laurel Blackwood than she lets on. And soon, he's
caught in the eye of the storm—falling under her sensuous spell, willing to put his
own life on the line to help her protect the mystical jewel.

But Devon will eventually have to decide which gem is his true object of desire...

It's not just reviewers raving about *Secrets*. See what readers have to say:

"When are you coming out with a new Volume? I want a new one next month!" via email from a reader.

"I loved the hot, wet sex without vulgar words being used to make it exciting." after *Volume 1*

"I loved the blend of sensuality and sexual intensity—HOT!" after *Volume 2*

"The best thing about *Secrets* is they're hot and brief! The least thing is you do not have enough of them!" after *Volume 3*

"I have been extremely satisfied with *Secrets*, keep up the good writing." after *Volume 4*

"Stories have plot and characters to support the erotica. They would be good strong stories without the heat." after *Volume 5*

"*Secrets* really knows how to push the envelop better than anyone else." after *Volume 6*

"These are the best sensual stories I have ever read!" after *Volume 7*

"I love, love, love the *Secrets* stories. I now have all of them, please have more books come out each year." after *Volume 8*

"These are the perfect sensual romance stories!" after *Volume 9*

"What I love about *Secrets Volume 10* is how I couldn't put it down!" after *Volume 10*

"All of the *Secrets* volumes are terrific! I have read all of them up to *Secrets Volume 11*. Please keep them coming! I will read every one you make!" after *Volume 11*

Finally, the men you've been dreaming about!

Give the gift of spicy romantic fiction.

Don't want to wait? You can place a retail price ($12.99)
order for any of the *Secrets* volumes from the following:

① online at **eRedSage.com**

② **Waldenbooks, Borders, and Books-a-Million Stores**

③ **Amazon.com** or **BarnesandNoble.com**

④ or buy them at your local bookstore or online book source.

Order by title or ISBN #:

Vol. 1:   0-9648942-0-3
ISBN #13 978-0-9648942-0-4

Vol. 2:   0-9648942-1-1
ISBN #13 978-0-9648942-1-1

Vol. 3:   0-9648942-2-X
ISBN #13 978-0-9648942-2-8

Vol. 4:   0-9648942-4-6
ISBN #13 978-0-9648942-4-2

Vol. 5:   0-9648942-5-4
ISBN #13 978-0-9648942-5-9

Vol. 6:   0-9648942-6-2
ISBN #13 978-0-9648942-6-6

Vol. 7:   0-9648942-7-0
ISBN #13 978-0-9648942-7-3

Vol. 8:   0-9648942-8-9
ISBN #13 978-0-9648942-9-7

Vol. 9:   0-9648942-9-7
ISBN #13 978-0-9648942-9-7

Vol. 10:   0-9754516-0-X
ISBN #13 978-0-9754516-0-1

Vol. 11:   0-9754516-1-8
ISBN #13 978-0-9754516-1-8

Vol. 12:   0-9754516-2-6
ISBN #13 978-0-9754516-2-5

Vol. 13:   0-9754516-3-4
ISBN #13 978-0-9754516-3-2

Vol. 14:   0-9754516-4-2
ISBN #13 978-0-9754516-4-9

Vol. 15:   0-9754516-5-0
ISBN #13 978-0-9754516-5-6

Vol. 16:   0-9754516-6-9
ISBN #13 978-0-9754516-6-3

Vol. 17:   0-9754516-7-7
ISBN #13 978-0-9754516-7-0

Vol. 18:   0-9754516-8-5
ISBN #13 978-0-9754516-8-7

Vol. 19:   0-9754516-9-3
ISBN #13 978-0-9754516-9-4

Vol. 20:   1-60310-000-8
ISBN #13 978-1-60310-000-7

Vol. 21:   1-60310-001-6
ISBN #13 978-1-60310-001-4

Vol. 22:   1-60310-002-4
ISBN #13 978-1-60310-002-1

Vol. 23:   1-60310-164-0
ISBN #13 978-1-60310-164-6

Vol. 24:   1-60310-165-9
ISBN #13 978-1-60310-165-3

Vol. 25:   1-60310-005-9
ISBN #13 978-1-60310-005-2

Vol. 26:   1-60310-006-7
ISBN #13 978-1-60310-006-9

Vol. 27:   1-60310-007-5
ISBN #13 978-1-60310-007-6

Vol. 28:   1-60310-008-3
ISBN #13 978-1-60310-008-3

Vol. 29:   1-60310-009-1
ISBN #13 978-1-60310-009-0

The Forever Kiss:
0-9648942-3-8
ISBN #13
978-0-9648942-3-5 ($14.00)

Object of Desire:
1-60310-003-2
ISBN #13
978-1-60310-003-8 ($14.00)

Red Sage Publishing **Order Form:**
(Orders shipped in two to three days of receipt.)

Each volume of *Secrets* retails for $12.99, but you can get it direct via mail order for only $10.99 each. Novels retail for $14.00, but by direct mail order, you only pay $12.00. Use the order form below to place your direct mail order. Fill in the quantity you want for each book on the blanks beside the title.

_____ *Secrets* **Volume 1**	_____ *Secrets* **Volume 12**	_____ *Secrets* **Volume 23**
_____ *Secrets* **Volume 2**	_____ *Secrets* **Volume 13**	_____ *Secrets* **Volume 24**
_____ *Secrets* **Volume 3**	_____ *Secrets* **Volume 14**	_____ *Secrets* **Volume 25**
_____ *Secrets* **Volume 4**	_____ *Secrets* **Volume 15**	_____ *Secrets* **Volume 26**
_____ *Secrets* **Volume 5**	_____ *Secrets* **Volume 16**	_____ *Secrets* **Volume 27**
_____ *Secrets* **Volume 6**	_____ *Secrets* **Volume 17**	_____ *Secrets* **Volume 28**
_____ *Secrets* **Volume 7**	_____ *Secrets* **Volume 18**	_____ *Secrets* **Volume 29**
_____ *Secrets* **Volume 8**	_____ *Secrets* **Volume 19**	**Novels:**
_____ *Secrets* **Volume 9**	_____ *Secrets* **Volume 20**	_____ *The Forever Kiss*
_____ *Secrets* **Volume 10**	_____ *Secrets* **Volume 21**	_____ *Object of Desire*
_____ *Secrets* **Volume 11**	_____ *Secrets* **Volume 22**	

Total _____ *Secrets* **Volumes @ $10.99 each = $**_____

Total _____ **Novels @ $12.00 each = $**_____

Shipping & handling (in the U.S.) $_____

US Priority Mail:	UPS insured:
1–2 books .... $ 5.50	1–4 books $16.00
3–5 books $11.50	5–9 books $25.00
6–9 books $14.50	10–31 books $29.00
10–31 books $19.00	

SUBTOTAL $_____

Florida 6% sales tax (if delivered in FL) $_____

TOTAL AMOUNT ENCLOSED $_____

Your personal information is kept private and not shared with anyone.

Name: (please print) _____

Address: (no P.O. Boxes) _____

City/State/Zip: _____

Phone or email: (only regarding order if necessary) _____

You can order direct from **eRedSage.com** and use a credit card or you can use this form to send in your mail order with a check. Please make check payable to **Red Sage Publishing**. Check must be drawn on a U.S. bank in U.S. dollars. Mail your check and order form to:

Red Sage Publishing, Inc.   Department S29   P.O. Box 4844   Seminole, FL 33775